For my Parents

THE CHRONICLES OF
NATHAN LAMB

Suffer the Little Children

IAN WRIGHT

authorHOUSE®

AuthorHouse™
1663 Liberty Drive
Bloomington, IN 47403
www.authorhouse.com
Phone: 1 (800) 839-8640

Cover by: Cletus Kuhn
1st Editing By: Rudy Carillo

Published by AuthorHouse 04/27/2017

ISBN: 978-1-5246-2460-6 (sc)
ISBN: 978-1-5246-2459-0 (e)

Print information available on the last page.

Special thanks to:

Michael Gideon and Dennis Woods. Your expertise was greatly appreciated!

Thanks to:
Arthur Boesiger
John Hill
Michael Johnstone
Floyd Montoya
Peter Phipps
Loni Singletary

My co-workers, workout partners, and former students.
Thank you all for your support. I could not have finished this novel without you all!

Table of Contents

Chapter 1

The Creation of CPAT

After graduating from the CIA academy, Victor Price stared at the badge in his office. His wife, Alice, was very proud of his accomplishments and had been supportive of Victor throughout his career. He was given an office and a take-home vehicle. This was nothing new to him; he had retired from the military as a Delta Force field-operations commander to join the CIA as a field-operations agent.

Agent Price opened his last box of office artifacts and retrieved something very special to him: the Medal of Honor, which he had received during one of his missions in Afghanistan. He stared at it for what seemed like eternity. Price remembered the pain behind what came with that medal—the kind of pain that continued to haunt him today. He refused to face it and let go.

Price took out a miniature bottle of whiskey and slammed it down, clinching it tightly in his fist and closing his eyes; his hand shook. He looked for more miniatures but did not find any inside the box.

Just then, he heard a knock outside his office. "Agent Price? Sir, I have your assignments."

"Leave them in my box outside the door, Cindy," Price replied to his secretary. "I'll get them in a moment."

Price knew he must focus on the task at hand. He searched for some breath mints or gum of any kind to rid his breath of the aroma of alcohol. He finally found a mint at the bottom of the box. Then he opened his door and saw Cindy. After giving her a quick, friendly smile, he took his folder out of the box, went back inside his office, and opened the folder to read the assignment.

> Escort and protect dignitaries to and from the following buildings in the San Diego district: Governor's Mansion, Drands Hotel, the Annex, and the Sars Convention Center on Main Street.

The assignment was spread out over a five-day period.

The next day, Price reported to his supervisor, Ryan Smalls. Agent Smalls headed the assignment of escorting the three dignitaries from meetings to conferences and then back to the governor's mansion. There were four agents assigned: Reeves, Schillings, Price, and Agent Smalls.

The week had gone by fast. The last assignment started off as a routine day, but that was when all hell broke loose.

As the team of agents was escorting the dignitaries from the convention center, shots rang out on the rooftop across the street. Agent Smalls ordered Price to take Reeves, go to the roof across the street, and investigate the shootings. Once Price and Reeves reached the rooftop, they observed two men lying down on the roof with their handguns drawn. The men were well dressed, wearing suits and ties. Both men had been shot several times in the chest; one was already dead. The man who was still alive told the agents he was an undercover FBI agent who had been working covert for almost a year, tracking down the individual he had shot along with the individual escorted by the CIA agents.

"Who?" Price inquired.

"The man who made you believe he is a dignitary from India is not who he says he is. He is an al-Qaeda terrorist. They are both al-Qaeda terrorists. I had to shoot him," replied the FBI agent. "Now, you've got to shoot the one down there. The one who calls himself Nance is very dangerous and is responsible for many, many lives lost. Many children … babies. You … you've got to st-stop him," the agent said with his last breath.

Price and Reeves were in shock and at a loss for what to do.

Just then, on the street below, the dignitary from India began to laugh. He pulled out a handgun and quickly shot Agents Smalls and Schillings in the head. He then turned and shot the two dignitaries in the head, instantly killing them. Reeves and Price opened fire on the terrorist from the rooftop above, but the bullets missed him as he ran. However, one bullet hit the pavement, ricocheted, and entered his right hamstring. He limped away while laughing evilly. Price ran toward the stairwell leading to the street.

Reeves called for medical assistance as Price pursued the terrorist and called for backup. Agent Smalls survived his wound, but everyone else was killed. Price observed Nance turning a corner and running down an alley. As Price tried to turn the corner, he was met with several shots from a machine gun. He dove into a pile of trash bags, using them as cover, and the firing stopped. He heard Nance laughing as a vehicle drove away.

The next day, Price found himself as the head of field operations after the briefing. They needed him because of his knowledge and experience in field tactics. Price accepted this new assignment and promptly went into his office. He pulled out a whiskey miniature to slam down before he began the rest of the day.

As the years went by, Price was moved from one division to the next. He advanced and learned these divisions well.

The terrorist, Abdullah Mohammed, was responsible for the deaths of the agents and dignitaries. He was also advancing in Al-Qaeda. After a period of ten years, Price had become the senior director of the CIA, and Abdullah had become the head of al-Qaeda.

It was graduation day for CIA agents. Price had had a long week and was ready to hand out certificates to the new agents. He was introduced by the master of ceremonies. One by one, each agent was handed a certificate. Price was ecstatic that more agents would soon be ready for the field. As Price finished handing out the last certificate, he walked to the back of the auditorium to speak to one of his agents concerning an assignment.

Meanwhile, a man in a blue suit called out to a girl in the hallway. Her name was Karen, and he hadn't seen her in years. Price's cell phone rang, and he answered it. A lost girl passed by, looking for her parents. Just as Price turned to engage her, the building exploded, and bodies were blown everywhere. There were sounds of horror throughout the area. The building became a graveyard for those who were blown up, crushed, and buried.

"Breaking news," the anchorman said. "There was an enormous explosion in the downtown Los Angeles CIA building at approximately 6:15 p.m. this evening. Intelligence has just received information of a terrorist by the name of Heiman Mohammed. Heiman is claiming full responsibility for taking the lives of two hundred fifty individuals; one hundred were agents, and fifty were graduates. The rest were family members there to see their relatives graduate. Among the victims was CIA Director Victor Price."

"Lieutenant, are you all right? Lieutenant, wake up, sir!" the sergeant cried in a frantic shock.

Lieutenant Nathan Lamb's eyes opened up slowly as he heard the voice of his sergeant. His eyes saw blurred figures in front of him, and his body trembled. The figures slowly formed into lieutenants, captains, and deputy chiefs.

"Lamb, are you all right?" Captain Escobel asked.

"I think so, sir. I'll be fine now. I just need to get a drink of water. I'll be just fine," Lamb said.

The supervisors looked at each other and then stared at Lamb as he walked out of the room and into the men's restroom. The chief's meeting had just ended.

As Lamb walked into the restroom, he closed the door behind him and locked it. *Was this a dream, or was it a premonition? Do I let it go, or do I take it seriously?* He thought.

Some officers already believed him to be some sort of freak. Others saw him as a hero because he had saved many officers' lives in the San

Francisco Police Department. Lamb was clairvoyant, and he'd had many premonitions. One involved his former commander from Delta Force, Victor Price. Everything was so vivid, so clear—*everything*. Lamb couldn't let that go. He did not want to learn about this on the evening news, knowing that he could have tried to prevent it and did nothing!

Once he regained his composure, Lamb washed his face, got a drink of water, and calmly walked back to the conference room.

"Everything all right, sir?" his sergeant asked.

"Yeah, everything is fine," replied Lamb.

Lamb spoke to his captain and explained what had occurred. Captain Escobel was very familiar with Lamb's premonitions and encouraged him to follow through on them; after all, Lamb had saved the captain's life on two occasions.

Lamb received permission from his captain to take the department's helicopter to CIA headquarters in Los Angeles. Captain Escobel contacted the CIA headquarters and warned staff to begin an evacuation, stating that the San Francisco Police Department had received reliable intel that there might be a bomb within or near the building.

In the meantime, Lamb phoned Price.

"This is Agent Price."

"Sir, this is Alpha Dog returning to the field in full gear!" Lamb said.

"Alpha Dog? Lamb, is that you?" Price said excitedly.

"Yes, sir. It's me," Lamb replied.

"How are you doing, Lamb?" Price inquired.

"I'm fine, sir, but you've got to start evacuating everyone out of the building. There is not enough time to explain. As a matter of fact, I don't know how much time you have."

"Is this concerning a premonition you just had?"

"Yes, sir. I'm very sure about it. I'm still trembling," Lamb said. "You just finished handing out certificates, and I interrupted you while you were speaking to one of your agents, correct?"

"Go on," Price said, surprised.

"There is a man who will pass by you and call out to a woman named Karen," Lamb said. Just then, there was an announcement stating the building was to be evacuated immediately. Price ran toward the exit along with several other individuals. "Sir, take the stairwell toward the basement. Go into the conference room. Grab the young girl who is coming up the staircase and take her with you, because she is lost," Lamb said. Price did what he was told. The young girl was terrified and thought Price was trying to harm her. Price shut the door behind them as the building exploded.

Approximately five blocks away, three individuals observed the explosion. They looked at each other and nodded with approval before they turned to walk to their vehicle. One has a limp, and turned to look one more time and smirked before entering the vehicle.

Those who did not get out in time were blown up and buried beneath tons of metal, brick, and rubble. Emergency vehicles arrived to take care of those needing assistance. Lamb could now see the rubble from the sky above the burning building. "Sir! Sir, this is Lamb! Are you all right?" Lamb said. He could hear coughing as Price answered his cell phone.

"I'm okay, Lamb! We are both all right," Price answered. The young girl embraced Price and thanked him for taking her with him into the safe room.

Lamb radioed the emergency units on the ground and directed them to search the north wing of the building. The search team found Price and the young girl along with several other survivors. Twenty individuals did not survive and eighty were wounded, but there could have been many more killed.

Lamb set the helicopter down near the north end of the building. The San Francisco Police Department was given full recognition for informing the CIA and taking action in alleviating casualties.

Price asked Lamb to transfer over and work under him. *It would be good to be with him again!* Lamb thought, however he kindly turned down the offer. "I hope you catch whoever was responsible for the shooting, sir," Lamb said.

"We will, Alpha Dog," Price replied. "We will." Lamb ran to the helicopter and headed back for San Francisco. As Lamb lifted off the ground, he looked down and waved good-bye to his former commander. Price waved back. "I wish we were working together again. I miss that!" Price said to himself.

Price began work on finding out who was responsible for the lives of those agents and civilians. The intelligence team informed Price that they had located Heiman Mohammed. He was observed on the CIA cameras entering a building adjacent to the CIA, carrying some items in both hands. The cameras zoomed in on what Heiman was carrying: he had five C-4 packages in each hand. He exited the building after twenty minutes.

Price received more information from intelligence: They had located Heiman. Price sent a taskforce out and arrested Heiman without any resistance. He was sent back to the Middle East to stand trial for crimes there. Then he was extradited back to the United States to stand trial for the murders of those who died in the bombing of the CIA building. They found Heiman Mohammed guilty of crimes against humanity and sentenced him to die by lethal injection.

On the day of Heiman's execution, Price walked up to Heiman and told him he knew most of those individuals murdered. Heiman looked at him and laughed. "Do you think I care, American?" Heiman said. "You are all doing me a favor. I'm going to see my creator, you fool. There are more of us—many more of us. You kill me, and twenty will replace me, and on it will go."

Price sat down as Governor Barry Barton gave the nod to the doctor, who administered the lethal injection needle. Heiman had convulsions and began to foam at the mouth. He made a long, gurgling sound, and then he died with his eyes open. The world news announced the death of Heiman Mohammed.

Lamb was at his apartment two days later with his dog, Tank, sitting next to his chair. He watched the world news. Al-Qaeda made an announcement on the Internet, and it was shown on national television.

"Americans, do you know pain? Have you any idea what pain is? I think not. You have destroyed a part of me. A part of my life," cried Abdullah. "Now I will take what is precious from all of you, Governor Barry Barton, starting with you and your family. I hope that you are listening very closely. I will destroy you and all who were responsible for the death of my son. I know damn well who all of you are. I lost my child, and I suffer. Now you will be annihilated. As the Bible says, 'Suffer the little children.' You will all suffer for meddling in our affairs for many years. I've lost family because of your police actions."

Lamb looked at his dog. "Wow, Tank! Do you think we should take him seriously?" Lamb said. Tank barked. "Yes, I thought you would agree, boy."

"I think I will start with these three agents who captured and beat my son," Abdullah said. He ordered them to be shot in the backs of their heads. His men opened fire, killing the three men.

Lamb received a phone call; it was Victor Price. Victor informed Lamb that he desperately needed help in forming a team of special agents who could escort and protect dignitaries in and out of the United States. "The CIA units have other tasks. This unit will have this main task. I don't know anyone more qualified to handle this special assignment than you," Price said. "You would have your own unit to supervise. Just you, Lamb—no one else."

"Why me, sir?" Lamb said.

"I trust that you can follow through on every assignment, just as you did for me in Delta Force," Price explained. "I need you, Lamb."

I would be closer to Arianna, and this would allow me to make up for precious time lost, Lamb thought to himself. "All right, sir. I will do this. When do I report to you?"

"I have the paperwork, and I have already been speaking to my units about you. I have also been speaking to your captain and chief. They do not want to let you go, of course, but everyone feels that this would be a great move for you," Price said. "Two weeks would be just fine. Transfer papers are ready."

"It seems like this was well planned out, sir," Lamb said. Price was silent. "See you in two weeks, sir."

"See you in two, Alpha Dog."

The bright LA sun reflected off the buildings into the apartment of Nathan Lamb, waking him up. His eyes tried to focus on the clock on the table his next to the computer. Nathan saw the alarm did not go off at six, and it was now six thirty. Lamb sprinted for the shower and began to wash. He had to be at work in thirty minutes. This was Lamb's first day with the CIA, and he wanted to make a good impression on his supervisor. He got out of the shower and put on his suit and tie. He almost forgot his ID badge and gun as he left the apartment. Lamb's dog wanted to follow. "Not today, Tank, you stay here. Lamb said.

He jumped into his blue Mustang and headed downtown. Lamb had a presentation to give today, and he forgot a folder that contained information on terrorism prevention. The lights were all green once he turned onto Main Street. Lamb headed for the underground parking and was soon outside of headquarters. He went through security clearance checkpoint using a biometrics hand access ID. He passed through several areas of security officers with cameras positioned in all directions of the building. Lamb was greeted by his secretary, Andréa House.

"Mr. Lamb, where have you been? Price is looking for you, and I've made phone calls to your apartment and your cell phone with no answer!" Ms. House said excitedly.

"I had my cell turned off, Ms. House. I forgot to turn it on," Lamb said.

"Don't worry, Mr. Lamb. I am here to see to it that you have good support on your first day at work," Andréa replied.

The walk in the corridor to the conference room took two minutes from Lamb's office. Lamb opened the door and saw an entire room full of supervisors and agents.

"This way, Lamb. My name is Mike Jennings. I'm the tech satellite operator working on your team. Step this way to the podium please."

"I'm pleased to meet you, Jennings," Lamb said.

"Where are your notes, Lamb?" Jennings said.

"Believe it or not, I forgot them."

Jennings had a look of surprise and fear at the same time for Lamb as he reached the podium and addressed the audience. However, this was not the only time Lamb had made a presentation without notes in front of him. His past experiences gave him confidence.

Price greeted Lamb. "It's so good to see you again, Alpha Dog. The stage is all yours."

"Thank you, sir," Lamb replied.

Lamb got through his presentation within the hour. The presentation ended with a loud applause. "Good job, Lamb," Price said. "I want you to implement those ideas you have into our agency's policies and procedures. I will have Andréa assist you in making some adjustments in them."

"That sounds good to me, sir," Lamb replied.

"I will see you at briefing." They shook hands as many more agents walked up to Lamb to welcome and congratulate him.

Lamb returned to his desk, where there was a pile of papers awaiting him; his answering machine was also full. There was a knock at the door. Lamb looked up to see a young, thin man dressed in a blue suit and red tie. "Hello, Agent Lamb. My name is Melvin Burns. I work in weaponry supplies. I was told to see you before you had your briefing," Burns said excitedly.

"Very good, then," Lamb said. "I definitely need a new weapon, and a good backup too."

"Step this way," Burns said as he motioned toward the hallway.

As the two men walked down the hallway, Lamb saw pictures of all the directors and agents who had worked at the CIA. He then saw a big burly man who had folders in his hands. The man reached out to shake Lamb's hand. "Hello. You must be the new agent Price informed me was coming today. Welcome. My name is Kolzak Volkov. I work in the intelligence unit, and I'm looking forward to hearing your presentation."

Lamb nodded and continued walking. He was very excited yet nervous because he had never before created and organized an entire unit.

Burns took a turn in front of Lamb. He stopped, turned to his right, and looked into a small window that scanned his eyes. A voiced overhead camera stated, "Voice recognition activated. State your name, please!"

"Agent Nathan Lamb."

"Agent Melvin Burns."

The scanner then stated, "Voice recognition complete." The door gave them access.

"What type of weapon would you like to use in the field, Agent Lamb?" Burns said.

"I think I'm a fan of the .38 Super," Lamb stated.

"Ah, yes, the Super," Burns echoed. "Good choice of weapon."

"I used that weapon when I was in Delta Force."

"What are you using as a backup?" Burns asked.

"I'll take this one, a Beretta. It's light and easy to hide."

"I have to get you to briefing now," Burns said. Lamb collected his weapons and then followed Burns to the briefing room.

Price gave Lamb a long list of names of individuals who were exceptionally good and very skilled in military and law enforcement training. Lamb looked over the lists of men and women who had impeccable records. He spent hours studying their careers and viewing their personality, psychological, and polygraph tests. He read their histories and backgrounds. Lamb knew some of the candidates, and he matched up their personalities and felt that the individuals he chose would be perfect for the field unit.

Lamb had a meeting with Price and gave him the list of the men and women whom he chose to be on the new field unit, Crime Prevention Against Terrorism (CPAT). Price gave the approval and sent for these individuals to be transferred, if they agreed, into the CIA one month later.

One by one, the agents of CPAT fill the room. Jenny Lee was Chinese American with black hair and blue eyes, and she sat in the front. She was five foot five and weighed 125 pounds, and she wore dark blue clothing. Jenny was a quiet and reserved twenty-six-year old. She walked with confidence, her head level and her eyes straight ahead. Jenny was a competitor and possessed a firm determination to complete a job. She was transferred from the US Army Rangers. Lamb chose Jenny because of the uniqueness of her technical computer skills. Jenny graduated from the University of North Carolina with a master's degree in cyber forensics. She had a black belt in Jeet Kun Do.

Jenny had many missions in Iran and Iraq; the most dangerous one was an operation extraction, which had to be completed at night. The darkness would be her unit's cover. The individuals who were to be extracted were US Ambassador Craig Johnson and his wife, Kate. The problem the unit confronted was that the ambassador and his wife were moved from the location intelligence had marked for them. Jenny Lee's team got lost in the city and came under heavy fire; they rode into an ambush. The convoy team leader's truck was hit with a bazooka shell, killing three soldiers. The third one was also hit, killing everyone aboard and making it impossible for the second vehicle, Jenny's, to escape. There was a young boy named Haji, aged seven years old, who wanted to be a part of the US Army. He took action by leading the surviving soldiers to safety. There were six rangers left, and they asked Haji if he knew the whereabouts of the kidnapped US ambassador. Haji said that he knew the location and promptly lead them to it. The team, except for Jenny Lee, wondered at first if they should trust Haji. Haji showed them the building, and they observed that the ambassador and his wife were tied up and sitting in chairs, facing each other. There were four terrorists with Ak-17s pointed at them. Jenny was now the team leader because the captain, lieutenant, and sergeant had been killed in action. Jenny had the team split up in pairs and surround the building. They entered all three sides of the building simultaneously, killing all four terrorists with AK-17s automatics. The ambassador and his wife were unharmed. Jenny Lee gave Haji one of her ranger badges because of his bravery, and she promised she would try to stay in contact with him.

Wendy Skypack sat behind Jenny Lee. She was five six and weighed 130 pounds. She was twenty-eight and had blonde hair and blue eyes. She was originally from England. She was nicknamed Six Pack because of her well-developed abdominal muscles. Wendy competed as a bodybuilder before her military service and had won Ms. International twice. Wendy used her intuition during many of her missions in the Middle East, saving many in her unit, just as Lamb did. Wendy brought attitude and weapons expertise to the unit. Wendy also had a black belt in Middle Eastern martial arts. She was transferred from the army commandos, which was a very challenging assignment for Wendy. She had to prove herself because her fellow soldiers had some doubts about her ability to carry out the assignments given to her. Wendy made sergeant after her third year.

During the launch of Operation Enduring Freedom on October 7, 2001, Wendy and her team of commandos parachuted behind the enemy lines of Al-Qaeda. The mission was to detonate the enemy supply depot. The ten-unit team landed safely during the night mission. The unit was wearing night vision devices. Wendy and her team entered the camp using M9 pistols with silencers attached. The first four sentries posted were taken out promptly by the team. Wendy and her unit successfully planted the charges on the targets and set the timers. Just as they were ready to exit the area, they were met with heavy fire from the enemy. There were about twenty hostiles outside the perimeter of the camp. The map showed that there were tunnels made for escape; the charges were not placed near those areas. Wendy guided her team back toward the area leading to the tunnels. There was an old wooden door, and Wendy opened it. She noticed a ladder that extended down into the darkness leading to the tunnels. Wendy rushed the team into the tunnel. The tunnel led them to a river bank, where a rendezvous ship was waiting approximately fifty yards away. Wendy and her team could hear the sound of explosions detonating, and the ground shook. She made sure everyone got out of the tunnel.

As she turned from the tunnel to run to the ship, Wendy came face-to-face with a hostile who held a knife in each of his hands. "I'm going to kill you now, American pig," he screamed. He lunged his knife toward her with his left hand, and with his right hand he tried to slice Wendy's head open. Wendy quickly moved to the side and executed a cross block, and she used a spear hand to target the hostile's throat. He dropped both knives and placed both hands to his throat as he gasped for air. He fell on both knees face first into the dirt. Her men, running in front of her, saw the terrorist on his knees holding his throat and falling down. Wendy ran to the boat and received a round of applause from her surprised team of commandos.

The next agent to walk in was Benjamin "Doc" Robinson, an African American. Robinson was six two and weighed 230 pounds. He shaved his head and had brown eyes. Robinson worked out regularly and had a muscular build. He could be aggressive yet gentle. Lamb chose Doc Robinson not only because of his strength and size but because of his medical skills. Doc served as a medic in the marines and, he just received his MS in nursing. Doc's skills would be of great assistance to the team for the missions ahead. He was twenty-eight and was experienced when it came to pressure.

During Desert Storm, Robinson's team leader, Sergeant Burk O'Bradovich, wanted his men to walk through a known mine field in order to take a shortcut back to base. Doc and the others knew that the Sergeant was being irrational and showing lack of good judgment. There were ten men in the unit who had just survived several attacks, and they were carrying three wounded back to base. They were not going to take orders from the sergeant, who they felt had gone insane. "We're going to take that hill, Corporal. Do you and the rest of the men hear me? We are going to take it now! It's the only thing between us and home base!" the sergeant said bluntly.

"We are not budging, Sergeant. The map clearly indicates that there are too many mines to cross in that field. We should just go around it and avoid more fire from that hill, which has a ton of artillery aimed at us. We'll head toward base because we have wounded," answered the corporal.

The sergeant was insistent and stubborn; he did not want to listen to reason. The sergeant said he was going to show them himself by going through the field and taking the hill. "I cannot allow you to do that, sir!" Doc yelled.

Just then, an enemy patrol truck came toward their position. The corporal looked into his binoculars and observed two men that had rocket launchers aimed at the unit, riding in the back of the truck along with five others. The corporal told the men to spread out. The enemy was trying to push the unit toward the mine field to get them in range of their artillery. The men scattered and took cover behind stone structures. Al-Qaeda began to fire at one of the units. The corporal ordered the bazooka man to take aim at the side of the truck where the gas tank was. When the bazooka went off, one of the terrorists saw it, his eyes widened as he said, "Shit!" before the truck exploded. Pieces of the truck and bodies were scattered on the road. The sergeant ran toward the field. Doc ran after him, catching the sergeant before he could get into artillery range. Doc wrestled him to the ground and punched him in the face, knocking the sergeant unconscious. Doc carried the sergeant toward the men. The corporal told Doc he did well, and the unit was greeted by a patrol looking for them. They were able to get the wounded assistance in time and were sent back to the States. Doc was a Gold medal winner in Boxing and Wrestling. Doc took a seat one over from Jenny Lee because his arms were so enormous.

Ajay Reddy and his twin sister, Ajeeta Reddy, were next to arrive. The Reddys were Indian; their parents were from Mumbai. Ajay was five foot nine and weighed 180 pounds. He had black hair and blue eyes. Ajeeta was five five and weighed 125 pounds. She had black hair and green eyes. Ajay and Ajeeta were twenty-seven years old, and they competed with each other in everything they did.

The twins graduated from UCLA and received master's degrees, one in business and the other in mathematics. The twins were sergeants and sharpshooters in the navy SEALs. They later joined the LAPD as snipers in the SWAT team unit, where Agent Lamb quickly took notice of their shooting skills. They had earned numerous awards for their shooting skills and also for valor in combat. The twins were very quiet and reserved. Both held black belts in Wing Chun kung fu. The twins were in several extreme combat missions. There was one that stood out in both of their minds. US reporters went to Afghanistan to investigate POW camps, where prisoners were tortured and murdered. Al-Qaeda denied such accusations. When the reporters were filming, they were approached by Al-Qaeda, and their driver was murdered. The two female reporters were raped. The five males were interrogated and tortured day and night. The navy SEALs sent in a team of six for a rescue operation. Intelligence informed the SEALs that the reporters were being held in a compound just over a week. The twins and their teammates moved toward the compound armed with weapons and charges. The compound was heavily guarded: there were two guards in the front and six covering the exterior, and inside were at least ten more guards. Two were guarding the men's cell house, and two guarded the women's cell. There were also two watchtowers, one in the front of the compound with a guard inside, and other tower in the middle of the compound with one guard. Ajay and his two men took the back, and Ajeeta's team took the front.

Ajeeta placed her night vision binoculars near her eyes. After peering into them, she noticed two guards, one smoking a cigarette and the other speaking to the smoker. Ajeeta aimed her rifle at the guard smoking; her private aimed at the other guard. Ajeeta counted down using her fingers. *Three … Two … One.* The SEALs took one shot each, hitting the guards in the head; the men fell lifeless to the ground. "Firefox to Wolfpack, entrance clear," Ajeeta said.

"Roger, entrance clear. All teams, go infrared!" Ajay commanded. Ajay and his men scaled the back wall by using grappling hooks and rope. Once the three SEALs had reached the top of the wall, they could see two prison shacks where the reporters were being held. Ajay observe four guards near the entrance areas of the prison shacks. Ajay motioned to his men using hand signals that there were four men they were are going to take out now. Ajay and his men took precision aim at the guards and counted down. *Three … Two … One.* They fired four shots, one from each of his men's weapons, and two from his own. The guards fell dead to the ground. The team jumped down to the ground and ran toward the prison shacks. Ajay and his men opened the prison shacks and found the reporters wounded, frightened, and hungry, but they were still alive. The team gave clothing to the female reporters. The reporters were overwhelmed with gratitude.

"The Americans are trying to free the prisoners. Kill them. Kill them all!" shouted one of the guards. Four more guards heard the outcry and ran toward the prisoners' shacks. One of Ajeeta's men placed a machine gun on the ground and shot at the charging guards, hitting each of them in the chest, face, sides, stomach, and face. When the smoke had cleared, all five of the Al-Qaeda lay dead on the ground.

Ajeeta and her men began setting charges inside of the compound; they also set charges at the entrance. "Everyone out at the rear!" shouted Ajeeta. One of Ajeeta's men took aim with his bazooka and shot out the back wall, which made a large hole for escape. As they made their exit, each of the SEALs threw a grenade over the wall and into the compound, exploding on the enemies running toward the wall. An enemy truck arrived with twenty men. As they tried to enter the compound, Ajeeta set off the charges. The truck exploded, sending bodies everywhere. The prisoners applauded and cheered the navy SEALs. The reporters were escorted safely to helicopters and sent immediately to the States. The team was given the Medal of Valor. The twins took their seats next to Wendy Skypack.

Adam "Running Deer" Wombush, the Warrior, was Cherokee, and he took a seat behind the twins. He was 5'11" and weighed 190 pounds. Adam had long black hair and wore it in a ponytail. Adam lived most of his life on the reservation and left home to go to the University of Arizona, where he received a master's degree in communications. Adam signed up to go into the Green Berets. He and Doc were in the Olympics at the same time. Adam received first place in archery. Adam "Running Dear" Wombush had a unique relationship with nature, particularly with animals. He held a black belt in jujitsu. Adam worked his way up to the rank of sergeant.

One day Sergeant Wombush received orders: he and his men were to extract ten wounded soldiers from the 101st Airborne, from behind enemy lines. Once Sergeant Wombush and his men arrived at their destination, they were greeted with heavy gunfire. His unit consisted of four vehicles, three men inside each. When all of the wounded were placed inside the vehicles, they immediately fled back to base. Sergeant Wombush radioed one of his men, who stated that Taliban reinforcements were approaching. The vehicles were undergoing heavy enemy fire. Adam ordered his vehicles to stop, and he transferred all of the wounded from his vehicle to the others. The sergeant then ordered his men to head for higher ground to take cover behind rock formations. His men did so and were able to return fire. Meanwhile, the sergeant drove off in his vehicle, luring most of the Taliban. Once he was far away from his men, the sergeant started the timer on the explosives. He suddenly made a ninety-degree turn and headed straight toward the enemies' vehicles. Sergeant Wombush pressed on the gas pedal to increase the vehicle's speed. The Taliban began to fire on his vehicle with AK-47s and grenade launchers. The first two grenades missed, however the third one did not. Cheering came from the Taliban as a grenade hit the sergeant's vehicle head-on and caused an explosion. The vehicle continued onward, hitting the first Taliban-occupied vehicle; the enemy cried for help. The second, third, and fourth vehicles continued to collide, causing explosions. The fifth Taliban vehicle was able to avoid this fate, and they were relieved—until they observed an eagle in the air approaching them with something in its claws. One Taliban fighter thought it was a sign of victory. However, the eagle let the object go. One of the men placed his hands out to accept whatever it was. The cylindrical object fell instead into the vehicle. They stopped cheering once they saw the lit numbers on the side of the cylinder counting down. Everyone attempted to jump out of the vehicle as the explosive device went off, killing everyone inside. The sergeant's men looked on and saw that there was nothing they could do. They believed that their beloved sergeant was killed in action. Sergeant Adam Wombush returned to base later that evening with cuts and bruises all over his body. He told his commander that he was thrown clear of the wreckage from the explosion.

Troy Anders and André Leblanc walked in together. Troy sat in the back next to the exit. Troy Anders was from the Special Air Service (SAS), a regiment of the British Army. Troy was 5'11" and had blue eyes with black hair. He weighed 190 pounds. Troy was a trained sniper and held a fifth-degree black belt in tae kwon do; he was also an accomplished kickboxer and MMA cage fighter.

Troy had a dangerous assignment in Afghanistan. His unit had just completed a search-and-rescue operation involving contractors from the United States and England. Troy's unit came under heavy fire after they had rescued the contractors. Troy was on the roof holding off an enemy attack with his sniper rifle when more Al-Qaeda reinforcements approached from the north side. Troy radioed his unit below to leave because there was no time for him to get down to their vehicles. Troy's commander radioed a helicopter to extract him from the building. Two other Tomahawk helicopters came to Troy's aid. One helicopter landed on the roof while being covered by the other two Tomahawks. They shot missiles all around the building, destroying all enemy vehicles.

Andre Leblanc was 5'10" and weighed 185 pounds. He had brown eyes and brown hair. He sat next to Troy. André was born in the United States, however his parents were both in the military and had been assigned to France, where André spent most of his youth. When

André was seventeen, he was influenced by gang members and joined them. He was told to steal some money from a local store cash register in order to prove himself. André's conscience bothered him, and he could not go through with it. One of the gang members decided that they wanted the money, and André tried to stop him. The youth pulled out a handgun and told the clerk to hand over all the money. The clerk pulled out a shotgun and fired. André ran out of the store while the gang member fell to the floor and did not get up. André was surrounded by the police. The clerk knew him to be a good and honest teen; he was simply involved with bad people. André's parents were furious, and he went before the judge three days later. The judge gave him the option of the D-home or the French Foreign Legion.

The French Foreign Legion was a good place to begin. André served there for five years, and in time he became a sniper. He excelled at his assignments and became known throughout the Legion. André studied the French martial art discipline savant and became a fifth-degree black belt. André transferred out of the Legion to become a Green Beret. André's unit was assigned to Iraq, and his mission was to take out ammunition supply areas and convoys. André used a G-3 sniper rifle in most of his assignments. This assignment was extremely dangerous because his unit was outnumbered by the overwhelming number of Iraqis who were sent to protect the ammunition depot. André and his men would surround the convoys, ambush them, and cut off any supplies that were en route to that area.

Mike Jennings was an African American, 5'7" and weighed 170 pounds. He had brown hair and brown eyes. Mike was very hyperactive and was also a perfectionist. Everything had to be done to near perfection and in order. A computer geek, Mike was the creator of the space satellite STARE DOWN (Scanning, Transmitting, Audio-Receiving, Evaluating, Defensive, Operating Weapon Neutralizer). This satellite was a virtual spy and weapon machine. Mike worked on this project for four years before it was approved by the brass and then the agency. Mike went to school at Harvard and received his master's degree in computer science. He held a black belt in karate. He was transferred from US Air Force, where he worked in computer defensive technologies. Jennings sat next to Adam.

Terri Martinez was a Hispanic Irish American, and she was thirty years old. Terri was 5'6" and weighed 130 pounds. She had black hair and blue eyes. Terri had a master's degree in criminal justice from the University of Colorado. She served in the Marine Corps for seven years as a lieutenant in the military police before transferring into CPAT. Terri was in command of CPAT's second team, Omega. Lamb chose her because of her leadership and decision-making skills. She was very detailed. Terri took a seat in the front row, one over from Doc.

"Good morning, everyone," Director Victor Price said.

"Good morning, sir!" the team replied in unison.

"My name is Victor Price. I am the chief director of the CIA. My background is as follows. I began my military career in the United States Army as a second lieutenant. I served during the Gulf War. I worked my way up in rank to a major and then transferred over to Delta Force, where I was introduced to your unit director, Nathan Lamb. After serving in the army for approximately twenty years, I joined the CIA. I have been assigned to nearly every field, from logistics to surveillance to field investigations. Today I am the director of the CIA.

"The war on terrorism has already begun right here, on our own soil. The war began with the bombing of the World Trade Center in 1993, and then 9/11 in 2001. The threat is here, people, and believe me, it is real. Al-Qaeda threatens our freedom and our very lives. I'm used to walking to places with my family freely, without fear. Now I have that fear. The fear of losing what I have, my family, and yes, even my country. We take what we have here for granted. Do you all not agree?" The room was silent, but they nodded. "Do you all see that flag in this conference room? Do you think that this flag will be here forever? Do you believe that this soil on which we stand today will always be called the United States of America? I'm here today to inform you that nothing is forever. Nothing! Only God is forever, people. However, I will tell you this. I will do everything in my power, to my last breath, to make sure that this flag will continue to wave. My hope is that you will do the same.

"Your unit is a part of personal security detail. Your PSD unit will work along with the counterintelligence unit. This unit has a name given by your director, CPAT: Crime Prevention Against

Terrorism. You are to escort dignitaries to and from their jobs, and to various activities throughout the day. This unit will also be involved in extracting individuals from hostage situations, either in the United States or overseas. Governor Barry Barton is your first assignment. Most of our time and resources will be spent protecting the governor and his family. The governor's oldest is twenty-four years old and is about to finish college to become a lawyer; his name is Todd. The governor's daughter, Jasmine, is about to graduate to college. His youngest are identical twin daughters, Brianna and Suzanna, both in the second grade. Governor Barton has had death threats sent from a terrorist named Abdullah Mohammed. Heimen Mohammed was Abdullah's son, and the governor put the son death for killing twenty men, women, and children in the bombing of the CIA building in LA." The director from the Counter Intelligence unit presented me with these slides that I'm about to show you.

"We have these profiles of eight individuals who are part of Al-Qaeda. Abdul-Aliyy is thirty-three years old with long black hair and brown eyes. He's an explosives expert. Many in this group seek his expertise in hiding and setting off bomb devices in strategic areas. Abdul can make just about anything into an explosive device. Oh, by the way, he majored in physics at the University of Cambridge. Adham Mohammed is twenty-five years old. He wears his hair to his shoulders and is a pyromaniac. Adham is the group's diversionist. Adham has relatives living here in LA; they have been under heavy surveillance for the past two years. He has not yet made contact with them. Emir Muhammed is twenty-eight years old with short black hair. Emir is the weapon's supplier; he has strong ties with countries such as Russia, China, and North Korea. Most of their weapons and ammo arrive via the black market by boat, planes, trains, and semis. Fakhir Chandra is twenty-seven years old with long black hair that is usually braided into a ponytail. Fakhir takes care of all the logistics for the group. Fakir speaks English and several other languages very well. He has taught English to his fellow colleagues who did not know English. Fakir majored in English at the University of Texas. Hakeem Sur is thirty-two years old. He has long black hair and brown eyes. He also wears his hair in a ponytail. He is a well-known impersonator in the Middle East. Be careful because he can impersonate almost anyone in this class." Doc looked around the auditorium and shook his head in disbelief.

Price continued. "Jabbar Anand is thirty years old. Jabbar has short black hair and blue eyes. He is their guide to anywhere and everywhere in the world because Jabbar has been everywhere. He trains this group on the firing range and also in martial arts, including grappling. Numair Verma is thirty-five years old. He has short black hair and green eyes. Numair is a chemist and likes to experiment with and invent toxic chemicals. Numair majored in chemistry at the University of California. Zafir Nasser is twenty-seven years old and is a Syrian military fighter pilot; he acquired training in Russia. He has brown hair and hazel eyes. Abdul-Rahman is thirty-four years old. He has black hair and brown eyes, and he works as their intelligence. He is well versed in being covert and is very dangerous! Last but not least, Abdullah Mohammed is the leader of this group. Mohammed is 5'9" and weighs 185 pounds. Mohammed is sixty years old with long black hair and blue eyes. Mohammed has loyalty from all of his men, and he is a perfectionist. Ever since his son, Heiman Mohammed, was put to death by Governor Barton, Mohammed has gone to great lengths to attempt to murder the governor and his family. Take a good look at them, agents; study these faces. Know that each and every one of them is very dangerous and is well versed in Middle Eastern martial arts.

"The commander of your operation is of course Nathan Lamb. He will disseminate all the information that you need daily. Agent Lamb will keep me well informed of your progress with all dignitaries, beginning with your first assignment. Agents, do you have any questions?" The agents looked at each other and shook their heads. "If there are none I will give the platform to Agent Lamb. Have a good day." Nathan Lamb shook hands with Victor Price before the director left the platform.

"Good morning, team," Lamb said.

"Good morning, Commander," the team said in unison.

"I have handed out the profiles on each of these individuals. I want you all to study them and get to know each of them well. Just as the director stated, each terrorist is very dangerous. Approach them with caution. I expect you to contact me immediately if you do come in contact with any of them. No "on your own heroics," either. Clear?"

"Clear, Commander."

"I will break you up into two teams, the Hades team and the Omega team. We need to also work on defensive shooting tactics on the range. We need to do this every day at 0800 hours. We will meet at the range at 0800 hours until we begin our assignment next Monday. If there are no further questions, you are dismissed." No one raised their hands. Lamb saw that some were smiling, some had blank stares, and some had looks of eager anticipation.

Andréa, Lamb's secretary, walked up to him and asked him to follow her to the archive files, to show him where more files were kept on Al-Qaeda. She took him to the other side of the building, and they walked past the area where old files were kept for missing person cases along with homicides before they arrived at the terrorist files. Lamb looked at some of the files' titles, and one caught his eye very quickly. "The Anderson case." Lamb opened the file cabinet and pulled out the file.

Andréa saw the file and asked Lamb, "Agent, do you remember the Anderson case? It made national news." Lamb looked at the file as he had gone into a trance. "Agent Lamb, do you remember the Anderson case?"

Anderson, Anderson, Anderson. The name echoed through Lamb's mind. Lamb knew this case too well because he was part of it.

It was Lamb's sophomore year in high school. The halls of the high school were silent, but not for long. The bell rang, and soon the halls were flooded with the sounds of teenagers rushing out of school. Lamb and his friends were in the parking lot watching girls walk outside and listening to the radio. "In the news today, federal and local officials are continuing their search in the rescue attempt efforts to find Carrie Anderson, who has been missing for six months. Tune in for more details on action news at six."

"Hey, Lamb. There she is—Sandy Williams. Go for it," Jim Thompson said.

"Yeah, buddy. Don't let this one get away this time," Andréw Coswell said.

Lamb gave his books to Jim and walked slowly toward Sandy. Her friends motioned to her that Lamb was advancing toward them. Sandy laughed with her friends. Lamb became more embarrassed as he turned to his friends for support; they motioned for him to continue. Lamb stopped by her side and attempted a simple, "Hello, girls." His voice was weak and soft spoken. "S-s Sandy," Lamb said with a stutter.

"Yeah, Lamb? What do you want?" Sandy said obnoxiously. "W-would you be willing to go out with me to the sophomore dance this spring?" Lamb said, his voice shaking.

"Me, go with you to the sophomore dance?" Sandy said. Her friends laughed. "Me, go with a dork like you? I don't think so, loser," Sandy replied.

Lamb turned around and ran back to his friends. "Hey, better luck next time, Lamb," Jim said.

"Hey, Lamb, let's go do something! Don't let her get to you. There are plenty of other girls to ask out!" Andréw said.

Lamb was too upset to listen. He took his books from Andréw, jumped on his Honda motorcycle, and peeled out in the parking lot. "Don't go, Lamb!"

The laughter echoes in his mind. Tears flowed down his cheeks as he remembered all of the rejections he'd received from the girls in his school. Lamb began to speed. He turned down a dirt road and sped towards an area he visited went to seek out serenity, calmness, and peace. He rode into the woods and observed dark green foliage everywhere. A small path became visible, and he turned his lights on while keeping up his speed. These were the woods where Lamb and his friends played army, cowboys, and Indians. This place was where he went to meditate. Lamb saw a clearing in the woods and a sign that reads, "No trespassing. Keep out." His parents always forbade him and his siblings from going past that sign. Lamb continued to ride on. He saw an old barn house, slowed down, and turned off his bike about twenty feet away. Lamb walked his bike the rest of the way toward the barn house.

The barn was very old and gray. The windows were all broken, but the front door still had a lock on it. Lamb saw a window with a light on the first floor. He peered into the window and viewed a body sitting in a chair; he noticed that it was a young woman. She was bound and gagged. She had on what looked like a yellow blouse that had blood on it. She made small soft whimpers, and tears flowed from her face as she desperately struggled to get free from her ropes. Lamb made his way to the back door. He found it locked, however he worked on the lock with one of his pins. Lamb opened it, walked cautiously toward the young girl, and removed the gag. "Are you all right?" he asked.

"Yes, I think so!" the frightened girl answered. "I've been here for a long time. One of them tried to rape me." Her voice was desperate.

"Hey, I know who you are. You're Carrie Anderson, the girl from our rival school in Camden, across the river. I just heard that the FBI and police have more information on your whereabouts. I can get you out of here, Carrie. Don't worry." Lamb said as he heard a click. It was a sound of metal clicking metal, and something pressed on his neck. Lamb turned slowly as his fear turned into reality.

"Turn around slowly, boy." Lamb turned around to see a man in trousers with a cowboy hat and a pair of black worn-out boots. Lamb was looking down the barrel of a shotgun. "Hey, Lester, Bo. It looks like we've got ourselves another one here. Heh!"

"What's all the fuss, Junior?" Bo asked.

"Well, well. Looks like we could use some more ransom money," Lester said.

"Look, we can't use them anymore. Her father don't wanna pay no more. So that means she ain't worth nothing no more, neither," Bo said.

"Well, what do we do with them, then?" Lester said.

"We gotta get rid of them all and leave no evidence," Bo said.

Lester and Junior began to tie up Lamb. The men placed them both inside the trunk of an old Chevy. The three criminals then left the premises.

"I'll never get out. I'll never see my parents ever again. Oh, God, please help us, please!" cried Carrie.

Lamb could not speak because he was bound and gagged. He did remembered what his father used to do, and what he told him to do if he were ever tied up. His father was an escape artist—and a very good one at that. Lamb remembered his father told him to expand his chest and hold his breath once the ropes were tightened, and to exhale to loosen the ropes. Lamb did so, and began to exhale slowly. The ropes were loose. Lamb untied himself and took off his gag. He then untied a very surprised and frightened Carrie Anderson.

"How, how did you get loose?" Carrie said with a gulp.

"My father taught me well," Lamb whispered. He found the latch and opened the trunk of the car. Lamb got out first and then assisted the young lady. "You've got to come with me, Carrie. I promise to get you out of here," he said. Lamb took Carrie by the hand and led her to his motorcycle. They both got on, and Lamb started the bike. They took off towards the woods, back from where he came.

As they were leaving, Bo arrived in his truck, and they passed him. Bo made a U-turn and went after the motorcycle. Lester and Junior were on their motorcycles and joined the pursuit. Lamb headed into the wooded area and increased his speed. It was very dark, however he knew every inch of the terrain. He also knew that a car could not make it there. Bo now saw two trees up ahead, but it was too late. His truck hit the two trees, turned onto its side, and then flipped end over end twice before coming to a violent stop.

Lamb remembered the ravine ramp that he and his friends used to challenge each other to jump from time to time. However, it was very different this time. It was dark, and Lamb must use his instincts to know where that ramp was. He decided to go to the right and increase his speed. He was well ahead of his captors. "Hold on, Carrie. We're jumping!" Lamb yells. Carrie tightened her grip on Lamb's waist. The motorcycle lifted off the ramp and into the air. They both felt the wind hitting them as they landed on the other side, safely. Lester and Junior did not see the ravine or the ramp. They fell into the ravine, surprised and screaming helplessly. The bikes both exploded upon impact.

Lamb took Carrie straight to the police station.

"Agent Lamb? Agent Lamb, I said do you remember the Anderson case?" Andréa asked.

"Huh? Yes, I do. I do remember Carrie Anderson," Lamb replied.

"For a moment I thought I had lost you," Andréa said.

Lamb was looking at the newspaper in the file that stated, "Local boy hero rescues missing Anderson girl. Gives most of reward money to charity." He placed the paper back into the file and closed the door.

Andréa and Lamb walked to the files that contained information on Al-Qaeda. She opened the file cabinet and handed the information to Lamb. They both walked back through the halls and toward his office, where he found Jennings, the unit's tech. "Commander, I have something to show you. I have connected your computer to our system's supporting satellite, called STARE DOWN. It stands for Scanning, Transmitting, Audio, Radio, Evaluator Defensive Operating Weaponry Neutralizer," Jennings said with enthusiasm.

"Can this satellite be compared to a spy camera?" Lamb asked.

"Exactly, sir," Jennings replied. "Not only will you be able to hear what individuals are saying behind closed doors, but you will also be able to see them and monitor their activities."

"Well, Jennings, it's 1700 hours and time for me to leave. I will see you and Andréa in the morning!"

"Good evening, Director," Jennings and Andréa said.

Lamb walked toward the exit and waved good-bye to the security officers. His phone soon rang. "Hello?"

"Hi, Daddy!"

"Arianna?" Lamb said.

"Yes, it's me, Daddy! Are you coming over to get me tomorrow? Remember, you promised me shopping!" Arianna exclaimed.

"I sure did, angel, and I sure will. I will be there at noon!. Sound good?"

"Sounds good to me, Daddy!"

Lamb heard a familiar voice in the background. "Nathan, are you *really* going to make it this time?"

"Daddy, here's Mommy," Arianna said.

"Well, are you?" Susan said.

"Yes, Susan, I will be there," Lamb replied. "This is for her birthday. I won't let her down. I've put aside my schedule tomorrow for her."

"We'll see!" Susan said. Lamb was somewhat frustrated at Susan's question, but he knew that she was right. Lamb had been so busy that he had neglected his family, and that led to his divorce. Lamb remembered when he'd first met Susan at UCLA....

Susan majored in business, and Lamb majored in administration of justice. Their roommates were dating and invited them to join them for a dinner and a movie. Lamb believed at that moment that Susan was the one. Susan was impressed by Lamb's personality: he was very respectful and had a good sense of humor. She was really drawn to the fact that, unlike most of the young men she'd dated in the past, Lamb had goals. He explained to Susan that after college, he wanted to join the military, move up in the ranks, and then become an officer. Lamb said that he didn't think he would make a career out of it, because someday he wanted to become a police officer and move up to a supervisory position. This made a good first impression on Susan. Lamb was drawn to Susan being independent and free spirited. She also had goals of working in a business or school organization.

Later, they became serious about their relationship and decided to get engaged. Lamb bought her an engagement ring and on a memorable Friday evening, and he proposed to her on a boat ride in the San Francisco Bay. She accepted his proposal right away, and they contacted family and friends. They were soon married and honeymooned in Vegas.

Lamb wanted to tell his new bride about his special ability but was very hesitant. He wanted to say something well before they were married but was afraid of rejection. Lamb was afraid that Susan would either think he was insane and laugh at him, or reject him and call off the wedding. The plane that they were waiting for at the airport had been delayed. Lamb was going to be flying out to Fort Bennington, Georgia, for military training; he had joined the army two weeks before. Lamb told Susan that he felt dizzy and had to use the restroom, however Lamb knew that this was no ordinary dizziness. He felt that he was going to have a premonition—a very strong one. He opened the bathroom stall, sat down on the commode, and covered his face with his hands. The room seemed like it was spinning. Lamb felt as if he had no control of his muscles, and his vision became blurred. He felt as if he were being drawn into a vacuum. These were the first signs of Lamb getting a premonition. Lamb's vision then began to come to a clear focus, and he slumped forward.

Lamb then slowly rose and opened the bathroom stall door. He promptly went to the sink to wash his hands and face. As he was doing so, he noticed a pilot beside him washing his hands and face. He glanced over at Lamb and said, "Hi. You know, this is my final flight. I have nothing left to look forward to in my life. My wife took the kids and left me for some young punk. She also cleaned me out of my bank account. I was also passed over for a great promotion. Someone's going to pay for that today. You'll see." The man began to sob uncontrollably and then picked up his briefcase, revealing an empty miniature whiskey bottle inside his coat pocket. As the pilot walked, he stumbled twice before exiting the men's restroom. Lamb immediately pursued and then observed the pilot wave to his fellow pilots and flight attendants. All of a sudden, the pilot grabbed one of the flight attendants by her arm, moved her to the side, and said, "You know I can't give you that kind of money, Sharon. You know I can't."

"Now look here, Marty," Sharon said as she pulled her arm away from his grip. "You're the one who forced me to be with you that night. When you play, you pay. You will pay, Marty. I'm not giving up that baby. If you want me to keep quiet, you're going to have to pay me what I want."

"But Sharon, my wife says she'll leave me if you don't."

"Well, I guess you should have thought of that before," Sharon said, snickering as she walked toward her co-workers who were waiting for her a few feet away.

Marty turned his attention towards the bar that was to his right. He walked towards it quickly and glanced at his watch. He knew the bartender and ordered a shot. Though the bartender noticed that Marty appeared to be intoxicated, he continued to serve him. "Take it easy, Marty. You still have a flight to take before you're off."

"Yeah, yeah. I've got this, and you know it, John," Marty said, annoyed. He then slammed the glass down on the bar hard, paid John, and left.

Lamb continued to follow him. Marty moved toward the gate where the plane was waiting: B-24. No one else seemed to notice that he was intoxicated and disoriented. He greeted his crew and took a seat in the captain's chair. His co-pilot glanced at him and shook his head in disbelief as he looked over the flight plan. Marty informed the co-pilot of his dilemma and sought his advice. The co-pilot replied, "You should have thought of that before." That was his only answer—no advice as to what to do now.

As the flight attendant completed her emergency procedures for the passengers, Marty went into his own thoughts about life and came to the conclusion it was time to end it here and now. He throttled the engines and asked for clearance from the towers. The plane moved quickly down the runway. The co-pilot told him to slow down because he was going too fast. Marty turned onto the flight runway without clearance from the tower. "What are you trying to do, Knoll?" the co-pilot asked. Marty ignored his comment and pulled up on the controls as the plane entered the air. He turned the plane, making a hard right in the direction of the air traffic control tower. The co-pilot wrestled Marty for control of the plane. Marty hit the co-pilot in the jaw and knocked him out. Lamb could not interfere—he was a phantom from another world.

Marty's supervisor was in that tower. "I've got you now, you asshole son-of-a bitch," Marty screamed. The people inside the tower tried to exit quickly, however they were too late. The plane crashed into the tower, the left wing leading into it as the plane descended. The nose hit the ground first and exploded into a fiery inferno. The passengers screamed as their bodies were scorched and burned.

Lamb's vision became blurred once again. Once it refocused, he saw that he is back on the toilet in the men's room. Lamb was no longer disoriented and was stable. Before he opened the restroom stall door, he peered through an opening and noticed a pilot washing his hands. The pilot has a name tag: Captain Knoll. Lamb walked out of the stall and washed his hands and face. The pilot turned toward Lamb and smiled. He said, "This is my last flight before the weekend. My wife ran off with a younger guy, some punk, and she took the kids. She caught me cheating—can you believe that? I was also passed over by my boss for a big promotion. He gave it to a guy who doesn't even deserve it! He's gonna pay for his bullshit. You mark my words: he'll pay."

Lamb noticed a miniature whiskey bottle inside the pilot's right coat pocket. "I know that you probably didn't want to hear my bullshit this early in the morning, but thanks for listening anyway, kid. Have a safe flight. I know I won't." The pilot picked up his briefcase and walked out of the restroom.

Lamb followed close behind him. He noticed a group of pilots and flight attendants walking toward Knoll. Lamb felt he has to act without hesitation. He quickly took one of the pilots aside and spoke to him concerning Knoll's drinking. "If you were to open his briefcase and check the inside of his coat pocket, you would find bottles of whiskey miniatures. He appears to be intoxicated and is extremely upset about his personal life," Lamb said.

The pilot whom Lamb spoke to motioned for his captain to join the conversation. They immediately called airport police. Captain Marty Knoll was placed in custody as he walked toward the bar after being questioned. The police and pilots were very grateful for Lamb taking the initiative. Many lives were saved that day. Lamb was told it was Knoll's supervisor who was in the air traffic control tower.

Lamb walked back to gate B-24, where he found his fiancée already in line to board the plane. "Hi, honey! Where have you been? You made it back just in time. We just started to board the plane. The service desk said that we were delayed because they had to get another pilot," Ann said. Lamb gazed into Ann's eyes and then gave her a kiss and a hug. When he slowly pulled away, she had a look of surprise. "Are you all right?" she asked.

Lamb said, "I'm fine. Everything is fine now."

Lamb began to have premonitions at the age of fourteen after an accident, It occurred because of a dare he took with his friend, David Jensen. It was David's birthday; he was turning fourteen one month before Lamb. Lamb was invited, along with all of David's friends and family, to his birthday party. David received many gifts from his friends and family. After the party was over, Lamb and David went for a walk through the woods to an open field where three electrical towers stood. Five boys from a rival school were at the bottom of the middle tower sitting on the metal girders. One boy said to them, "Hey, you kids.

Come over here. Don't be scared. We ain't gonna do nothing to you." The boys moved slowly toward the towers. The rival boy continued. "I dare you to climb all the way up the middle tower and come back down."

"I'll do better than that," an older boy said. "I'll bet you twenty bucks that you won't do it!" He pulled out twenty dollars and let it fall to the ground.

David didn't want to pass up the opportunity to get an easy twenty, so he also dropped a twenty to the ground; he had already received nearly a hundred dollars for his birthday. "Come on, Nathan. Let's do it," he said enthusiastically.

Lamb was ready and determined. The other boys were in shock because they didn't really believe that they would take the dare. David and Lamb proceeded to climb the tower. As they climbed, dark clouds began to form above them. When they reach the top, both boys cried out in victory. The group of boys began to shout for them to get down as thunder roared and lightning flashed across the sky above them. David and Lamb began a quick descent. As they did so, Lamb could feel his hair rising on his head and arms. David's hair did the same.

"Nathan!" David cried as lightning struck the tower. Both boys fell fifty feet to the ground. Two of the rival boys ran to get help. Lamb's and David's bodies lay lifeless next to each other on the ground.

Once Lamb woke up, he could see that he was in a hospital. There were flowers with cards on the table to the right of him. Lamb felt a bandage wrapped around his head. "So you finally decided to wake up, Mr. Lamb," his nurse said.

"How long was I out for?" Lamb inquired.

"Three days" replied the nurse. "You fell fifty feet, young man. You are very, very fortunate. I will get the doctor and inform your parents."

The doctor arrived and had Lamb go through an MRI and blood tests before he was released. His father told him that David wasn't so fortunate. David had died when he hit the ground. Lamb cried uncontrollably because he considered David to be his closest friend. Lamb was released from the hospital with a broken wrist, shoulder, and leg. Lamb's classmates would stop by the house to say hello and bring him homework. Once his leg healed, Lamb would take walks with his friends around the neighborhood.

One day as he was walking, his body began to experience tremors; they were almost seizure-like symptoms. He shook uncontrollably, and his eyes rolled to the back of his head. He nearly collapsed to the floor when his two friends caught him and laid him gently to the ground. One of his friends ran to get his parents. Once his they arrived, his mother, a licensed nurse, tried to revive him. "What is it, Nathan? What's wrong, baby?" Carol said frantically. Lamb was unresponsive.

"I'll call for an ambulance," Lucas said. Lamb saw darkness and then a light that began to grow brighter until he could see figures that were unfocused and unidentifiable. As the figures became focused, he could observe a large crowd sitting and applauding. He saw a ringmaster in the middle. "Ladies and gentlemen, welcome to the greatest show on earth! It's time now to turn our attention to the world's greatest magician, escape artist, and ventriloquist to ever walk the face of the earth: Lucas Lamb the Great!" It was Lamb's father! He had taught Lamb everything he could about his job and about life. Lamb saw him perform several acts of illusions and escape acts. The scene flashed to his parents driving down a winding road. A vehicle was headed toward them and swerving from side to side. Lamb's parents' vehicle was run off the road by the oncoming car. They were both ejected from the vehicle through the windshield.

Lamb shook as he came to, and he saw his parents and friends staring at him. The ambulance arrived and transported him to the hospital. The doctor could find nothing wrong after he finished his examination. "I want to keep him overnight for observation," she said. Lamb's parents show a look of concernment as their son lay in bed.

Lamb was frightened by what he saw. "Mom, I saw you and Dad in a bad car accident coming home from the show on Friday," he said. "I saw you both covered in blood. You were both dead!"

Laura glanced at Lucas and then turned to Lamb and said, "Now, now, dear. It was all just a bad dream."

"But, Mom, this was no dream. This happened when I went into that seizure. This was no dream!" Lamb said.

"Don't worry, son. It's going to be all right," his father stated assuredly. "I want to be frank with you, Nathan. Your mom and I plan to be with you as long as God wills it. Hopefully it's a long time. However, if it is time for us to go, then no amount of magic can prevent that from occurring. If that is our destiny or fate, nothing can prevent it."

"You don't have to go. You can cancel, and then there will be no accident. Mom, Dad, please don't go!" Lamb pleaded.

"Dear, it's going to be all right. You'll see," Laura said.

"Get some rest, son, and we'll see you in the morning." Lucas said.

The next day, Lamb's parents visited him until the hour before the show began. They both gave him hugs and kisses and told him that they would tell him all about the show the next day. It was five o'clock. About five hours later, Lamb received word from the hospital medical staff that both his parents had been killed in an automobile accident. The other driver was intoxicated and driving a rig. Lamb wept.

At the funeral, Lamb was taken in by his Aunt Rebecca, his father's sister. His two siblings, Jonathan and Ruth, were taken in by another aunt, Eunice, Laura's sister. Rebecca was single and lived alone and wanted Nathan to live with her. Jonathan and Ruth already had two children. There would be room for only two more. Rebecca was Nathan's favorite aunt. Rebecca made sure that the children kept in contact with each other throughout their teen years. The accident, however, made Lamb bitter. It changed him and gave him a negative attitude toward life. He was sent to detention several times for stealing. Lamb liked associating with gang members. It wasn't until Marty, a friend of Lamb's, was shot and killed by a rival gang that he removed himself from their affiliation. However, Lamb would continue to get into trouble with the law. He had a hard time respecting the law and authority. He was apprehended when he attempted to burglarize a home. The judge saw a young kid who was very bitter and needed discipline. He gave Lamb a choice of six years of jail time or four years of army life. Lamb immediately chose to join the army.

The army gave Lamb some discipline, but he continued to associate with the wrong crowd. He would later encounter someone who would have a profound effect on his life. Lamb had memories that helped him grow into the person he was today.

Lamb wanted to see how effective STARE DOWN was. He instructed Jennings to set all monitoring and tracking systems on him throughout the day. The satellite would monitor all of Lamb's activities; everywhere he went, STARE DOWN would be.

Inside a white van were four individuals who were planning something devious and destructive. "Abib, do you have the blueprint of the mall?" Adullah asked.

"I do, and we are ready to proceed as planned," Abib said.

"Numair, are you ready to carry out your orders?" Abdullah asked.

"I am ready, sir," Numair confidently stated.

"Good. We will begin to execute our orders as planned very shortly. Soon this country will bow down to our authority. They will be at our mercy once we cripple them by eliminating their leaders," Abdullah said. Abib and Numair were both captains in Al-Qaeda. They were the first wave of destruction to wreak havoc against leaders in the United States. This plot of terror had been in the making for nearly ten years. All terrorists involved had been trained proficiently in every aspect of their assignments. Each of them were loyal to the cause, and they had worked toward the goal of annihilating the enemy no matter the cost. They were commanded by General Abdullah Mohammed, the head of Al-Qaeda. He was the one who had given orders to strike.

The four men of the Al-Qaeda group were wearing overalls with name tags of a fake company, "Greg's Plumbing." Three of the men had tool boxes in their possession. Each box contained a filler along with C-4. They drove away from an old, abandoned building where they were devising the plans.

Lamb received a crash course from Jennings on learning how to operate STARE DOWN. Lamb's activities would be monitored. He was very anxious to test the satellite's abilities and to learn its limitations.

Jennings began to program the satellite's system by uplinking it to the system's monitor. "It's ready, sir. You are good to go," Jennings said. "I'm leaving now and will be on call this weekend. If there are any problems, I can always assist by using my laptop at home. I have full access to the satellite anywhere."

Lamb thanked Jennings. Jennings then shut down the other computers in the lab and closed the door behind him. Lamb continued to look over the manual. The system seemed to be very complicated. The satellite contained wiring and mechanisms that he had never seen before. Lamb picked up STARE DOWN's operational manual, and he read it and looked over the complexity of the system. From his own desktop computer, Lamb was able to get a sample of exactly how STARE DOWN operated. Lamb pressed the videotape button, and it revealed a vehicle with two suspects sitting inside of a dark SUV across from the bank. The two suspects were planning to rob the bank. Lamb was able to actually hear exactly how they were planning to rob the bank. They also revealed two individuals who were already inside of the bank and would be their backup in case they got into trouble.

STARE DOWN then used its visual system to reveal who was inside the bank. Individuals in the bank showed up on Lamb's screen as if he were looking at negative pictures. It showed the bodies moving around and carrying on with their activities. The suspects outside in the SUV began to phone their backups inside of the bank. One of the men answered the phone and began to speak. He was now the fourth one in line in front of the bank teller. The other suspect was writing out a form at a counter near the exit of the bank. STARE DOWN revealed that both men were carrying concealed weapons. The conversation they had concerned where the money was in the bank, and also if there was a security guard. They saw that there was no guard on duty, and they felt that this was a good time for them to act. Once they got their vehicles and placed on their hooded masks, they walked across the street to the bank.

They were intercepted by federal agents. Both men inside were apprehended by four federal agents. All four suspects were caught off guard and were surprised by the quick response of the federal agents. Jennings now appeared in the video. "Hello, my fellow law enforcement agents. This is just a small demonstration of how STARE DOWN operates. You can see how the system not only shows you the suspects but also reveals what they have on them and what they are saying. The system also has other features that no other satellite has. It has the ability to give clear pictures of individuals and objects such as license plates and street names from the satellite three hundred miles above the Earth's atmosphere. STARE DOWN can give clear pictures even though people are inside a building that is deep underground. The satellite system also has a defense mechanism that can launch missiles from the satellite into an object that is hostile. The system must be programmed to act in that way, but only if it is completely necessary and is an emergency. It can only be activated by me, the director, and of course Agent Lamb.

"In this next video demonstration, we are going to see just how the missiles can be used. The video shows a vehicle heading for a building. The vehicle is being shot at by federal agents. It will not slow down, and it is carrying C-4. The individuals are planning to destroy the building. STARE DOWN activates and targets the vehicle. The visual monitor is activated and reveals the C-4 inside of the vehicle. The defensive mechanism is now activated, and the target is located and fixed. The missiles are launched from the satellite and head toward the vehicle. The vehicle is immediately hit by the missile and explodes approximately a hundred yards away from the building." Jennings appears again on the video and gives the pros and cons of STARE DOWN's defensive mechanism. "As we have seen from the demonstrations, STARE DOWN can be very beneficial in our law enforcement activities. It could be used to prevent crime and terrorism taking place here in the United States. This system will be part of our new unit that is headed by our new supervisor agent, Nathan Lamb. Crime prevention is a big part of the new unit, and this will definitely assist federal agents in their field operations." The video ended, and Lamb continued to read the manual in order to get familiar with its operations.

Lamb now begins to unpack the boxes that he had in his office. He took out pictures, awards, certificates, and his degrees, and he began hanging them up in his office. Lamb reached into the box and pulled out a picture of him and his daughter, Arianna. He stared at her for a moment and then placed it on his desk. Lamb hoped that by him moving to LA, he would be closer to her not only physically but mentally and emotionally. He knew that he could now spend more time with her.

Arianna and Lamb had always been close—closer than anyone could imagine. Lamb and his daughter had the ability to telepathically communicate with each other. Lamb could also do the same with his mother. They had a special relationship. Lamb discovered their abilities to communicate telepathically when Arianna was about two years old. Susan had placed her down on the carpet floor in the living room and told Arianna that she was going to start dinner. Arianna could play with her toys, but she was to stay in the living. The phone rang, and Susan answered the phone and began to talk to one of her best friends. Meanwhile, Arianna got up and walked toward the kitchen, where she thought Susan was. Susan had walked into the back room for something. Their pet dog had just come inside through the doggie door to drink some water. The dog then walked back outside. Arianna saw this and also wanted to also go outside. She used the doggie door and exited the kitchen.

Once Susan got off the phone, she began to call out to Arianna, however there was no answer. She looked in every room of the house but could not find Arianna. She was frantic and ran to the neighbors; she looked in the backyard of the neighbors and could not find her. The neighbors also began the search. Susan then became very frantic and desperate. She called Lamb, who was just starting his career in the San Francisco police department as a rookie field officer. Lamb was just finishing up a call concerning a neighbor's complaint about loud music in the neighborhood. "Lamb, I can't find Arianna. I need help. You've got to help me find her!" Susan said, crying.

"Susan, try to calm down and control your breathing. Now, where was the last time you saw her?" Lamb asked.

"I saw her in the living room. I put her down in order to fix dinner. The phone rang, and I answered it. It was my friend Melanie. She needed the number to our financial office downtown. I went to our bedroom and found my address book. I then gave Melanie the number and walked back toward the kitchen. I looked for Arianna then but couldn't find her. I called out for her, and she didn't answer. I ran in the backyard and then the neighbors' yards and couldn't find her. Lamb, we've got to get her back now!"

"Okay, honey. I'm on my way home. My shift is about over. My sergeant will let me go early, I'm sure," Lamb said.

He went to the neighborhood and searched. He began to then think out loud, "Where are you, baby? Where can you be? Daddy is looking for you."

"Daddy? Daddy? Where are you, Daddy? When are you coming home?"

"Baby where are you? Can you hear Daddy?"

"I'm playing with Scruffy. I'm here inside his house."

Lamb drove home, and he saw family and friends at his house. When he saw Susan, he gave her a hug and kiss, and then he took her by the hand and told her to come with him. Susan wondered what Lamb was doing. They both walked out back as their family and friends watched them. He said that he had a feeling she would be back here. They walked towards Scruffy's doghouse and found her inside playing. Susan was relieved.

"Hi, Mommy, Daddy. I told you this is where I would be, where you would find me," Arianna said. Susan ignored her comments and hugged her tightly. However, Lamb looked at Arianna and knew that from that moment on, they were going to be close, and that Arianna was very special!

Chapter 2

Terrorist Attack on the Mall

Lamb hurried to his Mustang and took off through the parking lot onto the street. He first had to leave Tank in his apartment and then went to pick up Arianna. Lamb traveled through the streets of Beverly Hills. The sun was bright and glistened against the tall buildings as he headed toward the residential areas. On his way to see Arianna, Lamb thought about the task ahead of him. He thought about the terrorists, the atrocities they had committed, and how they wanted vengeance for their fellow countrymen. Lamb had the enormous task of training an entirely new team and making it functional. The only way the unit was going to succeed was if lives were protected.

Lamb arrived at his ex-wife's house and noticed an unfamiliar vehicle parked out front. "Daddy, Daddy!" Arianna ran outside excitedly, jumping into her father's arms.

"How are you, angel?" Lamb said.

"I'm much better knowing that we're going to be together this afternoon!," Arianna said excitedly.

Susan, Lamb's ex-wife, walked to the door. "I'm glad to see that you're not late for once," she said sternly.

"Who's your new friend?" Lamb asked.

"He's just a good friend. Someone I've known at the gym for years now. He's a lawyer and has his own firm," Susan replied.

Her boyfriend walked to the door and introduced himself. "Hi, I'm Jake Pennington. Susan told me a lot about you," he said as he reached out for Lamb's hand.

Lamb responded by giving him a firm handshake. He was a little surprised that Susan had started dating. He knew that with her busy schedule, it was difficult to meet new people.

Jake placed his arm around Susan. He began to talk about his firm and asked if Lamb needed any legal counseling. He told Lamb to feel free to come by his office. Lamb nodded as he held Arianna in his arms.

Arianna went back inside the house to get ready. She finished changing into her jeans and blouse. Susan told her to hurry, and then she asked Lamb if he had been dating. He replied no; once he settled into his new job, maybe there would be some time for himself. Susan spoke about a vacation that she and Jake were planning, and she wanted to see if Lamb would be able to keep Arianna for a week. Lamb replies, "Let me know at least two weeks in advance, and I will be able to make arrangements." Susan smiled, took Jake by the hand, and said, "We're going to see how Arianna's doing. We'll see you later."

"Nice meeting you Nathan," Jake said. Lamb waved at them. Susan had surprised him this time.

Five minutes went by and Arianna appears at the front door.

"I'm ready, Daddy! Let's go!" Arianna said.

"I'll have her back in three hours," Lamb said.

Susan nodded and waved good bye to Arianna.

"Daddy, don't be sad!" Arianna said.

"What makes you think I'm sad, angel?" Lamb replied.

"I know that you're still in love with Mommy. I want you to be with Mommy too. I can make that happen, Daddy, and I will!" Arianna said excitedly.

"Look, angel. Your mommy is very happy with Jake, it seems. I don't want you making it bad for him. I also want you to listen to Mommy just like you listen to me. We have had this conversation before, young lady."

"I know, I know," Arianna said with a sigh.

"Hey, I want my big girl smiling today. In two days you are going to be seven years old! Besides that, we're going to have fun today, right, angel?" Lamb said.

"Right!" Arianna replied, giving her father a high-five. Lamb looked briefly at Arianna as he made sure her chair was secured and her seat belt was fastened. Arianna folded hers arms and smiled as Lamb opened the driver's door, sat, fastened his own seat belt, shut the door, and started the engine. Lamb headed toward the mall cautiously.

It was Friday, and school was out. The number of children in the mall was huge. There were individuals dressed up as cartoon characters walking around in the mall, and there were games and prizes in front of the stores. Spring sales specials on clothing, video games, CDs, and DVDs were everywhere. The mall was full of activity and full of people. Lamb parked in the underground parking lot at the mall and began to walk toward the mall with Arianna. Lamb took Arianna to the clothing department and followed Arianna through the clothing department as she excitedly looked and smiled at the new clothing styles that were out.

"Pick out whatever you like Angel." Lamb said with a smile.

"Arianna turned and smiled back and said,"Thanks, Daddy!"

Arianna chose her outfits and went to the cashier with her father and purchased them

"Daddy can we get ice cream now?' Arianna said.

"We sure can angel!" Lamb stated.

They both walked to the ice cream shop that was across from the clothing store. They ordered ice cream and began to eat.

All of a sudden, Lamb got a flash in his mind, and pain exploded throughout his head. As his head cleared, he saw two men getting out of a van in front of the mall. The men were wearing track suits and were carrying gym bags while walking toward the men's room. Once they were inside, they went into separate stalls and opened their bags. They both pull out cylindrical devices and activated the devices by pressing a red button. They placed the cylinders inside the tile roofing and exited the room. The two men headed out the main door and got into a waiting van. The sign on the van read, "Greg's Plumbing." The van sped out of the parking lot and onto the ramp of the freeway. An explosion occurred, and metal flew everywhere.

Men, women, and children were thrown about and ripped apart. The ceiling and walls collapsed. Glass was imbedded in bodies. An individual was shooting two AK-47s and murdering men, women, and children. Medical emergency teams entered the area through the thick smoke that filled the mall.

Lamb's vision was blurred and then came to a focus as he felt Arianna's hand rubbing his head.

"Daddy are you alright? Should I call mommy now and get you to a doctor?" Arianna said concerned.

"No, no Angel!" I'm alright! I just feel a little hot. I'll get a cold glass of water." Lamb replied.

"You stay here and I'll get it for you daddy!" Arianna stated as she ran up to the counter and asked the young man there for a cup of water.

Lamb thanked Arianna and began to drink the water. He then told her that something has come up and has to call her mother to pick her up right away.

"Hello!" Susan answered.

"Susan this is Nathan. Something very serious has come up and I can't discuss the details with you right now. Everyone in the mall right now is in danger and I have to begin evacuation. I will get Arianna out of here now!" Lamb said desperately, as he began walking quickly with Arianna toward the mall exit.

"Oh my God! Where will you have me pick up Arianna?' Susan said frantically.

"On the North side of the building! Hurry! Lamb stated concerned.

Lamb saw two mall security officers walking toward him and Arianna. He stopped them. Lamb pulled out his badge and informs them of terrorist activity about to take place. He has positive intel that a bomb is in the building and they need to begin evacuation now.

"Please take my daughter Arianna with you toward that Northside exit. Her mother will be there soon to pick her up!" Lamb Stated.

"Do you know where the bomb is and do you need assistance sir?" One of the Security Officers asked.

"The only thing I need from you is to begin evacuation now!" Lamb said.

Lamb walked hurriedly toward the men's room. He looked in every direction as he entered the room. Lamb noticed a man and a young boy washing their hands. Lamb looked into the mirror as he washed his face and hands. An elderly man walked in, and the man and young boy left the room. Lamb walked into the last stall and waited. He then heard someone enter the stall next to him and use the commode.

Lamb saw hands lifting the ceiling tile. Lamb slowly pulled out his super automatic. As he stepped up on the commode, he noticed that it was the maintenance worker who worked regularly at the mall, and he quickly retracts his weapon and placed it into his holster. The maintenance man did not see him. Lamb started to think that it may be a different men's room.

Lamb saw a man in a track suit with a gym bag. It was exactly the same person he'd observed in his premonition

Lamb hurried through the mall in the direction the man wearing the rack suit was walking. Lamb noticed that the man had answered a call from his cell phone. The man in the track suit slowed and headed down a hallway toward the side door exit. Lamb followed. "Stop right there! I'm a federal agent, and you need to stop now," shouted Lamb. The man stopped quickly, turned, and kneeled on the floor. Lamb anticipated his move and dropped to the floor as he pulled out his super. The track suit man's shots went past Lamb's head and right arm. Lamb's shots connected in the man's leg and hip. The man fell to the floor in agony. "Drop the weapon now! Do you hear me?" shouted Lamb. The man lifted his weapon once more. Lamb's next shots went into the man's chest and head.

Lamb got to his feet and walked cautiously to the suspect. The body was quiet with no movement. Lamb did a body check from head to toe and found a passport. The name was Muhammed Iopo. Lamb looked into the gym bag and pulled out a cylinder. It was gray, and lights were moving across the sides of it.

Lamb called Jennings. "Jennings here."

"Glad you're still at the office," Lamb said.

"What's going on, sir?"

"I believe that I just shot one of Mohammed's men from Al-Qaeda!" Lamb replied.

"Where are you, Agent Lamb?"

"I'm at the Fashion Valley Mall. The suspect's name is Muhammed Lopo. I also found a cylinder in his gym bag. It is active with lights and some numbers that I can't make out," Lamb said. "I'll send you a picture on my cell phone."

Jennings received the picture of the numbers and transferred the information to the Diagnostic Scanning Analysis, or DSA. This program scanned the cylinder and made an analysis. "Lamb, this is a very complicated detonator. It cannot be defused, and there is no time to call the bomb squad. You must get rid of it," Jennings shouted. "You have approximately half an hour."

"Jennings, I need you to fully activate STARE DOWN because I believe that there is another cylinder here at the mall, and another terrorist," Lamb said.

"It's already activated, sir."

"I forgot that you had it operating."

The satellite turned in space to the coordinates of Lamb's cell phone. The satellite scanned the area, and Jennings could see the entire area of the mall. "Lamb! I have a visual on the second suspect," Jennings said. "He is located on the second floor, wearing a track suit, and carrying a gym bag. He is walking near the podium of a stage. Is there some type of performance going on today?"

"Yes," Lamb replied. "I need a helicopter here on the roof ASAP," Lamb replied.

"I will get you that copter. I'm also sending agents to assist you!" Jennings said. "Thanks, Jennings. I appreciate your support."

Lamb contacted the LA police department and his director, Victor Price. He explained the situation. "Carry on, Lamb. Find and contain that second suspect. You need to apprehend him for interrogation," Price said.

Lamb hurried to the roof of the mall, where the helicopter landed. Lamb gave the cylinder to Agent Smith. "Take it out to the Pacific! You've got approximately twenty-five minutes," Lamb said. This gave the agents time to release the device and save lives. Lamb then went back to the terrorist's body, where the LAPD was waiting. Lamb identified himself and hurried toward the second suspect.

"Jennings here, Agent Lamb. The second suspect has placed the cylinder underneath the stage. He is walking toward the south exit."

"Have the agents look for a van that has 'Greg's Plumbing' written on the side of the van," Lamb replied.

"Agent Martinez is right there with Thompson. There are three more suspects inside the van armed with automatic weapons. Agents are to approach with extreme caution," Jennings stated.

Soon, shots were coming from the van. Agents Martinez and Robinson took cover behind pillars and returned fire. Martinez shot the front-seat passenger, who slumped forward. The driver had an AR-15, opened his door, and shot at the agents. Robinson shot and hit the suspect in the arm, and his weapon fell to the ground. The suspect began to run, however he tripped and fell down. He reached for a backup gun. "Drop your weapon now!" Robinson shouted. The suspect pointed the weapon but was shot by Robinson and Martinez. The agents checked the van and found an arsenal of weapons and maps.

Lamb saw the suspect in the track suit leaving the stage area, and he told him to stop. The suspect ran, and so Lamb took a shortcut through the jumper area. Lamb ran through a crowd but could not see the terrorist. "Continue forward, Lamb," Jennings said. "Stop where you are and turn left. Look behind the sofa."

Lamb pulled out his super and slowly walked around the sofa. He placed the weapon to the side of the suspect's face. "Turn around slowly," Lamb said. "Place your hands on top of your head." Lamb took out his cuffs and secured the man's hand.

Agents Wombush and Skypack arrived on the scene. "Hold him. I've got to get to that cylinder," Lamb commanded.

"Agents Jones and Landon are at the stage area. Do you want them to get that second cylinder?" Jennings asked.

"Yes, Jennings. Do so now! We've don't have a lot of time!" Lamb said. Just then, Lamb heard automatic weapons from the center of the mall. "Jennings, do you have a fix on that?"

"Yes sir, there is a man with holding two automatic weapons approximately thirty yards in front of you" Jennings said.

There was now a crowd of people running toward Lamb. As the crowd dispersed, a gunman continued to shoot in their direction. There were sounds ripping of flesh

and screams of fallen victims from the gunman's arsenal. Lamb ran toward the gunman and took cover behind a card stand. "Stay down!" Lamb commanded the vendor. The vendor was too scared to respond. Lamb noticed the gunman was approximately twenty feet away, wearing military fatigues with full body armor. The man brandished two AK-17s. The gunman pointed his weapons toward the beauty shop, where several women and children had taken refuge.

Lamb cried out, "No!" and fired his weapon at the assailant. Three bullets hit the assailant, knocking him down on his back. However, the gunman recovered and calmly got to his feet, shaking a finger at Lamb. Lamb advanced toward the right side of the gunman and hid behind a pillar. The gunman shot at Lamb, and the bullets hit the pillar taking apart pieces of it. Lamb returned fire and got off five more shots, hitting the gunman twice in the chest and moving him two feet backward. He shook off those shots also and continued to shoot at Lamb. The assailant was now ten feet in front of Lamb. Lamb aimed at the assailant but found that his weapon was jammed.

"Now you will die, you American pig!" the gunman cried.

Lamb reached in his pocket for one of his strobe flash bombs. He threw it in front of the gunman, and there was a small flash explosion. The assailant was blinded by the flashing light, but he continued to shoot toward the area where Lamb was kneeling. The bullets hit the pillar and the counter behind it, destroying the glass merchandise. Lamb took cover behind a cell phone counter.

"I see you!" the assailant shouted.

"This is the LAPD. Drop your weapon now!"

"Die!" the assailant answered as he shot at the officers. The bullets hit two of the five officers, one in the leg and the other in the arm. The officers picked up their fallen and retreated into one of the stores.

Lamb got his .38 Super to function. He and the assailant continued to exchange fire. Two more police officers shot at the assailant only to watch their bullets bounce off the body armor. The assailant returned fire, and the bullets hit the officers in the chest; they both fell to the floor. Lamb took careful aim and shot at the assailant's legs. The bullets again bounce off armor. Lamb was getting frustrated and time was running out. He then took aim at the assailant's head. *There is no way that he can survive this one,* he thinks to himself. He hit the assailant twice in the head, knocking him to the floor. Lamb was relieved because he did not see the assailant moving at all.

Meanwhile, people were frantically running for the exits. Two officers walked slowly toward the assailant. Lamb cautioned them to take cover behind the pillars near him. The assailant began to move and then shot at the officers. Lamb noticed someone nearby left the restroom and seemed unaware of what was going on around him. The assailant then turned his attention to that man by firing upon him. Lamb yelled for him to get down and take cover. The man continued to walk as if nothing was going on. Lamb couldn't believe what he was seeing and continued to shoot at the assailant to cover him. Instead of aiming at the assailant, Lamb aimed at the weapon, and it worked. Lamb was able to hit one gun and knock it out of the assailant's hand. The old man was then assisted by one of the police officers, who moved him quickly behind a counter. They found out later that the man had not charged both of his hearing aids.

The other AK-47 that the assailant had in his possession jammed, and he dropped it. Meanwhile, Lamb reloaded his super. The assailant retrieved the weapon knocked out of his hand by Lamb's bullet. The assailant ran over toward Lamb and pointed the loaded AK-47 at him. "I've got you now, American dog. There is no one here to save you. No more officers—only you and me. You die now!"

Suddenly, two bullets simultaneously hit the assailant in the neck, killing him instantly. Lamb looked up towards the right and left sides of the balcony on the second floor and observed Agents Ajay and Ajeeta, waving. Lamb smiled and waved with appreciation. Jenny Lee ran toward Lamb with her weapon drawn, looking side to side and behind her for more assailants. "Are you all right, sir?" Lee asked.

"I'm fine, Agent Lee. I'm just concerned there might be more gunmen in the area. I want you to watch the back exit on this floor to make sure that we there are more surprises," Lamb replied.

"I'm on it." Lee sprinted toward the first floor exit.

Lamb looked up toward the twins and instructed them to split up. One covered the second floor, and the other covered the third floor. All agents were now in place, waiting for any more activity by terrorists. The agents were joined by more LAPD, who had arrived just after the team shot the second assailant. Lamb ran toward the beauty shop to see if anyone was hurt during the shooting. He saw mothers holding their children while lying on the floor. Many were frightened and in tears. Lamb saw that no one was hurt and instructed them to leave the mall immediately. They followed Lamb's orders and left right away.

Lamb saw the victims of the terrorists. Some were still alive. Lamb ran toward the area where the other agents had a terrorist in custody. Lamb wanted answers now.

"The agents have the cylinder and are on the way out of the building," Jennings said. Lamb began to interrogate the suspect, who did not answer.

Just then, an explosion occurred at the north exit. Glass and metal flew everywhere. The second floor of the main entrance of the mall crumbled. "We need emergency medical vehicles here on this side of the mall, ASAP!" Lamb said.

"They are on their way, Agent Lamb," Jennings replied. The smoke was very thick, and the sounds of frantic people were everywhere. Men, women, and children were shouting and crying for help. The suspect whom the agents had in custody fell to the bottom floor along with Agents Wombush and Martinez; they were all unconscious. Lamb's head was pounding more. Glass was imbedded on the right side of his cheek. Lamb touched his head, and it was bloody. He was surrounded by concrete and steel. He soon lost consciousness.

Medical emergency personnel were everywhere. Firemen sprayed the area with water, but fire spread throughout the mall. A team of emergency rescue workers reached Lamb and pulled his limp body out of the smoldering rubble.

Lamb regained consciousness. There were blurred figures in front of him as he was being carried off in a stretcher. Lamb tried to call Jennings, but there was no signal coming from his earphone. Lamb lost consciousness again. There was only darkness, with the sounds of sirens and people fading.

A lone figure limped into an alley four blocks away from the mall, unnoticed by anyone. He leaned against the wall and slowly slid down the cold brick as he pulled out a cell phone from his pocket and pressed a button that directly connected him to his leader. "General!"

"Yes, Abib, go ahead."

"We've accomplished our mission, sir. However it was not met without opposition," said Abib.

"What do you mean?"

"General, there were some men who I believe that were federal agents. They interfered with our plans. They appeared out of nowhere, as if someone knew our every move."

"Did the governor's wife and daughter get annihilated?"

"Yes, sir, I believe they did!"

"Then our mission is complete. Did we experience casualties of our own?"

"Yes, General. I was the only one who survived."

There was a long silence. "That was to be expected. They died for the cause. I need you to follow up on the plan. Make sure that they are truly dead by going to the hospital. If they are not, you are to call the Wolf. He will know what to do from there. Understood?"

"Yes, my general. It is fully understood." The general hung up.

Abib searched through his cell phone, looking for the Wolf. He located the number and made contact. "The air is clear for the Wolf to howl," Abib said.

"Then the Wolf will howl for only you," Wolf replied.

"We may be in need of your other contact at the hospital to ensure that the mission has been completed for the day."

"All right, that can be arranged. I do have some contacts already working at the hospital. I will make contact with my other source right now," the Wolf replied. He hung up and made a call to Japan.

"Hello, Wolf. Do you have a contract for us?"

"Yes, Your Excellency, I do. It will be the governor's wife and daughter. The contract came through. They may be still alive at the

Los Angeles Memorial Hospital in California. I will send you the exact directions from the airport. Will they need transportation, sir?" Wolf asked.

"No, there will be no need for that. We will have our own ready. Thank you for asking," the emperor said.

"I told Abdullah that you are the best and that there will be no mistakes," Wolf said.

"There will be none. My family makes no mistakes. We have been providing services for the black market for over fifteen hundred years. We are unique—there are none like us! Inform the general to have our money ready to be paid in full," the emperor said.

"I will do that, Your Excellency," Wolf replied.

The emperor disconnected the call and continued to walk through his garden.

The mall was a crime scene as well as a disaster area. Only the north side of the mall was destroyed. If the bombs had not been removed by the other agents, there would have been many more deaths.

The body count was twenty-six dead and fifty injured. Victor Price, Jennings, and Andréa were in Lamb's recovery room. Lamb woke and was surrounded by the agents, balloons, and cards. "It's about time you woke up, Lamb," Price said.

"Good to have you back," Jennings said.

"Glad to see that you're all right, Agent Lamb," Andréa added.

Lamb touched the bandage wrapped around his head. His right hand also had a bandage on it. Lamb had minor cuts and abrasions on his face. "It's good to see you all again," he replied. Two doctors entered Lamb's room and told him that he had suffered a concussion and would be released soon. They gave him a prescription for pain and told him to take off a week. They then left the room.

"What happened to the other agents?" Lamb inquired.

"The agents who found the detonator device are gone, Agent Lamb. The bomb exploded before they could dispose of it," Jennings said.

"There will be a memorial for them this week," Price added. "On a positive note, Agents Robinson, Martinez, and Thompson were able to contain the van and take out two suspects. The two men have yet to be identified, however I'm sure they are working with Abdullah."

"What about the suspect that I apprehended?" Lamb asked.

"He died once the bomb went off. Glass sliced through his throat during the explosion," Price answered. "Agents Martinez and Wombush are outside your door if you need anything."

"Daddy, Daddy!" Arianna cried when she entered. "Are you all right?"

"I'm fine, angel," Lamb answered as Arianna gave her father a choke-hold hug.

"Let's go, everyone. Give Lamb some privacy and rest," Price said. The three agents exited the room.

Arianna was so happy to see her father that she cried. "It's all right, angel. I'm all right," Lamb said with his arm around Arianna. As Lamb looked up, he saw Susan standing in front of his bed looking worried with her arms folded. She stared at him and told Arianna that she would be waiting outside. Lamb fell into a deep sleep with Arianna alongside his bed.

When he woke, he found that Arianna was no longer at his bedside. A card was left where Arianna had been. The card reads, "Get well soon, Daddy! I love you very, very, very, much!" He placed the card back inside of the envelope.

Martinez walked in the room and informed Lamb that his family had left two hours ago. Martinez handed him an envelope containing pertinent information on the terrorist attack. There were pictures that the mall security cameras took before and after the bombing. Agent Martinez also gave Lamb pictures of the van and everything inside that was confiscated. The items were six AK-47s, fifty boxes of C-4, and several maps. The maps had writing on them that neither Lamb nor Martinez understood. It was clear, however, that these were terrorist targets. The governor's mansion was on the list of targets along with the senator's home. The university was on the list along with state fair.

"I wonder just why the terrorists struck the mall today?" Lamb inquired.

"What do you mean, commander? The terrorists had the mall as part of their target because of the size of the population yesterday," Martinez replies.

"There is another reason. I believe that the terrorists knew that someone would be there who was of special interest to them," Lamb said.

"Don't you think that we would have been in on that?" Martinez inquired.

"Agent Martinez, I was there shopping with my daughter. It was a fluke that I was in the area at that time."

"I wasn't aware of that, sir," Martinez said, surprised.

"One thing is bothering me, Martinez."

"What is it, sir?"

"I noticed one of the terrorists I was following pause and slightly turn as if there was someone giving him information that I was tailing him. I do believe there was a spotter in the mall."

"What do you want me to do?" Martinez asked.

"I'm going to need pictures from those security cameras in that area. I'm going to also need the video from STARE DOWN to see what it picked up."

"I'm on it," Martinez replied. "I'm also going to have Agent Wombush outside your door."

Lamb thought to himself, *Where can they be now?* He soon fell asleep again. He saw individuals from his past and dreamed about Korea. Lamb visited the area at times when he was on leave in Korea and Japan. He learned the discipline of karate, tae kwon do, and ninjitsu. Many individuals came from far away to learn from Grandmaster Lin Po. Po taught Lamb many things concerning these arts, and Lamb learned quickly. Lamb was taught to break seven boards and bricks using the ancient art of DiMak, or death touch. Po taught Lamb how to fight in the dark. "Darkness, like light, can also be your friend. Adapt to your opponents fighting skills. Expect the unexpected. Become one with nature. Learn to win your enemies over with a gentle tongue. Learn many disciplines. Do not limit your mind because it is like the universe—endless. Become like the wind: silent, invisible, and gentle, yet strong and powerful. Always assist the weak and never ignore their cries for help. This is the mark of a true martial artist." These words of his grandmaster echoed throughout his mind.

Lamb then has dreams about his military life. He went back to the days of basic training and his drill sergeant's voice echoing commands. Eight-mile runs, calisthenics, lifting weights, and defensive tactics were all part of his training. He dreamed of an overseas mission that involved a seek-and-destroy of the enemy.

Lamb was on a special mission with Delta Force, working alongside the navy SEALs. They were to split up, flank the enemy, and then engage. Lamb's unit, which he was in charge of, consisted of himself and four others. The navy SEAL team also had five individuals. They were to take out the enemy's ammunition supply, which was important because it was at a strategic location; the majority of the enemy's ammunition came from this location. Lamb's team took the east side of the camp, and the navy SEALs covered the west.

There was one problem, however: the area was heavily guarded. Lamb's team was to be the one to engage first and cause a diversion, thereby giving the SEALs time to enter the west gate. Delta Force began to fire upon the guards at the east gate, and they were able to take out four guards. They also used grenade launchers that caused the enemy to return fire. This worked because the guards from the west gate began to assist the east side and abandoned their posts. This action gave the SEALs easy access for them to enter the west gate. They set charges off and gained access to the compound. Once inside, they began to place charges on containers of C-4, TNT, automatic weapons and handguns, grenades, grenade launchers, and other explosives inside and outside of tents. Once the charges were set, two hostiles began to engage the SEALs. The enemies were shot and killed immediately, however someone saw the SEALs and sounded the alarm.

Lamb's team radioed that they had been discovered inside the compound. His team was pinned down at the time because of the concentration of fire. The countdown of the charges had begun. Time was now beginning to run out. Lamb knew this and pulled out a smoke grenade. He got very close to the gate as his team covered him with return fire. The hostiles thought he was insane and began to shoot in his direction. Lamb threw a smoke bomb at his feet. Bullets began to hit in the area where he is standing, but there was nothing but a cloud of smoke. Once the smoke cleared, Lamb was gone. The enemy was in awe, wondering what had happened.

Lamb was now on the other side of the gate. He saw that the SEALs were engaged in heavy fire, pinned down by a 50-caliber gun. Two of their men had been shot and needed medical attention right away. Lamb pulled out two of his knives and threw them at the man handling the 50-caliber gun. The enemy slumped over on top of the gun, dead. Lamb radioed his unit and told them that he was going to exit with the SEALs out of the west gate, and for the team to leave the area immediately. The charges had been set, and time was running out. Lamb and the SEALs begin to exit the compound. As they ran, they could hear the men in the compound starting their Jeeps and beginning their pursuit. The compound started to explode. Lamb and the SEALs team hit the ground for cover. The ammunition supplies blew up, setting off a chain reaction.

The men could hear three Jeeps in pursuit. The SEALs team slowed down because of the two wounded men. Lamb told the SEALs team to move ahead while he slowed them down. Lamb set claymores in the path of the oncoming Jeeps, but he made sure that the enemy would see him first. His plan worked. They saw Lamb, began to pursue him, and fired upon him. Lamb returned fire. Two of the Jeeps were lined up straight, and one was coming toward him. Lamb immediately jumped of their way and set off the claymores. Each of the Jeeps were hit. The first Jeep flipped over, upside down. The second one hit the first one and then flipped over and exploded. The third Jeep swerved around and continued pursuit. They were angry and wanted vengeance. Lamb ran as fast as he could. He had a plan in mind that involved the Jeep chasing him. The Delta Force team watched through their binoculars. The SEAL team was almost near the lifeboat.

Lamb continued to run through the rain forest with the Jeep in hot pursuit. He then came to an area with which he was familiar; he had seen it when they had first landed. He arrived at an opening in the forest. The enemies saw Lamb standing by himself. They slowed down and came to a stop. Lamb simply stood there staring at them. They began to shout at him and swear. They started up the Jeep again and moved forward quickly. This time the driver stepped on the gas.

Lamb continued to stand where he was. They began to shoot at him, and Lamb took a smoke grenade and threw it at his feet. He disappeared when the Jeep was fifty yards away from him. The Jeep went through the smoke, and the enemy looked around to see where he went. They saw him off to the side, waving good-bye to them. As they turned to look in front of them, they noticed they were headed for a fifty-foot cliff into the rocks below. The Jeep flew downward, and the men's screams were suddenly silenced by the explosion. The Delta Force team and the SEAL team applauded Lamb. He rendezvoused with his team a few moments later. Lamb's team was given full commendations by the navy SEALs and the president of United States.

Lamb began to come out of his dream, and he heard sounds coming from the television monitor above him. His eyes slowly came into focus. Lamb looked around his room and sees that it was now evening. He slowly raised himself and sat up in bed. He turned his body to the left so that his feet touched floor. Lamb heard sounds coming from outside the door, and he shuffled toward his door and looked out the small window. Lamb saw two nurses walking by. He then noticed something else that caught his attention. Shadows were moving. These shadows resembled the likeness of snakes moving past him and down the hallway. Lamb rubbed his eyes and looked again. He observes the last part of the figure with a tail moving down the hallway to the right of him. Lamb was not convinced of what he'd just seen. *It must be the drugs,* he thought to himself. *Yes, drugs can make me see things and imagine things that aren't there. Though I always see things that are not there.*

Lamb decided to walk back to his bed and lay down. As he did so, he noticed a dark, shadowy figure entering his room. He closed his eyes and focused on his senses. The shadowy figure moved next to the IV unit. The figure then raised his hand with a long, sharp object in it. Lamb's leg was now in striking position, bent and ready. The sharp object caught light from outside the room, causing it to reflect off the walls in the room. The figure formed into a ninja and was fully solidified. Just then, Lamb executed a side knife piercing kick to the ninja's midsection. The ninja was knocked backward toward the wall and made contact against it. The ninja held his stomach in agony, and the knife fell to the floor.

Lamb got out of bed and now saw another shadowy figure enter the room. This time Lamb tried to punch the figure, however his fists went through it and into the wall. The first figure hit Lamb in the back of the head, knocking him to the floor. Lamb pushed himself off the floor and got into a defensive stance. Lamb knew this was not a dream because he felt pain throughout his body. He was still sore from the cuts and abrasions he'd received from the explosion, and his head also ached tremendously. Again, Lamb attempted to throw a punch at the shadowy figure but did not connect. Lamb was kicked in the stomach and face. He fell back onto his bed and felt excruciating pain. Lamb noticed that the first figure had no substance. Lamb stood up on his bed, facing the two shadowy figures. Each one was trying to flank him. Lamb saw the door and jumped toward it. One of the shadowy figures ran toward Lamb, but a light was turned on in the hallway. Now there was a light shining inside Lamb's room. Lamb was against the door, and the light was in front of him. The shadowy figure stood there, staring at the light. He did not want to get near the light.

Lamb had a plan. He executed a series of roundhouse kicks, knowing that he would miss both of the shadowy figures. He continued to move forward toward his pants. Lamb reached inside his right pocket and pulled out a flash bomb. When both of the shadowy figures approached him, Lamb threw the bomb to the floor. The bomb exploded, causing a bright, blinding light to appear. Lamb covered his eyes and noticed that both of the shadowy figures now had substance. Lamb attacked them with the IV pole. He hit them both in the stomach simultaneously and then upward in the chin, knocking them on their backs. Both placed their hands on their chins in shock, staring at each other. Lamb twirled the rod around in his left hand. He used it as if it were a staff, just like the one that he had used when he was in the Lin Po temple, training. Both of the ninjas pushed themselves off the floor at the same time and landed in standing defensive positions. Lamb wasted no time, executing a flying kick with his legs in a split position. He connected, hitting them both in the jaw. He kicked so hard that he sent one of them across his bed, crashing through his window and onto the street.

The second ninja pulled out a dagger and lunged toward Lamb. Lamb turned to the side and then executed a back kick, hitting the would-be assassin in his midsection. Blood flew out of the assassin's mouth as Lamb ran toward the man. The assassin quickly placed something into his mouth. Lamb shouted, "No!"

The assassin's body began to shake and jerk violently. Foam erupts out of his mouth. "Who sent you?" Lamb asked repeatedly in vain as he shook his adversary with both of his hands. Lamb soon laid the lifeless body down on the floor and examined the assassin's body. He removed the assailant's glove from his right hand and noticed that there was a tattoo of a red dragon on the inside of his wrist. The dragon had five claws with seven stars in between them. Lamb noticed something else very strange: the stars began to move out of the dragon's claws and form a circle underneath the dragon. The circle of stars moved three times and then stopped. Lamb was in shock and wondered what all this meant.

Lamb heard more footsteps down the hallway, coming toward his direction. He pulled the corpse out of sight and then peered out the small window of his door. Lamb saw another ninja dressed in black moving past his room. He could hear a silencer going off. Lamb reached inside his pants pocket, pulled out two more flash bomb devices, and headed quickly toward the door. Lamb slowly opened the door and then moved down the hallway.

Lamb noticed that there were two bodies outside a door, approximately five doors down the hallway. Lamb quickly moved down the hallway took the device out of his pocket, and readied himself as he looked inside the room. Lamb saw the assassin in the room with a gun that had a silencer, ready to shoot at the body inside the blanket. Lamb quickly pulled the pin out of the device and threw it to the floor. The device included a light that flashed like a strobe. The assassin was blinded and surprised. He tried to shoot, however the bullets missed several feet away from its intended target.

Lamb rushed the assassin. He jumped forward and executed a front snap kick, knocking the weapon out of the assailant's hand. Lamb turned the assailant around and placed him in a sleeper hold. The assailant struggled, but soon the man's grip weakened and his vision blurred. Finally, there was darkness and unconsciousness.

A second assassin entered the room and was surprised by the flashing strobe. Lamb punched him in the face, chest, and stomach until he was knocked to the floor. The assassin held his stomach in agony. "Tell me who sent you! Why are you doing this?" Lamb asked desperately.

"We will eventually kill them. We will kill them all. You are good, but you will not be able to stop us. There too many of us; we have been around for a long time." The assassin then turned his head quickly and snapped his own neck. Lamb stood over him in shock as the assassin slumped to the floor. Lamb once again examined one of the fallen ninja's wrists and noticed that the same red dragon tattoo was on the arm. The stars began to move out of the claws of the red dragon and underneath it. They formed a circle, moved around three times, and then stopped. The ninja expired once this occurred.

The two individuals who were hospitalized in the room were under heavy sedation and slept through the attack. Lamb called the front desk and asked for assistance. The nurse was horrified at what she saw upon arrival. Lamb gave her the number for Director Price and dialed 911. Victor Price hurried to the hospital and was shocked when he arrived on scene. He showed his ID as he walked past the secured area that LAPD had set up. Victor walked up to the third floor where Lamb was.

"Lamb, are you all right?" Price asked as he entered his room.

"I'm exhausted!" Lamb stated. "These guys are Asian. It doesn't make sense. I thought that Abdullah only used his own?"

"Not necessarily," Price replied.

"Where was Running Deer? I thought that he was right outside my door."

"Hello, sir," Martinez said as she walked toward Price and Lamb. "I saw him in the stairwell.

We both were in pursuit of men dressed in black outfits. I was knocked unconscious near the stairwell door. He was shot in the shoulder and was unconscious. He will be admitted here soon. He was able to get off two shots."

The LAPD arrived and asked Lamb a series of questions. He saw three bodies being placed inside body bags. The red dragon ninja who had fallen onto the street had disappeared. The two individuals who were on the floor in the hallway and were murdered were secret service agents. Price finally received information that the governor's wife and daughter were in the room the assassins had struck. Lamb's questions had been answered. The governor's family was at the mall two days ago. Abdullah had his assassins attack when they thought their targets would be vulnerable and surprised. "Good job, Lamb. I knew that you would be the right person for this job when I recruited you," Price said.

"Thanks, sir. Right now I need Jennings to connect us with STARE DOWN. I want to locate the spotter who alerted one of the terrorists when I was tailing him."

Price contacted Jennings and connected STARE DOWN to Martinez's laptop. The connection was quick, and they were able to view the mall two days ago. "Agent Martinez, I need you to go to Friday, 1430 hours. Zoom in on me in pursuit." Lamb was running through the children's play area, where a child is playing in the sandbox area. "Stop. There she is. Suzanna, the governor's daughter," Lamb stated.

"The secret service has disseminated information concerning the entire family," Price said.

"We should have had that information two days ago, sir," Lamb said.

"I agree," Martinez added.

"Now, move STARE DOWN to the third floor, a little to the left," Lamb directed.

There was a man wearing a track suit watching Lamb. He reached in his pocket and began talking to someone. Lamb directed Martinez to move STARE DOWN to the second floor. The satellite showed the terrorist whom Lamb was following reaching for his cell phone and slightly turning as if he were being notified that there was someone behind him. The camera now moved toward an individual on the cell phone. It was Abdullah. It showed him running on his bad leg out the exit door.

Agent Wombush walked inside the room and briefed the group on what happened. "Sir, I heard a sound down the hallway, and I then investigated. I noticed that there were two men dressed in suits. They had secret service badges. I also showed them my credentials. I informed them that I was going to investigate the sounds that I had heard in the hallway. They told me they did not hear anything. I wanted to make sure myself, so I continued to walk toward the stairwell exit door. As I began to make my way downstairs, I saw traces of blood going down the staircase. I saw the security guard face down with a knife in his back. As I turned around to look upward, I noticed a man dressed in a ninja outfit. He began to throw stars at me. I was able to move out of the way, and I could hear a silencer shooting off a few rounds. The sound came from the third floor. I then noticed another ninja walking up the staircase. They pulled out a silencer and shot me in the shoulder. I then returned fire and hit one in their upper torso. I collapsed to the floor. The next thing I knew, I was being revived by Agent Martinez along with the paramedic."

Lamb knew that Agent Wombush was telling the truth. This had been Lamb's first encounter with a real ninja. He had heard that they had existed centuries ago, however he had never encountered one himself. Lamb had to inform Grandmaster Lin Po at once concerning his confrontation with the red dragon ninjas. Everyone left the room for him to rest.

Agent Lamb requested a telephone be brought to him. He immediately dialed Lin Po's number. He knew he needed assistance because this was something that he had never encountered before. In fact, he wasn't sure whether his former Grand Master had even had such an encounter. Lamb contacted the Korean embassy, where Lin Po worked as the ambassador's assistant. His secretary answered and then transferred him to Lin Po. "Hello, sir. I want to come back and learn martial arts from the best," Lamb told Lin Po, disguising his voice.

"Is that you, Nathan Lamb?" Lin Po asked. Lamb was surprised. He thought he had fooled his old grandmaster. "Did you think you could trick me, young man? Remember that with age comes wisdom. Wisdom begets knowledge. Knowledge then begets awareness!"

Lamb stated the reason why he had called. He informed Po of the red dragon ninjas he had encountered in the hospital. Lamb gave detailed information concerning the ninjas, such as how they moved as shadowy serpents through hallways and were able to gain access to his room without using the door or window. Lamb also talked about his encounter when examining the ninjas and the red dragon tattoo on each of the ninjas' right wrists. He informed Lin Po how he had observed the Red Dragon with five claws and seven stars in inside their claws. Lamb went on to tell Po that when the stars moved, they circled beneath the dragon tattoo. Once it came to a stop, the ninja expired.

Lin Po informed Lamb that he had indeed encountered the red dragon ninjas. These ninjas were not traditional ninjas. The red dragon ninjas had been around for centuries. They involved generations of clans banded together—an entire family. They were evil and were murderers for hire. Traditional ninjas had nothing on them. "I would rather fight ten traditional ninjas than one Red Dragon ninja. They are very deadly, son. But if I were to fight them at any time, I would rather it would be with you. The Red Dragon Ninja Clan's leader was a man called Yang and his son, Ho. Some of them—very few of them—are able to remain in the light; that is because they are evil and belong to darkness. Legend says that they made a pact with the evil one himself, Satan. They were able to gain their powers once they made this pack and swore their allegiance to him. Some Red Dragons are more advanced than others.

My first encounter with them was when I had just become a grandmaster in Korea. I was on my way to the marketplace when I saw two dark figures pass me by in the night. By the time I reached the marketplace, Mr. Tae had been knocked to the ground unconscious. When I helped him to his feet, he stated, "It's all right, young Po. It was my fault for not paying the protection fee." The people in the town I was visiting had to pay a protection fee to the Red Dragon. They told Tae that if he did not come by, they would be back—and this time they would murder him and take over all his business. Mr. Tae wanted me to leave, but I had no intention of doing so. These people needed my help and had no one else to turn towards. I felt that I was obligated to assist them in any way I could. I informed Master G, my grandmaster, as to what had occurred in the village. He told me things were going to get worse. He also was on the Red Dragon's protection list, and he needed to pay an even higher fee because he taught and ran a martial arts temple. They felt that he was a threat and could lead a rebellion against the Red Dragon. He told me that they were very strong in numbers and also had advancements in their level of powers. Master G had me go on some errands the next morning. I wanted to hurry and get back before nightfall, but he had a long list for me to do. I believe he knew I could not complete the entire list in a day. My instincts told me to go back to the temple. Something was wrong.

"As I reached the top of the hill, I noticed fire and smoke coming out of the temple. I ran as fast as I could toward the temple. Once I arrived, I observed ten of Master G's disciples dead. I went inside and saw Master G on the floor near the front; he was barely alive, and his breathing was very shallow. He motioned me to lean near and told me that there were five of them who had arrived to collect the protection fee. Master G did not have the protection fee in full. The Red Dragon captain began to swear at them and curse the temple. They threw poisonous stars at them and were very accurate. His disciples were not trained to take on such evil. Master G said, 'I feel I have failed them because I did not train them.' I told Master G that he was the best grandmaster in the world, and I was proud to have him as grandmaster. There was no shame in what happened there. He told me that he felt dishonored in not being able to protect the temple and his disciples. He then turned to me and told me that I had been like a son to him, and that he could not have asked for a better student. Master G told me to continue with his teachings; I should teach others to be humble and never to use their newfound skills to harm individuals, only to protect them from evil. Master G then expired.

"I was very upset at the time. For the first time in my life, I felt alone and did not know what to do. I had vengeance in my heart and could not think clearly. I went to the town village and informed them what had occurred in the temple. They came back to the temple with me in order to give Master G and his disciples a proper burial. Once they were buried, I told the townspeople that we must band together in order to get rid of the evil in the town. One of them stated, 'Just look what they did to Master G and his disciples. Do you take us for fools? We do not have training such as you have had. We are peaceful, humble farmers who have families and want no trouble of any kind. We are willing to give the Red Dragon protection fees so that they will leave us alone.'

"I could not believe that I was standing alone. There is no one else but myself, I thought. I do remember the words of Master G when he said, 'One good act of another may lead others to follow.' I decided to remain in the village. After a month went gone by, it was time for the villagers to pay another protection fee to the Red Dragon.

"I had been staying with an elderly couple named Lu. The Lu's were like the village grandparents. Some of the Red Dragon members walked inside their hut one day, demanding the protection fee. They were very rude and disrespectful to the couple. When Mr. Lu tried to give the money to one of them, the man knocked it out of his hands and then slapped him in the face. I had had enough of their insolence and disrespect. I told them that if they were to raise their hand again, it would be the last time they raised it to anyone here. They looked at each other and laughed. They asked, 'Just who the hell do you think you are?' I told them that I was someone who was not going to stand by and let the elderly be harmed and disrespected. As one of them moved toward me, I told the Lu's to leave the hut. They quickly exited.

These Red Dragon members knew that I was a disciple of Grandmaster G. They both looked at each other and moved toward me. I saw their bodies transformed into shadows. I blew out all the candles inside the hut. I began to meditate and let my mind become one with my body. I sat down on the floor and released my inner soul, my spirit. My spirit became that of a fighting tiger. I was able to make contact physically with the Red Dragon members, striking them unconscious. I dragged their bodies outside the hut, tied them up, and placed them on their horses. I sent them all back to where they had come from. The people in the village observed what happened and were amazed. However, one of them made the statement, 'Look what you've done! Now they're going to come back in force and destroy us all. Our families will be threatened with death because of you!'

"I told them, 'If I can stand up to them, you can too. You should not be afraid of evil. Conquer evil with good by protecting yourselves, your families, and your village. Stand with me, and together we can conquer this great evil that is in your village.' One by one the people walked up to me and stood by my side. We devised a plan on how to rid the village of the Red Dragon. I did not have time to thoroughly show them how to meditate and separate themselves from their souls and spirits. However, I was able to teach them how to work together in harmony, in order to combat the Red Dragon. When more of them arrived, they began to transform themselves into the shadowy figures. However, the villagers came running out from their huts and formed a circle with torches in their hands. The Red Dragon clan did not know what to do; their bodies were now solidified. The villagers, all one hundred of them, pounced on the ninjas at once, and I joined them. I had to stop the villagers from killing the men. I instructed them to let some go, but to keep some of them hostage. I wanted to negotiate with their emperor.

"When they arrived back at their village, they informed the emperor of what happened and told him that Master G's disciple, who had become a grandmaster himself, said he wanted to see the Warlord and negotiate. After about an hour, the Warlord arrived with eighty guards. The Warlord was quite concerned because one of the captives was his nephew. "What do I need to do in order to get my nephew back?" the Warlord asked. I told him that he needed to promise that he would never, ever come here to demand protection fees, and that he would never attack anyone in this village. I also told him I knew that they were evil and could never be trusted, because the evil one was the originator of the lie and could never be trusted. The Warlord felt insulted but reluctantly agreed and released his nephew. His nephew then got onto the Warlord's horse. They turned around and went back to their own village. I remained in the village for a month until I knew they would not come back. They never did. Now you can see the reason why I have told you in the past to never give up when you fight, no matter what the odds are against you or what you are facing. Never give up and always have an indomitable spirit. This spirit cannot be defeated. This is how you confront the Red Dragon clan; this is how you win. I never did see any more members of the Red Dragon clan anywhere. Not until you have brought them to my attention at this time. I want you to be extra cautious when you're fighting them. I wish I had time off now, to train you."

"Maybe I will get that chance again soon, sir," Lamb said. Lamb went on to talk about the terrorist and the attack at the mall, intended for the governor's wife and daughter. He also mentioned he believed the Al-Qaeda had contracted out the Red Dragon. Lamb needed strong advice from his grandmaster. Lamb said that he would be in touch with him in the near future.

Just then, Victor Price walked into the room and gave Nathan Lamb an envelope containing directives for the governor's protection. While Lamb read the directives, Victor Price paced the floor with his hands clasped behind his back. The directives were very detailed and precise.

The governor was going to Korea within a week. Agent Lamb would have to separate his team. His Hades team, including himself, would go to Korea and protect the governor. The Omega team would stay behind at the mansion and protect the family.

As Lamb continued to read the directives, he noticed that Price was very nervous. "Why do you so seem nervous, sir?" Lamb asked.

"I guess I cannot hide what I feel right now. I never told you that the governor and I had once served in the army together, when I first started out in the military," Price said.

"No, sir. You never did mention that to me," Lamb replied.

"The Governor and I have had our quarrels in the past. You see, Lamb, we were in love with the same woman. I actually was engaged to Betty before I met Joan. Betty and I met in college. I also knew Barry in college. We were very competitive academically, as well as in sports. I would win some starting positions against him, and he would win some against me. We were very resentful of each other because we were competing for the same prize, Betty. When I went through the ROTC program, I got so involved that I didn't have time for Betty. I had to study, I had to make my grades, and I had to be the best there was in the military. I neglected her and became apathetic toward her feelings. I should not have done that. There were times she told me that she wanted to run far away from me. And do you know something, Lamb? She did just that. She ran right into the arms of Barry Barton, now governor of the state of California.

"I really didn't think that I would ever again run into both of them, especially in a situation like this. They have a beautiful family together. Todd is the oldest, Jasmine is the second oldest, and they have two identical twins, Brianna and Susanna. Beautiful children. Todd is about to graduate law school. Jasmine is graduating high school and is going to college. The twins are seven years old. I informed Governor

Barton that we didn't have to see much of each other unless of course there were problems in the unit. The governor looked over my policies, procedures, goals, and objectives of this unit. He was hesitant at first but later agreed. I believe that Betty had a lot to do with our unit being approved to protect the governor and his family as our first assignment." Price walked over to Lamb's bed and sat down at the foot of the bed. Price paused and said, "You see, Lamb, I really want this to work. I want this team to succeed and do its job. I feel that with you as the leader, it will be successful. I have the utmost confidence in you. I want you to look over the directives carefully, and if there any questions that you have, please feel free to ask. You can always call me on my cell phone."

"I do appreciate your kind words, sir. However, I feel you have had a big part in creating this team. I know that taking on this assignment must've been somewhat difficult. But your team is not going to fail you, sir. We will be successful."

"Well, I've got to be going. I think Joan has some good Italian food ready for me. I will see you in a few days," Price said.

"I noticed, sir, that the peace talks are in three weeks. I would like to go to Korea one week before the peace talks begin. I need to get in touch with Master Po in order to learn how to fight those Red Dragon ninjas. Will that be okay with you?" Lamb asked.

"I have seen what the Red Dragons are capable of, and I'm all for Master Po training you on how to combat them. I will have a plane ready for you at that time," Price told Lamb. He then got up and waved good-bye to Lamb.

After saying good night to the children, Governor Barry Barton opened the door to his bedroom, finding his wife, Betty, ready for bed. He quietly walked up behind her, placed his arms around her, and gave her a soft kiss on her neck. Betty saw Barry in the mirror and smiled. She placed her hands on his arms and rubbed them. "So how do you feel about Price being the one to take the lead in protecting this family?" the governor asked.

Betty paused and then said, "I know it may cause a strain, however I feel that Victor Price is the right person to protect us. I know that you and he have had your differences in the past, but you must put them behind you, Governor Barton. I believe in Victor Price. I believe he is the one who can get the job done. I know that you're only trying to protect me, however the past is the past, and I am married to you, not him. I chose you because I knew that we were right for each other."

"Do you think that his problems will come back to haunt us, Betty?" he governor asked.

"I really don't know. All I can say is that I believe that he will do his utmost to keep those problems away from his job, and to fully focus on the task at hand. He is a good man. He has a good wife who fully supports him, just as I fully support you, Barry Barton. This new team that he created sounds as if it will be successful. Besides that, the new leader, Agent Nathan Lamb, did save our lives. I'm looking forward to meeting all of them. I do want you to try to get along with them, and I hope that all of your jealousy diminishes, because there is no need for you to be jealous at all."

"I, I know that I shouldn't be. I just want to make sure that they do their job. It's so good to have you and Susanna home again. I missed both of you."

She turned to him and gave him a hug and kiss.

Anders and LeBlanc were at the mall working with the crime scene detectives because their background was also in CSI. They looked around in the rubble and found a plumber's toolkit. Next, they saw remnants of a radio and cell phone. LeBlanc continued to work on the right side, where the explosion took place. He saw a brown package and noticed a C-4 device that had not yet been set off. LeBlanc called over Anders to take a look. It looked as if the person planting the bomb did not have time to set the device because either he was running out of time or someone had interrupted his devious plan. Both men continued to look for more evidence.

A week went by, and Lamb was released from the hospital. Price picked him up at the hospital. Lamb gathered his belongings and packed them into a suitcase. Lamb signed papers and then left with Price. On the way to Lamb's apartment, Price asked about his well-being and if he was really up to reporting for duty on Monday. Lamb told Price that he was ready and would go crazy if he had to stay home for another week. Watching TV all day long with Tank wouldn't work for him.

Price informed Lamb that the suspect they were going to interview had swallowed a cyanide pill and died. "He made sure that he would not divulge any information to us." As they were driving, Price noticed that there was a vehicle behind them that may be following them. He wanted to put his curiosity to test. "Lamb, I want you to look cautiously into your side mirror. Act as if nothing is going on. I believe that Honda Prelude is following us."

"How do you know, sir?" Lamb replied.

"I know because the vehicle has been following us ever since we left the hospital. Hang on—I'm going to try something." Price continued to increase his speed through the city streets. He then took a sharp right turn down a small, secluded road where there was no traffic. The street narrowed as they continued to drive.

Lamb looked into his side mirror and noticed that the vehicle was no longer following them. "I think that you may have lost them."

"I don't believe I did, Lamb. Maybe temporarily, but I know they will be back soon," Price said. Just as he finished speaking, another Honda Prelude came toward them. There was nowhere else to go but forward. Price noticed there was another street to his left. He turned the wheel hard left. The Honda Prelude also took a hard left but overcompensated and hit a wall. The driver corrected and continued on.

The individual in the passenger seat shot at Lamb and Price. Price was driving a government SUV, and the vehicle's windows were bulletproof. As their assailants fired, Lamb pulled out his .38 Super and retaliated. Lamb hit the passenger in the chest, and he immediately dropped his weapon outside of the vehicle and slumps forward into the dashboard. The driver then smashed out the rest of the windshield so that he could see. The driver pulled out his own weapon and fired upon Lamb and Price. The vehicles continued to race through the back streets of the city.

Price knew he was coming to a clearing. Just as they were entering that clearing, another Honda Prelude cut off the exit. Two men quickly got out of vehicle and shot MAC-10s at them. The two men were aiming for the tires. Price told Lamb to reach into the back seat, open the footlocker, and use the grenade launcher on them. Lamb took aim at the assailants and opened fire. The grenade that was fired exploded and left nothing but blistering metal. The SUV went speeding through the fire and metal. Price then called for assistance from agents in the area. He also calls the LAPD and informed them of the incident that took place, adding that they were still being pursued by assailants believed to be Al-Qaeda. Price and Lamb continued to look out for the second vehicle that was pursuing them. Price knew they could not go to Lamb's apartment at this time, and he continued driving around the city.

After a while, they decided to stop inside a café for some coffee. "I guess they decided not to pursue us after all, sir," Lamb noted.

"I think they will be back. It's just a matter of time," Price said, concerned.

They took a seat with their backs against the wall in the corner of the café, where they could clearly see outside. They had a good visual on their vehicle. Price and Lamb began to discuss their directives and also how the two teams, Hades and Omega, would work together. They also discussed how unique the individuals on the team were and how they would complement each other with their skills and talents.

As they were speaking, two individuals entered the café and walked toward the counter. They were both wearing long overcoats, and one of them kept staring at Price and Lamb. The waitress immediately walked toward them and said, "What would you gentlemen like to order?" The one standing remained silent. The shorter individual spoke broken English; it was difficult to make out his language because Price and Lamb were too far away to hear. The shorter man was talking to the taller man, and then all the sudden both of them pulled out MAC-10s and shot at Price and Lamb. The agents had anticipated their movements and took cover behind the tables. The customers who were nearest the exits began to scream as they ran outside. The gunmen found cover behind the kitchen counter and continued to shoot at Price and Lamb. Lamb and Price turned over a metal table for cover and returned fire. Price called for backup, and agents were already near the café.

The taller assailant got up and ran to the left side of the café, taking cover behind a table. Lamb observed they are trying to flank them, and he hand signaled that information to Price. The bullets from each of their weapons destroyed the contents of the café. Lamb threw a smoke grenade in front of them. The two assailants continued to shoot and advance forward. When they did not hear any more rounds coming from Price and Lamb, they slowly moved from cover and advanced to the area where Price and Lamb had been. Once the smoke cleared, they cautiously moved past the table with their guns pointed in the direction of the agents. However, they found no one.

Lamb and Price were now behind them. "Drop your weapons and put your hands up—now!" Lamb commanded. The assailants were caught off guard. The taller assailant pointed his weapon at them but was shot to death by both Price and Lamb. He fell to the floor and did not move. The shorter one immediately dropped his weapon and placed his hands above his head as agents entered the café.

Lamb immediately began to interrogate the remaining assailant. "All right, whoever you are. I want answers from you. I want the truth!" he said angrily. Lamb placed his right hand around the man's esophagus.

"All right, all right. I'll talk! Just take it easy, will ya! We were hired by some guy named Wolf. I don't know where he comes from or where he lives. We just received this contract from him three days ago. We are murderers for hire and go to the highest bidders. We didn't even have information about who you are and what went down between you guys. All we do is carry out what the contract states, no questions asked. We didn't know who you guys were. He also didn't tell me we had to fuck with ninjas!"

Lamb ordered the agents to take the man away. Just then, a throwing star hit the suspect in his heart. He cried out in pain and died. Price, Lamb and the other agents were shocked and pointed their weapons in the direction from which the star was thrown. Price sent two agents to pursue the attacker. Lamb immediately pulled out the metal star and examined it. He noticed that the tips were dipped in some mysterious substance. "Well, at least we know that we are well-known at this time and have to watch our backs. We never know who's going to come for us," he said. "I just received a vision: I saw a split in the dragon. I don't know what that could mean, and I wonder who this wolf is?"

Price said, "I'm wondering if he is part of the Al-Qaeda or has some connection with them. I want you to inform your unit concerning what happened here, Lamb. It looks like we're not just looking at amateurs. There are professionals out there who certainly want to take us out of the equation. That reminds me: you have to get touch with Master Po and tell him that you will be on that plane to see him in two days."

"Thank you, sir. I do need the time to train with Master Po. I have a lot to learn, especially on how to fight these supernatural ninjas."

Price and Lamb got into the SUV and headed toward Lamb's apartment. Once they arrived, Lamb said good-bye to Price and then went inside his apartment, where Tank was anxiously awaiting his arrival. Tank wagged his tail as Lamb reached in the refrigerator and got some ice water. Then he fed Tank. Lamb sat down and turned on the TV. He then reaches for his cell phone and called the Korean embassy. Lin Po answered the phone, and Lamb informed him that his director would let him leave one week early for the training. Lin Po was very pleased at the news, and he arranged for Lamb to stay in the embassy during that week. Master Po had much to teach Lamb even though Lamb was a grandmaster himself. The Red Dragon was a very dangerous and evil clan.

Anders and LeBlanc continued their search for evidence. They were joined by Jenny Lee on the second floor of the mall. They informed her of all the work they had done up until this time. So far they had collected several bullet casings and shotgun shells. As Jenny Lee walked, she looked down and found a matchbox. She bent down and picked it up. It had strange markings of a pentagram around the box, and on the cover was a dragon. Jenny Lee used her mobile lab kit and discovered traces of sodium nitrate on the railing that had fallen from the third floor during the explosion. Anders and Leblanc found traces of PBX, plastic explosives, near the entrance of the mall on the first floor. The three agents then completed their investigations and went to the office to fill out their reports and to contact Lamb.

Agent Lee called Lamb to inform him of their findings in the investigation of the bombing. She informed him of the sodium nitrate and the PBX that they had discovered at the site. Agent Lee also spoke of the matchbox that she'd found. Lamb asked if there were any prints that were found. Agent Lee had dusted for prints but did not find any. Lamb then told Agent Lee to hold on to the matchbox; he would look at it in the morning before she turned everything in to the evidence room. The agents completed their investigation and were ready to retire.

Jenny Lee then said, "Hey, guys! I don't know about you, but I'm not that tired, and I'd like to get a drink before I retire. How about it?"

Anders looked at Leblanc and then turned to Lee. "You two go on ahead. I'm too tired, and I definitely need my rest. It's been a long day. I'll take a rain check and will see you both tomorrow!"

"It looks like it's just you and me!" Leblanc said.

"There is a bar called Stan's three blocks away. We could go there," Lee suggested with a smile.

Both agents waved good-bye to Anders and walked toward the bar. Leblanc talked about the day and the events that had occurred. However, Lee didn't want to talk about work while they were off the clock. They entered the bar and were greeted by two bouncers. Leblanc paid the cover charge as they walked into the club and took their seats near the dance floor. The club got crowded as more and more students from the nearby college arrived.

Leblanc had always wanted to get to know Lee, ever since he first saw her almost a year ago during their first briefing in the CIA conference room.

Lee asked Leblanc about himself. "So how did you end up on this assignment? And how did you ever end up in the French Foreign Legion?"

"Simple. I was very delinquent as a teen. I got into a lot of trouble, and my parents didn't know what to do. I ended up before a judge after getting into trouble. The judge gave me two choices: reform school or the French Foreign Legion. The judge actually chose the latter of the two for me; he decided that it was in my best interest. As for here in CPAT, Lamb saw my background, and I guess he found me worthy to be a part of the team," Leblanc said as he waved to the waitress. They ordered two martinis. "What about you, Chéri? Why did you choose the military?"

"I always wanted to be a soldier. My entire family is made up of soldiers, from the army to special forces. I made the commandoes when I was in England. I had to prove myself because, as you know, this is a male-dominated world, and I had to show them what I was made of. There was no time for me to let up; I had to go all-out. Once I did so, I earned the respect of my commander as well as my unit," Lee replied.

"I'm very impressed, Chéri."

"Why thank you!" Lee blushed. They raised their glasses in a toast to their success in their military careers, and to the success of their new unit.

Leblanc looked deeply into Lee's eyes. She noticed and quickly looked down. "Why do you stare at me like that?" she asked.

Leblanc smiled and said, "I was just admiring you. I've always admired you from the first day I saw you!"

Lee smiled back and looked down at her drink. She moved her hand towards his and holds his hand. "Well, Agent Leblanc, I guess the feeling's mutual."

Leblanc felt that this was a good ending to a bad day. They both got up to dance to a slow song.

As they danced, two individuals, a man and woman of Asian descent, kept a close watch on them. They were both dressed in dark clothing. "These are the agents from the new CIA unit, Meeko. We have to make sure that we eliminate them this evening and report back to the Wolf."

"Yes, Neto. We may have to split up. I don't think that they live together," Meeko stated.

After the dance, the agents walked out of the club hand in hand and then went to their vehicles. "We both have a long day ahead of us, and we should just say good night and get some rest," Lee said.

Leblanc gazed into her eyes and moved her body closer. She didn't resist him, so he leaned his head toward hers and parted his lips as she did the same. They kissed and embraced for a long time.

"Okay, all right. That's it, agent. We have to prepare early for tomorrow. Lamb goes went a week ahead of his team, and we have to prepare to protect the governor's family!" Lee whispered.

"Agreed, Chéri. I will try my very best to resist your love for the rest of this evening!" Leblanc said.

Lee smiled as she got into her vehicle. They kissed again, but this time it was brief. They waved good-bye to each other, and Leblanc entered his vehicle and started his engine. He noticed a car speeding away quickly, behind Lee's. At first he thought it may be nothing. He then gave her a call from his cell phone. "Hello, Chéri!"

"Leblanc, dear, I thought we already said our good-byes?"

"We did. However I just wanted to call your attention to your rearview mirror. There is a vehicle that took off very quickly after you pulled away from the parking lot. I think you are being tailed."

Lee sped up and took quick, sharp turns to the left and then the right. The vehicle behind her did the same and sped up as well. "I believe you. I'm glad you warned me," Lee said. She continued to increase her speed. Leblanc then asked her to put on the speaker phone. Leblanc increased his own speed and notices that he was being followed by a vehicle also.

The man in dark clothing tailed Leblanc and began to throw metal stars at Leblanc's tires. Leblanc swerved his vehicle to the right and the left. The stars barely missed the tires. Lee also performed the same maneuvers.

Meeko wanted to cause an accident for Lee. "I think that vehicle maneuver crossover eighteen is due now, Chéri."

"I believe you're right, hon!" Lee said. Lee drove toward a wall that surrounded an apartment complex. "On my mark. One … two … three!" Lee turned quickly to the right, and Leblanc turned quickly to the left. Both enemy drivers were caught off guard at the swift maneuver and could not react in time. They crashed into the brick wall, first Meeko and then Neto. The vehicles exploded into oblivion. Agent Leblanc quickly exited his vehicle and ran toward Lee, who also exited her vehicle. They embraced each other and watched the vehicles in flames. They ran over to see if there were any survivors and could already hear sirens en route to their location. Medical emergency vehicles, fire engines, and police officers arrived on the scene. The agents informed Lamb, who in turn contacted Price. Lamb sent a text to Price, but he hadn't answered it yet. The firemen quickly put out the flames from the vehicles.

While Lee and Leblanc were giving their statements to the police, Lamb arrived on the scene. He was concerned because he knew that Al-Qaeda would target his team at any time and in any place. Lamb walked over to the agents and noticed them holding hands. Agent Lee quickly released Leblanc's hand and continued to give her statement to the police. "Hello, sir. We're sorry to disturb you. We know you had a bad ordeal already," Leblanc said. "It's all right. I just want to make sure that you and Agent Lee are okay. You know that I have to know everything that goes on with my unit. Are you both all right?" Lamb asked.

"We're both fine, sir," Lee said. Lamb looked around for Price, but he hadn't arrived yet. The two agents told Lamb about had happened after they had completed their investigations at the crime scene in the mall. Lamb walked over to examine the burnt vehicles and asked if there were any bodies in the vehicle. The firemen stated that there were no bodies. Lamb noticed a piece of the broken glass had a picture of a Red Dragon on it. The piece had broken off during the explosion.

Price never arrived at the scene, and so Lamb called his cell and his office. He now sensed that something was terribly wrong. Lamb remembered observing miniature bottles inside Price's coat pocket. He didn't question him at the time, but now he believed he must do so.

Chapter 3

Price's Dark Secret

CPAT was back at the academy training facility. Lamb was about to teach the class grappling techniques when he received a troubling phone call from Alice Price, Victor's wife of twenty-five years. She informed him that Victor had not been home for two days. Alice and Victor had been arguing for quite some time now. Victor began to drink heavily again after going through counseling. "What could possibly be the cause for him to start drinking heavily again?" Alice had thought.

Lamb left the academy with Tank and arrived at the Prices' home. Alice greeted Lamb at the door, crying. She gave Lamb a hug. "I ... I just don't know what's wrong with Vic. He just hasn't been himself. He comes home and doesn't want to spend time with me. He's also been short tempered. He doesn't answer his cell!"

"Did Victor say where he was going at all? Are there any places where you both go to get away and relax?" Lamb asked.

Alice raised her head slowly, paused, and said, "There is a cabin in the East Mountains that used to belong to my parents. Victor and I use it for the summer months to get away and relax. The cabin is located in the mountains off of I-30. It's just east of the 125 mile marker. The cabin is located about fifty miles from here. Please bring him back to me safe and sound, Nathan," Alice said, sobbing.

"I will, Alice. Don't worry," Lamb said. He quickly ran to his SUV and took off toward the mountains. He also notified Jennings, who was at the headquarters' satellite command center. Jennings set the satellite to hone in on the SUV's tracking system. It revealed Victor Price at the location where his wife said he would be. Lamb thanked Jennings and increased his speed, heading toward the East Mountains. Lamb followed the winding hill. The terrain became progressively difficult to climb. The wet, slippery roads did not help.

Lamb was near the cabin when suddenly he could feel his body begin to shake. "Oh no! Not now, not now!" Lamb shrieked. Tank began to bark. The road became narrow as Lamb's vision blurred and then darkened. He turned his vehicle to the side of the road and parked it. Then his vision went completely dark.

He was now speaking to Victor Price in the cabin. Lamb held a cup of hot chocolate when a bullet hit the window near Price's head. Gas canisters were shot inside the cabin. Lamb pulled out his super, and Price pulled out his 45. Machine gun fire ripped up the cabin, breaking mirrors, pictures, furniture, and glasses. Lamb saw three men in the front and two more in the rear. Price got up and ran towards a back door. He opened the door, and Lamb yelled at him not to open it. Price was met with several bullets shattering his muscle tissue and bones throughout his body. He fell backward onto the wooden floor. Lamb ran toward Price and saw a grenade next to Price. There was a flash of light.

As the light diminished, Lamb's vision cleared and he saw images of deer crossing the road as they came into focus. Lamb turned his head, and Tank licked his face and wagged his tail. "I'm okay, boy. I'm glad I brought you with me," Lamb whispered. Lamb turned on the engine and drove back onto the road, continuing his upward track toward the cabin.

Price saw Lamb driving closer through his binoculars. Price took off into the mountains on foot staggering. Lamb parked the vehicle at the bottom of the mountain. Tank barked and took off up toward the cabin. Lamb yelled for him to stop, however Tank continued running full speed toward the cabin with a blanket in his mouth. Lamb ran toward the cabin too. Once he reached it, he saw Price was nowhere to be found. He found Price's binoculars, left on the table near beer and liquor bottles. Lamb ran around the back of the cabin and saw footprints in the snow leading into the woods. Lamb followed the footprints, running as fast as he could and calling Price's name. *He can't be too far away from here. There may not be enough time. Al-Qaeda is coming.*

The sun was beginning to set, and the temperature in the mountains got lower by the hour. As Lamb continued his search for Price, snow began to fall, and the footprints were getting covered. Lamb's body felt cold, and his hands and feet were going numb. "Where are you, Price?" Lamb muttered over and over. Just then he heard a familiar sound. It is faint at first but became louder. It was his German shepherd, Tank, barking. Tank was very resourceful, as his actions proved on the battlefield and in the streets as a canine soldier and officer. Lamb ran toward Tank's barking. The sun was down, and Price's tracks were completely covered. Lamb could now see Tank standing over a body on the ground as he continued to bark. Tank saw Lamb and wagged his tail. As Lamb approached the figure on the ground, he saw that it was Victor Price, covered in a blanket. "Tank, did you give Victor a blanket?" Lamb asked the faithful dog. Tank barked in reply. Lamb assisted Price to his feet. Price didn't speak but went along with Lamb to the cabin. Tank led the way.

Lamb wanted answers as to why Price had not been to work for the past three days, and why he had started drinking again. They soon reached the cabin. Lamb laid Price down on the sofa, and Tank sat next to him on the floor. Lamb gathered wood for fire and got coffee brewing. Lamb looked outside the window of the cabin, making sure there was no sign of Al-Qaeda. He then sat on a chair across from Price and stared at the man. Tank got up, walked over to Lamb, and sat at his side, staring at Price as well.

"Well, what?" Price asked sternly.

"I'm waiting, sir," Lamb said.

"I can remember when we first met, Lamb. You were so damned green then and thought you knew everything. No one could tell you shit, could they? But for some unknown reason, you wanted to spend leave with Lin Po in Korea. Now look at you. It seems they straightened your ass out more than the military did," Price said assuredly.

Lamb pauses and replied, "I believe that both entities assisted me in life, sir. They both made me the person I am today."

"I bet someday the CIA will be yours. You will be the next director," Price noted sadly.

"Sir, tell me what's going on. I need to know."

Price said, "You need to know, huh? Why I drink like a fool and can't stop?" Lamb nodded. "Well, then, I'll tell you. Years ago when I was green like you were, I wanted to be all I could be. I joined the army. My father wanted all of his boys to be like him, so all four of us were. Billy, the youngest, wasn't cut out for it, but Dad made him join anyway. Billy was always out of control, like you used to be. You remind me so much of Billy...." Price hesitated and then continued. "Billy and I were in that same unit in Beirut. I was a captain by that time, and Billy was assigned to my unit. I was called to a meeting with several high-ranking officers. My orders were then given to me—orders that were suicidal, unfeeling, and uncaring. I did not want to carry them out. Damn them, Lamb! Damn them all!

"I had to order troops into an area that is now called Slaughter Field because so many of our boys were killed there. I knew the area, so I decided to go around it. Besides, intelligence informed us that there would be no enemy contact if we did so. I ordered my troops around the field; I believed that by doing so, I could save many lives. I was wrong. I was so very wrong, Lamb. I walked us all into a trap we couldn't walk away from. We walked right into a minefield. My first squad was blown to shit. They retreated only to find us flanked by the enemy on both sides and coming straight toward us. My men retreated back toward the mine field. I even called for an airstrike. I was pissed because they screwed the damn coordinates up and began to bomb not only the enemy but us too. I was in the field with them and felt so damn helpless, Lamb. There wasn't a damn thing I could do except pray.

"When the fighting was over, I saw bodies everywhere. I think more than half of my unit was blown to shit. We gathered the dead and wounded. It was just like Dante's *Inferno*, like hell. I saw hell that day, Lamb. Bodies burning, men screaming everywhere. It stays with you always; you can't just turn it off. Billy's body was among them. When I returned to headquarters, the brass said that I was a hero. When I told them that the slaughter was my fault, they did not want to hear it. Instead, they slapped more stripes and medals on me. I went home after that, and that started the first series of binge drinking.

"Alice separated from me for two weeks; she went to live with her parents. I left the military after twenty years—retired. When we were in elementary school, my father required the three of us boys to be in sports and Boy Scouts. This had to be done because Dad said so. He was supportive, though and would go to almost every game we had. Dad would tell us, 'Hey, Johnny, run faster. Put more spiral into that ball. Robert, you can block better than that. Keep your body upright! Move it, Victor. What's wrong with you today? Grandma can run faster. Do you want to walk home?' Those words always haunted the three of us growing up. We didn't talk to anybody concerning our family life. Mom was very quiet and would hardly have a say in anything. Then there came Billy.

"Billy was born in 1960. He had the blond hair and blue eyes in the family; everyone knew he was going to be a lady killer. The pressure for us to perform to perfection was somehow relieved to a certain extent. Dad's attention was on Billy, and he wanted him to be perfect. Dad also put Billy in sports and scouts. Sports weren't Billy's forte. He did all right in Scouts. It was music that was Billy's specialty. He received a scholarship in music to a small college. However, Dad was bent on having all of his sons in the military. Johnny went into the marines, and Robert and I joined the army. Robert became a Green Beret. I later became a member of the Delta Force, as you are aware of. Dad knew that Billy wasn't cut out for the military, but he pushed him into it anyways. Billy accepted it only because he wanted to please Dad. Billy's wife, Lorraine, also knew it, and that caused friction between them. She told me to look after him. I tried, Lamb—I really tried. At Billy's funeral, people came from everywhere. Billy was given a hero's funeral. All of his classmates attended, as well as teachers, old girlfriends, co-workers, and relatives. I was asked to give part of the eulogy.

> Billie Jonathan Price. BJ is what his brothers would call him. BJ always wanted to hang out with his older brothers. He wanted to be just like us. We were all

very competitive; I guess it came from our father. BJ was a people person and cared about everyone. I can't recall anyone who he didn't like, or anyone who did not like him. BJ always helped others. He had a big heart and would do anything for anyone. BJ wasn't as competitive as the rest of us, but he would get the job done. He was a team player. He was an outstanding musician and continued his education at UCLA, where he graduated as valedictorian of his class. He then went into the military and made the rank of sergeant. BJ was engaged to a very beautiful and loving person, Lorraine. Lorraine, BJ loved you very much. Please don't ever forget that.

BJ will be missed by all of us. We learned so much from him by the way he lived his life. He loved God and his fellow man. BJ was a great role model for all of us. The X-Ray unit and Alpha unit salute you. We'll see you again in a better world.

"There was a gun salute for BJ. Mom couldn't take it. She nearly had a nervous breakdown. She would call out his name in the middle of the night and wake up. She would walk to his room, grab one of his pillows, and curl up in his bed. Dad didn't know what to do. Mom would tell him that it was his fault for pushing him into it. They separated for six months, and she stayed with relatives. Afterward, she was encouraged by her counselor to go home and get counseling together. Dad was never the same, though he did treat everyone better. What the hell? Did it have to take Billy's dying for him to do so? Dad was silent throughout the funeral, from the beginning to the end. The honor guard folded the flag on Billy's coffin and then gave it to Mom. She wept. Lorraine was clinging to her mother; she was three months pregnant. Robert, Johnny, and I also cried with our wives. No one said a word until after the burial. Mom and Dad cried uncontrollably.

"The wake was at our parents' house. When it was over, my brothers and I drove home with our wives. I will never forget that day, Lamb.

That day a part of me died with Billy. Billy, my little baby brother, was not going to be coming over to visit me and Alice ever again. Reality hit me so hard that I began to drink and drink. I continued to drink in order to forget. The drinking only worked until I sobered up. When I remembered, I would drink again. I tried to keep it from Alice. As I said before, she left me. Alice said she would return, but only if I got help. I did get help for a while. When I was assigned to the CIA, the incident with the terrorists changed everything. Things seemed to be going well until my new assignment of personal security detail.

"I was assigned to protect some diplomats during their stay in San Diego. We heard shooting outside of the convention center and immediately investigated. We observed someone on the building rooftop across the street from us. My director ordered my partner and me to pursue the suspect. My partner and I ran inside the building across the street and up the stairwell leading to the roof. Once we reached the roof, we observed a man dressed in a black suit and tie. He shot a man twice in the chest. The other man had also shot him in the chest, and they both had collapsed on the roof.

"My partner and I drew our weapons on the suspects. The man dressed in a black suit told me that I needed to shoot and kill Jack Nance. I informed him that Jack Nance was one of the diplomats whom we were protecting. The man said that he was misleading us. 'Not everything is what it seems to be. Kill him. Nance is responsible for many deaths, even the murder of babies. You have to trust me. Kill him!'

I heard laughter coming from the street below, where we'd left our other agents and the diplomats. I saw Nance pull a gun out and shoot and kill the two other diplomats. Then he shot my director and fellow agent in the head. The director survived the gunshot to his head. I immediately opened fire on Nance and hit him; I didn't know where at the time. I pursued him, and he tried to escape in a large crowd of people. I continued to pursue through the crowd. I saw him run around the corner into an alley. When I ran around the corner, I was met with a barrage of bullets near my feet. They were coming from a man armed with a machine gun. I observed some garbage bags near the front of the alley, and I threw myself behind them for cover. I heard Nance laugh. I never forgot that laugh. His laugh echoed as he drove away in a limousine. The FBI agent who was working undercover that day died after he arrived at the hospital.

"Nance later revealed his real name: Abdullah Mohammed. Ten years later, he became the head of Al-Qaeda. Ever since that incident, all those bombings, murders, and deaths happened because I didn't stop Abdullah when I had the chance. I should have also protected Billy because he couldn't protect himself. These are the reasons I drink, Lamb. I will continue to drink until the day I die. That is, unless I kill myself first!" Price started sobbing.

Lamb gave Price a solemn look. "You can't blame yourself—you didn't know. You could not have known. I don't think anyone being in your position could have possibly known what was going to occur in either one of those cases, sir. Listen to me. You were given orders by your superiors to carry out, and you did so, just like you should have. At the time you carried out your orders, you made a decision that you felt was in the best interest of your men, including Billy. It wasn't your fault; you were told there was no activity in that area. You wanted to protect Billy as well as your unit. As for the incident concerning Abdullah? I wouldn't have known what to do in that case either. I would've probably acted the same as you did, sir. I wouldn't have known who to trust. Who could know such a thing and the outcome in a situation like that? I would have done the same thing, sir! You've been walking around carrying this huge baggage of guilt on your back for years. It's time to let go of it all. I think—no, I believe it is just a damn excuse to drink and remain in the mire. You choose to stay in the situation you are in and want to throw away everything good that you have, including your wife, family, friends, and career. You just got so hung up on your self-pitying attitude that you forgot the real reason why you had me put this team together."

Price lifted his head slowly to look at Lamb as Lamb continued. "It was to apprehend Abdullah and other terrorists, and to protect those that need us. You call the shots—you put this together. I just brought the people here; you started the fire. Let's put an end to this together, sir!"

Price wiped the tears off his face and nodded. "Lin Po really fine-tuned you, didn't he, Lamb?"

"Yes, sir, he did!" Lamb replied.

Tank moved toward the front door. His ears stood up, and he growled. Lamb had almost forgotten about the premonition that he'd had before arriving. He informed Price about what was going to happen. Five figures in the dark moved toward the isolated cabin. It was Emir, one of Abdullah's captains, along with four of his men: Fahim, Riyah, Fuad, and Farid. They each carried AR-15s.

Lamb and Price set c-4 explosives to the front of the cabin. Lamb could see five men approaching. Two of them ran in opposite directions, engaging toward the rear of the cabin. Bullets ripped through the glass windows of the cabin. Lamb and Price returned fire. Lamb ordered Tank to open the back door of the cabin and run down the hill toward the vehicle. "We have to start running behind Tank because they are about to shoot tear gas at us, sir," Lamb said. Price did not question Lamb because he had seen too many premonitions become reality in the field. They quickly ran out the rear door and opened fire on two suspects, Farid and Riyah, hitting them in the chests. The suspects fell to the ground and did not move.

"I heard shots coming from the back. They must be trying to escape! Let's go around now," Emir commanded.

Fahim started to speak. "Sir, we almost have—" At that moment the door exploded. Fahim and Fuad were killed instantly. Emir was thrown to the ground but was unharmed.

Lamb and Price turned around for only a moment to watch the cabin explode in a violent fury. They continued running downhill toward their vehicles. Tank made his way to the vehicle and waited. "We're almost there, sir!" Lamb said.

Emir pursued Lamb and Price, and he radioed for assistance from his other men. "This is Captain Emir. They are both still alive and heading toward their government vehicles. They must not escape us! I repeat, they are headed west toward the vehicle. Stop them now!" Emir saw Lamb and Price, and he fired his AR-15 at them, barely missing them.

Lamb and Price stopped and kneeled down to return fire. Then they got up and continued toward the SUV, which was now in sight.

Tank saw Lamb and Price and he barked at them in a manner that was very different.

Lamb knew it was different. "Hold up, sir. Let's take a knee here," he said abruptly.

"What is it, Lamb?" Price asked.

Lamb motioned with his finger for Price to keep quiet so that he could listen to Tank's barking. "Take cover behind those fallen trees, and keep your head down, sir."

"What's going on?" Price demanded.

"Tank is barking in code. He's informing us that there are four hostiles trying to flank us, and there are booby traps forty yards in front of us at twelve o'clock," Lamb replied.

"You mean to tell me that you got all that from just those barks?" Price said, surprised.

"Yes, sir. I began to teach Tank to bark in code the day after I rescued him in that building that we destroyed in Afghanistan. Tank and I have always used code on the battlefield and while working on the streets in the K-9 unit."

"And to think I wanted you to get rid of that dog when you were in Delta Force!" Price remarked.

Four hostiles began to close in on their flanks. Lamb and Price checked their weapons and reloaded. Both were lying down between two trees on the ground. The trees were the best cover they could find. Emir signaled to his men by waving to them. They lowered their weapons as he approached. "What happened?" Emir demanded.

"I don't know, sir. One minute the Americans were running toward us, and all of a sudden they took cover as if someone had alerted them," Bashar said. The hostiles opened fire on Lamb and Price, who returned fire. Bullets whistled through the air on both sides. Lamb and Price continued to exchange fire against the hostiles, who had taken cover behind trees on both of the agents' flanks. Lamb radioed Jennings for backup, and Jennings dispatched teams to the area. Team copters one and two, Henderson and K-Hawk, responded immediately and were en route to the scene.

Lamb and Price tried to get off clean shots at the hostiles, however they couldn't because they were outflanked. Lamb suddenly remembered he has one strobe flash grenade left in his vest. He retrieved it from his right vest pocket, pulled the pin, and threw it at the hostiles on their right flank. The grenade landed near the feet of the two hostiles, but they couldn't see exactly where because of the dark. "Adil, can you see where that landed?" Basit asked.

"No, Basit. We have to search quickly. It may be a grenade!" Basit said. The two hostiles fell to their knees and searched for the grenade.

The grenade was two feet away from them and began to spin. "What is this magic?" Adil cried. The grenade then flashed light as the men backed away and covered their eyes from its brightness. They stood up and stumbled into each other. This gave Lamb a clear target. Lamb told Price to keep his head down. He opened fire on the men, hitting both of them in the chest. The two hostiles fall to the ground and did not get up. The two hostiles to the left of their flank continue to shoot and move toward the agents. Lamb and Price were beginning to run out of bullets. As the hostiles closed in on them, Lamb threw a smoke grenade at his feet. Smoke filled the area where Lamb and Price were trapped.

Tank heard the explosion and saw the smoke coming from the area where Lamb and Price were located. He began to bark and whine.

The hostiles held their fire and moved toward the fallen trees with no signs of movement from the agents. "Nasser, can you see them?" Emir asked.

"No. There are no signs of them here. We do not know where they have gone!" Nasser replied.

"They must be there somewhere. They could not have just disappeared! Find them and kill them now!" Emir cried. Emir took out his binoculars and began a visual search for the agents. He looked at the bottom of the hill and saw two figures and a dog entering an SUV. The vehicle sped away. "The agents have reached the vehicle and are getting away!" shrieked Emir.

"How? How did they get past us, Nasser?" cried Fahid.

"Get them! Get them now!" Emir demanded. He radioed for assistance. "Denwolf to Foxhunter, Denwolf to Foxhunter come in."

"This is Foxhunter. Go ahead, Denwolf," Basti said.

"Targets are trying to escape, moving west down mountain. Do not let them get away."

"Foxhunter reads you loud and clear, sir."

The SUV sped down the muddy, narrow, and winding road. "I forgot that you can do that ninja stuff, Lamb!" Price said.

"I knew that we were going to need it because we were running out of ammo," Lamb replied. As Lamb drove down the mountain, he noticed another SUV pursuing them. Lamb saw another vehicle coming head-on in front of them. They were trapped, but only for a moment.

Lamb made a sharp left turn off the road and down a steep embankment, moving around trees and breaking low branches. The hostiles in both vehicles also turned off the road and continued pursuit. Lamb saw that a hostile had a grenade launcher aimed at them. Tank began to bark. "I know, boy. I see it," Lamb told the dog. Price looked at Lamb and shook his head in amazement. Lamb initiated evasive action, making the SUV swerve to the left and right, in and out of the lines of trees.

"Emid, shoot them now!" shouted Basti.

"I'm trying, but that damn American won't let me get a clear shot!" cried Emid. Emid shot again and came close to hitting the SUV's right rear tire. The grenade hit the road, causing the SUV to swerve into a spin.

Lamb quickly got the vehicle under control. He saw a clearing and sped onto a side road. The hostiles were in hot pursuit behind them. The enemy continued to shoot the grenade launcher at them, barely missing them. "That does it—I'm done playing ball with these guys," Lamb said, frustrated.

"What are you planning to do, Lamb?" Price asked.

"You'll see. Tank, I need you to pull Hades for me. Pull Hades now, boy. Now!" Lamb commanded. Tank looked at Lamb and whines. "I know you don't like doing that because of the noise, but if we don't, we will all die," Lamb said. Tank whined once more.

"What in the world are you telling that dog now? Does he understand? What the hell is Hades?" Price inquired.

Tank reluctantly jumps over the seat and moved to the rear of the vehicle as grenades continued to explode nearby. Another vehicle joined the pursuit. Lamb became more frustrated. "Tank!" he shouted. Tank slowly moved his head above the seat. Lamb saw him in the rearview mirror. "Do it now! Pull Hades!"

Tank whined and pulls a cord with his teeth, releasing a small cylinder from the rear of the vehicle. Then the dog lay down and covered his ears. The small cylinder hit the ground and headed toward the first vehicle, where Emid had been launching grenades. The cylinder bounced on the dirt road underneath the pursuing vehicle, attached underneath the vehicle, and exploded, ripping the vehicle apart. The second and third vehicles collided into each other and exploded.

Price looked back and saw a fiery inferno along with pieces of flaming metal. "So that's why you named it Hades!" he said.

Lamb nodded. "Good boy, Tank. You did good!" he said excitedly. Tank let out another whine and wagged his tail.

"Damn, I feel left out because that dog of yours has two up on me!" Price said. Lamb and Price felt relieved, however there was another SUV, and this time a helicopter was also in pursuit. "Looks like there's more trouble above," Price noted.

Lamb looked up and observed a sniper on the wing of a helicopter. He immediately took evasive action as the sniper shot at the agents. "Where are my helicopters? Where is my air support?" Lamb muttered.

The helicopter moved quickly toward the agents' vehicle. The sniper steadied his weapon and aimed at the driver, Lamb. As the sniper placed his finger on the trigger, the helicopter exploded.

"What the hell happened?" Lamb wondered.

K-Hawk had shot a missile into the hostile helicopter. "Copter Two to Team Leader One. Sorry we're late, sir. We couldn't quite locate you. There was some type of radio-jamming device they used on us."

"You did good, K-Hawk. Is Copter One also with you?" Lamb asked.

"Henderson here, sir! We're going to take out that SUV for you." Ajay and Leblanc were in Copter One. Ajeeta and Anders were in Copter Two.

The remaining SUV continued to fire upon the agents.

"Copter One to Copter Two. This one is ours," Henderson said.

"Take the honors, Copter One," K-Hawk said. The hostile inside the SUV got another grenade ready and loaded it into the launcher. He moved toward the open sunroof and steadied the launcher. Ajeeta aimed her sniper rifle at the hostile and shot him in the head. The man fell inside the SUV.

Lamb floors his SUV. Once the agents' vehicle was further separated from the hostiles, Henderson, shot at the hostile vehicle, hitting it in the center. It exploded on contact. "Good job, Copter One. Good job, team. I think we have gotten all of them. We have to call our investigators in along with local law enforcement authorities to clean up this mess," Lamb stated. Lamb drove the SUV back to the main road that would lead them down the mountain. They first drove back toward Price's SUV.

"The vehicle is still there. There are no signs of any hostiles in the area. How about up there, team?" Lamb asked. Copters One and Two reported no activity in the immediate area. "Go ahead, sir. I will cover you. Here, take the AR-15 with you, just in case," Lamb said.

"Thanks," Price replied. He moved cautiously toward the SUV, opened the door, and then quickly moved inside and started the engine. He moved his car forward while Lamb followed close behind. It was still dark; the sun wouldn't rise for another four hours. Lamb radioed both teams and informed them that they could go back to headquarters. They needed to fill out reports and also get ready for another day at the academy.

Tank made his way to the front seat and sat next to Lamb. "Good boy, Tank. I didn't mean to be so hard on you. You did very well. I'm proud to have you as a part of this team," Lamb told the dog. Tank barked and wagged his tail as Lamb rubbed his head. The vehicles continued to move down the winding hill.

Price saw that his cell phone had been ringing; it was on vibrate. He noticed that Alice had been calling him—three missed calls. He picked up his phone and called her. "Hi, babe. It's Victor."

"Oh thank God, thank God you're alive! Where have you been, Victor? Where have you been?" Alice cried.

"I had to get away, Alice. I couldn't deal with all the guilt that I was facing. The pain and the memories were too much for me to handle," Victor said, sobbing.

"I'm here for you, sweetheart. You know that I care about you, and most important, I love you. Your family loves you very much. I wouldn't know what to do without you!" Alice replied.

"Don't worry, dear. Lamb came for me and set my mind straight. I'm going back to counseling. I don't know what I would have done if he hadn't found me. My mind just wasn't right. You sent for him, didn't you?"

"Yes, I did. He was my last resort. I knew he could find you. I'm so glad you are working together again."

"I'm also glad, dear. You don't know how glad I am to have him. Baby, I have to go now. I should be home in another hour or so. I just wanted to tell you how much I love and appreciate you. I really do!" Price said.

"I love you too!" Alice said, crying with joy.

Price hung up and concentrated on the road. As Price drove, he saw a dark figure in the rearview mirror holding a sharp object. He watched as the hostile man raised his hand with the object in it. Price turned the SUV sharply to the left and then to the right, causing the hostile's body to be thrown from one side of the vehicle to the other.

Lamb saw Price's vehicle swerving and radioed the director. "What's going on, sir?" Lamb asked.

"I think I have a passenger who wants me dead. Sorry, son, can't talk now," Price shouted. The hostile regained his composure and raised his hand up with the sharp object in it once again. This time Price slammed on his brakes. Lamb turned sharply to the left to avoid hitting Price. The hostile's body fell forward into the dashboard. Price hit him in the head, neck, and back with his hands. The hostile cried out and retaliated with elbow strikes to Price's chest and head. Price punched him in the face, knocking him toward the front dash again. The hostile reached for a handgun in his pocket, but Price hit him in the face. Price's AR-15 was on the passenger side where the hostile was, just within arm's reach. Price quickly opened the driver's door and exited the vehicle. Lamb had his AR-15 ready and motioned Price to take cover behind his SUV. Lamb had his handgun inside Price's SUV and retrieves it. Lamb saw the hostile trying to circle to the right of them, and he gave hand signals to Price regarding the hostile's position.

The hostile was Emir. He had stayed behind just in case the agents survived the main attack. Emir was very nervous and sweated profusely. He knew that he must kill both of the agents—or else he would be killed by Abdullah for failing his mission. Out of the ten men who had been assigned to him, only Emir remained. Emir couldn't face Abdullah as a failure. Failing wasn't an option. He quietly continued to the right of the SUV, believing he would catch the agents off guard.

Lamb and Price knelt down in their defensive stance positions with their handguns drawn and ready. Lamb could see Emir's feet walking slowly and moving forward awkwardly at times. Emir held his breath and then charged around the corner, praying that God would grant him victory. Emir was expecting the agents to be standing upright, however they were kneeling as the opened fire on him. Emir was shot in his chest, arms, and legs several times. His AK-47 shot several times into the air as his right finger pressed upon the trigger. Emir then spun around and fell to the ground.

Lamb and Price walked over to where his body had fallen. "He looked very determined to kill us, Lamb. I believe this guy was one of Abdullah's men. I gave you and your team the profiles on these terrorists. Emir was one of Abdullah's captains," Price said.

"I remember him now. They were very determined, sir. We have to get moving. Hey, can you hear that?"

"That sounds like something ticking. Emir planted a bomb in my vehicle!" Price said.

"Get back to the other SUV! Hurry!" Lamb shouted.

Lamb was parked only thirty feet away. They ran inside the SUV, and Lamb turned the ignition and placed the vehicle in reverse. He placed his foot down hard on the pedal as they went backward, flattening small trees along the way. Lamb placed the SUV in drive, turned around, and sped off toward the main road leading to town. Just then, a huge explosion occurred. Tank jumped in the back seat and covered his face with his paws. Price turned around and observed the SUV exploding.

Lamb continued to race down the hill. They finally reached the road and could now see the city lights. "I think we made it, sir," Lamb said.

"I think you're right," Price agreed. Both Lamb and Price were exhausted; they had had a long night. They both had black ash on their faces and clothing, along with several bruises on their bodies. Tank was annoyed by all the explosions and chaos surrounding them.

Lamb took Price home. Price phoned Alice and informed her that he was minutes away. "I want to thank you, Lamb. I couldn't have made it through this ordeal without you. When I first met you, I didn't think that you would pan out. I'm glad you proved me wrong, kid. I'm proud of you. I just wanted to let you know that!" Price said. Lamb nodded and gave his director a smile.

Once they arrived at the Prices' home, Alice was there to greet Price with open arms. "Would you like to come in, Lamb? Alice would love to thank you personally," Price said.

"I can't right now, sir. We've got a lot of things to take care of—reports and more reports. We also need intel on those terrorists. Besides, you need some alone time with her. I will definitely speak to her at another time," Lamb replied.

"Roger that, Lamb. See you tomorrow, then."

Lamb waved good-bye. He saw Alice and also waved to her, and she waved back.

Price ran to Alice and gave her a hug and kiss. "I've missed you so!" Alice said.

"I've missed you too. Things are going to be different from now on, dear. I promise," Price said, sobbing.

Lamb drove toward headquarters, where he would drop off the SUV, fill out a few reports, and then go home for a few hours' sleep before getting up and teaching at the academy at eight.

Approximately fifty miles away on the outskirts of the city was an abandoned house that had been set up as a headquarters for Al-Qaeda. Four individuals sat at a table with maps of the city and other items. The maps had marked targets on it. "I can't believe it. I have now lost both of my sons!" Maali said.

"This was not in vain, my husband. You must continue to fight for the cause. Our sons believed in it, and they both died honorably. They are in heaven now. We should both be happy for them!" Adan said. Maali stood up, walked toward the wall, and leaned forward with his head resting on it. Adan walked over and placed her arms around Maali to console him.

Just then, someone knocked. The couple asked the person knocking for the code name. The person answered correctly and was given access. A tall man walked into the room. The newcomer said, "I just wanted to say that I'm sorry for your loss."

Maali slowly turned around and said, "Thank you for your concern, Wolf."

"Here. Abdullah has given me these new orders for you and your men to carry out. There is a time limit as to when this has to be accomplished. You know the rules: there can be no mistakes, and failure is not an option," Wolf stated.

"We will carry out our assignments, Wolf. We have greater motivation to do so," Adan said as she cried.

"I know you do, Adan. But I'm not so sure about your husband. I believe that hearing about his son's deaths has made him weak," Wolf noted.

"I'll show you weak, you Russian bastard!" Maali shouted, and he lunged at Wolf's throat with both hands. The men fell to the ground, trying to choke the other.

Just then the door swung open. "What the hell is going on?" Both men jumped to their feet.

"We were just demonstrating American ground fighting techniques, sir," Wolf explained. Abdullah nodded and then gave his condolences to Maali and Adan. "We will avenge their deaths. You have a new mission, and I expect that we will have success this

time," Abdullah said. Everyone shouted in agreement with him. "Now, let's get to work, shall we?"

Chapter 4

Return to Korea; Protect the Governor

The Hades team had to escort the governor to North Korea for the peace talks. Lamb would take the team to North Korea. The Hades team consisted of Agents Robinson, Skypack, Ajeeta, and AJ Reedy. The Omega team consisted of Agents: Anders, Lee, Wombush, Leblanc, and Martinez, the team Leader. The Omega team would stay and protect the governor's family in California.

Lamb traveled one week ahead of the Hades team to Seoul, Korea, where he stayed with his former grandmaster, Lin Po. It had been over fifteen years since Lin Po had seen his former pupil, Lamb. Lamb waved down a taxi after he arrived at the airport to travel to the US embassy, where Lin Po worked as an assistant to the ambassador. The embassy was approximately an hour away. Once Lamb saw the embassy, he got excited and reminisced about his first introduction to Lin Po, who was from Chinese and Korean descent.

Lamb was a private in the army. He was an impulsive, headstrong, and self-centered individual. He and his army buddies were going to town to get intoxicated when on leave in Korea—and of course, to find women. Lamb and his friends went inside the local bar. Sammy, a huge private, began to speak loudly. "Hey, baby, come sit on my lap," he said boldly.

"Stop it, please. Stop, GI," the waitress cried, pushing Sammy away.

Sammy started to backhand her on the right side of her cheek. However, his right hand was held back. "Let go of me, dammit," Sammy said. He turned and saw a small, old man smiling.

"Please don't strike her. Women are gentle. You are strong. Of what benefit would it be if you were to strike a feeble woman? Besides, she is my one and only daughter," the old man said humbly.

"Well, then, I'll strike *you,* old man!" Sammy yelled.

The old man calmly placed himself in a defensive stance as Sammy took swing after swing at the old man, missing each time. The bar exploded with laughter because Sammy could not touch the old man.

Luke then lunged body at the old man. Like a tiger, the old man jumped straight up into the air as though it took no effort. Luke went sliding into the leg of the table, hitting his head and knocking himself unconscious.

Rudy said, "Okay, old man, let's see if you can get out of this bear hug." The old man took his right heel and targeted the instep of Rudy's foot. His heel connected to the instep, and Rudy felt pain as his grip loosened. The old man bent down and flipped Rudy over shoulder onto the floor, knocking him out. Sammy was now infuriated.

"Do not be angry, because anger is the god of fools. Now, you are not a fool, are you?" the old man asked. "Im gonna shove those words right down your throat old man," Sammy said as he charged. The old man grabbed Sammy's shirt as he lowered himself onto his back and placed both of his feet on Sammy's stomach, flipping him over onto tables and knocking him unconscious.

Lamb's mouth fell open. Never had he seen anything like this before, except in kung fu movies. "Are you among these young men?" the old man asked him.

"I, I°..." Lamb stuttered. He could hardly speak.

"Young man you need to find better companions. You also need discipline in your life," the old man stated.

"I don't need you or anyone to tell me what to do!" Lamb cried, and he stomped outside the bar. As he walked back toward the gate, he saw MPs on their way to pick up his buddies. Lamb runs through an alley, a shortcut to the base.

He was met at the end of the alley by two muggers. "Hey, soldier boy. We want your money—now!" one of them shouted while wielding a knife.

"Don't make us ask again!" the other mugger said.

Lamb tried to run but was tripped by one of the thugs. Lamb fell to the ground and was kicked in the ribs and stomach by both thugs. Lamb began to lose consciousness, but then he heard something odd occurring. The thugs were crying out as if *they* were in pain. One fell down, and then the other. Lamb saw a small figure looking down at him as he lost consciousness.

When he woke, he heard sounds of beautiful music, and he saw exotic green plants around him. There was also a small waterfall in the middle of the room. Lamb turned to his right to see the old man holding a tray with water in it and a washcloth. "I see you have finally awakened," Lin Po said.

"Where am I? What is this place?" Lamb asked.

"You are in the temple!" answered Lin Po. "I am Lin Po, one of the temple's grandmasters." Lin Po bowed, served Lamb some tea, and gave him a grand tour of the temple. Lin Po showed Lamb the training area of the temple, where young pupils were trained in the martial arts. Discipline and humility were highly valued here. Lin Po informed Lamb that these qualities were lacking in Lamb and in his spirit. Master Lin Po introduced Lamb to the grandmasters, Kwang-su, Man Soo, Sang-Jun, and Tae Won. All were masters of the temple and were one with the universe.

"Do you wish to remain with us, young Lamb?" Lin Po asked.

"Could I really, sir? You would really want me to?" asked Lamb surprisingly.

"The invitation will be open to you as long as you abide by our rules."

"I will, sir. I promise," Lamb said.

During the next month, as he was on leave, the masters taught Lamb the ways of the Shaolin. He learned fighting styles from the five masters. Lin Po also taught him Dim Mak, the death touch, and ninjitsu, the art of invisibility. Lamb learned the way of the Tao. Lin Po found Lamb to be a willing and apt student. Lamb already knew martial arts, however he was undisciplined in body, mind, and spirit. His method and skills needed to be adjusted and polished.

During the next fifteen years, Lamb trained, learned, and advanced incredibly quickly with the many disciplines in the temple. Whenever he had leave from the military, most of the time it was spent in Korea. Lin Po and the other grandmasters were pleased and surprised at how quickly Lamb progressed. Lamb wanted to remain in the temple after his service time was over. However, this day was a special day: Lamb would have to leave forever.

"Master, you wanted to speak to me?" Lamb asked.

"Yes, Lamb. Sit, please," Lin Po said.

"You first, sir," Lamb said.

"I want to first say that we are all very proud of you. You entered that door a boy, and now you have become a man—a real man," Lin Po said.

"Sir, why are my things packed and outside the entrance?" Lamb asked, surprised.

"You will be leaving us today, Lamb," Lin Po said.

"But, sir!" Lamb protested.

Lin Po placed his finger in the air and paused. Lamb bowed his head. "This day is a day of rejoicing, because you are going to become a grandmaster. Do you not know what that means, Lamb?" Lin Po asked. "You are no longer mine or anyone else's student. It is time for you to leave. You have far surpassed us in your skills."

Lamb looked up at Lin Po and had mixed feelings by the news.

"What is wrong, Lamb?" said Lin Po. "I thought you would rejoice at this news."

"Other than my family, no one has given me a break such as you have. I have no real friends, no family," Lamb cried.

"You do have your family. You need to find them, Lamb," Lin Po said.

"I want to come back on leave, sir. I want to continue to train here."

"We can no longer teach you. Just as water is poured into a bucket until it is full, we masters have poured all of our knowledge into you. We know that your time has come. There are five masters. You need to spar with all of us for three minutes each using the style of the master that you fight. It is time for you to focus now, turn your emotions into positive energy, and know the reason—the real reason— why you're leaving this day. It is to honor your masters and this temple. More important it is to stand up for what is right and to protect those who cannot protect themselves. After you have sparred with the last grandmaster, you will need to walk out this door, which leads to the path of your destiny."

Lamb prepared himself. He would miss this place; it had been a home away from home. All of the grandmasters walked into the room. Lamb now focused on his task at hand.

Kwang-su was the first he encountered. "Seijak," Lin Po said, which meant they should begin. Lamb was quick and countered Kwang's moves. Lamb was able to avoid Kwang's kicks and then counter his moves, and he was able to back him against the wall. His time was soon up.

Man-Soo was next. Man tried to snap kick Lamb. Lamb blocked Man's consecutive kicks and swept Man, who fell down. Man-Soo smiled as he executed several roundhouse kicks at Lamb, who was able to block all of them. The three minutes were soon up.

Next was Sang-Jun. Sang was quick with his hands and used a spear hand followed by a backhand, missing Lamb. Lamb used the same moves and knocked down Sang, who was surprised and quickly got up. He then used a series of back kicks and downward hammer strikes at Lamb. However, Lamb is able to block all of them. Their time came to an end.

Tae-Won jumped into a flying kick at Lamb. Lamb stepped out of the way, jumped, and knocked Tae-Won to the ground. Tae Won got up and smiled. He executed a series of butterfly kicks, and Lamb was able to block all of them. The three minutes were over. "I will miss you very much, Lamb," Tae-Won way said.

"Good-bye, sir," Lamb said.

Last but not least, Lin Po jumped in using ninjitsu fighting methods. Lin Po was very quick and executed punches, elbows, and kicks. Lamb was quick as well and countered all of Lin Po's attacks. The three minutes were up, and Lamb was exhausted and fatigued, but he was victorious.

"Good-bye, my son. You have far surpassed our expectations, and we're all very proud of you. Go now, and never forget to protect the weak and defend those who cannot defend themselves. Go now, my son," Lin Po said.

Lamb bowed his head and said softly, "Good-bye, my masters." He then took a look at the temple, turned, and walked through the door that led to his destiny. Lamb saw his luggage near the temple wall. Lin Po's daughter was waiting to take Lamb to the airport.

"Hey, are you in a trance or something?" the driver asked. Lamb's mind was now in the present time, and the cab had arrived at the embassy. He gave the cab driver the money, looked to his left, and saw the American embassy where Lin Po worked. Lamb was greeted at the door by security and was shown where Lin Po's office was located. Nancy Yang. Lin Po's secretary, told Lamb to sit and relax, or he could look around; Lin Po would be here shortly to greet him.

Lamb heard music coming from the back room; He was curious and walked toward the room. As he entered, he noticed candles lit on several tables. He also sensed that someone else was in the room. "Who is here? Is it you, master?" Lamb asked cautiously. Instinctively, Lamb moved to his right as a dark figure appeared and landed where he was standing. The dark figure threw several punches and kicks at Lamb. Lamb countered the punches and kicks as he advanced forward. Lamb then executed a crescent kick and turned into a spinning roundhouse. The dark figure went into the splits, and Lamb executed axe kicks down toward the dark figure. The dark figure rolled out of the way from the kicks, quickly rose to his feet, and threw stars at Lamb. Lamb moved to his right and then left, and he jumped straight up toward the light fixture in order to evade the three stars, which all landed in the wall next to the door. The dark figure took a spear from the wall and aimed it at Lamb. Lamb executed three backflips and grabbed a shield from the wall; the spear hit the shield and bounced off. Lamb heard laughter coming from the dark figure, and the light turned on.

"Master Po, is that you?" Lamb inquired.

"Yes, it is I. We all knew that you would continue in your advancement of your disciplines, and you have proven us correct!" Lin

Po said as he pulled off his mask. Lamb ran toward Lin Po and gave him a strong embrace. Lin Po then gave Lamb a tour of the embassy. Afterward, Lin Po took Lamb back to his office, where they reminisced about the old days and Shaol Lin Temple. All the masters were alive and well and teaching in the temple.

Lamb showed Lin Po pictures of Arianna and Susan. He informed Lin Po of his divorce. "I believe you still have feelings for her," Lin Po said.

"She is already involved with someone else," Lamb stated. "We were together for ten years." Lamb showed more pictures to Lin Po. He also showed the pictures that STARE DOWN took three weeks ago. The pictures revealed the terrorists in the mall. There were also pictures of Lamb in a hospital when he was attacked by the Red Dragon warriors. The pictures revealed, frame by frame, the shadow warriors' transformation from shadows to a human form and back to shadows again.

"What? This cannot be!" Lin Po said.

"What's wrong?" Lamb asked.

"I cannot believe what I'm seeing," Lin Po answered.

"I confronted them in the hospital, sir. They were very difficult to fight and defeat."

"Nonetheless, you did succeed," Lin Po noted with a smile.

"They have dragon tattoos on their arms, and there were seven stars in each of the dragon's claws," Lamb explained.

Lin Po informed Lamb that the shadow warriors were from the Red Dragon clan, the oldest and most evil clan on earth. They were said to be of an urban legend. Lin Po had fought one in his lifetime. Lin Po also informed Lamb that the Red Dragons were extremely deadly because of their invisibility and special powers, which they attained through a pact with the devil. The Red Dragon clan went back almost two thousand years. The Kagem (Darkness) had plottted to over throw the emperor of Japan. However, their plan was discovered by a spy that had worked covertly with them for months. The Kagem tried a surprised attack but was confronted by a large force of the emperor's army. The evil warlord, Yang was the leader of the Kagem. His warriors were being annihilated by the emperor's men. He wanted vengeance, and so he sought out a witch, who granted him powers from the evil one in exchange for him and his family's services for the rest of their lives. By doing so, the Kagem family became shadows. These individuals became very rich and powerful because they were sought out by various individuals throughout time in history. They were murderers for hire. Most of them could not be out during the daytime because light meant death to them. Some had advanced in their powers and were able to withstand the light; these individuals were few, however they were the deadliest.

Master Po stated that he had fought only one of them. The only way that Lamb could ever face up to one of these advanced Red Dragon ninjas was to become a spirit. He could not become like them because he was part of light. "You must separate his spirit from his mind and body. This will mean full concentration and focus on the transformation and separateness of spirit. That is one way you can hope to defeat this type of Red Dragon ninja. The other is to continue just as you have, using light to conquer the dark. I must now train you to fight a Red Dragon warrior." They had a short time because the peace talks began next week.

Lynn Po blindfolded Lamb. Lamb was now trained on how to listen with and without noise surrounding him. Lin Po taught him to listen to the sound of nature and become one with the universe. He told him to concentrate as Lamb sat still. That which was body became lighter and lighter, yet Lamb was still a solid object with a powerful force. "You cannot see the wind however, once it hits an object, the force can be devastating." Lamb opened his eyes and saw that his spirit had separated from his body. Lin Po now concentrated and separated his spirit from his own mind and body. He began to spar with Lamb. They started with the basic martial arts defensive tactics and then moved on to more sophisticated moves. Lamb caught on very quickly. They stopped and discussed the techniques that they had used, and also how Lamb would have to use them when fighting the Red Dragon. Whenever he was not in his spirit form, he must use light as an offensive and defensive weapon against the Red Dragon clan because that was their weakness, as he had seen before.

The rest of the day involved Lamb performing different techniques and styles of fighting. Lamb would also train some of his unit on fighting the Red Dragon ninjas. Lamb was a grandmaster, and now that he knew the technique of spirit separating the body, he could teach his team members how to use light against the Red Dragon ninjas in order to defend themselves. "Remember, Lamb, these skills can only belong to those spirits strong in faith and with a spiritual level on a higher plane such as your own!" Lin Po explained. Lamb nodded in agreement.

The next day, Lamb and Lin Po went to the airport to greet Governor Barry Barton and the Hades team. As the plane came to a stop, the door opened. Agent Lee stepped out, cautiously looking around for any sign of trouble. Lamb informed her that everything was clear. Agents Ajay and Ajeeta exited the plane with Barry Barton between them. Doc Robinson was seconds behind them. Lamb and Lin Po greeted the governor.

"Hello, sir. I'm agent Nathan Lamb. This is Lin Po, assistant ambassador for Korea. Your room is ready at the hotel near the embassy," Lamb said.

"Thank you, gentlemen. I think I'll rest for an hour and go over my notes before I see the ambassador," the Governor stated.

"All right, sir. You will always have us near you," Lamb said. They got into the SUVs that were at the airport and drove toward the hotel. Once at the hotel, everyone exited the vehicles and went inside. After the governor opened his hotel room door, the agents went through the room, making a thorough check. Lamb and Lin Po had already done so, but Lamb wanted to make sure.

Lamb gave orders to his team and explained the situation with the Red Dragon. "I don't have time to fully explain, however I can try to train and convey to you some information to take you to another level." Lamb gives each team member three strobe light boxes to be used sparingly if there were any encounters with the Red Dragon warriors.

Doc and Jenny Lee were somewhat skeptical. "You mean these things really are shadows that can harm us?" Jenny asked humorously.

Lamb revealed his bandaged arm. "Do you think this is a joke, Agent Lee?" he said sternly.

Agents Robinson and Lee were in shock. Lamb instructed AJ to take position on the roof of the embassy building across the street.

Agent Robinson would take position in the right hallway, and agent Lee would take the left hallway. Ajeeta would be positioned on the hotel roof. Lamb would watch the door, and Lin Po would be in the lobby area. Each agent, including Lin Po, was wired, having constant contact with each other. Each agent called a radio check on the half hour.

Lin Po walked pensively in the lobby. He then feels a sudden chill over his body, as though ice had gone through him. "Lamb."

"Yes, go ahead, sir," Lamb said.

"Is the governor all right? Please check right away."

Lamb knocked on the door and called out to the governor, who did not answer. Lamb was about to open the door when the door suddenly opened. "Agent Lamb," Barton said.

"Yes, sir?" Lamb replied.

"I almost forgot to tell you that I ordered room service at the front desk. They should be on their way up soon," Barton stated.

Lamb informed his team members to watch a for bellboy delivering room service. "I have the bellboy in sight now, sir," Robinson said.

"Bring him down this way, Robinson," Lamb ordered.

"Roger." The bellboy got out of the elevator and headed toward Robinson. All of a sudden, the lights went out. "Sir!" Robinson said frantically.

"Okay, team, go infrared," commanded Lamb sternly. Lin Po found the manager, who turned on the emergency lights in the hallway. The food table had been knocked over, and there was no sign of the bellboy.

"I no longer have the bellboy in my sight, sir," Robinson stated.

"Everyone, look sharp and stay focused," Lamb said.

"Help me! Don't let them get me!" cried the governor.

"Governor Barton?" Lamb yelled. The door was locked. Robinson ran down the hallway along with Lamb. When they reached the room, they kicked open the door. The room was dark. Lamb motioned Agents Lee and Robinson to shut their eyes. Lamb saw a Red Dragon warrior in human form approaching the governor with a knife in his right hand.

"Help! He's trying to kill me!" cried the governor.

"There will be no mercy for you, Barton!" the ninja said. Lamb wasted no time in throwing a strobe flash bomb at the feet of the ninja.

A cloud of smoke burst out, and then a bright light appeared through the smoke, spinning and flashing. It was very intense and blinding.

"I cannot see!" cried the ninja.

"That's the whole idea!" Lamb said as he executed two roundhouse kicks to the sides of the ninja's face. The lights were turned on by Agent Lee. Agent Robinson pulled the mask off the ninja. "A woman! How many more of you are there?" Lamb inquired.

Agents Lee and Robinson tied her hands and feet together. They asked questions, however she remained silent. There was only a mad glare in her eyes as she stared coldly into their faces.

"Tell us where and when you plan to strike again!" Lee demanded.

"You'll never know, you fools. You will all die soon. No one in this room will leave this place alive!" she cried. She bit down hard on an object in her mouth; it was a cyanide capsule.

"No, damn it! No!" Lamb cried. The ninja began to seizure as foam and blood poured out of her mouth. Doc Robinson tried to assist, but it was too late as her body convulsed and then stopped. Her head dropped to the right as she let out a whisper of air. Agent Robinson checked for a pulse but found none.

The governor was in his robe and was very angry. "Why didn't you people get here sooner? I could have been killed by that idiot!" he cried.

"Sir, we were right outside the door. Why was it locked?" Lamb inquired. "I didn't lock the door. I was in the bathroom the whole time."

Lin Po stood in the doorway. "I thought that I felt the presence of the Red Dragon in this hotel," he said.

"Sniper Two to Team Leader. Sniper Two to Team Leader, come in!" Ajay said.

"This is Team Leader. Go ahead, Sniper Two," Lamb replied.

"I see something on the roof, sir. However, I don't know what to make of it. It looks like a shadow running on the hotel roof," Ajay said excitedly.

"Sniper Two, this is Sniper One. I don't have a fix on it," Ajeeta said.

"We're on our way up now. Keep your eyes focused on it, Sniper Two, and keep us informed. Agent Lee, you are with me. Doc, watch the governor's door. Lin Po, stay inside the room with the governor," Lamb ordered as they ran toward the stairs leading to the roof. Once Lamb and Lee arrived on the roof, they observed a shadowy figure, which threw shiny objects at them. The objects barely missed Lamb and Lee. Lamb and Lee continued to pursue. The ninja was now running toward the north corner of the building.

"We've got him now, sir," Lee said confidently.

"This is Sniper One. I have subject in my sights," Ajeeta said.

"This is Sniper Two. Also have subject in sights," Ajay added.

"He's reaching for more stars," Lamb noted. Ajay and Ajeeta aimed with precision at the ninja's stars, and fired. The rounds connect with the ninja's hands. The ninja bent over in pain because both of his hands were bleeding from gunshot wounds. The ninja then turned around quickly only to lose his balance and fall off the roof, hitting the pavement.

"Sniper One to Team Leader: suspect is down," Ajeeta said.

"Let's go, Lee," Lamb ordered. The two agents raced down the stairwell, through the lobby, and out to the street, where they saw the shadowy figure suddenly change. The body became fully visible. The suspect was wearing a red ninja outfit just like the one the female had. Lamb rolled up the ninja's right sleeve and observed a tattoo of a Red Dragon holding five stars between its claws. The stars began to move outside of the dragon's claws and form a circle. The circle turned three times before it came to a halt, and the ninja expired.

Once Lamb and Lee arrived at the hotel, Lamb spoke to Lin Po and the governor. They went over a tactical plan for what they were going to do over the next week. The team would take extra precautions in protecting the governor and themselves. Lin Po informed the team that the Red Dragon clan was not to be taken lightly. Governor Barton had been very skeptical in the beginning, however this incident made him a full believer. The team would switch positions guarding the governor's door, with the exception of Ajay and Ajeeta, who had orders of watching the streets and rooftops. Both snipers remained on the hotel and embassy roofs.

The governor had his conference outline to look over the night before the conference began. He also needed to call home to speak to his family. Lin Po remained in the room next to the governor. The door inside the room remained open so that Lin Po could constantly check on him. Lamb and Robinson guarded the governor's door while Lee watched the front lobby area. The lights were left on in the governor's room, in the hallways, and throughout the hotel for the duration of the governor's visit.

The governor felt relieved and safe for now. He took off his shoes and loosened his tie. He took out his wallet from the back pocket of his pants and looked at the photos of him and his family. As he reflected on his career and family, he received a call on his cell. It was Betty, his wife. "Well, Barry, did you forget you have a wife and kids?" Betty joked.

"Oh, no, darling, not at all. As a matter of fact, I was just looking at the photos in my wallet of all of us together," Barry said with a sad tone.

"What's wrong, honey? Is everything all right?" Betty inquired. "Yes, sweetheart, everything's fine. It's those peace talks that have me worried. I just hope that what I have to bring to the table will do!"

"I'm sure that you will make us proud, as always."

"I can always rely on you to lift me up, dear," the governor said. "Where are the children?"

"They are all getting ready for school. Luke is going to his graduation rehearsals later today. Jasmine is getting ready for her senior prom this weekend; she wants me to go shopping with her and her girlfriends for dresses. The twins, Brianna and Suzanna, are missing their daddy every night when I tuck them in bed."

"Please tell the kids that I love them and will see them soon. I owe you all a big hug."

"Don't forget that you also owe them your time!" Betty exclaimed.

"Yes, dear. How could I forget that!" the governor said.

"Well, I won't hold you up any longer. I know that you are very busy getting your outline ready for the conference tomorrow. I'll just say good night. I love you!" Betty said.

"I love you too, Betty. Good night!" the governor said with a smile.

The next day the team was ready to escort the governor from his room to the embassy across the street, where he would be with the other dignitaries discussing peace talks with North Korea, China, and six other representatives. The embassy had its own security consisting of thirty guards. CPAT's perimeter of responsibility was inside the conference room. Ajay and Ajeeta were stationed in the balcony. Jenny Lee and Doc Robinson stood in front of the stage area. Lamb and Lin Po were backstage with the governor. Lamb, Lin Po, and the other agents were constantly looking for shadows in the conference room and anything out of the ordinary.

Governor Barton made his way toward the podium, looking around the room nervously. He cleared his throat and then began his speech. His audience listened attentively as he discussed the disarming of all nuclear bombs. Everyone was very impressed by the governor's ideas of peace, and they gave him a standing ovation at the end of his speech. The governor was informed that China and Korea were very impressed and would like to discuss his proposals later.

The conference ended without incident. The governor was then escorted back to his room at the hotel form across the street. Everyone was relieved for the time being. It was Agent Robinson's turn to sleep. Lamb and Lee stood together in front of the governor's door. Lin Po was inside the room with the governor. Both agents were very tired but fully alert. Agent Lee turned to Lamb and asked him why he had accepted this job.

Lamb paused and said, "I would like to be part of the solution to prevent and end terrorism."

"Why did you choose me to be a part of your unit, sir?" Lee asked as she lowers her head.

"Just as I stated earlier, you all have very special abilities. We are an elite team of special units from the United States Armed Forces. This means that we all came from some type of adversity to get where we are today. I chose you because of that. I knew that all of the harassment you went through to get your rank of sergeant in the Green Berets would be of great assistance to the team. When I read your background, I knew that you would make a great candidate, but most important you'd be a great agent."

"Thank you, sir. No one has ever given me the kind of recognition and respect as you have. I'm proud to serve in this capacity under you,"

Lee said with tears in her eyes. She quickly wiped them away from her cheeks. "Sorry, sir!"

"It's all right, Agent," Lamb assured her. Lamb was pleased to have her and the rest of the agents in his unit. Lamb glanced at his watch and noticed that it was time for roll call. "CPAT team, 1016 (Roll call and location)."

"Sniper One, 1016, embassy roof. Clear, sir," Ajeeta said.

"Sniper Two, 1016, hotel roof. Clear, sir," Ajay answered.

"Robinson here, 1016 adjoining room to the governor. Clear, sir."

"How's it going in the lobby area, sir?" Lamb asked Lin Po.

"Still waters are flowing calmly," Po replied.

"Ten-four, team. Over and out!" Lamb said. Before the night ended, Lin Po and Robinson relieved Lamb and Lee from their posts. The night passed quickly.

The next evening, many dignitaries would join the conference and contribute to the peace talks. Ajay and Ajeeta took their positions on the balconies. Doc and Lee had the front stage area, and Lamb and Lee were backstage.

Just then, the lights in the conference went out, and the emergency lights did not go on. The audience became frantic. The host immediately moved to the podium and took charge of the microphone. "Gentlemen, please walk calmly toward the exits." Agents Lee and Robinson escorted the governor to an area designated as a safe room.

"Everyone, go infrared now!" Lamb ordered.

Three figures moved silently throughout the hallway as though they were serpents. They moved in unison. The embassy security did not notice them as one slipped under the door of the entrance to the conference room. The other two rose from the floor and formed into humans. They each pulled out knives from the inside of their belts and started to stab two of the embassy security officers multiple times until they were dead. They placed the bodies inside a storage room that was to the right of the conference room.

The dignitaries were in a panic, running toward the doors. Many collided into each other and fell down. As Robinson and Lee protected the governor in the safe room, Lamb followed a shadowy figure down the corridor leading to the safe room. Lamb threw a strobe grenade at the figure. The shadow quickly increased its pace and moved underneath the door to gain access. Lamb could not gain access until the code was given for it to be unlocked. Lamb radioed the team, "Robinson and Lee, is everything okay?"

"Everything is good here, sir!" What's going on out there?" Lee asked.

"The Red Dragon ninjas are in the building. Do not let the governor out of your sight, not even for a moment. I saw a shadow enter underneath the door."

"Our lights are on, sir!" Robinson said.

Lamb ran back toward the conference room. "Snipers, keep on the alert. The Red Dragon is present here inside the building, so look sharp. I'm making my way toward you!"

"Sniper One to Team Leader, I may have one in my sights!" Ajeeta said. The ninja looked at Ajeeta and then disappeared.

"Sniper One, what's going on?" Lamb asked.

"I thought I just saw one of them in my sights, sir!" Ajeeta said.

"Sniper Two to Team Leader. I could have sworn that I also saw one!" Ajay exclaimed.

The doors were locked to the corridor, and all exits were completely locked. "Let's get them open now!" Lamb ordered.

"I'll take the east set of doors," Ajeeta said.

"Roger that. I'll take the west set of doors," Ajay replied.

Ajeeta got her G3 rifle in place and aimed at the center locks. She squeezed the trigger and split the doors open. Ajay did the same with the west doors. Lamb made his way around to the outside of the east doors, where he found a door open to the storage area. Lamb opened the door and found two embassy security guards dead from stab wounds to the heart and lungs. "Team, we have two of the embassy security guards dead inside of the storage area, just outside the east doors. Keep focused!" Lamb informed all of the dignitaries to stay down on the floor. Twenty-four dignitaries lay on the floor, frightened. One of the dignitaries tried to get up and make a run toward the exit doors. He was hit by a flying star in the back of the neck. He slowly turned around and got another one lodged in his back. He fell onto a chair, gasping and coughing, and then he slumped to the floor dead.

"Snipers One and Two, cover me as I head for the fuse boxes on the north end," Lamb said.

"Roger, Team Leader," they said.

Lamb ran to the north end. As he was running, he saw stars barely missing him and impacting the wall near his head. Lamb made his way to the fuse box. He wondered why the emergency lights hadn't gone on by now.

Lin Po was giving tea to the governor when he thought he had heard movement on the floor near the door. Lin began to write something on a piece of paper as he motioned for everyone not to make a sound. "I believe that there is a Red Dragon ninja near the door. He cannot completely form into a human because of being exposed to light!" whispered Lin Po. Robinson walked toward the door and suddenly tripped over something that was on the floor. Lee saw an outline of a human being. The figure was trying desperately to move. Lin Po told the agents to move away from the area. Lin Po took a blanket that was on the sofa and draped it over the figure. Robinson and Lee were surprised as the blanket draped over a full body. The body then moved underneath the blanket. "Darkness gives them power," Lin Po said.

"Damn, I had to see it to believe it!" Robinson said astonished.

The ninja tried to get up. "I think not," Lin Po said as he gave the ninja a front kick, knocking him into the wall. The ninja fell down, unconscious. "I must go and join your supervisor in confronting the rest. Tie him up, and don't let him bite down on his teeth. Ninjas have plenty of areas where they can hide cyanide capsules!" Lin Po explained.

As Lamb reached the fuse box, there was a hand that formed underneath a table behind him. A star flew past Lamb and hit the Red Dragon ninja in his right shoulder as he formed fully into a human. The ninja ran toward Lin Po and executed front kicks. Lin Po reacted by blocking the fast and furious kicks. Lamb then executed a leg sweep from behind the ninja and knocked him off his feet. The ninja pushed off the floor with his hands, kicking his legs straight out and landing on his feet in a defensive stance. The ninja noticed that the lights were beginning to turn back on, and he reached in his waistband and pulled out a round object.

"Be careful, Lamb," Lin Po warned.

The ninja threw it onto the floor, and a cloud of smoke formed. Lin Po immediately threw ninja stars into the cloud of smoke. The ninja took off running toward the exit door; a trail of blood led into the stairwell. The ninja placed his right hand on his right leg and limped away in agony. The trail of blood led Lin Po and Lamb into the boiler room. The ninja was nowhere to be seen, and so Lamb threw a strobe bomb inside the room. The flashing light exposed boxes piled upon boxes. There was no sign of the ninja. Lin Po and Lamb discussed what might have happened. He could have slipped through the window near the ceiling, using a stack of boxes near it. The ninja had escaped.

Lamb and Lin Po discontinued their search when power was restored to the entire embassy. Lamb and Lin Po returned to the governor's room. The other ninja had also escaped. The governor was very grateful to be alive and let Lamb know that there would be commendation letters to the director on behalf of the team. The team continued the task of protecting the governor throughout the night. Ajay and Ajeeta were on high alert with their sniper rifles, ready for any danger.

At a CIA desk on an unsecure line was an individual sitting in a chair chatting to a menacing character. "Bad news. That's all you offer, Wolf! These ninjas are supposed to be indestructible, deadly, and flawless at their job. Mistakes are not what I'm paying you for!"

"Yes, sir. I realize that. I did not know that we would come across interference with grandmaster Lin Po!" Wolf said, upset.

"You know what Americans say about excuses, Wolf?"

"Yes, sir, I do. Lin Po also knows the art of ninjitsu very well. I did not know that Agent Lamb is also a student of Lin Po. He is very well versed in the art of ninjitsu, as well as other disciplines of martial arts. Lin Po also knows the art of the Red Dragon's fighting style!" Wolf added nervously.

"This Lin Po—what is he doing there?"

"He is the assistant to the ambassador in Korea. He stays in the embassy. His student, Lamb, has been taught about fighting the Red Dragon ninjas."

"Let my people lead the assault at the airport. Give your ninjas a rest. Understood, Wolf?" the mysterious voice said.

"Understood, sir!" Wolf replied. "I will speak to you again when the governor and his family are dead."

The conversation ended abruptly as the mysterious man hung up. The man turned to several individuals in a dark room. "They have failed so far. It is time to bring in our own people. You are all in charge of your soldiers. As for those you choose to attack, tell them no kill, no return home. I want results, not excuses!" His fists hit the table hard, causing a loud noise. The men quickly dispersed out of the room.

Lamb and his team had a debriefing in the governor's room. Those who were doubtful were now believers because of what they had encountered. Lamb informed the team that Lin Po would assist him in learning how to fight and defend against the Red Dragon. The team was excited about the opportunity. The embassy's security was reinforced for the remainder of the conference.

Lamb contacted Price and briefed him on the incidents that had occurred at the conference. "I almost didn't believe it, sir, until I witnessed it for myself at the hospital," Lamb said.

"Sounds like you and your team went through quite an ordeal, but you handled yourselves well. I knew you were right for the job, Lamb. Agent Martinez has her hands full protecting the governor's family. The Omega team has had two incidents of terrorist attacks against the family." Price said.

"My God! Anyone hurt, sir? Lamb asked.

"There was an incident—a death involving both of Todd's friends and Jasmine's boyfriend," Price said. Lamb lowered his head as Price told him the news. "The family has been shaken up. Betty has just spoken to the governor as to the details of the incidents. I will also keep you informed. Meanwhile, you and your team need to focus on protecting the governor for the rest of his visit."

"Yes, sir," Lamb replied.

Price hung up the phone, stared at the bottle of vodka, poured it into the sink, and placed it into a waste basket.

Lamb informed the team of the incidents. There was no more sign of the Red Dragon that night; the threat from them seemed to be over for now.

Betty informed the governor of the incidents with the family that occurred over the past three days. The governor is very anxious to get home and see his family. He was relieved to know that CPAT Omega did a good job in protecting them.

The team was ready to leave the hotel and escort the governor and his two assistants to the airport. Ajeeta and Ajay remained at their posts until the escorts left the building. The sniper team would then be picked up by a helicopter and rendezvous with the rest of Hades team at the airport. Lamb was very pensive as the team left with the governor and his two assistants in an SUV. Lin Po would not be traveling back with them; he still had business to conduct and reports to write from the incidents that occurred in the embassy. Lamb was concerned about more attacks before they left.

They reached the airport within thirty minutes. The agents exited first, looking cautiously in every direction. The governor and his aides walk inside the diamond formation of the agents. Lamb was leading, Robinson had the rear, Lee and Ajay covered the left flank, and Ajeeta and Lin Po covered the right flank. As the escort reached the escalator, Lamb noticed a glare as they passed a window, and then sunlight temporarily blinded them. Once Lamb's eyes came into focus, he noticed a rifle barrel aimed at the team. "Everybody down—now!" he shouted.

The agents shifted the formation to the left, where there was cover behind the counters. Shots went off, and the governor was hit in the shoulder. One of his aides was hit in the chest. Doc quickly ran to administer first aid to the governor. "I'll be all right; it's just a flesh wound. Take care of Vernon," cried the governor.

The agents exchanged fire with the assassin, who shot from the third-floor concourse. People ran everywhere in a panic as the shooting continued. The team was now flanked by four more assassins who joined in on the shooting; the four were posing as airport porters. They dropped the luggage they were carrying and shot at the agents behind the counter. Two of the assassins were near the agents' left flank, and the other two were at their right flank.

The agents used boxes and luggage for cover. Lamb directed Ajay and Ajeeta to take out the sniper on the third-level concourse. The agents covered them as they took careful aim at the assassin. Ajay shot first, hitting the assassin twice in the chest and shoulder. Ajay hit him twice in the chest. The assassin fell forward and flipped over the railing, falling down to the bottom floor. Lamb and Lee hit two more assassins in the chest. Lin Po saw the last two assassins flanking to the left of them. He pulled out two ninja stars and threw them at the assassins, hitting one in the throat and the other in the head. They both fell to the floor.

Airport police arrived and secured the area as the agents searched the dead assassins' bodies. The team and the governor were delayed for another two hours after questioning and giving their reports to the airport police. CPAT then escorted the governor to a private plane. When they entered the plane, Governor Barry Barton was there; his double was the one who had gotten shot instead. He and the governor wore bulletproof vests at all times. The governor had a different route to the plane and was escorted underground by airport security. The governor was grateful for Lamb's plan. He couldn't wait to be home again to see and hold his family again.

Chapter 5

Protect the Governor's Family

CPAT arrived at the governor's mansion. Agent Terri Martinez briefed the team on who they would be escorting for the next two weeks. Secret service agents had the task of maintaining the safety of the perimeter of the property. Agent Skypack was assigned to protect Betty and the twins. Agents Martinez and Wombush were assigned to protect Jasmine. Agents Leblanc and Anders had the task of escorting Todd and his friends, who were heading out for a night out on the town. Todd had just passed his bar exam and wanted to unwind from all the studying. He asked his father if it was all right to take his friends out with him to relax at the clubs downtown. Both his parents agreed, as long as they followed protocol and listened to whatever the agents had to say. Anders did not like the role of babysitter. Leblanc was patient and soft spoken, yet he was cautious and possessed a heightened sense of awareness.

Todd's friends, Eric and Jay, arrived. Todd greeted them and introduced them to the agents. They entered Eric's vehicle and drove to the club downtown, with Anders and Leblanc following closely behind. They soon reached the Night Owl, a club that was located in the center of town. They parked near the front of the building. Anders and Leblanc quickly exited the SUV and flanked Todd as he got out of the vehicle. As they entered the club, there were three young Asian women observing them while sitting at a table. Todd and his friends noticed them and sat at a table across from them. Eric nodded at Todd and Jay, and they nodded back with approval. The waitress arrived, and the three young men ordered a round of beers. The young ladies continued to stare at them and talk among themselves. One in particular was interested in Todd. Todd decided to order the women drinks, Todd and his friends left their table and asked the ladies if they would like to dance. The girls quickly accepted the invitation. Anders and Leblanc kept an watchful eye on them.

The young lady whom Todd was dancing with was a young, beautiful Asian girl from Japan. She told him that her name was Aimi. She had on a dazzling black dress and black pumps. "What is your name, American boy?" Aimi asked.

"I'm Todd. My two friends dancing with your friends over there are Eric and Jay," Todd answered.

"You are all so nice. So very nice!" Aimi said as she pulled Todd closer to her and pressed her body against his. "My friend's names are Hana and Izumi. We are all from Tokyo." Aimi smiled.

"Pleased to meet you," Todd said. Todd looked over at his friends and noticed that they were also enjoying themselves. The music came to an end. Todd and his friends escorted the young ladies back to their seats, and Todd and his friends headed back to their table. "Hey, guys, let's ask them if they don't mind if we sit with them and get to know them," Todd suggested. Eric and Jay nodded and spoke to the young ladies. The ladies were delighted to have company.

Todd and his friends talked about their background and what they were planning to do after college. Eric stood up and said," We are here tonight to celebrate my best friend's graduation from law school. I would like to make a toast to Todd Barton. He will be the best lawyer that the state of California and the nation has ever seen!" Everyone raised their glasses to Todd. Aimi placed her hand on Todd's. He smiled and felt very relaxed.

The agents saw the evening was going to be a long one. "I wonder how long that's going to last between them," Anders observed.

"You never know. They do make a good couple," Leblanc replied.

Three young Asian males entered the club and gave hateful glares at Todd and his friends. "Look at them," Jun said.

"They think they are bad. *We* are bad," Dai agreed.

"Calm down, guys. Let's just wait and see what happens," Akio said.

"But that's your woman that he's with! Don't you even care?" Jun shouted.

Akio did not answer; instead, he continued to glare.

"Heads-up, mate! Those two chaps over there don't look too happy," Anders said.

"Looks like somebody just pissed in their pool!" Leblanc agreed.

The three couples walked out to the dance floor and begin dancing again.

Akio was now growing impatient. He got up and walked over to Todd and Aimi. Aimi had a look of surprise when she saw Akio. "Akio, what are you doing here?" she said.

"Never mind that, Aimi. What are *you* doing here—and with him? You know that you should stay with your own kind," Akio said.

Aimi continued to dance with Todd and tried to ignore Akio and his remarks. Todd asked about Akio and what he wanted. Akio suddenly pulled out a switch blade and told Todd to leave.

Just then, Akio felt cold steel against the back of his head. "You really don't want to do that, do you?" Anders asked bluntly.

The club's bouncers also interceded. "What seems to be the problem, gentlemen?" the head bouncer asked. Anders and Leblanc showed the bouncers their ID badges and explained the situation. The bouncers asked Akio and his friends to leave the club quietly.

"It's not over. It's far from being over!" Akio shouted as he was escorted off the premises.

Todd's friends asked him if he was all right. Todd nodded. Anders and Leblanc sat back down at their table. Todd was shocked and inquired about Akio. "He's just an old boyfriend who is angry because I broke up with him over six months ago. He needs to know that I'm never going to be with him," Aimi explained.

"He looked really mad. Does he belong to a gang?" Todd asked.

"He belongs to the Yakuza," Aimi replied.

"Are you sure you're over him?" Todd said.

"Does this answer your question?" Aimi pulled Todd closer and pressed her lips against his. Todd closed his eyes, and after sometime he opened them to see that his friends were also making out with Aimi's friends on the dance floor.

"Unit One to Unit Two. Come in, over."

"This is Anders. Go ahead, Unit One."

"Is everything okay there, agents?"

"We're doing fine, ma'am. We just had a small run-in with a lady's ex-boyfriend. Todd was dancing with her. It seems that the ex- didn't like Todd very much. It was nothing that we couldn't handle," Anders said.

"Is Todd all right?" Martinez asked.

"Not a scratch on him," Leblanc replied. "How are you and Agent Wombush doing, ma'am?"

"Fine, we're just waiting for Jasmine's date for the prom to arrive. Everything is quiet here so far. I will keep you posted. Unit One, over and out."

The nightclub continued to fill up with more patrons as the evening went on. Todd and his friends seemed to be getting along well with these young ladies. "Hey, guys. We're going to go to the hotel that is two blocks over," Todd said to the agents.

"We'll drive you there. You lads have had a lot to drink," Anders stated. The agents had the young men go with them in their SUV, and the ladies followed them to the hotel. Once they arrived, each couple checked into a room. They arranged for the rooms to be near each other.

Aimi informed Todd that she left her purse in her vehicle and would be right back. Todd wanted to escort her outside, but Aimi told Todd that he was being overly protective. Besides, her vehicle was only a few feet away from the hotel. Aimi ran quickly to her vehicle.

"Is everything all right, lass?" Anders asked.

"You startled me! Everything's fine. I'm just going out to my vehicle to get my purse," Aimi said.

"Would you mind me accompanying you?" Anders asked.

Aimi did not answer but quickly ran to her vehicle. She was joined by Hana and Izumi.

"What we do now?" Hana asked.

"We do what we were told to do," Izumi said.

"You are correct, Izumi," Aimi agreed. "We must carry out our orders no matter what. Get rid of your emotions for these young men—they are the enemy and are to be eliminated. Our master says so and has given orders to carry out."

Just then, Akio and his friends arrived. The young ladies quickly ran inside the hotel. "They will ruin everything!" Aimi noted.

"Aimi, please. Let me speak with you, babe. I still love you!" Akio cried.

Aimi turned around and gave Akio and his friends a glare of contempt. The young ladies walked faster. "It is time to eliminate them now, my sisters," Aimi said. The three young ladies ran down the hotel hallway and broke into three different directions. Hana went down the left hallway, Izumi ran to the right, and Aimi continued straight.

"Go after the girls now. Don't let them get away!" Akio shouted to Jun and Dai. Akio quickly ran after Aimi. All of a sudden, the lights in the hotel flickered.

"What's going on?" Leblanc said. "Get ready, mate. I believe some serious shit is about to happen here," Anders replied as both agents pulled out their M-9s. The lights then went completely out throughout the hotel.

"Babe! Aimi, come back! I'll make everything up to you, I promise! I'll even leave the Yakuza, if that's what you want me to do," Akio yelled. He reached out and touched Aimi. "Oh, here you are babe." He could smell the sweet perfume she always wore when they were together. "I just wanted to say that I'm a changed man. I want you back. I want you as my woman."

"Really, Akio? What about all those pictures you have of those naked women that I found? What about all those love letters and e-mails I found in your room and on your computer? And those messages from those sluts I found on your phone? How the hell am I supposed to trust you, Akio?" Aimi asked.

"Oh, baby, that's over! I promise you it's all over—history. Come back to me, and leave that stupid American," Akio pleaded.

"You were right about one thing, Akio," Aimi replied.

"And what's that babe?"

"It is over—and so are you!" Aimi said. She quickly moved behind Akio and placed a choke hold on him.

"Babe! What are you doing? Hey, I can't breathe. Aimi!"

Akio continued to struggle as Ami's grip tightened on his neck and throat. She continued to tighten her grip until Akio's body went limp and his last breath went out. "Good-bye, lover," Aimi said. She then let Akio's lifeless body fall to the floor. There were two more sounds of outcries that echoed throughout the hallways of the hotel.

"We'd better get back to the young lads' rooms," Anders said. The two agents ran quickly down the hallway to check on Todd and his friends. Todd answered his door. "Are you all right Todd?"

"I'm fine. What's going on?"

"We both heard screaming in this area. Did the girls arrive back with you?" Anders asked.

"I'm here!" Aimi replied as she walked out of the bathroom in Todd's T-shirt.

"How did you get back here without me hearing you come in?" Todd asked.

"You were really out of it, babe. You were passed out on the bed when I arrived," Aimi said.

Hana and Izumi were also with Todd's friends in their rooms. The lights turned on, and security arrived with the on-call maintenance man. "Someone had cut the power cable. I had to turn on the auxiliary power," he said.

The hotel security found Dai's and Jun's bodies on the west and east wings of the hotel, respectively. Both of their necks were broken. Akio's body was found by a receptionist in the janitor's closet a few moments later. The agents viewed the bodies and informed Todd and his friends of what occurred, suggesting they get ready to leave because they felt the hotel was unsafe. Leblanc informed Martinez of the situation, and she commended both agents on a job well done.

Aimi was frustrated that her plans were interfered with. She begged Todd to stay. "I have to listen to the agents because of protocol. Our lives depend on it," Todd explained. Aimi and her friends wanted more time with them. They begin to say their good-byes and exchange numbers.

"It was nice meeting you, Hana. I would like to see you again soon," Eric said as he drank some water she poured for him.

"I don't think that will ever happen!" Hana retorted.

Eric looks at her surprised and felt nauseated. He began to sweat profusely. Eric felt agonizing pain in his stomach, and his mouth foamed. He reached for Hana but fell to the floor on his back. His head turned to the right as he expired with his eyes open wide.

Izumi and Jay were in the room next to Todd and Aimi. Jay was about to walk out the door when Izumi pulled him back and kissed him. "What was that for, babe?" Jay asked.

"I'm saying my last good-bye to you, baby," Izumi said as she stabbed him in the chest and stomach with a butterfly knife. Jay looked at her in surprise as he placed his hands on his bloodied shirt. He lunged toward Izumi and fell to the floor face.

"I thought I heard a noise! You?" Anders asked.

"I heard it too. It sounded like it came from Jay's room," Leblanc replied. Leblanc and Anders knocked hard on Jay's door. "Jay!" they shouted, but there was no answer. They opened the door and hurried inside the room. They saw Jay lying in a pool of blood, face down. There was no sign of Izumi. Anders and Leblanc pulled out their M-9s and searched the room. Anders checked to see if Jay was still breathing, but he was already gone. Leblanc quickly ran to Todd's room and tried to turn the doorknob; it was locked. Leblanc then moved back to kick open the door.

Just then Todd opened the door. "What's going on?" he asked.

"I was trying to open your door. I also tried knocking, and there was no answer. I was about to kick it in. Jay and Eric have been murdered, and Hana and Izumi are missing." Anders said. "Where is Aimi, Todd?"

"I ... I don't know. I was standing near the door when she told me that she had something very important to say to me. Then I turned around to speak to her. That's when I heard you agents coming in."

"It seems we arrived just in time," Anders said.

"But where did she and the rest of the girls go?" Todd asked. Leblanc radioed the headquarters and the local police for backup. Todd began to cry as he walked to each room to observe the bodies of his friends. Anders and Leblanc took Todd out of the hotel, and after giving their reports to the LAPD detectives, they headed toward the governor's mansion. Leblanc informed Agent Martinez of what had occurred.

Martinez and Wombush were escorting Jasmine and her prom date to the prom. The agents informed Martinez that Todd was unharmed and that they were en route to the mansion, where the family doctor would examine Todd as a precaution.

Three blocks away, two shadowy figures moved down the street and finally turned into an alley. They materialized into human form. "Hana, where is Aimi?"

"I don't know, Izumi. I thought she was right behind us."

"I thought I heard a door kicked open by one of the agents trying to get into the room that Aimi was in," Hana said.

"I think you're right! That means a light must have gone on inside the room at some point. We should go back there to see if Aimi is all right."

"No, Izumi! Remember what the Wolf said? We may blow our cover trying that. We cannot risk that even though we have failed this part of the mission," Hana said. The two women walked toward a van they saw at the end of the alley. They both recognized it: the van belonged to the Wolf. The Wolf was their main contact and the one in charge of operations.

"Ladies, where are you going? Why could you not stop the agents and do away with the governor's son?" Wolf demanded to know.

"They had help," Hana answered nervously.

"They had help from those CIA agents," Izumi added.

"Those agents should not have been a problem at all. You could have exterminated them with ease. You both have failed! Abdullah has ordered your termination."

"No! You cannot do that. The clan will avenge us!" Izumi said.

"You bitches will pay!" Wolf yelled. He opened the doors to the van as the young ladies turned into shadows and tried to escape. Wolf turned on a large spotlight that lit up the entire alley. The ladies were immediately immobilized. Wolf pulled out a .45 and shot both ladies in the head. They fell lifelessly onto the pavement. "Incompetence is unacceptable!" Wolf said as he walked over the two corpses and disappeared into the darkness of the alley.

The detectives dusted for prints at the hotel, and the coroner examined Eric's and Jay's bodies. No one noticed a transparent figure trying to make its way to the door, crawling painfully. Aimi was in severe pain. The light felt as if needles were going through every nerve and fiber of her body. Aimi made her way around all the law enforcement officers, and she finally reached the exit.

I ... I've got to tell Todd the truth, she thought. As she moved into the dark, she transformed into a human body. Aimi continued on even though she was in pain and was weak. Aimi pulled out the directions to Todd's house. She got up and walked, limping, as she looked at the directions to the governor's mansion.

Once Aimi was ten feet in front of the door, Wolf stepped in front of her. "Now where do you think you are going?" he said.

"To finish my duty and kill him," Aimi said nervously.

"Where are the weapons you were given? And why are you so nervous, ninja?" Wolf asked angrily.

"Please, Wolf, give me another chance. I know I let my emotions get the best of me. I will not disappoint you this time," she cried.

"It's not in the contract, and you will have to be disciplined for your incompetence," he said sternly.

"No, you cannot harm me. I am of royalty. Stop! No!"

Wolf stabbed her many times. Aimi, in her weakened state, could not fight back. She fell down, and Wolf took her body and buried it in a secluded area.

Todd's family doctor examined him at the governor's mansion, making sure that he was not somehow poisoned. Agent Martinez arrived at the prom and was fully briefed on Todd's situation. A dark vehicle waited outside the building where Jasmine's prom was being held. Jasmine got pictures taken with her date, Brad. Agents Martinez and Wombush stood nearby, scanning the room and looking for anything out of the ordinary.

The evening soon came to its conclusion. Brad and Jasmine were announced and crowned as the prom king and queen, and their friends and classmates applauded. This served as a perfect opportunity for them both to exit the dance hall and try to elude the agents, which they had earlier planned. As the crowd dispersed, Martinez and Wombush noticed that Jasmine and Brad were no longer in the crowd. The agents began to panic.

"Where are Jasmine and Brad?" Martinez shouted at the crowd. The kids stared at them; some tried hard not to laugh and others simply turned and walked away. "You kids don't understand. They may be in grave danger if we don't find them!" Wombush said, agitated.

"We have to start searching now," Martinez said. The agents ran outside and searched for a red Mustang, but he could not locate it. The crowd was large, and most were driving away from the parking lot in haste, causing confusion for the agents. The agents noticed three red Mustangs in the parking lot, parked near the same area where Brad had parked. The agents called in the plates. Martinez turned on the tracking device that was on Jasmine's bracelet. "They are moving east toward the freeway." Wombush and Martinez started their SUV and pursued the Mustang.

"Did you see the look in their eyes when they couldn't find us?" Brad said.

"Yeah! It was fun watching Martinez freak out and panic, wondering where we were!" Jasmine chuckled. Brad and Jasmine were looking for a secluded area. Brad wanted to stop right away, however Jasmine remembered that she has to first get rid of the tracking device in order to be free of the agents. Jasmine removed the bracelet from her arm and threw it out of the window.

The agents noticed the tracking device stopped working approximately three miles away.

"There they are, Jabbar—alone, as you predicted," Alq said.

"Americans, as you can see, are very predictable," Jabbar noted.

Brad observed headlights behind them. "Who could that be?" Brad said nervously, wondering if it was the local sheriff. Or had the agents found them before Jasmine threw away the tracking device? The vehicle following them was a Jeep Cherokee and sped toward them. The vehicle hit Brad's Mustang on the rear bumper. "Hey! Watch it, you asshole!" Brad shouted. The Jeep hit them again, harder. Brad sped up, and Alq shot an AK-47 at the couple. Bullets ripped through the vehicle, tearing the vinyl seats. Brad made a hard right turn off the main road and into a wooded area.

The agents arrived at the scene where the tracking device was located. They noticed that the tracking device was on the ground near a pine tree. "What now?" Wombush asked.

"We switch the tracking device to Brad's Mustang. I knew those two would be trouble, so I placed a tracking device inside Brad's car, near the front wheel."

Brad took more evasive action, turning his wheel and causing his vehicle to move side to side on the road. The terrorists were joined by another Jeep, and one of its passengers possessed a grenade launcher. Bullets shattered the back of Brad's rear window. Jasmine screamed continuously as the chase moved on through the woods. Brad drove over rocks and fallen branches. Alq continued to spray more bullets at the Mustang, this time hitting Jasmine in the back and arm.

"Oh, my God! I'm hit and bleeding, Brad! I'm bleeding!" Jasmine cried.

Brad reached inside the glove compartment and found some paper towels. In the back seat he had some rags that were clean. He made a compression bandage for Jasmine. "Press this against your wound and keep it there," he yelled.

"It is time to end this now," Jabbar said over the radio. The terrorist passenger in the second Jeep aimed the grenade launcher at the right rear tire and fired. The grenade hit the tire, causing an explosion that made the Mustang swerve out of control. Brad frantically turned the wheel as the Mustang hit a tree and rolled over three times before coming to a stop upside down. The terrorists stopped thirty yards away. Brad was badly injured, and Jasmine was unconscious.

Jabbar got out of his vehicle and calmly walked toward the demolished Mustang. He placed the gun to Brad's head and fired, killing him. Alq walked over to the passenger side where Jasmine was and saw that she was unconscious. Suddenly two bullets hit each of the terrorists, Alq in the head and Jabbar in the neck. The terrorists in the second Jeep fired on the newly arrived agents; there were three enemies inside the vehicle.

Agent Martinez called for backup as they took cover behind two large pine trees. Bullets hit the large tress. Wombush ran to the Mustang and pulled Jasmine out of the vehicle as Martinez covered them. Jasmine sustained head injuries along with bullet wounds to her back and arm. Martinez took cover behind the SUV as Wombush carried Jasmine behind it. Wombush joined Martinez in shooting at the terrorists. The terrorists had no more grenades; instead, they used .45s and MAC-10s. Martinez concentrated on taking out the MAC-10 enemy first. The one who carried the MAC-10 ran to the right, trying to flank the agents.

Wombush kneeled down and carefully targeted the Jeep Cherokee. One of the terrorists lifted up his head to see if he had a clear shot at the agents. Wombush aimed his M-9 and hit the terrorist between the eyes. Wombush couldn't see the third terrorist as he advanced toward the Jeep Cherokee.

Martinez continued to shoot at the terrorist with the MAC-10. They exchanged fire as she made her way toward the terrorist. The bullets from the MAC-10 sprayed all around her, delaying her efforts at advancement, but only for a moment. She found a fallen tree and took cover behind it.

Wombush ran for cover behind a large pine tree. Bullets rained down, hitting the tree he was using for cover. Wombush slowly looked up and saw the second terrorist perched in the tree. He pulled out his knife and threw it at the assailant. The knife hit the assailant in the chest; the man cried out in agony as he held the knife with both hands and fell to the ground, breaking his neck and several ribs. Wombush moved quickly to the fallen terrorist as Martinez covered him. As Wombush pulled out his knife from the terrorist, a shadow quickly moved toward him. He saw something moving toward him in his peripheral vision. As he turned, Wombush found himself face-to-face with the third terrorist, who immediately hit Wombush on the right side of his face. The strike was so hard and fast that Wombush did not see it coming. Wombush shook off the blow and returned with a closed-fist strike to the assailant's nose. His fist went through the terrorist, who then executed a leg sweep on Wombush, taking both of his legs out from beneath him and causing him to land on his back.

Wombush quickly used both hands to push off the ground and kick outward, landing on his feet. The terrorist quickly moved behind Wombush, placing him in a deadly choke hold. Wombush struggle to get released. His assailant continued to apply pressure on his neck and throat. "Die, American! Die!" the terrorist screamed.

Wombush concentrated and called on the great spirits of his ancestors. The power surged deep from within him. All of a sudden, the terrorist felt himself being lifted off the ground while trying to keep the choke hold. He felt his grip loosening because Wombush's neck was too big. Wombush became a large black bear. He then easily shrugged off the terrorist from his back and threw him to the ground. The terrorist quickly got up, reached into a pocket, and threw stars at the bear. He missed as the bear charged him. The terrorist ran toward a tree and jumped onto a large branch.

One of the terrorists whom Martinez and been exchanging gunfire with looked up to see what had occurred. Once he did that, Martinez shot him in the chest. The bear pushed the tree violently, and it uprooted and landed on the ground. The terrorist also landed on the ground.

Martinez ran over to the fallen terrorist. "Place your hands behind your head and interlace your fingers—now! Don't you dare move an inch, or I will shoot. Wombush, where are you?" The black bear turned toward Martinez's voice but then ran up the mountain. Martinez noticed a Red Dragon tattooed on the arm of the terrorist. She knew this was no ordinary terrorist. "Who is your leader? How many more are there like you?" Martinez asked sternly as she held the M-9 to his head.

"You are very good. You remind me of my wife—very agile and aggressive. What kind of human is your partner?" "I've never encountered a being such as him!" the Ninja said.

"Keep your hands behind your back. I'm not going to repeat myself!" Martinez warned.

"You know that I'm a Red Dragon! You must also know that I cannot be taken prisoner." With these words, the ninja threw a smoke bomb at the agent's feet and disappeared.

Emergency vehicles and other CIA agents arrived on scene. Martinez instructed the agents to search for Wombush. She directed the medical personnel to transport Jasmine to the hospital. They placed Jasmine on a stretcher and then in the ambulance, making preparations for transport. The agents reported back to Martinez and informed her that there was no sign of Wombush.

"Unit two team leader to control, over," Martinez said.

"Control here. Go ahead, team leader two," Jennings said.

"I lost Wombush in a skirmish we had along I-94. Can you get a fix on his location?" Martinez asked.

"I'll try." Jennings replied.

Martinez wanted to continue to search for Wombush, however she had to leave in order to escort Jasmine to the hospital. Jasmine was priority one. "All units, begin heading for Memorial Hospital."

"Control to team leader two."

"Go ahead, Control," Martinez answered.

"There is no location for Wombush. His tracker must have come off during that skirmish you had. Unable to locate at this time." Jennings said.

The agents were now en route to the hospital. The second ambulance transported Brad's body to the morgue. Agent Martinez rode with Jasmine on the way to the hospital. She had to inform both sets of parents about this disastrous event. Barbara Barton cried hysterically when she learned what had occurred. Martinez informed her that Jasmine was being taken to Memorial Hospital.

As they moved along the highway, Martinez noticed that they were not going to the hospital but instead drove onto a dirt road. The medical staff riding in the back with her also noticed and banged on the glass between them and the driver. "Driver, turn this vehicle around now!" Martinez demanded. The driver ignored their pleas. The ambulance broke through a construction barricade; a sign read, "Do not enter.

Road under construction." The driver sped up. The medical staff were terrified as the vehicle headed toward an unfinished bridge.

A hawk flew toward the ambulance and landed on it.

"Something hit the top of this vehicle," Sal, the driver, said.

"You must be hearing things," Sai stated.

Wombush turned back to his human form and reached his arm down as he lay flat on the roof of the ambulance. He opened the door and grabbed Sal.

"Let go of me! See? I tried to tell you, Sai. Let go of me!" Sal cried.

Sai was surprised and pulled out a handgun.

"Let go! Damn it, let go!"

"All right, I will," Wombush said. He let go of Sal, Sal fell outside and rolled underneath the moving ambulance.

"You will die for that, you American dog!" Sai said. He tried to pull the trigger on his gun, however the chamber was empty. "You will all die! Allah is my God!" Sai then jumped out of the vehicle.

Wombush took over the wheel and turned the vehicle around twenty yards before the end of the bridge. The medical staff and Martinez applauded Wombush. "How was he able to get inside the ambulance?" one of them asked. Martinez wonders how Wombush was able to maneuver such a feat at seventy miles an hour.

The ambulance arrived at the hospital where Barbara Barton was waiting. The hospital staff immediately transported Jasmine into the emergency room and began to operate on her. Agents were placed outside of the room as well as around the perimeter of the hospital. The doctor removed bullets from Jasmine's neck and shoulder. Once the operation was over, the doctor informed Barbara that her daughter was going to be fine.

As Barbara held Jasmine's hand, Victor Price walked in. "Victor? I didn't expect to see you," Barbara said, surprised.

"When I heard over our radio what happened, I had to come. How is she?" Price asked.

"She's doing fine. The doctor removed two bullets." Barbara began to cry. Agents Martinez and Wombush quietly walked outside the room.

Victor headed slowly toward Barbara and then moved a chair to sit next to her. He placed his hand on hers. "I'm sorry that I wasn't strong enough to always be there for you, Barbara. I should've been strong enough for you." Price wept.

"It's all right, Victor. I forgave you a very long time ago. Now you've got to forgive yourself. You've done a marvelous job getting together this team of brilliant agents. The children love them. I thank you for them. We thank you." Victor slowly looked up at Barbara and nodded. "Just stay with me, Victor. Right now I need you by my side." Victor smiled and agreed to remain by her side until the governor arrived.

"All right, Wombush! I want answers, and I want them now!" Martinez demanded.

"I cannot explain what happened back there, ma'am, because your mind cannot grasp what my ancestors can do at times," Wombush said.

"Look, this is an empty waiting room. We are going inside, and you are going to tell me everything," Martinez said. Both agents walked inside and sat on sofa chairs across from each other. Martinez sat with her arms folded and her legs crossed, waiting for Wombush's explanation.

"My tribe and history goes back over three hundred years. We are a proud people of Cherokee descent. We have survived many battles and wars. These wars were between other tribes and of course the white man. In my tribe, which has several elders, there was a medicine man who was very powerful. The medicine man to my people the power to change into almost any animal. The power of change was to be done only if someone's life was in danger, or if your own life was in danger. My tribe was full of peace and tranquility until there was trouble.

"Our chief, Thunder Bull, took his family into town to buy food and supplies. Some of the townspeople did not like our people, especially the sheriff's department. When the chief went inside the general store, one of the sheriff's deputies also walked in and planted an item on him. When the chief was through shopping, the deputy told him that he saw the chief place something inside one of his pockets. The chief of course denied any of his accusations. He did comply and pulled out a cigarette lighter from his right back pocket. The chief and his family were shocked and immediately knew that the lighter was planted on him. The deputy drew his revolver and told him that he was under arrest. He brought the chief over to the jail and would not let him go until the judge arrived on Monday; it was Friday. The chief was very upset. He told his wife to take the children, leave, and come back for him on Monday. His wife, Nadine, would not leave his side. Instead, she and her children got a room in a hotel not far from the jail.

"The sheriff and his deputies were drinking one night and saw the chief's wife and daughter out walking. They took them into one of the stables and raped and murdered both of them. When the chief found out that they had been violated, he lost it. He broke out of the cell by transforming into a bear, and he approached the sheriff and his deputies. They opened fired on the chief, fatally wounding him. Before he died, he gave Sheriff Smith a long scar on his face. The chief's surviving children, Nina and Jacob, were brought back near the tribe and released by the sheriff's deputies and released. They told the tribe what had happened, and we were all enraged over what had occurred. Strong Bow, an elder in our tribe, said that we should let the law of the land settle this. Another elder named Black Eagle said that it was the law that did the chief wrong, and it was up to us to make things right. I then spoke out against Black Eagle. He then told me that I was speaking out against not only him but our ancestors, and that it was our duty to exact vengeance upon a town of murderers. My reply was that it was not our way to exact vengeance on a whole town where innocent people resided and had nothing to do with our chief's murder. Elder Strong Bow commended me on my stand and conviction. Elder Black Eagle was blinded by bigotry and hatred but convinced half the tribe to take his side.

I decided to go into town that evening to warn the sheriff and the townspeople. The town consisted of many young and old people. They were doctors, businessmen, ranchers, lawyers, and school teachers. They were not, however, warriors. They had their own preconceived ideas about Native Americans. I was not received by anyone, except this one special family, a preacher and his family. I told the preacher about Black Eagle and what he was planning to do by the end of the week: eliminate the entire town because of the sheriff's actions. The pastor kept me safe at his house. He told me that this was the Lord's house, and I had nothing to fear here because I was protected. I was surprised by his words and hospitality. I was only sixteen and had not come across a white man such as him. The preacher's wife was Ann, and she taught Sunday school. They had three teenage children: Johnny, James, and Priscilla. The good pastor had me stay overnight because the word was already out that there was an Indian stirring up trouble in town. I remained out of sight during the next day and got acquainted with the family, especially Priscilla. She was very beautiful and had long black hair that flowed with the wind. Her smile always brought comfort to me. Pricilla and her brothers taught me the ways of Christianity, and to love all people. Her family reminded me of my own. Both of my parents and elders taught me to love all. I was there for almost a week.

"I spoke to the pastor and told him that we must send word out to the rest of the townspeople to evacuate. The pastor had already been talking to the townspeople, starting with his own congregation. Many had left already to nearby towns. The sheriff had deputized several other men when word got back to him that Black Eagle was after him. Priscilla urged me to stay and leave with her family. We talked one night in her backyard on a hill overlooking the town. The stars were out, brightly glistening in the sky. It was then I spoke my heart to Priscilla. I told her that I had never met a girl like her, and I wanted us to be together forever. Her heart was one of gold. When she spoke, she had the voice of an angel. She placed her hand on mine, and it was soft and smooth as porcelain. For the first time in my life, I felt loved. This beautiful young lady from a different culture worshipped a very caring God, and she loved me. As I was speaking, she gazed into my eyes, placed her hand on my chin, and then turned my head towards her. Priscilla then gave me my first kiss. She pressed her lips upon mine, and I was stunned. I was hers and felt my body tingling. I could not speak; she told me not to. Priscilla then told me that she was falling in love with me. I told her that my feelings were the same and held her in my arms for a long time. She said that she did not want the evening to end. We continued to talk and then kiss once more.

"As the evening went on, Priscilla's mother called for her. She left to answer her mother's call and then returned, to my surprise. We continued to talk about each other, our families, and what was about to take place in town. Priscilla told me that she had never met a young man who treated her with such respect and honor. I told her that we had better get some rest, because it was near midnight.

"I had to sneak out of town during the night and return to my tribe. I had been gone for five days. My cousin, Running Bear, told me that there had been physical fighting going on among our tribes over the murder of our chief. Our tribe continued to be split, half with Strong Bow and the other half with Black Eagle. I wanted to know where my cousin stood. He answered, 'With you!' I then told him that I had to try to see if I could convince Black Eagle to cease pursuing his mad course of vengeance.

"When I confronted Black Eagle, he told me that I was too young to understand, and I must make a choice soon. The warriors of his tribe were planning to attack soon. I then went to speak to the elders. They told me that Black Eagle was hardheaded and determined to wipe out the entire town. Strong Bow said that he would try to stop him. Black Eagle had weapons of war that the white man had used in previous battles and wars: machine guns, grenades, and various explosives. He would also use bows and flaming arrows! I was advised by the elders to go to Arizona, where my parents were.

"I decided to end this by confronting the sheriff and finding out what really happened when Chief Thunder Bull was murdered. I made my way to the pastor's house and explained to him all that had taken place. He told me that his family was getting ready to go on their way, and the Lord would protect them. He was going to remain in town as long as he could and then join his family later. Priscilla and the rest of her family were almost finished packing their belongings when I arrived at their home. They were happy to see me, especially Priscilla. I told her that I had to see the truth behind the chief's murder. Priscilla cried and hugged me. 'Don't leave me, Adam! Please don't leave me!' We embraced and then kissed. I promised her that we would meet again and that I wouldn't forget her. I then hugged her brothers and her mom before I departed. As I turned to walk towards town, I heard Priscilla say, 'Good-bye, my love, my Running Deer.'

"Once I arrived at the sheriff's office, his deputies pulled their shotguns on me and asked what business I had there. I told them that I needed to speak to the sheriff. The sheriff opened the door to his office slowly, and I saw the barrel of a Winchester rifle. He asked who I was and why I was here. I told him that I wanted no blood to be shed. I wanted answers—the truth from the sheriff's own mouth. I told him that I was for the law, and as a lawman he should tell me the truth. The sheriff turned to his deputies, pointed at me, and laughed. He said the truth was that I was under arrest for trespassing. His five men moved toward me with their shotguns pointed at me. I placed my hands in the air. One deputy handcuffed me and escorted me into a cell. I was told I would have to stay there until Monday, when the judge would return.

"In the same cell was an old man who had on clothing that was torn and dusty. He told me that he knew the truth of what happened in town with Chief Thunder Bull and his family. He then asked how much the information was worth to me. I told him that the truth meant more than money. I then told him that I could get us both out of this jail. He told me that would be his price, and I agreed. His name was Sam, and he was a miner in town. He said he was thrown in jail a year ago for panhandling. The truth was he had discovered some gold in the mine he claimed. Once the sheriff found out about Sam's mine, he framed him and said that Sam had stolen the mine from someone else. Sam went on to say that the sheriff and his two deputies got drunk. After they arrested Thunder Bull, they went to the hotel and violated his wife and daughter. Chief Thunder Bull lost it and broke out of jail using his bare hands. Sam went on to say that he couldn't believe his own eyes as he saw the chief transform into a bear. Thunder Bull nearly killed two deputies and the sheriff before being shot three times by the sheriff and once by his deputy. Sam could see the whole incident from the window in his cell.

"Just then, Sam and I heard gunshots and explosions outside. The sheriff's vehicles were being destroyed by Black Eagle's followers. The deputies were being shot left and right. The sounds of panic and chaos rang throughout the town. Many people had already left, but some remained because they had nowhere to go. Arrows darkened the sky, raining down into flesh and other objects. I then knew it was time for me to act. I told Sam not to be frightened about what he was to see, and I called upon the power of my ancestors. Sam observed spirits appear above me as I chanted. I closed my eyes and transformed into a black bear. I broke the cell door and ran toward the front door, knocking it down as well. The sheriff was trying to escape in his vehicle. I turned it upside down and transformed back to my human form. Sam assisted me in pulling the sheriff out of the Vehicle and placing him into another one. Flaming arrows fell all around us; the entire town was in flames. We observed the two tribes fighting each other. Many of my brothers from both tribes were killed during the fighting. Sam and I had to shoot our way out of town.

"Once we reached the outskirts of town, I saw the pastor lying on the road. His vehicle had been hit by a grenade, and he was covered in blood. He was barely alive. He told me to find Priscilla. 'Go marry her, because she loves you,' he said. 'You're a good young man. I'm proud to have known you, son. You go now with God.' Those were the pastor's last words as he expired in my arms. Tears flowed from my eyes, and I placed his body in a nearby field; I would later bury him there. I had to find Priscilla—I had to know if she was alive.

"Five miles down the road, we observed the pastor's station wagon on its side. We stopped the vehicle ten yards away, and I quickly got out of the vehicle and ran toward the badly damaged station wagon. I saw Priscilla's mother and two brothers were already dead. I called to Priscilla, but there was no answer. She then answered me. She had been thrown from the vehicle into a nearby field. 'Don't be mad at them, Adam. Don't take vengeance. I'll be all right. Leave it to God. Promise me you will,' she said. I nodded as tears flowed from my cheeks. I told Sam to take Priscilla to the hospital; she would survive her wounds. I had to find Black Eagle. Sam took off right away and delivered the sheriff to the state police, and he turned in evidence convicting the sheriff and his deputies. The sheriff received eighty years to life. Sam got back his mine and the gold that belonged to him.

As I ran toward the town, I observed a band of warriors on the hill where Priscilla and I had sat two nights ago. I issued a challenge to Black Eagle. I asked Chief Strong Bow to let me finish this once and for all. We both ran toward each other and fought. We wrestled, and I was winning until he transformed into a bear. I also did the same. We hit each other in a furry of blows. In the end, I was the victor. Black Eagle told me to kill him, but I couldn't. Priscilla had changed me. Black Eagle told me that nothing had changed between us. Chief Strong Bow banned Black Eagle from our tribe forever."

"Did you ever see Priscilla again, Adam?" Martinez asked anxiously, trying to keep back her tears.

"I did visit her at the hospital. We were together for another two years. She went into missionary work and today, I'm a Federal agent. We stay in touch by phone and e-mail, but live very different lives." Wombush said.

Just then Agent Martinez's cell phone vibrated, and she answers. It was Lamb. Unit one had just arrived at the airport along with the governor. Martinez informed Lamb of all events that took place when they were away as Lamb escorted the governor to the hospital. "We have a lot to talk about, Agent Martinez," Lamb said. "We sure do, sir," Martinez agreed as she glanced at Wombush.

Chapter 6

CPAT Compromised

The governor arrived at the hospital along with Hades team. The governor opened the door and saw Victor Price sitting alongside Barbara. Barry hugged his wife as they both watched their daughter lie in the bed, unconscious. Agent Martinez and Lamb briefed each other. They were surprised at how much opposition both teams had encountered. The doctor informed the Bartons' that Jasmine would be released from the hospital the next morning.

The governor did not want to speak to any of the agents; he took Barbara by the arm and went inside a waiting room. Barry told his wife that he no longer wanted CPAT to protect his family. He wanted the secret service back.

"Why? Why, Barry?" Barbara inquired.

"Just look at the mess that happened to our daughter! Look what happened to me, for God's sake!" Barry shouted.

Barbara paused and thought for a moment before speaking. "Barry, our daughter is here because she and her boyfriend did not follow protocol. They chose this, not CPAT. As for you, you're still alive, aren't you? Alive, Barry Barton! Isn't that good enough for you?" Barbara had tears in her eyes. Barry reached out and pulled Barbara close to him. "The children, especially the twins, will miss those agents, Barry," Barbara added while wiping her tears.

Barry told her that everything would be better once the secret service was back protecting their entire home. Barry told Betty that he would call Victor Price on Monday to make the necessary changes.

The CPAT team was exhausted. Price gave the team time off for the weekend. He ordered them to go be with their families and friends. Lamb spent time with Arianna and Tank. Arianna and Tank were glad that Lamb had time for them. Lamb read to Arianna, played ball with her, and went over her homework. Arianna was skipping the second grade and moving on to third. The school counselor urged Lamb and Susan to consider her being placed in a school for the gifted.

Once the day ended, Arianna hugged and kissed her father and Tank. As they pulled out of the driveway, Arianna spoke telepathically to her father. "See you soon, Daddy! I love you!"

Lamb replied, "Good-bye, angel! Be good and listen to your mother! I love you too!"

Once Lamb and Tank arrived at their apartment, they found messages on the answer machine. One was from Director Price. Victor requested to see Lamb first thing in the morning.

When Monday came, Lamb and Tank arrived at CIA headquarters and went through the usual security entrance at CPAT using biometric security clearances. Tank followed Lamb through security. Once Lamb and Tank arrived at Price's office, they noticed that he was uptight and pensive.

"Have a seat, Lamb," Price said. Lamb took a seat in front of Price's desk; Tank sat next to him on his left. Price sat down and stared at the papers that were on his desk.

"All right, what's going on, sir?" Lamb asked anxiously. There was no answer as Price remained silent for the moment.

Just then, the door to Price's office opened abruptly, and Agent Martinez ran inside quickly. "I'm sorry I'm late. I had to get a babysitter at the last minute for Shanna!" she said.

Price told her to take a seat next to Lamb. He paused and then said, "It looks like CPAT will be reassigned from being the governor's escort. We will be escorting the ambassador of Japan starting this Friday."

Both agents turned to look at each other and then looked at Price. "Why?" they asked.

"The governor complained that we should have prevented his daughter from getting into that accident, and he felt that Lamb and his unit could have done a better job at protecting him in Korea," Price said angrily.

"That ungrateful SOB," Martinez shouted.

"I just don't get it, sir! We did all we could do under the circumstances, and we get rewarded with this?" Lamb said.

"You know this is bullshit, sir," Martinez protested.

"I know that, and I'm sorry to have to be the one to give you this news. I also know he has the right to choose whoever he wants to be on protective service detail for him and his family. In this case, he is bringing back the secret service. There's nothing else we can say or do in this matter. He has the power to make these decisions," Price said.

"I'll bet that Barbara is pissed off at his impulsiveness," Martinez noted.

"Well, we have a graduation to attend to in an hour. I just wanted you both to know how great of a job you have done with this case, and how proud I am of you and your teams. I couldn't have asked for a better group of individuals," Price said. The agents smiled, and Price continued. "The orders for the ambassadors are on your desks if you haven't already seen them. It's time for graduation, agents. That means you too, Tank." Tank looked at Price and then barked in the affirmative, wagging his tail.

As Lamb walked toward the auditorium, he heard his name paged to call the front desk. Lamb saw a phone in the corridor and called the receptionist. He was informed that there was a package addressed to him that had just arrived from the post office. Once Lamb reached the front desk, he examined the package. He placed it to his ear and could hear faint ticking sounds. He let Tank sniff the package, and the dog had no reaction. Lamb was unsure of its contents and ordered the receptionist to have the bomb squad meet him in the basement, where there was a bomb containment room.

Lamb told Tank to wait with Carol, the receptionist. He ran into the stairwell and down to the basement. The bomb containment room also had biometric access. Lamb placed his eyes next to the screen in the entryway to gain access. He gained access, placed the package inside the room, and quickly exited. Six bomb squad members arrived, and Lamb informed them of what had developed so far. The captain had his agents activate the bomb robot. The robot was remotely controlled using voice activation commands. The containment room was opened from the reception desk. The robot moved quickly inside the containment room. The robot cut the package string and ripped open the package to reveal an alarm clock, but no bomb. There was also a small object inside. When the agent commanded the robot to pick it up, they saw it was a cell phone. The robot affirmed there was no bomb inside of the package, and it handed the phone to Agent Lamb.

Once the cell phone was in Lamb's possession, it began to ring. Lamb stared at it in shock and then answered. "Hello?"

"Why hello, Agent Lamb."

"Who is this?" Lamb asked.

"You already know who I am. I am just getting to know who you are. You are a very interesting individual and a very worthy opponent. However, my quarrel isn't with you. This is between the governor and me," the man on the phone said sternly.

"What exactly is it that you want?" Lamb asked.

"What I want is for you and your new unit in the CIA to back off, or you will all die. I know how to cause pain that will last for what will seem like an eternity before you die. Tell this to your Director Price."

"You know that I can't back off," Lamb answered.

"Take heed of my words, American," Abdullah warned. The phone went dead.

Lamb looked up and observed Agent Martinez with a bewildered look on her face. She quickly ran toward Lamb. "Are you all right, sir? Who was that?"

"An old nemesis of Director Price's. The situation is going to have to be handled by the secret service from now on," Lamb said.

The bomb squad cleared the area. Both agents walked toward the auditorium and were joined by Carol and Tank. They walked inside and took their seats at the back of the auditorium. The master of ceremony introduced the keynote speaker, Kate Hudson, a retired agent who was now a private consultant. She soon completed her presentation, and the audience filled the auditorium with applause. The master of ceremony introduced the director, who began handing out certificates to the graduates. Among the new agents that would be working along with CPAT were Brian Keller, communications operations, and Doug and Doreen Fitzpatrick, field operations, counter intelligence. They would undergo training in the field before they could join the unit. Agent Keller would train with the satellite system's in-house operations, learning about STARE DOWN and how it operated. The Fitzpatricks would also work in-house and in the field with their field- training officers (FTOs); they would assist and respond with other agents on calls in the field.

Brian and the Fitzpatricks had known each other for years and were planning to go out to eat at their favorite restaurant along with Brian's fiancée, Tina Murphy. Tina told everyone to wait outside the building while she used the ladies' room. "We'll be outside in the parking lot, babe. Don't take too long," Brian said. The graduates headed to the parking lot.

A dark SUV pulled into the parking lot, unnoticed by all. It moved behind a big tree near Brian's vehicle. "You can go ahead of us and get seats. We'll meet you there," Brian said.

"That sounds good. We'll go ahead and get a table," Doug replied. Doug and Doreen waved good-bye, and Brian was left in the parking lot by himself. He opened the door to his vehicle, a 1979 Ford Mustang, and reached inside to take a file from the passenger chair. As he turned around, he was hit on the head with a blunt object. Before he fell to the ground, two men grabbed him and placed him inside the SUV. Another figure appeared out of the SUV wearing the same clothing as Brian Keller—in fact, he looked exactly like him.

"Brian? Brian where are Doug and Doreen?" Tina asked when she came out.

"They went ahead of us and said they would get a table," the imposter Brian replied.

"Oh, how wonderful. I'm ready to eat, babe." Brian opened the door for her. Tina pulled him closer and gave him a passionate kiss. "This is to let you know how much I'm proud of you, and that I love you," she said.

"Thanks, babe," he replied. Tina sat in the passenger seat and Brian closed the door. He walked around to the driver's side, opened the door, and went inside. Brian turned on the ignition and they sped to the restaurant.

Agent Jennings had told Brian and Tina that he couldn't stay for the whole ceremony and had to take care of some office work; he would meet them later on at the restaurant. As Jennings exited the building, he saw that everyone had gone and then got into his vehicle. He called Brian.

"Keller here!"

"You mean Agent Keller," Jennings said.

"Huh?"

"From now on its' Agent Keller," Jennings explained.

"It's going to take some getting used to," Keller said.

"Hey, which restaurant have you decided to go to for dinner? I'm hungry!"

"Hun, where are we going?" Keller asked his fiancée.

"Stop joking, babe! We're going where we always go when we eat out with Doug and Doreen," Tina replied.

The fake Keller began to panic and sweat. He bit his lower lip, hoping he didn't blow his cover. He noticed a flyer on his dashboard that had coupons from a seafood restaurant called "The Shoreline Buffet." He took a chance and said, "Look, honey, I won't forget the coupons!"

"I hope not. It's a good deal for buy two, get two for free," Tina said.

Keller breathed a sigh of relief and told Jennings that he would see him at the restaurant.

Once they arrived at the restaurant, Jennings joined them at their table. Brian received a phone call and excused himself from the table. He walked outside of the restaurant and stood behind a pillar. "Yes, comrade?" Keller said.

"I take it that the operation is going well?"

"Yes, comrade, very well," Keller answered.

"Very good. Are the files where we thought they would be?"

"Yes, they are."

"Good. You sound and look exactly like him. Very good. Carry on."

"Thank you, comrade." Keller smoked a cigarette before walking back inside of the restaurant.

"Are you already getting messages from headquarters?" Doug asked.

"Where are our calls, babe?" Doreen asked.

"Some individuals are just more important than others," Doug joked, and everyone laughed.

After they were done eating, Jennings excused himself because he had to get up early the next morning for work. He had to speak to his supervisor in person because he'd discovered a security breach earlier that day; they would address the problem in the morning. The Fitzpatricks also said good-bye because they had to rise early and learn about field operations and intelligence gathering. They had to pick up Keller in the morning because they would carpool every morning together.

Tina wanted to stay over with Brian, however Brian told her that he needed to get some work done and would feel distracted. Tina promised she would stay in his bedroom and not disturb him, and so he agreed to let her remain there overnight. Brian made sure that the door to the den was secured, then he searched for the secret files in the laptop. He came across a file about Operation Terminate, which would be carried out soon. This file contained terrorist involvement, locations of CIA and FBI headquarters, and the names of agents. Brian yelled to Tina that he would join her shortly. Brian pulled out a memory stick and copied the files. Tina continued to call to him. The Brian imposter noticed that it was going to take a long time for the download. Brian turned off the laptop, secured the door and went to bed.

Jennings looks at his alarm clock as it went off at 5:45 a.m. He had to meet Lamb right away. The Fitzpatricks were also up and getting ready for a long day ahead. Doug made sure he placed an extra clip on his belt for his .45. "Could you check my gun too, honey?" Doreen asked.

"Sure," Doug replies. The couple finished getting ready and were soon on their way to pick up Brian.

Brian was waiting on the front steps of his apartment. "Hello everyone," he said as he entered the vehicle. Doreen noticed Brian was using an unusual aftershave. "What is that you have on, Brian? I've never smelled that on you before!" she said.

"Oh, that's new, from overseas, called Avi-air," he replied.

"It is strong. I guess it's for us masculine guys," Doug said. Both men laughed.

Doreen observed Brian writing on a pad—using his right hand. She knew Brian was left-handed. Once they arrived at headquarters, Brian told them to go ahead of him because he needed to make a phone call. The Fitzpatricks went inside to begin security entrance procedures.

The Fitzpatricks had met on a call concerning a bank robbery over ten years ago while working in the LA police department, and they had been together ever since. Doug was 6'3", had brown hair and brown eyes, and weighed 190 pounds. Doreen was 5'4" and weighed 125 pounds. The bank robbery was in progress, and Doug and Doreen were riding in two separate vehicles. There were three bank robbers according to the bank manager on site. Each robber wore black ski masks, black long-sleeve shirts, and BDUs.

Once the units arrived, they positioned themselves out of site from the bank's view, unnoticed by the three robbers. The manager had informed dispatch that there was a side entrance on the north end of the building that was occasionally used. There was also a metal ladder on the outside that led to the roof of the bank. The officers could use it to gain access to the roof and then enter the vents, which led to the front area above the tellers. Doug and his partner, Ray, took the ladder leading to the roof; Doreen and her partner, Chris, took the north entrance. The robber watching the front door did not have a visual on the officers. Doreen and Chris were the first to reach the manager, who was hiding inside his office. They could see the robber, who wore a ski mask, pointing a gun at the clerk. The second robber was covering the first robber as he looked around the room, making sure that no one moved or made a sound. There were ten customers lying face down on the floor. Both robbers wielded AK-47s. The officers then made their way quietly toward the counter, crouching down and taking cover behind each desk and counter. They watched the clerk place money into a bag.

"Hurry up! We don't have all day, damn it!" the robber blurted. The cashier nervously placed the money into the bag, dropping some bills. "Clumsy bitch! You'd better hurry it up!"

Chris took careful aim at the first robber. The first robber was very irate and began to move toward the clerk, placing the barrel to her head. Chris opened fire on the first robber, hitting him in the chest and shoulders; the man fell to the floor. The second robber opened fire at Chris, hitting him twice in the shoulder. The sounds of gunfire echoed throughout the bank as Doreen returned fire. Doug and Ray got closer to the gunfire and positioned themselves over a counter approximately thirty feet away from Doreen and Chris. They dropped behind the counter and aimed their weapons at the robbers. The second robber heard them fall on the floor and turned around. Doreen then stood up and shot two rounds at the robber, hitting him in the head and chest. He fell backward, hitting the counter and then the floor. Doreen called, "Officer down! Need paramedics now!"

The third robber fled the scene, and Doug and Ray took pursuit. Doug and Ray told the robber to stop. He didn't, and they hit him twice in the back. He fell down and did not get up. Ray stayed with the fallen suspect while Doug ran back into the bank to see how the other officers were doing. "Good shooting!" Doug said to both of them.

"Thanks. We have to get Chris to the hospital," Doreen said.

"Did we get all of them?" Chris asked.

"We got them, partner," Doreen said. "You just stay quiet."

Doug asked Doreen out after they got off shift, and they had been together ever since.

Agent Keller finished his phone call and walked through security. Doreen saw Keller behind her in the concave mirror. Keller quickly threw a cigarette on the ground before he entered security. He emptied his pockets to go through the metal detectors. Doug and Doreen waited for him on the other side. Doreen had a puzzled look. "What's wrong, Doreen?" Doug asked.

"Since when did Keller start smoking again?" Doreen asked. Doug shrugged his shoulders and excused it as Keller having nerves, just as they all did with new jobs in the CIA. As Keller was about to gain access. He forgot his entry code. Doug and Doreen looked at each other. Keller was given a temporary code that day.

Jennings could hear everyone getting closer to his office in the hallway. He walked out of his office and saw Keller; they shook hands. Jennings informed Keller that he had a meeting with his supervisor and would meet him later for lunch. Jennings had a puzzled look because Keller didn't seem too excited to be here, as he did before. Jennings greeted the Fitzpatricks and then excused himself. He walked into Lamb's office and explained a possible security breach and compromise in the security systems. Jennings showed Lamb using the computer where the compromise came from—an outside source. The sites that were looked at were top secret, and information was extracted.

"Just how could that be?" Lamb asked.

"It was overridden by someone who knows the codes to gain access," Jennings said. There were only two individuals who knew how to gain access to those files: Jennings and Baker. Baker was replaced by Jennings six months ago and had retired.

Lamb called in Agent Lee because she was experienced in cyber forensics. He instructed her to look at Jennings's computer. Twenty minutes later, Agent Lee reported back to Lamb. "Sir, I discovered that whoever modified these files was using a virtual private network. I will have to use a protocol trap. It will detect where it came from, and we will discover exactly who is behind this conspiracy." Lamb nodded as Agent Lee walked back to Jennings's computer to continue her work.

Lamb had two agents visit Baker's place of residence and question him. They also looked at his computer and laptop using instruments that could detect activity connected to the security systems, including the satellite. Lamb then questioned Jennings. Jennings was surprised that Lamb would think that he could do such a thing. Jennings said that he was home over the weekend and did not leave his apartment; he had no alibi. Jennings lived alone in an apartment with no roommate. Lamb had Jennings's neighbors questioned. No one saw him that weekend. The computer showed that the compromise took place on Friday at

5:30 p.m., when everyone was gone out of the building, and then again from an outside computer on Saturday at 2:00 p.m. Jennings said that he left the building at that time, however the video footage showed him leaving at 6:00 p.m. and returning and entering the building at 1:45 p.m. on Saturday! Lamb must now call agents in to have Jennings placed into temporary custody, and he confiscated his computer and laptop.

Volkov knocked on Lamb's door. "Did you hear everything in the next room?"

"Yes, I did. Everything I informed you about is very true of Jennings," Volkov said. "Jennings did have full access to everything. He knows where to look for all files. He knows all the codes and how to override and circumvent any security system."

"But why?" Lamb said.

Price stood at the entrance of Lamb's door. "It's your call," Price said.

"Before I make any rash decisions concerning Jennings, I'm going to have to have a full-scale investigation done," Lamb said. Lamb and Price walked out of the office and headed toward the investigations unit. Volkov peered through the one-way glass window, where he observed Jennings sitting with his hands clasped together, looking nervous and bewildered.

"How the hell could this have happened?" Jennings said to himself. Lamb and Price sat and spoke with the investigations unit. The unit began to gather information and evidence concerning Jennings. Jennings was held in confinement for the time being.

Doreen walked into Doug's office and closed the door. "I need to talk to you—now!" she said.

"Okay, hon!" Doug replied.

"Brian doesn't seem to be Brian."

"I know. What bothers me is that is that code he missed. Brian is an individual who knows numbers; he has a great memory," Doug said.

"He also told us that he had stopped smoking for good. I say that we keep a close eye on him," Doreen suggested.

"You're right. I've got your back as usual, babe," Doug said.

Doreen smiled and walked back to her office.

The day was long but productive. The Fitzpatricks drove home with Keller. Once they dropped him off at his apartment, they quickly called Jennings. They informed Lamb of Keller's odd behaviors over the past two days.

The imposter Keller quickly locked the door. He took out of his pocket three memory sticks that contained secret files concerning CIA agents' plans and activities, names of agents, and locations throughout the world. He downloaded the information onto his laptop as his cell phone rang. It was his contact, Wolf.

"All is well. I have the memory sticks from the office, and I'm downloading them now!" the imposter said.

"Good. Make sure that your identity remains covert throughout your mission. Keep me informed," Wolf said, and then he turned off his phone.

The imposter continued to download the information. Just then, someone entered the den and stood in front of the fake Brian as he continued to focus on the laptop. "Hi, babe! I didn't hear you come in!" The imposter quickly pulled out his .45 and pointed it at Tina's head. "What the hell?" Tina cried.

"Oh, sorry! I thought that you had left for work. I didn't realize that you were still here!" he said, surprised, as he quickly minimized the laptop screen.

"You know that I was going to take today off in order to be with you," she said.

"Sorry, I forgot. There has been so much on my mind lately," he lied. The imposter gave her a gentle hug and calmly told her to go in the bedroom and wait for him while he finished his work; he was almost done now.

The phone rang. The imposter picked up the landline phone and shouted to Tina that he would answer. He was unaware that Tina had picked up the phone at the same time. "Hello?" "Jet, what's going on? How was your first day on the job? It's me, Lance. Jan and I are sorry that we couldn't make it to your graduation. However, we are planning a barbecue this Saturday, and you and Tina are invited. How about it?"

"Well ... all right. That sounds good, Lance!" the imposter replied.

"See you this Saturday at 1:00 p.m.," Lance said.

Tina made sure that she was quiet as she placed the phone back on the receiver. Tina wondered why Brian couldn't recognize his own friend, whom he had known since high school. Lance was Brian's quarterback on the football team; Brian was nicknamed Jet because he was the fastest wide receiver on his team. Tina became very concerned about Brian's behavior. It couldn't be just work. *Why has he really changed?* She thought to herself.

The next day Jennings was to report to the investigations unit, where he would begin to plead his case. The investigations team was able to get the video of Jennings leaving for work from his apartment complex. However, there was no footage of him arriving back at the apartment complex. Agents Tai and Ross presented the evidence to Lamb and Price, in front of Jennings. Agent Jennings was shocked at what he observed from the footages. He knew that he was being framed by someone who did not want him there, but why? The investigation agents walked outside the room into an adjoining one with Lamb and Price. Lamb shook his head in disbelief. Volkov also joined them.

"It looks bad for Jennings," Agent Ross said.

"You saw the evidence, Agent Lamb. It looks like the evidence will stick," Agent Tai agreed.

"I know, I know. I still believe that something else is at work here. Jennings wouldn't compromise for anyone, and I intend to find out what's going on," Lamb said sternly. "Remember, Lamb: it's not what you know—it's what you can prove," Volkov snickered.

Lamb gave Volkov a stare and said, "I'm still not convinced. I believe he's innocent. However, I know that you men must do your job."

Jennings was placed into custody and was allowed to contact his lawyer. Lamb asked to speak to Jennings before confinement. "I didn't do it, sir. I swear I didn't do it," Jennings said nervously, lowering his head.

"I know that, Jennings. That's why I'm going to get you out of here and back in the unit, where you belong. I promise you that," Lamb vowed.

Jennings looked up at Lamb and smiled. "I know you will, sir."

The agents informed federal corrections, and they arrived to transfer Jennings to a holding cell, to await trial.

Tina was too curious about Brian's behavior. She saw when he had switched screens but did not know what the original screen was. *IS There something that he is hiding from me?* she thought to herself. *Brian has never been so pensive before.* Tina began to investigate after he left for work. She looked through his drawers, clothing, and one of his wallets he left behind. She found nothing out of the ordinary. She then searched his bookshelf. Tina observed a book that was not placed all the way on the shelf. She looked at the title: *Terrorism, Fear, and Power.* Tina thought it was one of Brian's textbooks for one of his classes last year.

Something fell from the shelf from that same area. It was a memory stick. Tina made sure that all the doors were locked and the curtains were pulled together. She placed Brian's laptop facing the street near the window so that she would know when Brian arrived. Brian and Tina had shared everything up to this point; there were no secrets. She was shocked to see the files that were on the drive were the names of undercover agents and areas where they resided. *This would be a horrific security compromise,* Tina thought. Tina also discovered video footage showing Jennings entering the CIA satellite building on a Saturday. She moved the camera closer and saw that he has several memory sticks on his lanyard; one resembled the memory stick that Brian had. Tina turned off the computer. She was very upset and wondered if Jennings was in on this with her fiancé. Tina felt hurt and betrayed.

Lamb could not get Jennings off his mind; he knew that the man was innocent. Lamb went to speak to Director Price privately. All evidence pointed to Jennings, however something seemed wrong. Lamb felt that Jennings was somehow being framed and wanted to find out who and why. Price reviewed the evidence and asked Lamb what he wanted to do.

"I would like to be a part of this investigation, sir. After all, I had him transferred into CPAT.""I trust your judgment and instinct. You know that. If you feel that Jennings is innocent and can prove it, I'll back you up 100 percent!" Price stated.

Lamb thanked his director for the vote of confidence. Lamb needed something he could go on, something that would give him solid evidence in favor of Jennings. But what would that be?

As Lamb was about to leave Price's office, Agent Volkov walked in. Volkov said that they would be in dire need of a replacement for Jennings. "Who would you suggest that would be?" Price said.

"Why, it would be Brian Keller, of course. He has such great knowledge in communications and satellite systems background," Volkov stated.

Price turned to look for Lamb's approval. "Well, Lamb?" Price said.

"I'll take him into consideration, Agent Volkov," Lamb said. "If you will excuse me, I have a self-defense class to teach for my unit." Lamb walked out of Price's office.

The next day Tina woke up early. She wanted to find out more by accessing Brian's computer. She made sure that he was sleeping, and then she quietly got up from the bed and entered the den, locking the door behind her. Tina placed a memory stick of her own into the computer and downloaded information from several files. As the files were being downloaded, she entered an unknown file. This information contained a plan to take over the CIA by going through CPAT. The plan also gave great detail as to when and where the terrorists were, including their names. Tina made a chilling discovery: a terrorist named Hakeem Sur had the ability to impersonate individuals using makeup and his voice. The plan stated that his part would be to take the place of an academy graduate—Brian Keller on his graduation day on becoming an agent in the CIA! He was to find all top secret files and gain access and control over CPAT's STARE DOWN satellite systems. Tina was again in shock. Could this be why Brian hadn't been himself? He actually *wasn't* himself at all! Tina then sent off an e-mail to a very reliable source. Tina quickly moved toward the door leading to the hallway to see if the imposter had woken. She reached for the phone that was on Brian's desk and called the Fitzpatricks. Doreen answered, and Tina frantically confided in Doreen all the evidence she had discovered from the files concerning espionage of the CIA through CPAT. Doreen placed the phone on speaker so that Doug could also hear.

"Brian is really an imposter working for Al-Qaeda, and he has been sent to destroy the CIA and eventually our national security! He has to be stopped!" Tina said frantically.

Doug told Tina to try to act like everything was fine. He and Doreen would inform other agents on the way to the apartment.

Once Tina unlocked the door to the den, she was in for a surprise. Standing in the hallway was Brian. "So, dear, you like to snitch, as you Americans say," Hakeem said in his Arabic voice.

"I-I don't know what you're talking about," Tina said nervously.

Hakeem headed slowly toward Tina as she moved backward, taking glances behind her and trying not to trip over anything. Hakeem observed that Tina had begun transferring the files on his laptop to a memory stick, and this made him furious. "I will make you pay for that, bitch!" he said angrily.

"No, please don't!" Tina pleaded, and then she added, "CIA agents will be swarming this area soon."

"I'm going to cut you into tiny pieces," Hakeem said as he pulled out a knife and held it above his head. Tina quickly kicked Hakeem in the groin. He fell to his knees and clinched his groin as he cried out in pain. Tina walked toward Hakeem and kicked him in the face, knocking him unconscious.

When the Fitzpatricks opened the door of their home to leave, they observed two SUVs arriving in front of their home. Men with ski masks exited the vehicles armed with automatic weapons. Doug and Doreen quickly shut the door and retrieved their AR-15s from the gun safe in their bedroom. The masked men shot at the agents; bullets broke glass and embedded into the walls, furniture, and other objects. Doreen and Doug shot back; there were eight terrorists altogether.

"Move in, move in!" Ra's Ba commanded.

Doreen shot and killed two men. Doug killed two more, shooting them in the head and torso. They continued to exchange gunshots as smoke filled the home and street. The terrorists shot a gas canister inside the home, and then another. Doug told Doreen to stop shooting because he saw that one of the men had an RPG aimed at the house. He took Doreen's hand as they ran. The house exploded as pieces of metal, glass, and wood flew into the air and then fell to the ground. The terrorists shot off another round, destroying anything that was left standing. They looked for survivors and found none. The terrorists quickly left as emergency vehicles, along with CIA agents, arrived on the scene.

The Counter Intelligence Director, Sharon Crow, had received the Fitzpatricks message and relayed it to Victor Price. Price informed Lamb that the Fitzpatricks were murdered by terrorists. Many agents knew the Fitzpatricks; the funeral for the agents would take place the following weekend.

Lamb sat in his chair in his office, and he went through his email and observed a mail entitled "Urgent!" The mail had come from Brian Keller's computer. Lamb first scanned it for viruses, and once cleared, he opened it. The file contained information on the Al-Qaeda and their plans of espionage and ultimate overrun of the government. Lamb also saw that Hakeem Sur, the terrorist impersonator, was a key figure in this operation. Lamb knew that he was the culprit in framing Jennings. He also saw the plans for Hakeem to impersonate Agent Keller, a new graduate who would have access to all files in logistics and satellite communication systems. It would be a perfect plan to strike into the heart of the agency.

Tina was getting ready to leave the apartment after she found the keys to her car. She also made sure that the imposter was confined to the den by pushing a cabinet in front of the door. Tina opened the front door but was met by the Wolf. "I have something to give Agent Lamb. He knows that I'm coming," Tina said nervously.

The Wolf pushed Tina back inside the apartment. Tina tried to kick and punch Wolf. He backed away, but only for a moment. He glared at her in his anger and charged like a raging bull. Tina ran into the living room, however Wolf caught up to her and grabbed her hair, pulling her down to the floor. He slapped her face. Tina got to her feet and hit back, only to be punched in her right cheek. She fell to the floor again. Wolf pulled out his 9 mm as he hovered over her, and then he shot her twice in the chest. She lay on the floor, lifeless.

Wolf could hear Hakeem screaming to be free in the next room. "The bitch! Where is she?" Hakeem said furiously as Wolf freed him from the room.

"Why do you want to know? So she can beat your ass some more, Hakeem?" Wolf replied. Wolf slapped Hakeem on his right cheek and told him, "No more screw-ups, or I'll be the one killing you, not Abdullah." Wolf turned Hakeem's attention to Tina's corpse. "Get rid of her!"

Hakeem nods and continued with his mission. Wolf found the memory sticks in Tina's purse and quickly left.

There was an old, abandoned warehouse approximately thirty miles away, on the outskirts of town. The real Agent Brian Keller had been held captive for the past three days inside a small room. Brian knew that time was running out for him. Once the terrorists got what they wanted, they would have no further use for him. Brian heard a knock at the door, and it opened. Brian was blindfolded, and his hands and feet were tied. Every day the terrorists would untie his hands so that he could eat. Brian felt that it was now time for him to make his move. Once the two terrorists opened the door, they would routinely move the blindfold off his eyes and place it on his forehead. Brain waited patiently as the rope loosens on his wrists, and he began to eat.

"Hurry up, American pig. Eat like the pig you are," one of them said. Brian ate quickly. He noticed that the terrorist closest to him would take his eyes off of Brian to speak to the other. Once he did that a second time, Keller grabbed the man's shirt quickly and pulled him close. Keller then used his knees to flip him over onto his back while at the same time grabbing the man's ARr-15. He shot the terrorist who was guarding the door twice in the chest. The terrorist whom Keller had thrown to the ground reached for his sidearm, however Keller shot him three times in his chest.

Keller untied his feet and searched for vehicle keys in the pockets of the fallen terrorists. He found a set. He looked cautiously through a window to see if there were any terrorists outside. He ran to the vehicle, started it, and took off toward his apartment. Brian tried to call the Fitzpatricks but could not reach them. He used the cell phone that was inside the SUV, but the battery soon died.

When Keller reached home, he noticed the front door of his apartment open. He walked inside and saw Tina's body soaked in blood on the sofa. Brian was in shock. He held her in her arms and cried. He got up, walked toward the fireplace, and removed a piece of the floorboard, revealing his .45. Keller retrieved it and looked around the apartment. Brian discovered that his computer was left on, and files were on his computer that he had never seen before. Some files were written in Arabic. He had to have them translated and decoded. Keller found the name "Hakeem" in the file. Keller discovered that Hakeem was the impersonator, and his plans were to impersonate Jennings and frame him; then the man would impersonate Brian Keller in order to take over CPAT. Abdullah's name was also there. He discovered the plans to destroy the CIA using CPAT. The satellite was the key to sabotaging the CIA and the government. Keller also saw the names of other agents and their hideouts. This would be disastrous if it fell into the wrong hands. Brian sent this information to his supervisor Sharon Crow and to Agent Lamb. He tried to use his cell phone but found it was inoperable. Some information had already been sent out by Hakeem to other terrorists throughout the city. Keller knew that no more information could leak out. Many lives were at stake, and the compromise had already begun.

As Keller continued to work on his computer, a figure sprung out of the closet with a sock in his outstretched arms, wrapping it around Keller's neck. Keller pulled the sock away from his windpipe with his right hand. He grabbed his adversary by the shirt and threw him over his right shoulder onto the computer desk, breaking it. Keller noticed a gun in the man's right hand as he tried to get up from the floor. Keller began a series of kicks to his ribs, stomach, and chest. The man turned to look at Keller, and Keller was shocked. It was as if he were looking into a mirror! This must be Hakeem, the impersonator. Keller punched Hakeem in the face, knocking him unconscious. Keller tied him up and placed the sock that Hakeem had tried to strangle him with in Hakeem's mouth. Keller felt that the terrorists must have studied him and Jennings in order to impersonate them. Both of them had knowledge of satellite communication systems and satellite conversions. He had to get to Lamb and his team to show them this evidence—and to warn them of the terrorist attack.

Keller heard a sound at the back door. He observed a man wearing a ski mask outside the back door. He squatted down and looked in the kitchen. He saw the man trying to pry open the sliding door. Keller could also hear someone trying to open the front door. He went back to the computer; it was not damaged. He quickly sent off an e-mail to Sharon and Lamb, hoping that they would see his 911 call on their phones. He needed assistance now. Keller made sure that he had extra clips with him as he packed his duffle bag. He positioned himself behind the sofa as he placed Tina's body behind it. Keller touched her lifeless body gently as tears ran down his cheeks. He had to focus because many lives were at stake, not just his own.

The first terrorist opened the back door, looked around, and heard the TV on. As soon as he walked into the living room, Keller shot him in the head. The second terrorist broke the glass of the sliding door and entered the apartment. Keller saw him and began to shoot. The first bullet hit the terrorist in the shoulder, and the second hit his chest. He fell backward, hitting the refrigerator and sliding down onto the floor, lifeless. The other two terrorists shot at Keller, who returned fire. Bullets ricocheted everywhere. Keller was pinned down; the terrorists had him in a crossfire. Keller continued to shoot until he emptied one clip. He replaced it with another and continued to return fire.

Keller frantically searched for another clip when he ran out of his second clip. He remembered that he left his duffle bag full of clips inside the den. He couldn't go there now—one of the terrorists took position there. Keller slowly moved toward a broken piece of glass. He would not go down without a fight. He moved toward one of the terrorists, keeping low and holding the piece of broken glass in his right hand. He saw a foot at the end of the sofa and plunged the glass into it. Keller looks up and saw the terrorist scream in pain. The terrorist took aim at Keller, but Keller quickly got up and ran out the back door. The terrorist was angry and in pain as he shot at Keller. Keller ran into the kitchen, heading to the back sliding door. Another gunshot went off, this time hitting Keller in his left side; he collapsed onto the backyard grass.

As he looked up, he noticed several men in suits were relieved to see him alive. "Let's get this man some medical attention!" Agent Sharon

Crow shouted. The agents opened fire on the terrorist who shot Keller. Several bullets hit the man's body, and he fell onto the grass facedown. Keller told his supervisor that there were two more inside, one with whom he'd had a confrontation, and the other was tied up. However, there was no one else in the apartment; the terrorists were able to escape. Keller was taken to the hospital.

Once Lamb finished his defensive tactics training with his unit, he went to his desk to check his e-mail. He saw the 911 message and quickly contacted Sharon Crow for information. She briefed him in on what had occurred.

Volkov arrived at Lamb's office with a suggestion. Lamb invited him into his office. "I just want to say again that Keller would be a good choice to have for now running STARE DOWN. We don't know if Jennings will be back," Volkov stated.

Lamb looked at Volkov and replied, "Volkov I really don't think that you know my agents the way I do! I'm going to find evidence to free Jennings of this setup. He is a good man with good ethics, and he would never commit any crimes. Jennings has knowledge of all computer software that pertains to STARE DOWN. The system is very complex. I do respect Keller, and he has a very good and long resume. However, Keller does not have the knowledge or expertise to be able to take on the schematics involved in such a short period of time."

"You should reconsider—"

"I don't think so," Lamb interrupted.

Just then, Price walked in to speak to Lamb. "Am I interrupting?" Price asked.

"No, I was just leaving," Volkov said, frustrated.

Price needed to go over the compromise of the files with Lamb. As Price spoke, Lamb went into one of his seizures. The room spun around him, and his body stiffened and shook. Price tried to make sure that Lamb didn't fall out of his chair.

Lamb's vision soon cleared. He saw a laboratory with individuals wearing white suits and respirators. He observed large, round cylinders marked "sarin." The sarin was being transferred onto trucks on a loading dock. The warehouse had been made into a laboratory, and the sarin gas was being refined there. The premonition became blurred. Lamb saw the canisters released by someone wearing a respirator. The vision then fades.

Volkov had observed what had happened because the door to Lamb's office had not been closed. "Does Agent Lamb need assistance?" he asked.

"No, he'll be fine. Thanks," Price answered. "You can get some water. That would be helpful."

Volkov quickly went to the water fountain to retrieve water for Lamb. Price took a handkerchief and wiped the sweat from Lamb's forehead.

"I'm all right, sir. I did see some things that are of interest to us," Lamb said. Lamb's secretary walked in holding Tank on a leash; she took Tank for a walk every day. Tank saw that lamb just had a premonition by the look on his face, and the dog placed a paw on Lamb's shoulder as he stood on his hind legs and leaned on the chair. "I'm all right, boy. I'm fine," Lamb said. Tank barked intensely at the door. Lamb wondered why Tank was so angry. Who was there?

"Here is your water, sir," Volkov said.

"Easy, boy! It's all right, Tank. Thanks," Lamb said.

"Your dog doesn't like me?" Volkov asked as Tank continued to bark.

"Could you leave the room for now? I think he's just a little tired," Lamb said. Volkov immediately exited the office and shuts the door. There was another knock at the door, and this time it was Agent Martinez. Tank wagged his tail and went over to her. Martinez bent down and gave him a hug. Price and Lamb knew something was wrong. Tank never barked or acted out aggressively with anyone except enemies, or if someone had a type of weapon or illegal drugs.

Agent Lamb received a phone call from Special Agent Henderson, who informed Lamb that Keller had files on him pertaining to Al-Qaeda and terrorist activity. He also told Lamb to check his e-mail and look for a priority message. Lamb checked his mail and saw the message. It had an attachment containing the secret files. It also had information on a briefcase that had makeup, wigs, masks, and molds. Hakeem was responsible for framing Jennings! He was also trying to gain control of

STARE DOWN. This was the hard evidence that Lamb was looking for, and it would free Jennings of treason. He quickly informed Price, who stood across the room from him. He and Price would bring this evidence to the federal judge, who would then set Jennings free. "Sir, there are many terrorists involved in this operation. I'm wondering how they were able to get into our country without us knowing it," Lamb said.

"Maybe they had some help," Martinez said.

"Good point," Price conceded.

"Hakeem here."

"They did not fall for it. Your disguise has been compromised," Wolf said. "It looks like Plan X must be carried out immediately. Do you understand?"

"I do. This will be done now, as we speak. I need codes for entry, just in case," Hakeem said.

Price informed Lamb and Martinez that they must first take care of the sarin gas. The canisters must already be here, unloaded onto a dock, but where?

Chapter 7

Hostile Takeover

The imposter made his way to the CPAT building of the CIA. He used codes in order to circumvent the security system. Hakeem also used Brian Keller's prints from a synthetic hand to gain access into high-security areas. Hakeem carried an attaché in his left hand and a newspaper covering the synthetic hand in his other. Security observed Hakeem and believed it was Agent Keller walking through security. Hakeem knew that soon agents would inform headquarters that someone was impersonating Agent Keller in order to sabotage the satellite. Hakeem immediately went inside the electrical room and cut all power off in the building. All communications were non-functional at the CPAT building. Security, agents, and maintenance personnel worked frantically, searching for the problem. Hakeem informed his countrymen that the operation was now underway. "Begin the blitz!" Hakeem commanded on his cell phone.

Four terrorists entered the lobby area armed with MAC-10s. "Code red, code red, code red!" cried the front desk security as bullets sprayed the two men. There was no time for them to draw their weapons in defense. As soon as the terrorists secured the front lobby, they informed Hakeem.

Agent Jenny Lee had just completed running a protocol trap and discovered the files that were manipulated by Volkov. He was the mole that Al-Qaeda placed in the CIA—and his code name was Wolf! She relayed this information to Martinez and Lamb.

Lamb tried to contact Volkov, however no one knew his whereabouts. All agents were now looking for him.

Jennings had been working on upgrading the satellite's locating system. He installed devices that would also enhance surveillance abilities, up-close focus enhancement visuals, and audio relays. Jennings accidently dropped a pen onto the floor. When he bent down to pick it up, he observed on the security camera four armed terrorists gaining access to the east entrance corridors. Jennings immediately contacted security. "Team one, come in. Team one, come in. Reeves, Smith, Rollins, where are you?" he cried. He received no answer from them. Rollins was one of the agents killed by the terrorists as they made their way into the east corridor.

Jennings closed the corridors on the second floor beneath him in order to contain their movement. He tried to use the landline but found it inoperable. He then tried his cell phone, and it did not work either. Jennings sealed off the fifth floor, where he was located. Jennings looked at the monitor again and saw Agent Keller running toward the main access entrance of the STARE DOWN office. Keller looked up at the camera and waved. "Jennings, it's me, Keller. Open up! Those terrorists are right behind me. Hurry!" Jennings was hesitant because of Keller's odd behavior. He watched Keller up close. He then moved the camera to zoom in on Keller's hand. Keller always wore a zodiac ring that his fiancée had given him on the anniversary of their first date. It was something very sentimental to him, and he wouldn't go anywhere without it. Jennings became more hesitant about pressing the access button.

"What's wrong?" Hakeem asked.

"I'm not sure. You can never be sure, you know," Jennings said.

"Be sure of what?" Hakeem inquired.

"You can never be sure of whom you are speaking to," Jennings replied.

"It's me, Keller! I escaped from those terrorists. One tried to impersonate me in an attempt to sabotage the CIA. Let me in, buddy.

I can hear them down the hallway. They are right on my ass!" cried Hakeem.

Jennings wanted to be sure and decided to put him to the test. "I can remember back in the day, we had situations like this one in the academy. Remember, Keller?"

"Yes, I do," Hakeem stuttered.

"I remember the time you received almost enough demerits to get you kicked out of the academy. You always wanted me to cover for you," Jennings said.

"Well that's why you were always my friend—my best friend," Hakeem replied.

Jennings knew that Keller was the best student in the academy, finishing first in his class. "You might as well cut the shit now! Exactly who the hell are you, and what have you done with Keller?" Jennings demanded.

Hakeem knew that he was exposed and could no longer fool Jennings. He grew angry and pulled out his 9 mm to shoot at the glass. However, the bullets bounced off because it was bulletproof. Hakeem cursed at Jennings, demanding access.

Jennings continued to try to make contact with other agents and CPAT. Power had yet to be restored. Hakeem looked around the entrance and observed a console to the left of the door. There was a control panel release for the corridor sliding doors. He immediately engaged the button with one touch of his finger and opened the doors, giving access to ten more terrorists. They moved toward the fifth floor, where STARE DOWN satellite control was—and also Jennings.

Hakeem informed his men that they needed to use explosives in order to get to Jennings, because the door had been sealed and secured. His men placed C-4 next to the door and set off the explosive device. The doors collapsed and broke into several pieces.

As the smoke cleared, Jennings observed several terrorists who had joined with Hakeem; they stood next to the outer door, demanding entrance. "Let us in now!" cried Hakeem. Two of the terrorists placed C-4 charges at the bottom of the entrance and quickly moved out of the way. Jennings retrieved his 9 mm from under his desk and made sure it was loaded. He then closed off the satellite control console area.

The terrorists would have access to the room, but not the control area where the satellite was operating.

The C-4 exploded, and the doors blew apart. Hakeem was very angry. "Now you will die for your insolence!" He reached inside his coat and pulled out a .45. He shot at Jennings, who was behind another set of bulletproof glass. Bullets bounced off the glass and ripped into the walls and windows in the room. Two bullets barely missed several of the terrorists in the room. "Damn you, American. Damn you all!" Hakeem screamed. "I will soon kill you myself!" Hakeem observed someone hiding behind a desk. "Look at what I found, Jennings!" Hakeem cried. He pulls out a young lady who was hiding behind a desk; her name was Sandra Flemmings. She had been unable to get out of the building. The doors had been secured, and she saw the code red signal indicating that there was an unauthorized physical security breach inside the building. She had been terrified and hid behind a desk.

"Look, Jennings. I know you Americans care about each other. I will give you two minutes to open that damned glass. You will do it, or you will see me blow this bitch's brains all over the floor. Do you hear me, American pig?" Hakeem said as the rest of the terrorists pointed their weapons at Jennings and waited for his response.

Jennings saw that he had run out of options. Protocol stated, "Under no circumstances are the satellite doors accessible during hostile takeover." Jennings observes Sandra trembling as Hakeem had a choke hold on her, and the other terrorist had a gun pointed to her head. Tears ran down Sandra's cheeks as the terrorist continued to apply pressure to her throat.

"Two minutes are over, American. I guess the bitch dies." Hakeem snickered.

"Wait! All right, all right. You win, you win!" Jennings cried reluctantly.

"Checkmate, American!" Hakeem said.

Jennings pressed the release button to the doors leading to the control console. He dropped his 9 mm and placed his hands on top of his head as one of the terrorists cuffed him and placed him in a chair. "You see? This is what happens when you don't listen the first time, American dog!" Hakeem said. He took the gun away from his comrade and pointed it at Sandra. Hakeem pulled the trigger, releasing a bullet into Sandra's head and shattering her skull. He then pushed her lifeless body to the floor.

"Damn you! Damn you, you asshole!" Jennings shouted.

Hakeem struck Jennings on the right side of his face. "Now I give you pain, American dog. Pain is what I enjoy giving."

Jennings was worked over by two of the terrorists. They punched him in the face, chest, and stomach for five minutes. Once he lost consciousness, they threw water on him. Hakeem retrieved a kit from one of his men that contained makeup removal. He took the kit and sat away from everyone as he applied it.

"Keller, how are you doing?" Lamb asked.

"I'm better. Thanks for asking," Keller said. "What types of terrorist activities are they planning?" Lamb inquired.

Keller told Lamb, "The gas is to be released in various strategic locations in the United States: the White House, the Pentagon, and several federal buildings. The sarin gas is to be shipped from the Middle East to some of the ports here in LA. The gas will be placed in cylinders and then into a large warehouse on the docks, ready to be distributed by semi-trucks. Finally, the CPAT satellite division is to be overrun by hostile takeover. They plan to use the satellite to their own advantage."

Lamb commended Keller on a job well done. He consoled Keller concerning his fiancée and his friends, Agents Doug and Doreen Fitzpatrick. Lamb had been informed of the Fitzpatricks' fate on his way to the hospital. Lamb immediately called Jennings at CPAT division. "Jennings? Jennings, are you there?" Lamb said.

"I'm here, sir. Can I help you with something?" Hakeem said.

"We have intel concerning terrorists planning to overrun CPAT, and they plan to place and release sarin gas at the capital and the surrounding DC area. "Is everyone there all right?"

"Everyone is all right, sir," Hakeem stated.

Lamb was reassured that there was no hostile takeover at this time; the area was secure.

Hakeem, posing as Jennings, informed Lamb that the sarin gas was being held inside two warehouses, one in LA and the other in

San Francisco. Lamb immediately dispatched the Omega team to San Francisco Bay area; the Hades team would go to the warehouse in LA. The Omega team used the CPAT helicopter piloted by Hawk. Agent Martinez, Wombush, Leblanc, Skypack, and Anders were transported to a warehouse in San Francisco.

Before he landed, Hawk saw there were no hostiles on the roof. He landed safely there. The team exited the building. Agent Martinez saw three vents and ordered everyone to take one in order to gain access to the building. The vents led to the center of the auditorium, where they could hear music.

Leblanc observed two men walking down the hallway wearing masks. "Team Leader Two, I have two hostiles in my view moving toward the north entrance doors," Leblanc said.

"Copy," Martinez said. "You copy, Wombush?"

"Copy that, and ready to engage," Wombush stated.

"They are headed your way, Wombush. On my call … Engage!" Martinez commanded. The three agents simultaneously kicked off the vent covers and jumped onto the floor. Agent Wombush jumped onto two hostiles, knocking them to the floor.

Just then, the door swung open, and music rushed into the hallway. A short man with a mask on walked into the hallway and said, "Just what is the meaning of this?" He took off his mask. Agents Martinez and Leblanc looked at him in shock. It was the governor! He was having a masquerade ball for charity, and everyone present was wearing masks. Wombush got up from the floor and assisted the two men wearing masks to their feet, apologizing to them. "This is an outrage, and you will certainly hear more about this!" Barton cried.

"There must be a mistake. We received a call from STARE DOWN satellite that there was terrorist activity going on at this address!" Agent Martinez said, puzzled.

"*You're* the mistake! You're all the mistake!" Barton snapped.

"Barry, what are you saying?" Betty asked.

"I'm saying that after today, I'm going to see to it that Price and his project of folly imbeciles are fired. They're all incompetent and have no clue about protection and safety."

"I think that it is you who has no clue, Barry," Betty replied as she walked back with the guests to the ballroom.

Embarrassed by what had just taken place, the Omega team apologized and took the elevator to the top floor. They walked up a staircase to the roof, where Hawk waited to transport them back to headquarters.

"Team Leader Two to Team Leader One, come in," Martinez said.

"Go ahead, Team Leader Two," Lamb said.

"Sir, it seems that we have made a very big mistake. That building had no hostiles, just civilians. It was a ballroom masquerade party put on by the surprise host of the night."

"Who was that?"

"It was our friend, the governor," Martinez replied.

"Damn. We're going to hear it from Price now." Lamb cringed. He was stunned and wondered just what could have gone wrong. He tried to make contact with the CPAT satellite control center to speak with Jennings, but this time he received no answer.

Robinson, Jenny Lee, Ajeeta, Ajay, and Lamb were now en route to a warehouse where STARE DOWN had located terrorists possessing sarin canisters. The Hades team put on their full body armor and armed themselves with AR-15s. The call was being transmitted from the STARE DOWN satellite computer into Ajeeta's laptop. The message was that terrorists had the sarin canisters and were storing more inside a warehouse near Long Beach Harbor, getting ready for them to be transported. The team took the SUV and arrived there within the hour. Ajeeta turned on STARE DOWN's X-ray visual device so that the team could monitor movement within the building. They observed six men wearing hazmat gear and masks moving the canisters and placing labels on the sides. The team put on their hazmat gear and got ready to engage the hostiles.

They went to the south side of the warehouse, which was in the back. Ajeeta placed a petard explosive device on the door, and the team move to the side as the door exploded. They then stormed the warehouse. "This is the CIA! Place your hands above your heads and don't move!" Lamb commanded. The hostiles had a look of surprise as the agents searched them for weapons.

All of a sudden, a voice came from above. "Cut, cut! I told you guys that you don't enter until you see me give you the signal from outside—and that's in about thirty minutes. We've been over this before! What the hell's wrong with you guys?" the director cried.

Lamb turned to look at his team and then turned to the director as they took off their masks.

"I-I didn't even know that was part of the script," one of the actors said, surprised.

"Wait a minute. You mean to tell me that we were dispatched to movie set?" Lamb said, shocked.

"You mean to tell me that you guys are real feds?" the director asked.

"Yes, we are," Ajeeta said.

"Didn't you guys read the signs concerning our shooting of the movie? They are all over town. We have signs near the building too," another actor said.

"No, we did not see one sign. We apologize. It looks like we've been played again, people," Lamb said. The team left in haste as the actors had a puzzled look.

"Pardon me, sir, but I thought that STARE DOWN was supposed to be reliable," Ajeeta said.

"It's *supposed* to be reliable, Agent Reddy. Why it gave us bad intel twice is beyond me. I have to immediately contact Jennings to see what's going on," Lamb said.

Jennings, now barely conscious, began to talk to the imposter. "You'll never get away with this. Lamb will figure out this whole scheme of yours. Then it will be all over for you!"

Hakeem slapped Jennings hard on the left side of his face. "We've planned this for years. By the time Lamb or any agents figure this out, it will be too late, you American dog."

Lamb is able to make contact with Jennings and informed him that STARE DOWN had given him false Intel twice. "There's something wrong with the satellite systems. We can't afford any more mistakes. You have to correct this problem now!" Lamb said sternly.

"I just don't understand, sir. How could the intel be false? It is practically flawless when it comes to disseminating information. I will get on it right away," Hakeem said with a smirk.

As the Hades team was on its way back to headquarters, Lamb's body began to shake, and his head dropped forward. His eyes rolled back, and he kicked violently. Doc Robinson had Ajeeta pull over to the side of the road. "What's wrong, Doc?" Ajeeta asked.

"Lamb is having a minor seizure. He's going into that trance he's told me about that precedes a premonition," Doc stated.

"Here's a pillow for his head," Ajay said.

Lamb's eyes were now closed. However, in another realm he could observe six C-4 explosives being planted at a power plant in LA. Lamb also observed the CPAT satellite control base being overrun by a group of terrorists along, and Jennings was being interrogated and tortured. Lamb saw terrorists on TV demanding the release of all terrorist prisoners worldwide, not just in the United States. Lamb stopped shaking and slowly came to full consciousness.

"Are you all right, sir?" Doc asked.

Lamb nodded and informed them that the satellite systems base had been over run and that Jennings had been taken hostage. The team planned to take action.

Jennings was in pain from the constant punches to his face from Hakeem. His vision was at first blurred, and then it slowly came to focus. He observed three terrorists guarding the door, and Hakeem was at the satellite's control panel. "Emir, come here. I need your expertise," Hakeem said.

"What is it, Hakeem?"

"Do you think that I should send them further out, to give us more time?"

"Yes, of course you should. This will give us more time to distribute the canisters. By the time they figure out where they are, it will be too late!" Emir said.

Hakeem smiled as he said into the microphone, "Jennings to Hades team, come in."

"This is Hades team. Go ahead," Lamb said.

"We have a code red. Repeat, we have a code red. Ambassadors from China and Ecuador are in need of escort. They have been threatened by Al-Qaeda and received more death threats five minutes ago. You are all needed at the Chinese embassy now," Hakeem said.

"We copy," Lamb said.

"This is K-Hawk, Copter One. Omega team copy!"

Lamb then switched the frequency to one-on-one. "This is Team Leader One. Do not engage. Repeat, do not engage!" Martinez turned to K-Hawk with a surprised look. "I believe that we have been compromised and overrun at CPAT. That person you have been speaking to is not the Jennings we know. It is Hakeem, the impersonator."

"Are you positive, sir?" Martinez asked.

"I'll prove it right this moment," Lamb said. "Ajeeta, place this call on speaker." He made a call.

"Hello, this is Agent Matthews, escort detail. Can I help you?"

"Agent Matthews, this is Agent Lamb. Those two ambassadors whom you are providing protection today—were they threatened by Al-Qaeda today?"

"No, sir, not at all. There were no threats. As a matter of fact, they left for their countries thirty minutes ago. Is there something wrong, sir?" Matthews asked.

"Yes, and we're handling it right now. Good job, Matthews. Lamb out."

"What now?" Doc asked.

Copter Two now joined Copter One in the air. "Henderson here."

"Standby, Copter Two," Hawk said.

Lamb remembered seeing a warehouse in his premonition. The warehouse was in a familiar part of town. The side of the warehouse had the word "Emergence" on the side of it. Lamb sent a text to Martinez and informed her of them being listened to by STARE DOWN's audio and visual tracking systems. They immediately switched to their radios.

"What do you think you will gain from all of this?" Jennings asked Hakeem.

"We will gain prestige and honor. We need to have all of our fellow countrymen released. Our main goal is to cripple the United States so that you can no longer interfere in foreign affairs or harm anyone," Hakeem stated.

"What kind of harm? What the hell are you talking about?" Jennings asked.

"I'm speaking about the innocent lives that have been lost due to your bombings and countless attacks. Innocent people have died because of your ignorance and stupidity. Our great leader, Abdullah, lost his family because of attacks from you Americans. We have a plan to do away with many of your leaders, and with other leaders of other countries who have meddled in our affairs. We will succeed. Abdullah wants the governor put to death because he murdered his son, Heiman."

"That's because Heiman was a murderer himself!" Jennings snapped.

Hakeem struck the captured man again. "One more stupid word from you, American pig, and you will die. We have no more need for you. I know this satellite system. I'm just waiting for the word from Abdullah to execute you," Hakeem said laughing. Jennings's head slowly bowed forward as he fell unconscious. Hakeem continued to try to locate where CPAT was in order to keep them away from the satellite base.

"Copter One to Team Leader One, come in, over," Hawk said.

"Go ahead, Hawk," Lamb said.

"Intelligence just informed me that they have the location of the meeting place: the entire operation is there. The address is 7166 Eagle Tower Road. Go north toward the end of town. Should we engage, sir?"

"Go and engage now, Copters One and Two," Lamb commanded.

The helicopters headed north toward the warehouse, where there had been reports from intelligence concerning terrorists planning attacks throughout the United States.

Ajeeta also headed north and engaged the GIS map system. "Copters One and Two, ignore all calls coming from the satellite base—they are hostile. Repeat, they are hostile," Lamb commanded. Hawk and Henderson acknowledged as they flew toward their destination. The intelligence team was the first to arrive and immediately surround the warehouse. The ware house was located at the end of the street, and it was isolated and near a field. The STARE DOWN satellite systems monitored the agents' every move.

"Zafin, the agents have arrived. You know what to do," Hakeem said.

"Yes, my captain. We are ready," Zafin answered. The terrorists positioned themselves outside and made a perimeter flanking the agents.

Agent Lamb to Agent Crow, come in."

"This is Crow. Go ahead, Lamb."

"Sharon, stay where you are until we get there. Copters One and Two will be there in five minutes. Wait for them. I have a bad feeling about this one."

"Copy that, Agent Lamb. Standing by," Crow responded.

The terrorists had two snipers lying in the field watching the agents with their scopes. Agents Olsen and Smith covered the rear door while Agents Wallace, Johnson, and Worthington covered the front door. The agents were using AR-15s.

Olsen began to get restless. "What's taking CPAT so damn long to get here? By the time they get here, it will probably be too late."

"We have orders to sit tight and wait, and that's what we have to do!" Smith said sternly. "Orders, hell! I wish I was running this outfit. I would have had all of these terrorists annihilated by now," Olsen growled.

"Tell me something, Olsen. How in the world did you ever pass the psychological testing?" Smith asked.

Olsen ignored her comment and contemplated his move toward the front door. "Cover me, Smith. I'm moving in now!" Olsen said as visions of promotions and medals dashed through his mind.

"Get back here now!" She got on her radio. "Agent Smith to Crow, come in."

"Go ahead, Smith."

"Ma'am, it's Olsen. He is attempting a code red now, and I tried to make him stand down," Smith said.

"Agent Olsen, this is Sharon Crow, your supervisor. You are ordered to stand down now!"

"I can't hear you, ma'am. You're breaking up," Olsen lied as he turned his radio off.

Smith ran up behind Olsen to try to stop him. Olsen and Smith had gone through the academy together, and developed a bond. She had no idea that their relationship would be put to the test at this level.

Olsen ran to the back door and stepped back to kick the door. As his foot made contact to the door, it exploded, sending Olsen's body thirty feet into the air and into the nearby field. Smith was also thrown to the ground as she tried to stop Olsen.

"What's going on? Smith, Olsen, come in. Come in!" Crow cried. Just then, the snipers received orders by Hakeem to begin taking out the agents.

Sharon Crow was hit twice in the shoulder. The other two agents were hit in the neck and head. Copter One arrived on the scene. "Copter One to Agent Lamb."

"Go ahead, Hawk," Lamb said.

"There has been active shooting in the field and an explosion at the abandoned home. I can see that our agents are down. Only Agent Crow is moving."

"Search for hostiles and take out them out," Lamb commanded.

"Agents Anders and Leblanc, you are up!" Martinez said.

Leblanc readied his sniper M-107 semi-automatic and peered through his scope, searching for hostiles. He at once observed movement in the field and fired three shots where the tall grass was moving. Leblanc hit the hostile in the arm and leg. The hostile tried desperately to crawl away.

"Take him out," Martinez said. Leblanc aimed and pulled the trigger. The hostile went down as the bullet made contact with his head.

"Anders, I see a hostile behind the SUV. Hawk, can you get us around that vehicle?" Martinez asked.

Hawk nodded and maneuvered the helicopter to the rear of the SUV. The terrorist shot at the agents, hitting the underside of the helicopter. Anders took aim and misses the terrorist, however the bullet hit the gas tank. The SUV exploded and instantly killed the terrorist. Agent Leblanc was surprised.

"Team Leader One to Team Leader Two, come in."

"Go ahead, Team Leader One," Martinez said.

"What's your status?" Lamb asked.

"Right now we are searching for more hostiles in the area. We've already taken out two, but we have five casualties of our own," Martinez said.

"How did that happen?"

"I don't quite know, sir. It seems that one of the counter intelligence agents jumped the gun and disobeyed orders from Agent Crow to stand down."

"Damn it! Why can't people just follow orders? Is Agent Crow all right?" Lamb asked.

"She is, and we have called for emergency vehicles to stand by while we secure the area," Martinez replied.

"Hades team will be there in ten minutes."

"Copy that."

Agent Martinez was ordered to engage at ground level. Hawk began to land in the field fifty yards away from the house. Before Hawk landed, he observed a terrorist holding two grenades in both of his hands, along with a string of grenades wrapped around his entire body. "Check out the hostile with the grenades, Team Leader Two," he said.

"I see him, Hawk. Take him out now!" Martinez commanded. Hawk engaged the automatic machine guns on the right side of the helicopter. He sprayed the terrorist from head to toe with bullets, and the man's body was blown to pieces. Hawk set copter one down, and the agents exited quickly and cautiously. The agents came to the aid of Sharon Crow and administered first aid until the paramedics arrived. Wombush stayed with her. The agents turned their attention to the house. They readied their M-9s and slowly entered the house. Martinez entered the house first, and Leblanc followed closely behind.

The explosion destroyed the hallway, and part of the ceiling hung down. Once they reached the end of the hallway, Martinez observed a table with a map on it. She motioned Leblanc over to see her discovery. They were shocked to see the plans the terrorists had for US citizens and the government. The plans revealed the times, places, events, and names of individuals involved. Leblanc searched the next room. As he walked into the room, he found a large amount of munitions along with several handguns and MAC-10s. There was a large map of California and one of the United States. There were also several names of leaders from different parts of the world, like a hit list.

Martinez searched the fallen terrorists and found maps and pictures of their families. Anders, Wombush, and Leblanc joined her in searching the bodies. Agent Martinez found something very vital to their operations: she discovered the location of the sarin gas canisters on paper. She immediately contacted Lamb and informed him of their discovery. "The canisters are in located in a factory. The terrorists have turned it into a laboratory."

"Good job, Agent Martinez," Lamb said.

"Oh and one more thing."

"What's that?" Lamb inquired.

"The warehouse is titled 'Emergence in Production.'"

"Don't wait for us, Martinez—get going now," Lamb ordered.

"Sir, the location is, pier 19." Agent Martinez stated.

"We're on our way." The SUV turned south to its new destination, the piers. Omega team was also en route.

Hakeem continued trying to communicate with CPAT. Just then, a transmission came over the radio: it was Abdullah. "What is your status, Hakeem?"

"Sir, I'm trying to communicate with CPAT."

"I believe that by now Lamb has found out you are not Keller. You have been compromised. You should locate and notify our fellow countrymen in their designated areas. Give word to destroy all American agents now. All of them! Do you hear?" Abdullah commanded.

"Yes, my leader. I hear and obey you," Hakeem responded.

Omega team arrived at pier nineteen. Agent Martinez instructed Anders, Leblanc, Skypack, and Wombush to surround the building. Martinez also called for more agents as backup in order to cut off anyone trying to escape.

Fahd observed the Omega team exiting Copter One on the pier and nearing the warehouse perimeter. "They're here," he said.

"We're ready for those American fools," Adnan said.

Martinez and Wombush entered the warehouse through an open window. Martinez entered the east side, and Wombush entered the west side. As they moved cautiously inside the warehouse, they were immediately confronted by terrorists. Anders and Leblanc were on the north end and searched for an entrance but could not find one. The windows were five feet out of reach.

"Team Leader Two to Leblanc. We are taking on hostile fire. Withdraw—I repeat, withdraw now!" Martinez commanded.

Anders and Leblanc noticed two oak trees near the building, and they quickly ran toward them. Martinez fired several rounds as she took cover behind crates. Wombush was also using crates as cover, and he fired off round after round at the hostiles. The terrorists were well protected by the metal barriers set up in front of them. Each side exchanged gunfire. Martinez informed Lamb that they had come across hostile fire and had been set up.

Lamb realized that STARE DOWN was being used against them, and he had Doc pull apart the tracking device. He placed the vehicle into stealth mode by hitting a button to initiate the process so that the satellite could not track them. The SUV went off the satellite's scanner. The stealth mode could last up to one hour. Lamb hoped that it would be sufficient time to take care of what had to be done.

Martinez and Wombush ran out of ammunition. The terrorists realized this and moved in slowly. The agents surrendered. The terrorists hit them with their fists to their faces and then kicked them in their backs. "Enough!" Fahd said. "Tie them up."

"Abdullah's order was to kill all of the Americans, Fahd," Adnan said.

Fahd raises his .45 to Martinez's head and cocked the hammer. A shot went off and hit Fahd in the neck, ripping through his jugular vein. He fell to the floor. Agent Leblanc fired a shot from the tree next to the warehouse, and Anders also got off a shot. The other terrorists immediately dropped to the floor. Adnan informed the terrorists where

Anders and Leblanc were located and sent out two men with a grenade launcher.

Anders and Leblanc exchanged fire with the terrorists, but this was only a diversion. The terrorist with the grenade launcher moved toward a different window to Leblanc's far right, where his peripheral vision was nonexistent. The terrorist took careful aim at Leblanc and squeezed the trigger. Leblanc noticed a glare to his right and instinctively jumped out of the tree; the tree, which exploded. Wooden projectiles flew everywhere. Leblanc and Anders were hit on their heads by pieces of the flying debris, and they fell to the ground, unconscious.

The satellite camera zoomed in on a close-up both agents. Leblanc was lying on his back; his face was covered in blood from the impact of the debris. Anders was lying face down and was not moving. The terrorists begin to interrogate Agents Martinez and Wombush. They beat the agents into unconsciousness, revived them, and then beat them again.

Hades team arrived approximately fifty yards away. The SUV was still in stealth mode. Doc noticed Anders and Leblanc on the ground and quickly drove the vehicle next to them. Doc and Lamb exited the vehicle to assist Anders and Leblanc. Doc administered first aid as Lamb assisted. They then carried the downed agents into the SUV.

"Ajeeta, I need you and Doc to hold this perimeter unless you need to get them to the hospital right away," Lamb said.

"They'll be all right, sir," Doc said.

Lamb ran toward the warehouse. He reverted to his ninja training with Grandmaster Lin Po, who had taught him to make his body blend into the darkness. The terrorists' attention was not on them, and so Martinez ordered Wombush to escape, but he refuses to leave her. He was limited to his power of change, and the timing was not right for him to do so.

Lamb entered the building through the east window. The terrorists had no idea that he had breached the perimeter; there were no guards on post. Lamb observed hundreds of canisters being placed inside large crates. He used the crates for cover as he moved from one to the other cautiously without being detected. Lamb swiftly moved behind a group terrorists, executing the ninja death hold on three of them.

He continued to move toward a door, where he could hear a hostile interrogating someone.

Lamb heard a familiar voice say, "I don't know. I really don't know. Please stop."

"Tell us where they are going next, agent! I will give you just one more chance," Fahd said angrily. He slapped Martinez twice on her right cheek. Lamb observed that Wombush had been knocked unconsciousness, so he got close behind the door, chambered his right leg, and executed a front kick targeted at the middle of the door. The door collapsed into two pieces. The two terrorists reached for their weapons. Lamb quickly grabbed one of the terrorists and used him as a shield. The second terrorist shot his counterpart and looked on in shock. "Oh, shit! No!"

Lamb took the MAC-10 out of the dead terrorist's hand and quickly fired a round into the shocked hostile, killing him instantly. Lamb untied Martinez and then Wombush. Lamb revived Wombush by shaking him. "You're going to be all right," Lamb whispered.

"Let's get the hell out of here," Martinez said.

"You'll never get out of here alive. You are surrounded!" Fahd yelled.

Lamb turned the metal table over on its side to use it as cover. Several more terrorists joined Fahd. Lamb and Martinez used the dead terrorists' weapons, and both sides exchanged fire. They were close to the windows, and Martinez saw her chance. She jumped out of the window as Lamb covered for her. Bullets barely missed her as she escaped.

"Will you be all right, sir?" Wombush asked.

"I will. Now get going. I'll be right behind you," Lamb ordered.

Wombush pulled himself up and through the window, and he jumped down. Lamb fired off his last set of rounds and tried to pull himself up toward the windows, however he took one bullet to the shoulder and one to the leg. Weakened, Lamb let go of the ledge of the window pane. He fell to the floor and was immediately grabbed by the terrorists. He was beaten and interrogated.

Many Federal agents closed in on the warehouse; Hakeem saw this and began to program STARE DOWN's defensive missile mechanisms to target the agents. STARE DOWN was now programmed in defensive mode; if there was any type of hostile action toward the warehouse, STARE DOWN would take defensive action against the attackers. The agents were warned by Hakeem to stay back, or they would all perish.

"Now hear this! Come out with your hands up now. There will be no negotiating with you, Hakeem," Price said over a bullhorn. The agents began to move in. Just then, a missile was deployed out of the satellite. The agents were surrounding the warehouse, and the bay area was closed off. Price warned them and to give up their weapons.

"*You* surrender, you American dogs!" Hakeem countered. Just then, the agents observed what looked like a ball of fire falling out of the sky, approaching them. "Pull back, everyone! Pull back!" Price cried, but it was too late. The missile hit eight federal SUVs, destroying all vehicles. The agents screamed in pain and agony as some were thrown out of their vehicles; others were killed instantly on impact.

Lamb revived in time to see this horrifying event. His vision was partly blurred, and his shoulder and leg were numb. The terrorists continued to interrogate him, asking questions concerning CIA secrets and future missions against Al-Qaeda. When Lamb didn't answer, they hit him on both sides of his face. The terrorists grew tired of Lamb's endurance of pain. Lamb laughed at them because of their frustration. "You! I should have known it was you when Tank got upset," Lamb said.

"Look, you do not care about your own life. But I know someone whose life you damn well care about," Volkov said. "Get Hakeem. Have him pull up "1577 Walnut Grove" for me. I have to take care of something. I'll be right back."

Lamb's smile was now completely gone. He focused on what he was seeing on the laptop screen. He saw the satellite pull up his ex-wife's house. Her vehicle was not there in the driveway, but there was a different one: it belonged to Barbara Nelson, a young girl in her early teens who was Arianna's babysitter. The satellite's visual X-ray monitoring system was now activated, targeting the home. Lamb observed Arianna watching television with her friend, Shelly Ortiz. "Ah, now I see that we have your undivided attention. You will have to pay for your insolence. Your defiance will be short lived, Lamb," Volkov said as he returned to the room.

"Go to hell, you traitor!" Lamb said as he was punched in the face by Fahd.

"This is what we will do to the rest of you American dogs," Fahd stated. "Please don't! Not her. Kill me, but don't kill my daughter. She's done nothing to you and your cause!" Lamb pleaded. He had to find a way to save his daughter.

"It's too late to plead for mercy. You had your chance. Now watch as your family is sought out, tortured, and killed right before your very eyes. There is absolutely nothing you can do about it! This is better than killing you." Volkov sneered. The satellite camera viewed a vehicle with two terrorists en route, two blocks away from Susan's house.

Lamb knew what he must do. He relaxed his mind and body and descended into a transcendental state. Lamb's eyes fluttered, and his body shook violently. The terrorists believed that he was having a seizure. Lamb wanted them to believe this. Lamb turned his head to its side, and his eyes remained open.

"What the hell is going on?" Fahd cried. Fahd and his men were shocked as they stood there and stare.

"Arianna, Arianna, Arianna," Lamb's thoughts called out to his daughter.

"Daddy?"

"Hi, baby! How's my sweetheart, my angel doing?"

"I'm fine, Daddy! Where are you?"

"I'm at work and very busy right now, angel. What are you doing?"

"Barbara is babysitting me, and Shelly is visiting. We're all watching TV."

"Good, angel. That's very good. I want you to listen very carefully. I want you to take Barbara and Shelly into the safe room that I built for you and Mommy. Go to where the den is and get the remote from the top drawer. Press the enter button and part of the wall will open for you. When you go inside, shut the passage door behind you. I have some new dolls just for you sweetheart, but go right now."

"Okay, Daddy, I'll take them with me. Oh, and Daddy?"

"Yes, angel?"

"Am I going to see you soon?"

"Yes, of course you will. I promise. I love you, angel."

"I love you too, Daddy. Bye-bye."

Arianna informed her friend Shelly and her babysitter that she would like to show them something. She took them to the safe room that Lamb had made for Arianna and her mother five years ago. Arianna uses a remote that opens a passage way that is part of the wall near the den. Once inside, Arianna closed the door. The girls were so surprised and excited to see so many dolls that they sat down to play with them. Barbara looked around the room and observed several cases of canned food, a radio, two flashlights, twelve jugs of water, a television, and a cell phone. Barbara turned on the TV and watched her soaps, unaware of what was about to take place inside the home. The room was soundproof; individuals outside of the room could not hear what was going on inside. Cameras were outside, stationed on the roof, but they were not on the safe room monitors at this time. The door of the safe room could only be opened by Lamb or Susan.

Volkov called Fahd on his cell phone. "What's going on now?"

"I believe Lamb has had a seizure," Fahd said.

"You fool! That's no seizure. He must be having another premonition. Wake his ass up—now," Volkov commanded.

Fahd's men arrived at the house. They quickly moved inside by kicking open the door. They discover the TV was still on and dirty dishes were on the kitchen table, but there was no sign of the girls. They continued to search through the house and could not locate anyone. Volkov was upset and informed them not to come back without the girls. Fahd's men finally gave up after searching through the house for almost twenty minutes. Volkov believed that they were warned by someone, or they have a place somewhere inside the house that they could hide. He instructed the men to burn down the house and continue their search in the neighborhood.

Fahd's men were about to set the place on fire when a lookout radioed that the mother was returning to the house, and there were three other vehicles following behind her. One was a police unit, who was a neighbor two homes down the street. The terrorists quickly exited the house.

Wolf received a call on his cell phone. "What is it?"

"The men could not locate the girls, and Lamb is still out. Should we kill him now?" Fahd asked.

"Yes, kill him. It is a good time to do so. I want you to leave his body in the river so that the fish and rats will devour it. When you have completed this task, meet me at CPAT."

Fahd thought that he had heard a noise coming for the outside hallway. He then motioned for two men to investigate. As they walked outside the door, he shut and locked it immediately. Shooting began in the hallway. Fahd became nervous as he heard his men screaming. Fahd walked toward the door to make sure it was secure, but all of a sudden the door was kicked in, hitting Fahd in the forehead and knocking him unconsciousness.

Lamb slowly regained consciousness. As his eyes focused, he saw two familiar agents whom he thought were long gone: Doug and Doreen Fitzpatrick!

They were both pointing their weapons at Fahd, who by now had regained consciousness. Fahd quickly pulled out another weapon that was in his pants. They demanded that he surrender now. "Never, you American dogs. I will never surrender!" He pointed his weapon at the Fitzpatricks. They quickly opened fire on Fahd. He did not move after that. Doreen checked the man's vitals: Fahd was dead.

Lamb was grateful for the Fitzpatricks' timely rescue. The Fitzpatricks had called for backup and showed up at the warehouse with several other agents. Lamb asked them how they had survived the explosion in their home. They explain to Lamb that when the terrorists bombed their home, they quickly went into their basement, where there was an old bomb shelter designed by the people who had lived there before them. The Fitzpatricks survived for three weeks underground because they had plenty of food and water. They had to stay off of radar to make the terrorists believe that they were killed in the explosion. Doug informed Lamb that his team was all right. They also were in the thick of things and had called for backup.

Agent Robinson arrived along with the rest of the unit. Doc gave first aid to Lamb. "It's good to see you again, sir," Doc said. Lamb was going to be transported to the hospital, however he refused to go.

Agent Martinez arrived with Tank. Tank ran over to Lamb and licked him. Lamb immediately embraced him. "I'm all right, boy!" Lamb said as Tank wagged his tail and barked. Tank then ran out of the room and barked more. "I think he wants us to follow him," Lamb said. The agents followed Tank as he ran through the hallway to the outside where the docks were. Tank tapped his paw on a crate. The agents opened the crate.

"These are the sarin gas canisters!" Leblanc cried.

Ajeeta immediately radios the hazmat team to contain the gas canisters.

Tank continued to bark, and the agents noticed that there was some type of a device wired up to the canisters. The wiring was connected to one canister after another. The agents walked along the pier as they observed the canisters. The count came to twenty-two canisters rigged together.

"Abdullah wanted to make sure that no one would tamper with these canisters," Lamb noted.

Martinez immediately radioed the bomb squad.

The hazmat team arrived first and planned a protocol for transporting the canisters. The bomb squad agents also arrived and began to disarm the explosives wired to the canisters.

Just then, Numair held up an activator in his right hand. "Get back, you American dogs! Back the hell up!"

"We don't want this to happen, Numair. I want you to go home to your children. I know you want to see your family and not have to deal with this anymore," Lamb pleaded.

"Shut the hell up! You don't know what I want. One more move, and I will blow you all to hell! Is that understood?" Numair cried.

Lamb and his team slowly walked backward. Lamb signaled the hazmat, bomb squad, and others to stand down and move away.

"This device will set off all of the canisters with just one push of my thumb," Numair said.

"What do you want us to do?" Lamb asked.

"I want you to all die!" Numair answered.

"Tank!" Lamb said. Tank turned to look at Lamb with his ears pointing forward. "Go flank, boy. Flank, Flank!"

Tank moved slowly off to the side, undetected by the terrorist. He crawled, making his way ever closer to the terrorist.

Numair's cell phone rang. "Numair, are the canisters ready to be transported?" Volkov asked.

"No, Volkov, We ran into a situation with these American dogs," Numair said, frustrated.

"Situation? The only situation you have now is to do what is to be done. The other canisters will make their destination."

"I understand, Volkov. It was a pleasure serving with you," Numair said.

Lamb knew what was coming next. The terrorist held up the device in his right hand and stated, "Death to America. Long live Al-Qaeda!"

At that moment, Tank jumped up and clamped down hard on Numair's arm with his teeth. Tank's bite broke Numair's skin, causing him to drop the activator to the ground. "You'll pay for this!" Numair cried.

Martinez quickly jumped on to the platform of the dock. As Numair stood up, Martinez delivered a roundhouse to the right side of his head, knocking him to the ground unconscious. The agents placed Numair in handcuffs and took him in for interrogation. The hazmat team was given the affirmative to move in and contain the canisters. The bomb squad worked to defuse the explosives attached to the canisters, and they secured the area.

There were two terrorists who fled the area once the agents arrived. Abdullah received word concerning the canisters. He was furious and threw furniture around in the room. He also broke mirrors and turned over chairs and tables. "Is there *anyone* in this room who is competent enough to carry out my orders?" Abdullah screamed as his men looked on in fear.

Just then, his cell phone rang. "This had better be important—something that can save your life, Hakeem," Abdullah said.

"It is, sir! I can activate the laser that will destroy the governor's mansion and his entire family along with it. The victory will belong to you, sir, and no one can do anything about it. For you and the cause!" Hakeem said.

"For the cause. Excellent, very good," Abdullah echoed in agreement.

Lamb tried to contact CPAT in order to locate agents in the building. He received no answer. Lamb began to think the worst concerning Jennings; he may have been already killed.

Doc gave Lamb some pain medication. He observed that the bandages he placed on Lamb earlier had blood seeping through them. He continued to advise Lamb to go to the hospital.

"That's why you're here doc!" Lamb said. He then contacted the CIA building and gave orders that no one was to respond to any radio contact coming from CPAT until further notice.

Price had already been informed, however he was also called on a false report of canisters inside a small airport hangar. Lamb notified Copter Two to take him back to CPAT with his team. Lamb gathered both units together. "We don't have much time now. Those remaining canisters must be intercepted. Omega team will take Copter Two with K-Hawk. Hades team will remain here and try to take back CPAT. You've got to get going now," Lamb commanded.

"We're ready, sir," Martinez answered. Omega team was now picked up by K-Hawk in Copter Two, and they headed to the canisters on Highway Ten.

Chapter 8

CPAT's Counterattack

Abdullah walked across the room as he held the plans for destruction in his right hand. Then he rolled them up and hit his left hand with them. He swore and yelled at his remaining captains.

"We are not here to fail. Failure is not an option. I will have the remaining heads on a platter for those who now fail!" Abdullah said angrily. His remaining captains listened in silence, slowly lowering their eyes to the floor as if the law itself walked by each of them.

"Sir," Jabbar said.

"What is it? And it'd better be good!" cried Abdullah.

"We still have the canisters on the way to the Pentagon, and Hakeem still has full control of the satellite. We also have agents in our control as long as we have the satellite, sir," Jabbar offered nervously.

Abdullah was very pensive and concerned. He knew CPAT was counteracting their every move. It was a matter of time before their entire plan failed.

Lamb called a briefing for Hades team. They had to take back the satellite building soon, before the terrorists could cause any more damage. "Team, keep me informed of your status regarding the canisters," Lamb said.

"Roger," Martinez replied.

Wolf informed the imposter that it was time for them to set the destruction sequence on the satellite and target it at the Pentagon. When Abdullah overheard Wolf on the radio, he tried to change the orders for a car to target the governor's mansion instead. "Abdullah, you must not let your emotions get the best of you, brother. You must remain focused," Maali explained. "We will get the governor later, but not now. We have to finish our real mission: destroying the American leaders. Then victory will be ours."

Abdullah turned his head slowly toward his brother and then nodded in agreement.

The terrorist who was captured was interrogated by Agents Doug and Doreen Fitzpatrick. They questioned the terrorist and were able to get the information they needed by using truth serum. The serum worked slowly but ended with positive results. The terrorist gave the exact route where the sarin canisters would be going to the Capitol and the Pentagon.

The semi-trucks separated and continued toward their destinations. Copter One arrived at the federal building's landing field at 1300 hours to meet the rest of the Omega team. Lamb was informed of the route and directed them to carry on. Hades team was now minutes away from the CPAT satellite building, ready to carry out plans to retake the building. Martinez briefed her team concerning the Sarin gas and how they were going to use their tactics in order to stop them. The Omega team got back into the helicopters, leaving for Route Ten to intercept the semi-trucks.

Jennings continued to loosen the ropes on his feet. The pin he was using slipped out of his fingers and fell onto the table nearby.

"I can't believe it, Wolf. We have not received the orders to destroy all of the leaders by using the satellite system," Hakeem bellowed.

"That time will come. Stop being overly anxious," Wolf said.

Jennings couldn't believe it. "Wolf? *You're* the Wolf!" Jennings exclaimed.

"Yes, I am the Wolf—the big, bad Wolf!" He then punched Jennings in the jaw, knocking him unconscious.

As the helicopters sped toward the semi-trucks a half hour away, the team conversed with each other. Leblanc spoke of the recent incidents that occurred with CPAT and Agent Keller. Agent Wombush pulled team leader Martinez aside and spoke with her in private. "Ma'am, I've told you almost everything about my personal life, and my secrets. I'd like to hear about yours now," Wombush said as he checks his weapon.

"My story? What do you mean?" Martinez asked with a puzzled look.

"Everyone has a story, ma'am. I'm sure you have one too."

Martinez glanced down for moment, took a breath, and turned to Wombush. "I guess I do have one," she said. Agent Wombush looked at her and listened attentively as she spoke. "I come from a large family. I have four brothers and three younger sisters; I am in the middle. We were poor. My father and mother both worked hard. We lived on a farm, and I hated the work but loved the animals. I didn't date until my senior year of high school, when I met Jim Whitfield. Jim was my first real crush. After high school, we got married and did everything together. All of our interests were the same. We joined the army together too! "There was one problem, though—a big problem. Jim drank and didn't know when to stop. At times he would resort to violence, hitting me. He made sure that I had long sleeves on at the time. However, my peers could see the abuse in my face. They knew that I was not happy with my life.

"I was working MP detail one evening when we received a call from the bar on base. Once I arrived, I saw my husband beating up another sergeant. We had to throw Jim in the brig. Jim was released after a week and was reprimanded for his actions. I became repulsed by his behavior and didn't want him to touch me or come near me. When I was cleaning the apartment, I found several photos of women, two of whom were close friends with Jim. The photos were shot without me being present, and the women were in bikinis and negligee. I told Jim I'd discovered the photos, and we argued. We both decided to separate.

"My captain, McIntyre, called me into her office one day to speak to me in private. She stated that someone was stealing top-secret documents from our high-security filing room. McIntyre wanted me to be the lead investigator on this case. The cameras were turned off at the time the documents were missing. I ordered a sting operation for the security filing room from 2000 hours to 0600 hours, when no one was on duty. We stationed ourselves in specific strategic areas inside and around the building so that we would have clear visual of possible theft. Nothing occurred the first three days. However, on Thursday evening we observed someone using an access card to enter the building. Our cameras showed him getting access for someone else: two individuals wearing black outfits, their heads covered with a black ski mask. We continued to be patient as we observed them making their way to the room where the documents were located. The camera showed them gaining access to another door and led them to the file cabinets. They placed the documents inside an attaché and began to exit the building. I told my team to wait for my signal; I felt that we should wait and see where or who they would lead us to.

"The two individuals took off in separate vehicles. I ordered my team to follow the other vehicle while my corporal and I followed the one who had the documents. We followed the vehicle to the outskirts of town, before it slowed down. We turned and parked behind some bushes off a side road. We then observed another vehicle pull up next to the one we were pursuing. The individuals took off their ski masks. I was in shock as I looked through my infrared binoculars. It was my husband and one of the girls from the photos! I recognized her to be one of the girls who worked in the security document room. I used my bullhorn and told them to drop their weapons. I noticed that the other two individuals were Middle Eastern.

"The two Middle Eastern men immediately shot at us. My partner and I returned fire as Jim and his girlfriend took cover behind his vehicle. My partner and I were able to fire off two shots that hit one of the Middle Eastern men in the chest. I was able to shoot the second one in the leg and shoulder; he threw his weapon to the ground and surrendered. Jim and the girl shot at us. I told him it was over. He said that they offered him a lot for the documents—money that would last them a lifetime. He asked me to be with him and forget about everything else. He said that he still loved me and would take me back. His girlfriend took a shot at me, and Corporal Stone shot her in the neck and chest. Jim said that he was going to get rid of her anyway. Jim continued to try to convince me to leave with him. As I began to move from cover, Corporal Stone covered me with his handgun. I glanced at him and continued to walk toward Jim. Jim placed his gun down on the hood of the vehicle. He then said, 'That's it, baby. It will be like old times together.'

"I saw him reach inside behind his pants, and I fired my weapon immediately. I hit Jim twice in the chest. He fell to the ground on his knees, then face forward to the ground. 'I didn't enjoy the old times we had, Jim, and you of all people should know that,' I said.

"We recovered the documents and were given commendations. It was a bittersweet feeling for a mission accomplished. I had to let go of someone I had loved at one time. Believe it or not, it was not easy even if he was a prick."

Wombush said, "That was a good and amazing story. I'm sorry for your loss. I just want you to know that I have the deepest respect for you, especially as our team leader."

Terri glanced at Adam as tears rolled down her cheeks. She gave him a smile and a hug.

The helicopters arrived at I-10, where they had to split up. "Copter One to Copter Two. This is our split-up point, Hawk," Henderson said.

"Roger that, Copter One. All the best, guys. See you when we see you," Hawk replied. The two helicopters now went in separate directions, hoping to intercept the semi containing the sarin gas canisters. They had no real leads at this time, only instincts to go by; there was no help from technology.

Wolf and Hakeem continued to wait on Abdullah's orders, but they were growing impatient. Lamb's team rendezvoused with other CIA agents five blocks away on the CPAT building. Lamb briefed his agents on how they were going to take back the building. He ordered four agents to cover the back of the building; the remaining agents would watch the rest of the perimeter. Lamb's team would enter a side door on the second floor. Ajay and Ajeeta would separate and be on top of two buildings that were to the north and south of CPAT.

The agents positioned themselves at their tactical locations and waited for the signal from Lamb. "How are you feeling, brother?" Ajay asked.

"I'm doing fine, sis. I just hope that you don't keep nagging me throughout this operation," Ajay said, sounding irritated.

"That's what sisters are for. I'm just making sure that you're on top of your game, brother."

Jennings continued to struggle, but quietly. He sweated as he tried to maneuver the small pin into his hands and unlock the handcuffs. Jennings had a terrible headache and a broken nose, along with two black eyes and a sore jaw. As Hakeem and Volkov continued their conversation, Jennings concentrated and finally had the pin under control. He was able to retain it in his fingers and moved the pin into the key hole of the handcuffs. Jennings took a deep breath and then turned the key; it makes a small click. Unnoticed by the terrorists, he got his other hand free from the cuffs. Jennings slowly removed his hands from the cuffs and pushed them to the side. He reached underneath the table for his 9 mm.

Jennings quickly ran behind Volkov and hit him hard in the back of his head; Volkov fell to the floor, unconscious. Hakeem glanced over and tries to yell, however he was hit in the face with Jennings's 9 mm several times. Jennings then secured the inner area of the control console section with the touch of a button. Glass doors closed off the area. Jennings handcuffed both Volkov and Hakeem. The other terrorists were furious and tried to shoot the glass, to no avail; it was bulletproof. They were frustrated and contacted Abdullah.

"Sir, this is Saif."

"Go ahead."

"Hakeem and Volkov have been captured by Jennings. We cannot get to him because of the bulletproof glass," Saif said nervously.

"Blow it up, you incompetent idiots! If we lose control of CPAT, I guarantee heads will roll," Abdullah said furiously.

Saif told the others to set up C-4 and place it near the entrance doors.

Jennings took a cell phone out of Volkov's pocket and tried to contact Lamb. "Hello, sir, it's Jennings."

"Jennings! We thought you were dead," Lamb said excitedly.

"I'm okay, sir, just a little beat up. They're trying to get into the console area, but I sealed it off. They're trying to use C-4 to gain access, sir. I don't know how long I can hold them off."

"We're coming now, Jennings. Hang in there," Lamb said. "All units, execute plans now."

Ajay took a look through his sniper scope and observed two hostiles walking on the south side of the roof. He aimed and breathed slowly. The shots hit each of them in the head. Ajeeta also had two hostiles on the north side. She hit one in the chest and the other in the head, killing them instantly. Both sides of the roof were now clear. Lamb, Lee, and Robinson diverged near the west side of the building.

Robinson, who was on point, observed the terrorists walking near the side entrance. He motioned for the others to stop. Robinson waited until the hostile walked past him. He then engaged by placing him in a choke hold, cutting off his air supply and rendering him unconscious. The terrorist's body twitched and became completely still. Lamb gave a grappling hook attached to a rope to Robinson. They both threw the grappling hooks at the second-floor balcony ledge. The hooks connected and became secured as they both pulled on the ropes to ensure stability. Robinson pulled on his rope and motioned Lee to get in front of him and move up as he secured the rope. Lamb began his hike up the building also.

As the two agents reached the top, Robinson made his climb. Lamb used his infrared binoculars to see whether there are any hostiles on the second floor. Robinson reached the top, and Lamb motioned for the agents to follow his lead through the window. As they walked through the corridors, Jenny saw a hostile and shot him in the head before he could react.

"Agent Lamb, Agent Lamb!" Jennings said.

"Go ahead, Jennings."

"Please hurry up, sir. These assholes are almost ready to blow up this part of the building," Jennings cried in desperation.

"You hang in there. You're doing just fine. We're almost there now," Lamb reassured him.

The rest of the corridor seemed empty and hollow as they ran toward the elevators. Once inside, they went up to the third floor. Lamb informed his team to cover their eyes. As the doors opened, Lamb threw a flash bomb outside of the elevator.

There were two more terrorists waiting for them outside the elevator. The flash was so intense that the terrorists dropped their weapons and covered their eyes; the bomb had caught them off guard. Lamb kicked one terrorist in the throat, killing him. Robinson threw a punch at the other terrorist and connected on his right cheek, knocking him out. Lamb and his team could hear screaming coming from down the hallway, in the CPAT room. The remaining terrorists were doing everything they could to gain access to the console control area while Jennings held them off. There were four terrorists shooting at the glass.

Lamb and his team returned fire. Two terrorists were critically injured, but the rest took cover behind tables. "Hold them off while I set off the C-4!" Ayman said. The C-4 was set and went off within thirty seconds. Ayman, who set off the C-4, took cover behind a counter off to the right side. Glass flew everywhere, and Lamb and his team could not get clear shots because of the smoke from the blast. The three terrorists got up and made their way into the console area. One of the terrorists, Ayman, tried to uncuff Volkov and Hakeem. He was shot three times in his chest by Lee and Robinson.

Jennings looked at the fallen corpse only for moment as he shot the remaining two terrorists several times. There were no more terrorists alive other than Ayman and the traitor Volkov.

"Jennings, are you all right?" Lamb asked.

"Yes, sir, I'm all right," Jennings replied. "We've got to help the Omega team locate two semi-trucks that are carrying deadly canisters containing Saran gas. They're headed toward the Capitol and the Pentagon."

Lamb informed Jennings that they had knowledge of the terrorists' plans. Jennings and Lamb worked on the coordinates of the satellite in order to track them. Robinson and Lee secured the area. Lamb informed Ajay and Ajeeta that the building was clear, but they should continue to watch the perimeter in case other hostiles came back and engaged. Other agents entered the building, assisting the Hades team.

"Lamb, here's a transmission coming from Volkov's pants. It's Abdullah. He wants to know their status."

Lamb spoke into the radio in Volkov's voice. "Everything is working out as precisely planned, sir! Hakeem and I have terminated CPAT."

"Very good, Volkov. Your superiors told me that I could count on you to complete this mission and further our cause. I will never forget this, and you will be richly rewarded for your services."

"How, how did you do that sir?" Jennings asked Lamb, astonished.

"My father was a magician and a ventriloquist," Lamb explained. Lamb turned and looked at Jennings with a grin. "I learned from the best."

Jennings set the satellite's coordinates to match the semi's path to the Capitol. He used the transponder from the satellite to locate the semi-truck. "Coordinates are locked, sir. It looks like Copter One is heading in the right direction. They just need to follow these coordinates: one hundred fifty degrees northwest, forty miles southeast."

Lamb contacted Copter One. "We have control of CPAT." Agents Skypack and Anders applauded. "I need you to follow these coordinates." He gave the location.

"All right, sir," Henderson replied. "Roger that sir, en route."

"Also, set up roadblocks. We need you to use the transponder to locate the semi heading toward the Pentagon," Lamb said. Jennings programmed the transponder, and it signaled the path of the semi-trucks. Jennings locked in on the signal and read their coordinates. Lamb relayed these coordinates to Copter Two, which Hawk was flying.

"Roger those coordinates. En route now, sir," Hawk said.

Lamb began to interrogate Volkov. He would later interrogate Hakeem. Lamb uncuffed Volkov and then interrogated him until he became very nervous. "Where is Abdullah? We don't have a lot of time. There are thousands of lives are stake here, Volkov. Don't play games! I want to know everything there is to know concerning Abdullah, what other plans he has, and where else he will target."

Volkov began to stare and tried to intimidate Lamb. Lamb stared back and informed him that he would now take severe action. Lamb broke two of Volkov's fingers on his right hand. Volkov cried out in agony. "Tell me where Abdullah is and what his future plans are—now!" Lamb yelled.

Robinson and Lee turned to look over their shoulders as Volkov screamed in agony. Finally, Volkov agreed to talk and said the Capitol and the Pentagon were targets. "However, Abdullah hates the governor so much that he intends to go off the original plans in order to execute vengeance for deaths of his son and of his other family members during the American air raids and rescue missions." Volkov stated nervously.

Lamb gave Volkov some water and placed him inside a holding cell.

Next was Hakeem. Hakeem's interrogation began with Lamb slapping him in the face. Lamb asked the same questions he asked Volkov. Lamb took Hakeem's hand and bent his arm. "What are you doing? Stop it now! I'm not going to say anything. I do know my rights here!" Hakeem said, frightened.

"Too bad you are never going to use these fingers ever again," Lamb said.

"No, no! All right, I'll talk. No more, no more, sir. I'll talk—please stop!" Hakeem cried.

"All right, Hakeem. Hurry up because we don't have a lot of time," Lamb said.

"It's just like Volkov said to you: all these things he spoke of are underway."

"Sir!" Robinson said. "Volkov is gone from the holding cell." The agent who was guarding him was knocked unconscious, and the cell door was unlocked. Agent Lee informed Lamb that the name, Kolzak Volkov meant "Slippery Wolf."

Lamb placed headquarters on full alert. The agents conducted a full search but could not locate Volkov.

Hakeem continued talking. "Abdullah wants to cripple the United States by using the sarin gas and eliminating all the leaders. Abdullah calls this a moral victory for our cause. What he really wants is the governor's head on a silver platter. Maali always tells him to focus only on the cause: elimination of the US leaders. Abdullah has already begun the final step." Hakeem laughed.

"What are you laughing about, you sick psycho? Lamb asked.

"I'm laughing because a few minutes ago I set the satellite to go off in an hour, to destroy the governor's mansion. There's nothing you or anyone else can do to stop it!" Hakeem said.

Lamb hit him in the jaw. He placed him in the interrogation chair and strapped him down.

Jennings started to work on shutting down the countdown. The STARE DOWN system was brand-new. The special feature on this satellite system was the laser function—a feature unequal to any satellite that had ever been established.

Copter One was getting ready to engage the semi. "Copter One to CPAT, this is Agent Sky Pack. We are ready to engage. Please downlink the satellite's audiovisual transmitter to our computer so that we can have a visual on them and hear their conversations," Agent Skypack requested.

Lamb gave the approval, and Jennings began to downlink the satellite's audiovisual transmitter to the computer that was inside Copter One. Skypack and Anders viewed the data.

"How much longer?" Hakim asked.

"We only have thirty minutes more," Alq said.

"Good. Victory will be ours soon!"

The agents observed a gray truck hauling the canisters inside. The agents also observed two more figures moving around where the canisters were, making sure that the canisters would remain stable and not fall and break open. "Team Leader Two, we are going to engage the hostiles now. We'll keep you informed. Sky Pack out!"

"Roger that," Martinez replied.

Copter One lowered down toward the thirty-foot semi-truck, hovering above it. "Let's go, Anders!" Sky Pack said. They jumped out of the copter and landed near the front of the vehicle. They crawled slowly. Alq was driving and conversing with Hakim, who was on the passenger side. Anders moved toward the driver's side, and Sky Pack eased toward Hakim.

"This is the CIA! Listen to my commands. Stop this vehicle and put your hands above your heads." Anders ordered over the loudspeaker. Alq and Hakim were startled. Alq suddenly slammed on the brakes, throwing Anders off of the roof of the truck and onto the pavement as the truck jackknifed. Sky Pack hung on tightly; she clenched the truck's top lights with both hands as the truck slid across the road and into the trees before coming to a stop.

"Alq, are you all right?" Hakim asked. Alq's head had hit the steering wheel, knocking him unconscious and causing a large lump on his forehead. Agent Sky Pack pulled out her M-9 and ordered Hakim to slowly step out of the vehicle as she moved off the roof and onto the pavement. Hakim slowly exited. "You're making a mistake. You have nothing on me, American," Hakim said.

"Oh, but we do. We have everything on camera, everything you're attempting to do. Give up, Hakim. Everything is over," Sky Pack said. She then called for Anders, but there was no answer from him. Hakim slowly tried to reach into his pocket. "Keep your hands up where I can see them!" Skypack ordered. She felt something hit her hard in the back of her head, causing her to collapse onto the pavement. Staredown disengaged the SUV's communications.

Abar and Salamon had been driving in an SUV behind the semi and saw that Hakim was in trouble so they subdued Agent Skypack. "Where's the other American dog?" Hakim asked.

"We don't know; we have only seen her," Abar replied.

Hakim was furious and told them that they would remain on schedule if they could get back on the road soon. The truck was able to back up and turn onto the road. Hakim then moved Skypack onto her back. "This is going to be my pleasure, putting you away for good," he said as he stood brooding over her.

Just then, Copter One was behind Hakim. Anders had him in his scope and pulled the trigger of his sniper rifle. The bullet went through the back of Hakim's head and exited through his forehead. Hakim fell over Skypack. Abar tried to shoot, but he was shot in the chest, along with Salamon.

Skypack came to as she observes Hakim lying dead on the pavement. She looked up and waved at Anders with a smile. There were two more terrorists they had to fight. Copter One landed. Anders joined Skypack on the ground; they moved toward the back of the semi. They cautiously opened the doors of the semi, revealing the canisters of sarin gas. Salem and Salahad told the agents if they stepped any closer, they would release the sarin gas. Skypack tried to reason with them, and Salem was hesitant and frightened. He was told their mission may call for sacrifice not only of their time but their very lives, and he was not prepared for this.

"Salem, let's do this. There is no other way out for us. This is our fate, our destiny!" Salahad said.

Skypack and Anders had their weapons drawn on both hostiles. "I cannot go through with this, Salahad. I don't want to die! My girlfriend is pregnant, and I want to live to see them," Salem cried. He let go of the valve that contained the deadly sarin gas.

"Now you can also back away from that canister," shouted Anders. Anders and Skypack moved in toward the hostiles.

Salahad was furious and began to yell and scream. He called Salem a traitor and said he would never make it to Paradise because of his actions. Skypack and Anders ordered Salahad to let go of the valves and step back.

Salahad simply said, "Go to hell!" He gripped the valve tightly and proceeded to turn the valve as several bullets entered his head and torso. Anders and Skypack ordered Salem to turn around and place his hands behind his head. Salem was in tears; he would be deemed a traitor by his people, and his family would be shamed and disgraced.

As Salem was being handcuffed by Anders. Skypack said, "We are going to need to know the plans for the rest of his attacks on the United States. Will you tell us what other targets he has planned?"

Salem paused and lowers his head. He looked at the agents and said, "I will tell you all that I know, however you must promise to protect my girlfriend and my baby."

Skypack and Anders immediately contacted Lamb. "We have the situation under control," Skypack said.

"Good job, Skypack and Anders. I'll contact the hazmat team to join you. There are several other agents en route to assist you in securing the area. Everyone all right?" Lamb asked.

"We're both all right, sir," Skypack replied. "We also have captured one of the terrorists, a young man named Salem."

"Bring him in as soon as the other agents arrive. We need him for questioning."

"Ten-four, en route after agents arrive," Skypack replied.

Jennings informed Copter Two that the semi was only a mile away. "I have a visual. The semi is headed off of I-80 toward the Pentagon," Hawk said.

"It's our turn to rock 'n' roll." Wombush said.

This semi was joined by two black SUVs. "The others on the radio are saying that we are being followed, Jabbar. What should we do?" Fahl asked.

"Destroy them with what we have. I want them eliminated as soon as possible!" Jabbar said.

As the helicopter descended, one hostile emerged from the SUV on the right side of the semi with a grenade launcher. Jennings notified the agents of the situation; he could see what was inside the SUVs and could hear the conversations.

"When they get close, shoot!" cried Jabbar.

K-Hawk took evasive action. The hostile didn't have a clear shot as the helicopter moved from one angle to another. He aimed and tried to steady the weapon. K-Hawk had a clear shot and took it. Before the hostile could pull the trigger, K-Hawk's small missile hit the SUV and overturned the vehicle. K-Hawk sent another missile to the rear of the vehicle; it exploded furiously as metal and glass flew everywhere.

"Good job, Hawk. Now we have the other SUV to contend with," Martinez said.

Leblanc aimed his M-107 at the remaining SUV and shot out the left rear tire. The vehicle swerved from side to side and crashed into a guard rail. LeBlanc and Wombush opened fire on the hostile. Several bullets hit the hostile in the chest, and neck. LeBlanc and Martinez moved cautiously toward the corpse and pulled off the mask, revealing a young woman. LeBlanc noticed a sound coming from her back, and he saw a device with lights and a beeping sound. He cried as he ran away. He leaped behind the thick shrubbery near the suv and the bomb exploded. Martinez was slow to react and was thrown across the road and onto the pavement. Wombush ran over to assist her. She was unconscious but breathing.

Copter One was now over and above the SUV. "Copter Two, is everyone all right?" Henderson asked.

"We've got one agent down, but she's going to be all right. One hostile is still alive inside the SUV," K-Hawk said.

"Team, there are two small canisters with sarin gas and explosives inside the SUV. Be extremely cautious," warned Jennings. Other federal agencies had arrived on scene and surrounded the SUV. The perimeter was secure. Agents had the enormous task of trying to stabilize the situation without releasing the sarin gas or causing an explosion. The hazmat team also arrived.

Martinez slowly regained consciousness, and the agents briefed her on what had happened. Martinez rose to her feet and told them that the hostiles may blow up the semi if they felt there was no way out for them. She ordered agents to shoot tear gas inside the SUV's front windows. Agent Martinez sprinted toward the SUV and climbed all the way to the top of the roof of the semi. She opened the door and quickly threw a teargas bomb inside. This caught the hostiles off guard because once the agents opened the hatch, the hostiles were barely conscious. Martinez's plan worked. "We've got to subdue that other semi now, before it reaches the population!" Martinez said. She and her team headed back to Copter Two and raced toward the semi.

After five minutes in the air, the team located the semi with the help of Agent Jennings. As K-Hawk tried to maneuver Copter Two near the semi, Fahl shot his forty-five at the helicopter. K-Hawk once again took evasive action. "Let me take out a couple of tires, Hawk!" LeBlanc stated. K-Hawk nods his head in agreement and maneuvered the helicopter to the rear of the semi. LeBlanc shot out two tires on both sides of the semi.

"They have shot out our tires, Jabbar!" Fahl said.

Jabbar grew angry and placed his foot all the way down on the gas pedal, shifted into a higher gear.

"He's not going to slow down. This one is definitely determined!" Wombush noted. They could see the city lights as they flew over the hill that led to the populated area. Fahl continued to fire off rounds at the helicopter, and one bullet hit the engine. K-Hawk was able to manage to continue to fly evasively.

Martinez leaned over to Wombush and said, "I believe it's time for you to do your thing, don't you?"

Wombush nodded. He looked over to LeBlanc, who was returning fire at the semi. He then glanced at K-Hawk, who was also busy maneuvering the crippled helicopter around the semi. Adam sat on the ledge. He slowly closed eyes and called upon his ancient ancestors. His body began to shake.

Martinez observes an eagle in flight, descending downward. Adam's clothing had been left behind. The eagle soared down with its wings spread. The eagle grabbed Fahl's hand with its claws. Fahl screamed in agony as the bird clawed into his skin, cutting deeply into the forearm. Fahl released his .45 automatic and grasped his hand in agony.

"What the hell was that?" Jabbar asked.

"It was an eagle, I believe," Fahl said.

The eagle continued to fly next to the semi. K-Hawk moved in front of the semi and hovered in the middle of the road. Jabbar did not want to slow down; Nothing was going to get in their way to complete their mission. Suddenly, Fahl screamed as he was pulled by Wombush toward the door. Wombush opened the door to the semi, standing on the platform and reaching for Fahl's jacket. LeBlanc shot at Jabbar as he continued head-on toward the helicopter. Fahl was thrown out of the semi while it was going seventy-five miles an hour, causing trauma to his head and other vital organs. His body rolled over and over on the pavement until it came to a stop.

Jabbar cried, "Nothing will stop me! Nothing. You Americans will die! You hear me?" Jabbar reached for a revolver underneath the driver's seat.

Wombush punches Jabbar twice in the face, and Jabbar dropped the revolver. Wombush turned the wheel hard to the right, avoiding the helicopter. Wombush gave Jabbar an elbow jab to his stomach and then his face, rendering him unconscious. The semi swerved back and forth until Wombush gained control of it by engaging the brakes. The semi came to a complete stop off the road. "Agent Wombush to Team Leader Two. I have control of the semi!" Wombush reported.

"Good job, Wombush! We will be setting down in the back of you. There may be more hostiles in the rear of the semi," Martinez said.

"How did you get down there so quick?" Leblanc asked Wombush.

Wombush ignored the question and told the snipers, "Job well done!"

Hawk was standing by. Wombush waited for the team to get near the doors. Leblanc opened one side of the doors, and Wombush did the other at the same time. Agent Martinez was ready, holding her weapon. When the doors opened, they were met by machine-gun fire. Agent Martinez got hit with three shots to her chest and fell backward. The other agents shot the door as the bullets continued to go everywhere. They disengaged and carried Martinez away to the helicopter. Wombush radioed Lamb that they were engaging hostile fire and awaiting further instructions.

Lamb had several agents en route to them, including Copter One carrying Anders and Skypack. Leblanc assessed Martinez's injuries and discovered that she had on her protective vest; she was merely unconscious from the hits that she took to her chest. The agents saw the doors slowly open. Two terrorists emerged from behind a crate and fired upon the agents inside the helicopter. The terrorists ran quickly to the front of the vehicle and tried to start the semi, but Wombush had taken the keys out of the ignition. The hostiles were furious, and they got out and ran toward the agents, pointing their AK-47s at the agents. The agents commanded them to drop their weapons, however the terrorists ignored their warnings. The agents opened fire on the hostiles, killing them.

Chapter 9

The Kidnapping of the Twins

The semi was secured. One of the hostiles who died was a young girl of sixteen years; her mother had died alongside her daughter. Lamb had his team return to CPAT'S headquarters for debriefing. He also had to continue interrogating their prisoner.

After debriefing, Safi gave Lamb information that indicated the governor would be the next target. Mohammed insisted that his brother not concentrate on eliminating the governor and his family; the focus should be on using the canisters containing the sarin gas on the US leaders and Washington, DC.

The governor opened the door to his children's room and watched Susanna and Brianna sleeping peacefully. The twins had a long day ahead of them because they were going on a school field trip to the carnival. "The children do miss the CPAT agents very much. They've been asking for them today!" Barbara said.

"I know they do. However, they are getting along without them just fine dear." Barry said as he rubbed his wife's shoulders. "Those agents are just an experimental project created by Victor Price. I think that they won't last in the federal agency. Maybe they would do better as mercenaries."

Barbara shrugged his hands off of her shoulders, stood up, and folded her arms. She turned to Barry and said, "Those so-called mercenaries saved your life, Barry. They have saved *all* of our lives. You of all people should never put down them or Victor Price. You should swallow that pride of yours!"

The governor rubbed her shoulders again, gave her a small apology, and went to bed. Barbara rolled her eyes at her husband and also went to bed.

When morning came, Brianna and Susanna rose out of bed in anticipation of the day ahead. They went through their morning routine, brushing their hair and teeth. The governor also got out of bed and prepared for work. Betty assisted the twins, and their oldest daughter, Jasmine, got ready to go to the school library and study for her finals. Once the twins were ready, they ate breakfast along with Jasmine and Barry. Todd moved into an apartment not too far away, and he had two secret service agents assigned to protect him. This day would prove to be very eventful.

Both CPAT teams were ready for some time off. Lamb was approached by Anders and Leblanc, who had both put in for time off. Lamb was willing to give the entire team a vacation if he could. Victor Price was very proud of Nathan Lamb and the team he had organized. He was very perturbed when the governor no longer wanted the services of CPAT and reactivated the secret service to their duties. The team awaited their new assignment from Victor Price in a briefing room.

The governor kissed the girls and his wife good-bye, and then he headed off to work escorted by two secret service agents. The twins were now ready for departure. They gave their mother a hug and kiss and ran into a limousine, driven and escorted by two secret service agents. The twins waved good-bye to their mother as the vehicle drove away. Barbara went to her computer to e-mail her friends and manage charity functions.

Two hours later, a dark van pulled up at the back of the mansion. Three figures exited the van wearing dark clothing. They had name tags on their front right pockets and were in the same uniforms worn by the maintenance people contracted by the governor. One of the agents observed them walking to the west side of the gate, which was the back entrance of the mansion. The maintenance man punched in a code. A secret service agent viewed the code on his computer screen and verified it. Once the codes matched, he granted access. The men hurried into the mansion; they made sure the cameras did not have a good view of them by looking down at the paved sidewalk. One of the maintenance men entered the code that gave access to the west side of the mansion. As he entered the code, another walked toward the screen.

"Who's that entering the mansion on the west side, Agent Scott?"

"Those are the maintenance men," Scott replied. "What's wrong, Smith?"

"They're usually here on Wednesdays. Call the governess to verify!" Smith said nervously.

The men gained access to the mansion. They reached into their pockets and retrieved their 9 mm guns. The guns had silencers attached to them. Two of the men walked up the staircase leading to the bedrooms. The other two searched for agents. As Scott used his cell phone to call Barbara, he was struck twice in the neck and back by two bullets. He drops the phone and fell to the floor. Agent Smith walked around the corner and saw Scott lying in a pool of blood. He quickly reached for his gun but felt a sharp pain in his back. Smith turned around and saw two men with guns in each hand. One had already shot two bullets in Smith's back. The second man fired two more shots into Smith's chest.

The third man contacted the other two men upstairs, informing them that the first floor had been secured. The two men moved quickly from bedroom to bedroom. They looked into the twins' room and then the governor's bedroom. No one had yet been found. They opened Jasmine's door and saw her gathering her books for school. They immediately grabbed her. She tried to scream, but they covered her mouth. They used chloroform, and Jasmine was soon rendered unconscious. One of the men threw Jasmine onto his shoulders.

As they left, Barbara saw them and cried, "Where are you taking Jasmine? I demand to know what's going on!" One of the men struck Barbara on her cheek, and she fell backward down the staircase. Her body continued to tumble until she reached the bottom of the staircase.

She slowly opened her eyes and observed two figures that walked past her.

Two more agents were walking the grounds when they observed Jasmine being carried off. They both tried to stop the men, demanding they stop. One of the terrorists had a MAC-10 and sprayed bullets in their direction. Agent Rivers was hit several times and fell to the ground. Agent Ross was able to take cover behind one of the statues in the yard and call for backup. The terrorists' damage was done. They took Jasmine and hurried off.

Once backup arrived, they secured the perimeter. Agent Ross notified EMS to transport Barbara to the hospital. Her body was found twisted at the bottom of the staircase. The governor was notified, and he quickly arrived at the hospital. Barbara was upset and crying hysterically. Barry tried to console her, and he gently touched her hand, lifted it to his lips, and placed a gentle kiss on it.

"Oh, Barry, they took our daughter. They took our daughter!" Barbara cried.

"I know, dear. We are working on getting her back. We will have her back with us soon, honey. You'll see!" Barry said.

Barbara pulled her hand away from the governor. "It's your fault!"

"My fault?" Barry repeated. "Why do you say that, dear?"

"Because you got rid of Victor's team, that's why. It's your fault because of you and your damn pride, along with your jealousy. I want CPAT back! Do you hear me, Barry? I want them back now! You won't ever touch me again until my child is safe with me."

Barry saw the note left behind by the kidnappers. Barry's head sank low. He walked out of the room as Barbara gave him his cell phone to call Victor Price. Barry had to swallow his pride. He knew that although CPAT was in the beginning stages, it was well equipped to handle any job. Besides, they'd saved his life and his family's before.

CPAT was ready to depart for the day when Lamb received a call from Victor Price explaining what had happened to the governor's family. Lamb and his team went to the hospital. Once they arrived, Agents Lamb and Martinez walked over to Barbara's room, where

Governor Barton was waiting. "Here is the note that the terrorists left behind," Barry said. Lamb took the note and let Martinez read it too.

> Americans, you are to release all Al-Qaeda prisoners all over the world. The United States will also no longer meddle in foreign affairs. Our actions are none of your concern. You will abide by this order, and we will give you twenty-four hours to comply, or you will never see your daughter again!
>
> The order of Al-Qaeda.

"Please, *please* get our daughter back, Lamb. Please get her back!" Barry cried. He then stood near the foot of the bed, where Barbara was lying down. Barry covered his face with both hands and wept bitterly. Barbara's eyes were also full of tears.

Lamb took her hand. "We will get your daughter back, ma'am. I promise you!"

Lamb called Jennings. "Jennings, are we still recording the governor's mansion?"

"Yes sir. You never told me to stop. Why did you ask?"

"The governor's oldest daughter, Jasmine, was kidnapped at approximately 0900 hours. I need you to replay that window of time for me."

Martinez opened her laptop and waited for the satellite transmission relay. They observed the terrorists entering the grounds of the mansion. Martinez activated the infrared audiovisual program that allowed them to see and hear the details of the incident inside the mansion. They observed Barbara getting hit and falling down the staircase. They also observed Jasmine being taken and placed inside a dark van. Martinez was able to get the license plate. The number came back as stolen and belonged to a man named Randall Watkins. Martinez programmed a downlink on the van and then initiated the tracking system. Her laptop screen showed the dark van heading west toward a rural area. Lamb quickly informed the governor and his wife.

Lamb and Martinez ran to the vehicles, where their teams were waiting. Lamb went with Hades team, awaiting him in the dark blue

SUV. Martinez got inside a white SUV, where her Omega team awaited her. Anders and LeBlanc followed both SUVs in the pickup. Lamb contacted Copters One and Two for air support.

At the warehouse where Jasmine was being held hostage, Maali met with Abdullah because he felt their cause had come to its end. "We will never get our demands met, brother. These ten years of planning have failed," Maali said.

"You have a great lack of faith. We have lost battles but not the war. This is far from over! If our needs are not met, the governor will suffer greatly—starting with his family!" Abdullah cried.

When Jasmine came to, she began to cry, making muffled sounds through the cloth that they had placed in her mouth.

Copter One and Two had located the warehouse and observed the van alongside it. Information on the van was verified and relayed to Lamb and Martinez. The terrorists guarding the perimeter saw the helicopters and informed Abdullah of their arrival. The units were on scene and split off in different directions. Lamb's team went north, and Omega team went south. Copters One and Two were instructed to take the east and west sides of the warehouse. The two guards began their assault by firing at the helicopters. Henderson wasted no time returning fire, tearing the terrorist's bodies in half. The team had the warehouse surrounded. Jenny Lee and Robinson shot teargas through the windows. The terrorists reacted by shooting at both teams. Jennings activated the infrared program and observed eleven individuals inside the warehouse. He could also see Jasmine in a corner, tied up in a chair with a gun to her head. Both agent teams were using AR-15s. The terrorists returned fire with MAC-10s. Two of the terrorists were shot in the head and chest.

Jennings told Lamb where Jasmine was, and Lamb ordered the team to cover him. He ordered the Omega team to hold fire as he entered the warehouse area from their side and made it to the window, where he had a visual on Jasmine. He shot and hit her assailant in the head with a round. As Lamb climbed through the window, Maali noticed him, and the confrontation continued. Lamb sensed something wrong, and he immediately threw a smoke grenade onto the floor and disappeared.

"Where did he go? I saw him in front of me. I know he was just here!" the terrorist cried, shocked.

The shooting continued, and three more terrorists were killed by the Hades team. Omega continued to hold fire. Lamb reappeared behind the two terrorists and opened fire. The bullets hit them both in the back and instantly killed them. Lamb threw another smoke grenade to the floor and disappeared again. Maali was furious and yelled, "I'll kill you, you American dog!" He sprayed several bullets in the direction where Lamb had been, however his fellow countrymen were in the same area. They were hit and wounded by the bullets.

Jasmine felt her ropes loosen as her gag slipped off. Lamb walked in front of her and said, "You're going to be all right now, Jasmine! You're safe!" Jasmine hugged him and did not let go. Lamb informed his teams to move in.

Maali continued to yell as he ran toward the Omega team, shooting off several rounds. Anders and LeBlanc took careful aim and hit him in the head and chest. Maali fell to the ground and turned over to lie on his back. Martinez and Jenny Lee were the first to reach him, and Lee kicked the weapon away from the terrorist's reach. "It wasn't supposed to happen this way. Not this way!" Maali said, as he expired.

Lamb continued to search for other terrorists who may had been still in the building. Both teams met inside the building. Abdullah Mohammed was nowhere to be found.

Agent Robinson noticed that the floor looked uneven where he was standing. It was a secret doorway. He pulled it back and observed a ladder that led to a basement. He alerted the team to his findings, and the team followed Robinson into the dark hole. The basement led to an underground cave. Robinson heard an explosion and ordered everyone to turn around and run back. The sounds of rubble, rocks, and glass were heard throughout the tunnel, which had been sealed off by Abdullah. The team returned to the surface, where Jenny Lee and Martinez were comforting Jasmine.

"My younger sisters too. You've got to protect them!" Jasmine said.

"Where are they now?" Martinez asked.

"They are going on a class field trip to Caspian's Carnival, about ten miles from their school."

"Anders, you and Leblanc can go now. We can take it from here!" Lamb said.

"We are here for the duration, sir!" Anders replied.

"We want to see the twins get back home safe, sir," Leblanc agreed.

They got into their truck and headed toward the carnival. "Team Leader Two to Team Leader One."

"Go ahead, Martinez," Lamb said.

"We have a fix on Brianna and Susanna, sir!"

"Now how did do you do that so quickly?" Lamb asked.

"I gave Brianna a bracelet that has a tracking device that uplinks to our satellite, just in case she was to ever lose her ankle bracelet."

Lamb nodded his head and then smiled. Ajay and Ajeeta also nodded in the affirmative. Lamb knew he chose the right personnel for his team.

The teams soon arrived at the fairgrounds. Hades team searched the west side, and Omega team took the east side. There were large crowds of children there, accompanied by adults from various schools in the area. As Lamb and his team searched the crowd, Jenny Lee peered into an open tent and saw the twins, Brianna and Susanna, sitting together in the third row. She motioned the team to stop. Lamb looked in and had the team sit in the back row. The show was a group of knife throwers and escape artists.

"Hey, look, sir! Wasn't your dad an escape artist?" Ajeeta remembered.

Lamb nodded with a smile. The escape artist had his assistant placed inside a compartment, tied up. Then he was placed in another compartment and tied up. They were facing each other. Two other assistants walked in front of both compartments and held up a curtain covering the front of the compartment. At the count of three, they dropped the curtain, and the escape artist had switched places with his assistant. Both were standing up, and the ropes were at their feet. The children applauded and shouted approval as the magician and his assistant took a bow.

Lamb went back in time, to when his father was rehearsing for his performances. He would watch his father practice, with his mother assisting him whenever she had time off from work. What really fascinated Lamb was when his father would perform his escape act. He was locked inside of a trunk with handcuffs on him. Lamb's father, Lucas, would also perform the Houdini act of being tied up in a trunk underwater. Lamb would always ask his father, "Show me, Daddy. I want to learn to do that too!" When he was young, Lamb's father would take time to teach him how to escape from almost anything. Lucas told young Lamb to never escape from his fears but to confront them and conquer them.

Lamb's mind focused back on the present. As he saw the next performers walking on stage, he noticed two knife throwers. The assistant was placed on a vertical platform that spun. Another assistant turned the platform and threw knives while it spun. The knives hit between her arms and legs, and inches away from her head. The children were amazed by this act and applaud. The two performers tossed their knives back and forth to each other. Lamb sensed strong feelings throughout his body indicating that something was not right. He turned to his right and quickly pushed Jenny Lee off of the bench. She fell to the floor. A knife hurled through the air where she was sitting and struck a post holding up the tent. Jenny was shaken and confused. Another knife was thrown, but this time it was caught by Lamb, who returned it to its owner. Lamb targeted the suspect's left side of the neck and hit his target. The performer fell to his knees, and the children screamed and cried.

A teacher instructed the children to run outside and into their buses. The twins ran outside and disappeared into the sea of children. Confusion began to set in along with chaos. Children were falling down and trampling each other. The last teacher to board the bus began to count. There was a shot fired, and a bullet enters his back. He fell backward outside the bus and onto the grass. Two terrorists with AK-47s entered the bus. "Now listen to me, children. You will not get hurt as long as you listen and obey. Understood?" Imad said. The children continued to scream. Catlin Romero, the teacher's aide, informed the terrorist that she would comply. She was allowed to talk to the children and try to calm them down as best as she could.

Lamb informed the Omega Team of their status. The Omega team observed the bus and began to converge, however bullets were sprayed in their direction by a fifty caliber gun. The agents scrambled to grab children and head for the nearest tree to take cover. Children were getting hit by bullets, and many bodies were down. Martinez called for assistance to the Hades team. The bus left the carnival and headed toward the freeway. As Lamb's team converged, he had them flank the fifty caliber gun, which was mounted on a Jeep. There were four other men armed with AK-47's near the Jeep. Lamb called for air support from Copters One and Two, and he told Hades and Omega team to take evasive action. The terrorists shot at the helicopters, and both helicopters returned fire, annihilating the Jeep. Robinson administered first aid to the children who were wounded; luckily none were killed.

Both teams pursued the school bus. The satellite had the tracking signal on Brianna. Copters One and Two were also in pursuit. Omega team was in the lead SUV, and following them was the Hades team, with Anders and LeBlanc behind them in the pickup. The terrorists shot at Omega team. Agent Skypack took evasive action by swerving left and right. Jenny Lee also maneuvered Hades team's SUV. The terrorists continued to fire upon CPAT.

"Copter One to Team Leader One!"

"Go ahead, Henderson," Lamb said.

"The road you are on is not complete. The bridge is out. There is still construction going on approximately twenty-five miles ahead on this freeway."

"That means we have to act now if we are to save the children!" Lamb said. "Did you copy that, Team Leader Two?"

"Copy!" Martinez replied.

Martinez turned to look at Wombush, and he knew what he had to do. Wombush lowered his head in prayer, asking for assistance from the ancient elders. The window was open on the passenger side where Wombush sat. In the next moment he was no longer there; a crow flew out toward the bus.

Meanwhile, the terrorists wanted to make sure the bus would make its destination into destruction, carrying the governor's twins. Caitlin was ordered to keep the children quiet. Each of the terrorists knew to sit in the bus seats close to the children, in case of snipers. The terrorists knew CPAT had snipers but would not take the chance of hitting children. The terrorists felt this was to their advantage. "The Americans are weak. Children are their Achilles heel," Imad said.

The children tried not to cry after Caitlin Romero spoke to them. They thought they would never make it home to their families. Ms. Romero assured them they would. "These guys are having a bad day!" Jimmy Hansen said. "Are they going to get a timeout for this?"

The terrorist looked at him sternly and then turned away.

The crow makes its way inside the rear window, where the emergency door was. Adnan saw it and tried to catch it with his hands. The bird quickly flew out of his reach. The children began to laugh and cheer on the crow. "What's going on back there?" Imad demanded to know.

"There is a black bird back here. I have to dispose of it!" Adnan said. The crow flew out of the window, and the children cheered because of its escape.

"Shut the hell up, or I will throw you out of the bus, one by one!" Imad threatened. The children quieted down, and some began to cry softly. They were comforted by the other children and school teacher

"Let me take your position now, Team Leader Two!" Lamb said.

"Ten-four, giving you the lead."

The Hades SUV took the lead. The bus driver was shot trying to take the exit before the road's end. Imad pulled the corpse out of the driver's seat and threw the body to the floor, near the exit; he took over driving. Imad began to disable the brakes. Lamb had Jenny Lee pull closely behind the school bus.

"You have no brakes now!" Imad cried.

The children screamed and cried.

The crow now gained access to the bus, and the children did not say anything but observed quietly. The crow positioned itself behind Imad and pecked at his neck. The bus began to swerve. Lamb was trying to reach the side door. The bus swerved right and then left. Lamb waited until it is steady. He found an open window and got inside the bus. Jenny backed off the SUV and drove to the rear of the bus. Lamb bent his knees and peered into the window of the rear of the bus. Imad began fighting with the crow, and Adnan walked over to assist. Lamb pulled out his .38 super and carefully aimed at Adnan. He fired two shots into the bus as Adnan tried to grab the crow. Adnan fell forward onto the steering wheel and did not move. The bus moved to the right, however Wombush quickly removed Adnan's body and took control of the wheel. The children wondered how Wombush appeared so quickly. Lamb motions for someone to open the rear exit door. The children at the rear of the bus slowly opened the back exit door for Lamb. A boy and girl let him in. Ms. Romero was crying and shocked.

"You're all going to be all right now. We are here to help!" Lamb said. The children applauded. Lamb made his way to the front of the bus where Wombush was. "Okay mister, How in the world did you get inside this bus? Are you a magician too?" Lamb asked.

"Right now, sir, I believe our main concern is how we are going to get us all off this bus. The other problem is that the freeway we are on is not complete!" Wombush answered.

Lamb looked down at the exit door and observed the bus driver and Adnan near the exit door. He contacted Anders, who had been driving alongside the exit door. Leblanc knew right away to get into the bed of the truck and get ready for extraction. Ms. Romero assisted in getting the children ready for transfer into the pickup truck. One by one they lined up and were moved, with the help of Anders and LeBlanc. Next was Ms. Romero. She was hesitant at first but managed to get into the truck. The wounded bus driver also made it across slowly but surely.

"All right, agent. I will take over the wheel. You can go now!" Lamb said.

"No, sir. You go. I can handle this. Please trust me on this. Go—leave me!" Wombush said.

Lamb knew that there was no time for arguments. They were getting near the end of the freeway. Lamb positioned himself and leaped onto the bed of the truck. The children applauded. Lamb looked around for the twins, but they were nowhere to be found even though everyone had exited the school bus. The bus increased speed as it headed downhill. Lamb pleaded for Wombush to let go of the wheel and jump. Wombush motioned that he was going to be all right. Martinez informed Lamb that Wombush had everything under control, and

Lamb should trust him. Lamb could do just that, because every one of his agents was gifted and trustworthy. Lamb ordered Anders to turn vehicle around. Anders slowed down and made a U-turn before the road ended. The children were sitting close and clinging to each other and to Ms. Romero. Hades team also slowed down, turned around, and stopped to see the runaway bus.

Agent Wombush was now alone as he continued to make sure the bus remained steady on the road. There was no time left. He closed his eyes as he focused on transforming his body into an eagle. There was now only fifty feet of road left. An eagle exited the bus, ascending high into the clouds. The bus came to the end of the road and ran off the incomplete bridge. The front of the bus hit the concrete and created a loud explosion. Everyone except Martinez thought that was the last they would ever see of Agent Wombush. They peered into the sky and observed a white eagle soaring above them and disappearing into the clouds. Martinez assured them that agent Wombush would be all right.

CPAT transported the children back to school, where parents and the media were waiting. Once they arrived at their destination, the children exited the pickup assisted by the agents. "This is Jerry Bird, Channel 9 News, on scene here at Bradford's Elementary School at 15 Lincoln Boulevard. Federal agents have successfully rescued all of the elementary children involved in an attempted kidnapping during an annual field trip to Caspian's carnival. The media went on to talk about the successful rescue of the children, but the reporters wanted more information. Price, Lamb, and his team dispersed as the crowd applauded. Lamb received a call from Jennings stating that there was a situation concerning STARE DOWN. The system had been turned to auto defensive mode, launching missiles. The main target was the governor's mansion.

"What is the launch time of those missiles, Jennings?" Lamb asked.

"Approximately two hours. We have two hours left, sir!" Jennings replied. "We have to get to work and resolve it soon. Did you locate the twins?"

"They were not on the bus. We believe that they never got on and were taken by Al-Qaeda during the confusion at the carnival." Lamb said.

Jennings used the tracking system, which picked up a beacon signal heading south from Los Angeles. Lamb had a team travel in the direction of the signal.

The STARE DOWN system began to shut down. The signal became weaker and weaker. "What's going on, Jennings? The signal is going out!" Lamb said angrily.

"I know that, sir. I'm working on it!" Jennings said. He was also frustrated, because the system had been sabotaged by Volkov and Hakeem.

The system went completely dark; communications were also cut. Lamb tried to use his radio to communicate with Jennings, but to no avail. Each member knew what to do when communications were out: they used the one-to-one radios. Lamb needed a convoy of vehicles south to where the signal was last detected. "I believe that Brianna may still have my bracelet on, sir. Yes, I can see the light going on and off!" Jenny Lee said. Lamb took a look at the laptop and observed the light also moving south. They were on the right track. The governor had taken all of the tracking devices off the children. However, Jenny Lee had placed one inside Brianna's bracelet just in case something happened to the other tracking device.

Abdullah paced the room as he looked at the monitor, viewing the satellite. He anxiously awaited the final countdown that would destroy the governor. "He has not heeded my requests by releasing all Al-Qaeda prisoners and promising to stay out of our affairs."

Karif, one of his captains, tried to plead with Abdullah to leave now and regroup. They could put together another plan later. Abdullah was furious, knowing ten years of planning had come to this. "These infidels will pay for their arrogance. They will die!" Abdullah cried.

Karif slowly backed up and then ran for the hallway and the back door. "Karif! Stop, traitor!" As Karif desperately tried to open the door, Abdullah shot him several times in the back.

Karif turned in agony and looked back at Abdullah. He said, "It is all for naught, brother. All for naught." He then slid down in front of the door and expired.

Two more of Abdullah's men left the cabin and headed for the outskirts of the town, toward a small airport. They left in a pickup truck, a 1976 red Chevy. The two men were almost there when they saw a roadblock, put in place by two sheriff's officers.

Officers Gary Anderson and James Whittington were given orders by Victor Price to set up a roadblock on roads leading to the private airport. They had already apprehended the pilot. "Amin, what do we do now?" Jaheed asked.

"We do nothing. We remain calm." Jaheed uncovered a revolver from a cloth on his lap and showed it to Amin. He nodded and placed the cloth back over it.

Officer Anderson asked for license and registration, and Amin slowly reached for it. Officer Whittington walked by the passenger side of the vehicle. Both officers had their hands on their weapons. Officer Anderson took the license and registration and walked back to his unit to run the information. The information showed that the vehicle had been stolen. The two suspects matched the description of terrorists they had been searching for. Officer Anderson called out, "Ten-eighty!" It was a code red. They both drew their weapons and ordered the suspects out of the vehicle one at a time. Amin slowly exited the vehicle but then quickly drew his weapon. He was shot several times by the officers in the chest, stomach, and legs. Amin fell to the ground, dropping his weapon.

Jaheed opened the door and tried to run, and the officers fired upon him and took up pursuit. Jaheed ran toward one of the hangars a mile away. The officers were in hot pursuit. Jaheed's legs began to tire, but he was almost at the hangar door. He thought he could fly out of the United States and go back home, if he could just make it to the hangar. He made it to the door.

The officers shouted out warnings to stop, but Jaheed ignored them. All he could think about was freedom. He wanted to see his family again. Jaheed shut the door behind him, but could not secure it. He saw a small plane, got inside, and started the engine. The officers heard the engine start and quickly entered the hangar with their weapons drawn. "Stop, or we will shoot!" ordered Officer Whittington. Jaheed was not going to stop and continued to move forward. The officers gave their final warning and opened fire. The bullets pierced the doors and windshield, hitting Jaheed's arm and shoulder. He leaned forward and turned off the engine. The officers pulled Jaheed out of the plane and detained him for CPAT.

Federal units were now closing in on the tracking device. The signal became stronger as they neared the harbor. "The twins cannot be far away now!" Lamb said. Three vehicles surrounded the pier, making sure that no one could escape. As soon as the vehicles approached the pier, they were greeted with a barrage of bullets. There were two machine guns spraying the entry into the pier. The agents were pinned down, and it was getting dark. Darkness was exactly what the agents needed, especially Lamb. He radioed his team and ordered them not to engage just yet. The terrorists could hardly breathe, and some ran out and shot their weapons at the agents. Soon darkness fell upon the city.

Lamb distributed strobe and gas grenades to his team. Lamb ordered them to open fire and throw the strobe and gas grenades around the pier and into the windows. The terrorists could hardly breathe, and some ran out and shot their weapons at the agents. The CPAT team returned fire and killed three of the enemy. Anderson and Leblanc positioned themselves on top of the SUVs in order to give them a strategic advantage. The enemy continued to return fire.

Lamb ran near the window followed by Robinson and Lee. The three agents threw strobe grenades inside. When the grenades exploded, they created an extremely bright, flashing light. The agents observed six more hostiles blinded, stumbling and falling down as if they were intoxicated. They surrendered as they dropped their weapons to the ground. Martinez and Skypack moved in. Lamb heard Tank barking.

"What is it, boy? Tank, what have you found?" Jenny Lee asked as Tank continued to bark at a crate. The agents quickly ran to the SUVs to retrieve crowbars in order to break the locks. Once opened, they were terrified at what they saw. There were several young girls packed inside of one of the metal crates; they are malnourished and dehydrated. The agents removed them quickly from the smoldering prison.

"What is your name, little one?" Martinez asked.

"My name is Nina. Ma'am, I'm scared. You are not going to hurt us, are you?" asked the frightened young girl.

"Oh, no, hon. we are here to protect you from those bad men. They can no longer harm you!" Martinez said. Nina clung to Agent Martinez. Robinson administered first aid to the girls who needed it, and Lamb had paramedics called to the scene. The unit handcuffed the suspects and interrogated them once the children were placed in the paramedics' care.

"All right, you pieces of scum. Where are the governor's daughters?" Anders yelled. The suspects were kneeling on the pier with their hands cuffed behind her backs. Their heads were down; no one wanted to speak.

"Let's start with this one!" Jenny Lee said. She pulled him by his hair toward the edge of the pier.

"No! No please! I talk. I talk now!" the man said in a heavy Mexican accent.

"Well, start talking, mister. My people don't take kindly to child abuse and human trafficking. There are many of my agents here, as you can see. I can't hold back all of them!" Lamb said.

"All right, I talk. Don't hurt me!" The man looks at the rest of his cohorts, whose heads remained bowed; some were shaking in fear. His mouth quivered as he looked up at all the agents. The agents had hate and anger toward these men, and he felt it. He also knew that he had to give his answers now. "We are from Mexico. We were given orders from the Ortega family to kidnap these young girls. They are to be sold into the black market as sex slaves. We're going to deliver the crates to Europe, England, and France." He pauses and added, "We do not know of any governor's children. I swear we do not know!"

"Look! This bracelet was found on one of the children. Why does she have this? Once opened, they were terrified at what they saw. I want to know!" Martinez said.

"There was this man. I believe he was from the Middle East. I remember him speaking to Manny."

Manny was the second man down from him. He said, "The man gave us money to place a bracelet on one of the girls we had taken hostage. We did not know that it was someone of high importance!"

"Where did he say he was going?" Lamb asked as he grasped Manny by his shirt collar.

"I–I don't know! All he said was that this country must pay for its arrogance. He left in a black SUV!"

"You idiots helped him get away?" Martinez cried. They remained silent.

The Federal ICE Agents arrived on scene and were briefed by CPAT. The team saw two figures emerging from the dark. Everyone turned their attention in that direction with their weapons drawn. As the figures moved into the light, one man appeared handcuffed, and a familiar face was behind him. "It's just me, sir. I caught this one trying to escape in a speed boat!" Wombush said. Lamb the team were relieved to see Wombush.

"Lucy, you got some 'splaining to do!" Robinson joked.

"I want to know where Abdullah is going with the twins!" Lamb said.

"This man knows as much as we do, sir," Wombush reported. "Nothing."

Jennings informed Lamb that the STARE DOWN systems were still targeting the governor's mansion. He contacted the governor, and no one was in the mansion; Jasmine and Todd were safe at CIA headquarters. Jennings informed Lamb that he was going to have to initiate Operation DX: disconnect the entire system. It would take months to bring the system up to speed again. Lamb told Jennings to do whatever it took to keep those missiles from leaving the satellite.

"Now what, sir? We have no visual recognition transmission because our satellites are down, no reliable witnesses for information on Abdullah's whereabouts, and no leads!" Martinez said frustrated.

"If there was ever a time we needed a miracle, it's now!" Robison agreed.

Just then, Skypack ran toward Lamb and Martinez. "Sir, here's a call that came across our phone in the SUV. It's a sheriff from Orange County!" Skypack handed the phone to Lamb.

"This is Agent Lamb of CPAT."

"Hello, sir. I'm Officer Gary Anderson. I'm here at the Grand Airport along with my partner, Mike Whittington. We had to set up roadblocks near LAX. Well, my partner and I came across a Chevy truck that came up as stolen. We ran it through NCIC. When we told them to slowly exit the vehicle, one of them opened fire on us. We had to return fire and shot one of the suspects dead. The other suspect fled to the field hangar, where we were able to apprehend him. He is here now with us in custody. He told us that he and his buddy were running from Abdullah. I take it that you want him?"

Lamb was silent only for a moment. "Yes, we will be there right away. We need to interrogate him because he may know the whereabouts of Abdullah. Abdullah has the governor's twins. We're on our way!"

Lamb's team quickly drove to Orange County, using sirens and lights all the way to the scene. Lamb informed Price about the new lead they had on the twins. They traveled for two hours to the airport, where they saw police officers, detectives, and OMI on scene. The agents exited their vehicles and approached the officers. Lamb asked for Officer Anderson.

"Hello, Agent Lamb!" Anderson said as they shook hands. "This is my partner, Officer James Whittington."

"This is my team, sir," Lamb said.

"What a fine group of agents you have. My goodness!" Anderson said.

Lamb interrogated the suspect, who did not resist and fully cooperated. Lamb informed him that he would see what he could do for him, for his cooperation. Lamb learned that the girls were being held in an abandoned factory on Old Grove Road, going west out of town.

"You agents must sure be busy nowadays," Anderson noted.

"Yes, we are," Lamb replied.

"Just like my daughter—she's a marshal now," Anderson said.

"Really? What is her name?" Lamb asked.

"Carrie Anderson."

Lamb stared at him in shock.

Chapter 10

The Recovery of the Twins

Jennings was in a dilemma. He discovered that the satellite was still moving as the countdown continued. Jennings informed Martinez of the situation. "I don't know what's going on. My guess is that the governor somehow had a tracking device placed on him. The satellite moves in the direction he is moving," Jennings explained.

Martinez verified the location of the governor and took a look at her laptop. It showed where the governor was. He was going to visit the ambassador of Korea. Wombush looked at Lamb, who was involved in an intense conversation with the sheriff.

"So you're Nathan Lamb?" asked the sheriff.

"Yes," Lamb replied.

"I'm sorry that I never had the opportunity to thank you personally. So much has happened since the time of Carrie's kidnapping and her mother's death. Carrie and I have been heartbroken. Her mother had a heart attack and passed away shortly after you rescued Carrie from those kidnappers. We both needed change. Per doctor's orders, we packed our things and moved to Orange County. Carrie went on to college and graduated from UCLA. She received her master's in business and minored in criminal justice. Afterward, Carrie applied for the US Marshals. She met a man named Pat Douglas and got married after courting for one year. Douglas was a marshal also. Those two hardly ever saw each other. As you can guess, they broke up and later divorced. Carrie said at least something good came of it."

"What is that, sir?" Lamb asked.

"They had a beautiful daughter named Ann Marie. Carrie went back to her maiden name, Anderson."

Lamb finally discovered what had become of Carrie. He'd always wondered after all these years, and now he knew.

"Well, here is your prisoner. He's ready for interrogation!" Sheriff Anderson said. Lamb reached for the sheriff's hand to shake it, however the sheriff gave him a hug. "Thank you, son. Thank you so much for saving my daughter's life. I don't know what I would've done if I'd lost her. She is all I have," he said with tears in his eyes.

Lamb informed the Sheriff that he had gone to the University of California and received his bachelor's degree in criminal justice; then he joined the military. After ten years of service, he was discharged and moved to San Francisco. While there, he became a police officer in San Francisco. He also married and then later divorced, and he had a daughter named Arianna. Lamb told the sheriff that he was transferred from the police to the CIA, where he worked now.

"Carrie would be tickled pink to hear that, son. I'm proud to hear of your accomplishments. I'll tell Carrie that I spoke to you."

"Thank you, sir. I appreciate that," Lamb said.

Martinez informed Lamb of Jennings's status and how the satellite moved with the governor. Lamb had Omega team go to the embassy where the governor and ambassador were. He also informed Price of the situation. Skypack took the prisoner back to headquarters for interrogation. Victor would relieve the secret service and give the personal security detail officially back to CPAT.

Hades team transported the suspect back to CPAT headquarters and began interrogation. Price was also present and joined Lamb during the interrogation. Lamb placed a map in front of the prisoner. "All I can tell you is that Abdullah is planning to take the governor's daughters to a secluded area. This is our main hideout. Shipments we get are brought there," Jaheed said.

"I want to know what, when, why, and how. I want to know your whole operation," Lamb said sternly.

"I will tell you, but I want immunity. Before I speak, I want your word that my family will brought over to the United States unharmed."

Lamb paused and then turned to glance at Price. Price nodded because time was expiring. Price then walked quickly out of the room to call the president of the United States.

Jaheed sat nervously with his hands folded together. Lamb paced the floor behind his chair. The rest of the team sat outside the room and observed through a glass window. After nearly an hour, Price received documents of immunity for Jaheed Ahmet. Two CIA field agents arrived at CPAT to hand the immunity documents to Director Price. Price looked it over carefully with Lamb and then handed the document to him.

Lamb sat down across from Jaheed and looked at him for a moment. Lamb placed the document on the table and slid it across the table. Jaheed read it carefully and then signed it. He saw that the document of immunity had been already signed by the president. It was official.

"All right," Lamb said. "Start talking now, and I want every detail."

"The factory is along a secluded road off I-24," Jaheed began.

Just then, a window broke, and Jaheed was struck in the esophagus. He quickly reached for his throat with both hands and fell off his chair. Lamb quickly ran over to Jaheed and placed a handkerchief on the wound; Robinson assisted him. Agents Lee and the Reedys ran to the roof to look for the shooter. Ajay and Ajeeta took positions on the roof across the street. An agent was shot in the arm as soon as she exited the door of the first floor. She then took cover behind a pillar outside. More agents emerged outside. One was hit immediately in the chest; he fell to the pavement and did not move.

Ajay and Ajeeta now had the sniper in their sights. They were positioned on the roof across from the sniper and on opposite ends of each other. Lamb and Robinson joined the agents outside. Robinson administered first aid to the agent who was hit in the arm. Agents Ajay and Ajeeta, discharged their weapons and the bullets connected with the sniper's right leg and side. Robinson tried to resuscitate the fallen agent, but he died.

Lamb radioed Ajay and Ajeeta. "Keep them occupied while Robinson and I try to make it into the building. We're going to the roof." The agents covered Lamb and Robinson by shooting at the sniper, pinning him down behind the wall on the roof. Lamb and Robinson ran up the staircase to the fifth floor and then to the roof. "This is Team Leader One to any agents with a visual!" Lamb said.

"No visual, sir. We've lost sight of him," Ajay stated.

As Robinson and Lamb moved to the roof, Volkov carefully took aim. They were both now clearly in his scope. He began to pull the trigger, but a dark shadow appeared in front of him. Volkov became very frustrated. The figure transformed into a man and became fully materialized. Volkov heard a familiar voice. It was Sushi, one of the emperor's imperial guards. Sushi was one of the most powerful ninjas among the Red Dragon. "You just interfered with my kill!" Volkov said, startled.

"I have no interest in your selfish schemes," Sushi said as he coldly stared into Volkov's eyes. "Why have you not contacted the Warlord, and why did you murder his daughter princess Aimi?"

"I-I don't know what you're talking about," Volkov said nervously.

"Do you know what we do to traitors? You are pathetic scum!" Sushi said.

As Sushi moved forward, Volkov backed up into a wall. He could go no further. "I had to discipline her! It says that I can do so here, in the contract," Volkov said nervously. He slowly pulled out a document. At the same time, Sushi pulled out his butterfly knife and held it beneath Volkov's throat. "I was told to discipline the girls and anyone who failed their assignments," Volkov repeated.

"It doesn't mean that you *murder* them, you arrogant piece of filth!" Sushi said angrily. "She was the emperor's daughter."

Volkov quickly shined a flashlight into Sushi's face, who was blinded but only temporarily. Volkov tried to run, but he was cut off from the fire escape by another Red Dragon. "There is nowhere for you to run," the second Red Dragon said. Volkov then turned and saw the anger in Sushi's eyes—and the torment that was to come upon him.

Lamb, Lee, and Robinson converged on the roof. They heard the sound of someone screaming in agony. The agents observed Volkov's sniper rifle on the roof next to the wall, and they continued to search to roof. "Over here, sir!" Lee said. They had finally caught up to Volkov, who was hanging by a long rope. His stomach was ripped open, his neck was sliced, and his heart was cut out.

The Omega team arrived at the embassy and relieved the secret service. The governor had a sense of serenity; he was beginning to let go of his doubt about Price and his newly formed unit. Agent Skypack approached the governor and informed him that they believed he had a tracking device on him that activated STARE DOWN's missile system. The device commanded it to move wherever and whenever he did. "How did it get on me? Where is it?" the governor asked as he stripped down to his underwear.

Martinez and Skypack turned around while Wombush and Leblanc searched the governor for the tracking device. They used a tracking detector wand that would beep if it located a tracking device. As they moved their wands to the front and back of the governor, then upward to the back of his neck, the wand went off. "It is located in the back of your neck, Governor!" Wombush said.

"My neck? How in the hell did It get back there?" the governor asked.

"I think that the danger you encountered when you were in Korea for those peace talks has something to do with this," Martinez replied.

"We have to remove it ASAP"! "Skypack said.

A shadow moved behind the Hades team they walked across the building. Agent Lee was pushed from behind, and Robinson was kicked in the stomach. Lamb was hit in the shoulder with a pipe. All three were shaken up but were ready to retaliate. "Get ready, everyone. This must be a Red Dragon," Lamb cried.

"Damn! Those things are back again?" said Robinson.

Lamb glances at Robinson and nodded.

The shadows ran in retreat. The first shadow leaped across to the next building. "Sniper team, do you have a fix on those shadow warriors?" Lamb asked.

"We see them, sir!" Ajay replied.

"If you have a shot take, it at any time!" Lamb commanded.

Ajay and Ajeeta took aim and shot at the shadowy figure that ran across the building. The rest of the team was in hot pursuit. The shadow slowed down when it was hit by several shots. "Give up! There is nowhere to run," Lamb said.

The Red Dragon knew that there was always a way out for ninjas. He stepped onto the ledge and jumped to his death. The other Red Dragon observed the building across to his right, looked at the team, and disappeared.

Lamb turned and began to feel dizzy as his body shook and convulsed. The team gathered around him. Robinson caught Lamb from behind and gently lowered him to the ground. He supported Lamb's head by placing his jacket underneath it.

Lamb had a vision. He saw many weapons being carried inside a large factory building. There were three men behind them carrying automatic weapons Lamb's vision became blurred, and his body stopped convulsing. His eyes were closed but only for moment. Lamb opened them and saw blurred figures above him. He notices that his team had surrounded him and stared at him in amazement. Lamb informed them of the twins' whereabouts. I saw a dirt road leading to a factory building. He got to his feet and asked for a map of the city.

"There is an old dirt road that is under construction," Jenny Lee said, using her laptop. Lamb had Jenny Lee inform Agent Martinez of their encounter with the two Red Dragons and the location of the twins. Martinez requested medical aid from Robinson, who had to remove the tracking device from the governor's neck. Copter One was notified and arrived on the roof top to transport Robinson to CIA headquarters, where he would remove the tracking device from the governor's neck.

Omega team arrived at CIA headquarters with the governor. Betty, Todd, and Jasmine, were already there awaiting his arrival. "Oh, Barry, I'm terrified. I want our babies back!" Betty cried."

We will get them back soon!" Barry assured her.

The twins were bound to chairs. Brianna tried to loosen the rope around her wrists by moving them in a circular motion. "I want the government agents to understand that there is no way out. We are at the end of negotiations. I have been patient with them long enough. Our fellow comrades have not been released at all. It is time we began executions!" Abdullah said.

"But, General, our objective is to get them out and rebuild our great army. We need to hold off on those executions!" Alta said.

"I agree with Alta. We need them, sir. Just a little longer!" Ahmed stated.

"Only a little longer, then!" Abdullah relented.

Susanna began to weep. She missed her mother and father, and she cried out for them. "Susanna, don't cry. We will see mommy and daddy soon. You'll see. We'll get rescued. Don't worry," Brianna said.

"You promise?" Susanna said.

"Promise," Brianna answered as she continued work on her ropes. Soon she was able to wriggle her wrists free.

There was a guard who looked inside the tiny room where the girls were held captive every ten to fifteen minutes. Brianna carefully watched the window. She then bent down quickly to untie the rope around her feet. She turned around and places her finger on her sister's lips to keep her quiet, and she untied Susanna. Brianna moved a chair next to the small window. The guard was about to glance inside the window, however another guard spoke to him concerning last night's soccer game. Brianna reached the window and opened it. She looked out as the wind blew against her cheeks and hair. She felt freedom nearby.

Brianna took hold of her sister's hand and assisted her to the ledge. They proceeded to walk on the ledge to the end of the building. Brianna and Susanna moved toward the fire escape and climbed down. Brianna went first. She looked up and observes her sister shaking. "Come on, Susanna. You've got to do it if we are going to see our family again. Come on, sis—you can do it!" Brianna coached her every step.

With each step, Susanna grew braver and increased her speed until she was finally able make it to the bottom. Brianna took her sister's hand, and they ran into a nearby field of wheat. They did not run far before they had to stop and catch their breaths.

"I don't know how much longer I can run, Brianna!" Susanna said.

"We have to run into the woods and hide, sister!" Brianna insisted.

The guards were laughing until one decided it was time to look inside the room where the girls had been held captive. "No, it cannot be! They are gone!" he said, surprised. He ran to inform Abdullah.

"You stupid idiot! They are just children! I give you a simple job, and you act like an imbecile!" Abdullah said as he punched and kicked the guard into unconsciousness. "Get those little devils. Get them both now!"

The terrorists ran into the field and searched desperately for the twins.

Brianna and Susanna found a log, and they hid inside to rest. "I don't think they will find us here, Susanna," Brianna said. The girls cuddled up together inside the log. They heard Abdullah's men as they ran past the log. The movement of leaves and sticks snapping made the twins terrified as more men joined the search.

Agent Robinson administered anesthetic to the governor, who became lethargic. Agent Robinson then made an incision just above the device. He used tweezers to carefully remove the tracking device. When Robinson was finished with the operation, he informed Lamb.

"Congratulations, Robinson!" Lamb said.

"Thanks, sir. But there is one problem."

"What is that?"

"The light on the chip is still continuing to blink. I believe that it's still counting down." Robinson described the mechanism to Lamb, who contacted the bomb squad. The bomb squad informed them to get the device away from others as far as possible. There was no way to disconnect this device in time. Lamb contacted Copter Two in order to pick up the device and dispose of it in the Pacific Ocean. K-Hawk arrived within five minutes. Agent Robinson handed the device to K-Hawk, who transported it toward the ocean. The device turned red, and K-Hawk increased his speed. Fifteen minutes went by.

"K-hawk! Are you near the destination now?" Lamb asked.

"Right over the designated area, sir!" K-Hawk replied.

"Drop it and get the hell out of there—now!" Lamb commanded.

"Roger that, sir!" The device had been placed near a closed hatch. K-Hawk opened the hatch and then pulled a lever. The device fell from the hatch and into the ocean. K-Hawk quickly sped away from the area as the device exploded. The explosion was like one hundred sticks of dynamite. "Mission accomplished, sir!" K-Hawk said.

"Good job, Agent K-Hawk!" Lamb said as both teams applauded.

The twins saw that all the terrorists had gone. They decided to run in the opposite direction. As they ran, some of their clothing was torn by the long branches. The twins did have one thing in their favor: they were both in the Girl Scouts and were taught survival skills at a young age. Susanna found some berries to eat as it became dark. They knew not to make a fire in the open area, and they decided to move east toward the mountains.

Abdullah had his men continue to search. "See what I have found!" Azul said.

"What is it?" Ahmed asked. Everyone in that area gathered around Azul to observe a piece of torn clothing: it was a piece of Brianna's white sweater. They continued to walk west.

The twins headed toward the mountains. As the girls walked, they noticed a dirt road off to the right and followed it. Brianna saw a truck driving toward them. She ran frantically in front of it, hoping it would stop.

The driver slammed on his brakes. "Are you crazy, little girl? What in tarnation are you to doing out here by yourselves? Where in the hell are your parents?" he asked.

"Please, mister, you've got to save us from those bad men. Our father is the governor of California. Those bad men are terrorists!" Brianna said tearfully.

"Well, get in quick. My God! You *are* his twin girls. I saw y'all on TV!"

The girls quickly got into the truck, and the man sped away. "Now, now. You're safe with me. Ol' Lester Hudson is my name. I won't let anything hap—"

Just then a bullet went through the front windshield, hitting Lester in the head. A second bullet hit him in the throat. The twins screamed as the truck swerved into a ditch.

"Are you ladies trying to go somewhere without us?" a voice said as the smoke cleared.

Brianna had hit her head on the dashboard and received minor abrasions. Suzanna also hit her head. The girls were scared and began to cry. "Now, now. You are going to be just fine!" Amin said as he took the twins from the truck.

The terrorists took the twins back to the old, abandoned factory. Abdullah was relieved that the twins were recovered by his men. He made an example out of the guard who was assigned to the twins by torturing him and then placing him inside a sweat box. Abdullah's men began to grow weary, and they started more bickering among themselves, and questioning why the negotiations were taking so long.

Doc walked outside the recovery room and slowly closed the door behind him. He turned and observed Barbara, Todd, and Jasmine waiting outside the room. "How is he doing, Doc? Can we see him now?" Todd asked.

"You can see him now. He's going to be fine, but he needs to rest. Please only stay for ten minutes," Doc said. The family agreed.

Omega team received the information about the abandoned factory and was soon en route to the area. Lamb informed Copters One and Two to follow them to the factory. The Fitzpatricks and three other agents were assigned to watch over the governor and his family while CPAT pursued Abdullah and his men.

The twins were exhausted and were escorted to the restroom. Adan made sure that the twins were clean and also fed them. The twins ate quickly, and Susanna began to cry again. Brianna placed her arms around her sister to console her. Abdullah instructed Adan to tie them up once they were finished eating, and she did so.

The Hades team was the closet to the factory. They arrived and held their position approximately three miles from the target area. Copters One and Two landed and received briefings from Lamb. Lamb also informed Price of their location and progress. Price said that he would join them again soon. Omega team arrived shortly and joined the briefing from Lamb.

"All right, team. We have a positive location of the twins and Al-Qaeda." Lamb then pulled out a map displaying the logistics of the factory. "Hades will converge on the back of the building, which is the south side. Omega will take the north side, where the parking lot is. The south side and front entrance will be covered by Copters One and Two, respectively. Sniper teams will be placed in the tree lines once we secure the outside perimeter. I want the helicopters to watch for movement in the trees. This is a good place for an ambush, and we sure as hell don't want that. We are too close. Any questions, team?" There was silence as the team glanced at each other and then turned to Lamb. "Good! Then let's all take our positions."

"Jennings to Team Leader One, come in!"

"This is Team Leader One. Go ahead."

"Sir, all systems on STARE DOWN are up and fully functioning," Jennings stated.

"Great job, Jennings! I knew you would be right for this job."

"Thanks, sir! There is already engagement occurring at the factory."

"How could that be, Jennings? We should be the only agency that has been assigned to engage," Lamb stated. He was at a loss.

"I'll try contacting them, sir!" Jennings said. Approximately three minutes went by. Jennings then informed Lamb that the US Marshals were confronting Al-Qaeda because one of them had escaped the state penitentiary, and he had led them to the factory. Lamb had his units take their positions, and the helicopters begin to sweep the tree lines. Once CPAT arrived, they discovered that several marshals were wounded or killed. One of the marshals tried to enter the building and stepped on a mine, setting it off and killing several other marshals. The front area was full of mines.

Tank became anxious and wary. "Soon, boy. Soon. I'm also anxious. Your job is to locate the twins once the perimeter is secured. Got it?" Lamb said to Tank. Tank barked an affirmative." "Good boy, Tank."

The helicopters began shooting in the tree lines and eliminated four snipers in the process. Lamb also instructed them to fire rounds at ground level twenty yards from the front entrance. This set off several mines and booby traps. Doc Robinson arrived first to aid wounded marshals; Hades and Omega also helped with the wounded.

"Who's in charge here?" Lamb asked one of the marshals.

"It's Marshall Anderson, sir!" one answered.

"What is your name, Marshall?"

"It's Marshall Lisa Thomas. Our lead marshal is right over there!"

Lamb turned around and headed toward the marshal in charge. As he approached, he could see she was hit by a bullet and was being assisted by Robinson and Lee. "Marshall Anderson!" Lamb cried out. She turned around and was surprised to see Lamb. Lamb's heart beat fast as she moved toward him with open arms. Tank began to growl. "Easy, boy. This is Carrie Anderson, a friend of mine!" Lamb said. Tank wagged his tail as they embraced. "Where did you move to? I tried to look you up recently," Lamb said excitedly.

"I tried looking you up too. I wanted to see you after my kidnapping. My parents felt it was in my best interest that we move far away. Father texted me ten minutes ago and told me you were in this area!" Carrie said. "I wanted to stay and get to know you. I really felt a connection between us that night."

"I felt the same way, Carrie," Lamb replied. Just then a bullet went by. Lamb pushed Carrie down behind a SUV. "I almost was lost in conversation," he said.

"You and me both!" Carrie cried.

Lamb said that the reason they were here was because of a lead they got from an informant, formally a part of Al-Qaeda. Abdullah, the head of Al-Qaeda, also had the governor's twin daughters held hostage. Carrie said that the marshals were there because her prisoner had escaped from the federal prison, and one of the marshals had tracked him here. Lamb wanted confirmation on that particular terrorist and received it from Carrie. Carrie looked at Lamb and smiled. She never thought she would ever see him again. Lamb explained to Carrie that he had come across her father in Orange County when he apprehended the terrorist attempting to leave via the private airport, outside the city limits. Carrie did not have a chance to speak to her father yet because she had just arrived back from a trip out of town.

The Hades and Omega Team snipers took out four terrorists on the factory rooftop. "Hear me now, American dogs. If you continue to assault us, we will begin executing the four senators and the governor's twins. Now, what a tragedy that would be. Back the hell off, dogs!" Abdullah cried. Lamb ordered the helicopters back to base, and everyone stood down and held the perimeters for now.

"General, they have backed off and heeded your words!" Ahmed said.

"Only for now," Emir said. "They will try again, Uncle. They will test us to see if we are strong or weak."

"Bring me one of the senators!" Abdullah ordered. "Set up the cameras. It is time to show the world we mean business!"

Brianna and Susanna hear the sounds of bullets whistling in the building. "Listen, the shooting stopped, Susanna!" Brianna said.

"The good guys are here now!" Susanna agreed. "We don't have to cry anymore."

"Team Leader to Jennings," Lamb said.

"Jennings here. Go ahead, Team Leader One."

"You need to get a visual of where the hostages are in the building now, because we need to know!"

"It's coming up, sir. We had some interference because of the weather," Jennings explained. Martinez pulled out her laptop and waited for the downlink to arrive. Jenny Lee was also waiting for the downlink on her laptop. "It should be coming to you very soon, sir," Jennings said. There on the screen showed a blurred picture, and it soon came into focus. Lamb observed the four senators in place sitting on chairs tied and blindfolded. There were two terrorists with ski masks standing behind them with MAC-10s pointed at their heads.

"Team Leader to all units. I'm going in with Tank at this time. I want Wombush, Skypack, Lee, and Robinson to enter the building and secure and hold the inside perimeter. Team, place silencers on your M-9s. Let's move," Lamb commanded. The ground team converged on the building. Lamb was able to monitor terrorist activity with a small video camera; each of the agents had a camera in their possession.

The video cameras were ready, and the lights came on. "Attention to all you American agents. This message is for you. As I have brought up before, it is your meddling in our homeland that has cost thousands of innocent lives. I want an answer now! I have lost all patience. You will respond, or they will die one at a time." The camera turned and shows all four senators: Nelson, Burns, Nolan, and Kiddman. They had been missing for three days. "What we are demanding now is that you release our country fellowmen and sign papers agreeing to your noninterference in foreign affairs. There has been too much bloodshed. Many innocent children have died—mine included. If I do not hear back within five minutes, one of these men will die!"

The rest of the team moved to their assigned areas. Hades team moved to the south side of the building. Lamb peered into a glass window and saw two men holding MAC-10s guarding the door. He quickly turned to Lee and Robinson, holding up two fingers to his eyes and then pointing in the area where the terrorists stood. Lamb picked up a chair and threw it into a window, to distract them. Lee and Robinson shot through the glass window, hitting both terrorists in the chest. The Hades team entered through the windows. Lamb picked up Tank and helped him into an open window. Lee and Robinson held that perimeter. Lamb and Tank continued on.

"Team Leader One to Jennings!"

"Go ahead, sir."

"You have visual on the twins?"

"They are on the third floor, on the east side!"

"Good job Jennings. Switch to our visual frequency to that direction as soon as we rescue those senators." Lamb said.

"Ten-four, sir." Jennings said.

"I'm going in with you. I have an escaped prisoner to catch!" Carrie stated.

"But you're wounded and should be looked at by a doctor!" Lamb protested. Carrie looked at Lamb, loaded a clip into her Glock, and moved past Lamb. "All teams, move in now!" Lamb ordered.

The teams moved to the second floor, where the senators were being held hostage. The teams were on opposite ends of each other. They arrived and observed a server room surrounded with glass windows. They had to crawl in order not to be seen. "Martinez, do you have visual on hostages?" Lamb asked.

"Yes, we do have visual—and a clear shot at the hostiles!" Martinez replied.

"Get ready to shoot on my command." Lamb and his team did not have a clear shot on the other side because of pillars blocking their view.

"Now that I have your attention, Governor Barton, call this number we have placed on screen. You only have five minutes to respond!" Abdullah said.

Martinez, Skypack, and Lamb took aim at Ahmin and two other terrorists. Martinez gave the go-ahead as a terrorist placed a gun to Senator Burns's head. The team fired their weapons, and the bullets reached their intended targets, hitting the terrorists in their heads, chests, and necks and killing them. The dead men fell backward through the glass behind them.

Hades team converged through the side door. The senators were safe. The team checked to see if any terrorists were alive; all three were dead. Lamb and his Hades team untied the ambassadors. Abdullah was not inside the room, as Lamb had thought. The broadcast was coming from somewhere else inside the factory. "Jennings, I need a fix on the whereabouts of Abdullah now," Lamb said.

"I'm working on it, sir!" Jennings stated.

Lamb turned to Carrie and asked, "Are you sure you're all right, Carrie?"

"I can do this, Nathan!" Carrie said in a low voice.

Lamb was not convinced and took her outside, where paramedics were standing by. Hades team continued to move upstairs. Lamb instructed Omega team to also move upstairs on the opposite side of the building.

"Sir, I have a visual on figures on the second floor's east entrance. They are next to the window," Jennings said.

"All right, teams. Converge now!" Lamb ordered. The teams rushed down the stairs. Lamb, however, began to have second thoughts, and his deep instincts kicked in. "Team, I want you to bypass the first floor and exit the building—now!" Lamb ordered.

"Ten ninety-nine that call, sir? I say, repeat that call," Agent Martinez said.

"Exit the building. We have a ten ninety-two call!" Lamb cried out. All agents exited the building. Lamb had a slight but vivid vision of both entry doors on the second floor being booby trapped with C-4.

Lamb and Tank moved downstairs to the first floor. Lamb noticed a fire escape on the outside of the building. He and Tank quickly ran up the stairs. The door was locked, however there was a window that was slightly open. Lamb widened the opening, picked up Tank, and assisted him through the window. Lamb then made his way into the warehouse. He saw a light on down the hallway, far away. He noticed the dim light coming from a room at the end of the hallway. As he neared, Lamb could hear voices coming from the room, and started to crawl. Lamb commanded Tank to slow down and crawl as well. They both reached the door.

Lamb peered into the room and could observe three individuals inside. He could also see the children, however there was still no sign of Abdullah. One of the terrorists left the room, saying that he had to see what Abdullah wanted next.

The girls looked very afraid, and Susanna was in tears. "Try not to cry, Susanna. I know that God will send someone to save us. I just know He will. Don't cry, sister. I love you! God loves you too!" Brianna said.

"Ali, get over here. I need to speak with you!"

"Who is that? Is that you outside, General?" Ali said.

"Of course, you fool. Stop stalling and get over here now!"

Ali immediately walked outside and turned to the left and then to the right. He soon found himself in a choke hold. Ali struggled only for moment and then slipped into unconsciousness. Lamb dragged his body around the corner to the back of the crates and then made his way to the door. He opened it.

One terrorist asked, "Is that you, Ali? What are you doing? What are we going to do with these American kids?"

Lamb executed a front kick and broke the door. A piece hit the terrorist in the head, rendering him unconscious. Tank pulled the weapon from his hands using his teeth. "Help me untie the girls, Tank!" Lamb commanded. Tank ran over to the twins and worked on the ropes using his teeth. "Good boy, Tank!"

"Are you here to save us?" Susanna asked.

"Yes, we are here to save you and your sister!" Lamb said.

"See? I told you that someone would come, Susanna," Brianna exclaimed.

"God did send someone after all!" Susanna agreed with tears in her eyes.

As Lamb untied Susanna, Tank began to growl. "What is it, boy?" Lamb asked. He turned to see a rifle pointed at his head.

"You stupid American fool! Always trying to save the damsels in distress. Always believing in a happy ending!" Ali said, sneering.

Just then, Tank's ears raised upward. He lowered himself to the floor and covered his ears. A bullet passed through Ali's head and impacted the wall. Ali fell to the floor.

"Talked too much, didn't he?" Price said. Lamb was surprised but glad to see Price. The twins were now free of their ropes.

As they walked outside the room, bullets sprayed near their feet. Lamb and Priced moved the girls behind the crates. They could hear footsteps getting nearer.

"Why hello, Price!" Abdullah yelled. "Long time no see. It's been at least ten years!" Abdullah held an AK-47 in his hands, pointing it toward them as he walked. "You and I have made great progress in ten years. You move through the ranks, up to director. And me? I am head of Al-Qaeda. Two men to be feared, no?"

Lamb and Price took the twins in the opposite direction, away from Abdullah, as they moved quietly toward the door leading to the stairwell.

"And your protégé, Nathan Lamb. My, my. What can I say? He has been an excellent fighting machine, if I do say so myself. Where did you ever get such a fine soldier? He should be in my army, serving me. We could all work together. I could make you both wealthy men. You would like that, wouldn't you?" Abdullah sneered.

Lamb and Price continued to move the girls quietly toward the door. Just as they reached the door, Abdullah fired on the agents and the twins, separating Price from the rest. Lamb took the twins down a different aisle, to the right of the door, and Abdullah followed them. Lamb told Tank not to attack and stand down. Tank whined but reluctantly obeyed.

"There is no escape, Lamb. Just stay where you are. You are cornered, trapped like an animal! You and your director have been worthy adversaries, but it ends here and now!" Abdullah said.

Lamb looked around the room and saw two large mirrors in a corner next to a pile of boxes that contained tnt. He told the girls to trust him as he devised a plan.

Abdullah turned on the lights in the room and saw the twins, however Lamb was nowhere in sight. "I have you now, children. There is nowhere for you to run. Come here now, and you won't be harmed," Abdullah said. The twins looked at each other and then climbed into a crate and secured the lid. Abdullah called the governor.

"Hello?" Barry answered. The cameras were turned on in the room.

"Hello, Governor. This is Abdullah. What is your answer?"

"You know that I cannot make any deals with terrorists. I just can't do it. I can't!"

"I want you to hear this, you fool!" Abdullah said.

"Daddy, please save us! Daddy, help us! We don't want to die!" The girls' voices were muffled, coming from the crate.

"Oh my god, Barry, he's got our babies in that crate! Barry, do something, for God's sake! Do something!" Betty cried.

"You'd better listen to her, you fool. You've got only one minute left," Abdullah said with a sneer.

Barry looked at his wife. Betty had tears streaming down her cheeks, and Barry's own eyes were wet. He answered Abdullah. "No deal!"

"Damn you Americans. Your children will die, just as mine did!" Abdullah screamed.

"No, Daddy! Don't let us die. No!" the girls cried.

Abdullah stepped back and pulled the trigger of the AK-47. The bullets ripped into the crate and went through the other side. Pieces of the crate flew everywhere. Abdullah continued firing and laughing until the clip was empty. Lamb used the mirrors to cause an illusion to make Abdullah believe that the twins had actually climbed into a crate near him!

Just then, a voice came from behind a crate. "You forget that the children belong to God. Game over!"

Abdullah saw a grenade bouncing on the floor next to him. As he looked up, it continued to roll into a supply of TNT. Abdullah's eyes widened as he screamed. His voice was lost as the room exploded. The explosion set off a chain reaction. Lamb and Price each had one twin in their arms as they ran out of the factory. Tank was already outside barking, encouraging them to run faster. As they ran, Lamb and Price knew that they could not slow down. Every part of that factory was exploding until it ended in the lobby area. They made it outside during the last detonation.

Lamb and Price covered the girls. Pieces of metal and glass fell around and on top of them. Tank whined and ran to Lamb and investigated his condition. Both teams ran to assist Lamb, Price, and the twins. They were shaken up, but they were safe. Carrie also joined them, and she embraced Lamb. "Nathan Lamb, don't you ever scare me like that again!" she scolded.

"I'll try not to," Lamb said as he slowly stood up.

Price ordered the team to secure the area. There were no more signs of terrorists in the area. The country was safe for the moment.

"You have been shot!" Carrie cried.

"I know," Lamb said softly.

"Agent Price, did you know that your agent has been shot?" Carrie asked. She examined Lamb's body. "You've been hit twice, once in the shoulder and on your right side."

Price said, "No, I did not know that. But somehow that doesn't surprise me at all."

"How so?" Carrie asked.

"He always follows through with his assignments, injured or not. It's always mission accomplished first," Price said proudly.

Fire trucks arrived along with medical emergency vehicles. The wounded agents were assisted. The twins' parents arrived. "My babies! My precious babies!" Betty cried.

"Mommy, Daddy!" the girls cried as they hugged Betty and Barry.

The governor turned his attention to Director Price and stated, "I don't know what to say, Victor. You and your team proved me wrong. They are a highly qualified and talented team. You will all be given full commendations and recognition. I promise you that."

"Thank you, Governor. I appreciate that. They have earned it and will appreciate the commendations," Price said.

Lamb was transported to the hospital as Tank whined. "You will see him again soon, boy," Martinez said.

Carrie rode with Lamb to the hospital, holding his hand all the way. "So tell me more about your daughter, Ann Marie," Lamb said.

"Well, she likes being in the Girl Scouts. She likes to bake and sing. She will be singing in the spring polychoral concert at Millville Elementary School," Carrie said.

"What did you say? Millville? That's the same concert that Arianna will be in!" Lamb said excitedly. "Arianna plays the piano."

Carrie looked deeply into Lamb's eyes and said, "You know, I never properly thanked you for saving my life, Agent Nathan Lamb." She gently kissed him on his lips. They continued kissing all the way to the hospital.

One week later ...

"Next up for commendations is the director of the CIA, Victor Price. Director Price put together a unique team of agents consisting of individuals from various military and law enforcement backgrounds throughout the United States. They were formed to combat terrorism, and they saved my family and myself from terrorist acts. I will be forever grateful. Lets' give a warm welcome to the men and women who serve in the CIA in the newly formed unit called CPAT, Crime Prevention Against Terrorism. Ladies and gentlemen, I present to you Victor Price."

The agents walked onto the stage and sat down. Victor Price walked up to the governor, shook his hand, and took the podium. "It was about a year ago today I asked a retired soldier who served under my command for five years for his assistance in forming a unit in order to combat terrorism. He did just that. I couldn't have done a better job than he did. Nathan Lamb was one of my best soldiers, and I was proud to have him in my unit in Delta Force. Now, I'm proud to have him as a part of the CIA as head supervisor of CPAT." Director Price called Lamb to the platform.

Lamb received his commendation, and the audience applauded loudly. He then had the honor of calling all of his team members to the podium to receive their commendations. First up were Brian Keller and Doug and Doreen Fitzpatrick, followed by the Hades and Omega teams. Last but not least, tank walked up to the podium, bowed his head as Lamb placed a medal around his neck. Tank raised his his right paw to his forehead and saluted Lamb. Lamb smiled and shook his head. Tank fell back into line. The audience gave the unit a standing ovation. Carrie and her father were in the audience, smiling, along with Arianna, Price's family and the governor's family.

Epilogue

Two weeks later, Lamb was at Millview Elementary School, ready to sit down and listen to his daughter's recital in the choir. Susan and Steve arrived along with Arianna. "Hi, Daddy. You came!" Arianna said excitedly.

"Angel you know that I wouldn't miss this for the world," Lamb said. Arianna gave her father a big hug.

"Where's Carrie? Running late?" Susan asked.

"She will be here soon," Lamb said.

They walked down the aisle and sat on opposite sides of each other in the third row. Arianna kissed her father. "Go get them, angel," Lamb said. Arianna smiled and skipped toward the stage.

Lamb received a call from Jennings. "Sir, I have Agent Martinez on the line for you."

"Go ahead and put her on, Jennings."

"Hello, sir!" Do you know a Yanni Seraphim? He says that you met each other about ten years ago when you took some type of joint military training. He's here in LA," Martinez said.

"Yes, I do remember Yanni from Russia. But what is he doing here?" asked Lamb.

"I don't know, sir. However, he gave me his number to give to you and said that he needs to speak with you as soon as possible."

"I will call him as soon as Arianna's recital is over." Lamb took down the information and thanked Agent Martinez.

The lights dimmed, and an outline of a woman in a dark blue dress moved toward Lamb and sat down next to him. Carrie was ravishing, and her blonde hair was down. She looked radiant in her blue dress with

sparkles outlining it. Everyone looked at her as she sat next to Lamb.
"Which one is she?" Carrie asked.

"She's playing the piano," Lamb replied. "Which one is Ann Marie?"

"She is the second girl in the second row from the left. Ann will be singing a solo!"

"Carrie, Ann Marie is very beautiful, just like her mother."

Carrie smiled. "Arianna reminds me of a beautiful angel."

Lamb glanced at her and smiled. Carrie crossed her leg and placed her hand in Lamb's. The children then began to sing.

THE END

About the Author

Ian Wright is from southern new England and now resides in the south west. He holds a Masters' degree in Criminal Justice and has background in Law Enforcement and Security. Ian has taught classes at community colleges in the criminal justice field. He also teaches personal safety and self-defense classes. The Chronicles of Nathan Lamb: "Suffer the little children," is part one of a trilogy series.

Printed in the United States
By Bookmasters